D1103040

THE PYRAMID

THE KURT WALLANDER STORIES

Translated from the Swedish by
Ebba Segerberg with Laurie Thompson

Henning Mankell

ISIS
LARGE PRINT
Oxford

First published in Great Britain 2008
by
Harvill Secker
part of The Random House Group Limited

Published in Large Print 2009 by ISIS Publishing Ltd.,
7 Centremead, Osney Mead, Oxford OX2 0ES
by arrangement with
The Random House Group Limited

British Library Cataloguing in Publication Data
Mankell, Henning, 1948–
    The pyramid
    1. Mankell, Henning, 1948– - - Translations into
    English.
    2. Wallander, Kurt (Fictitious character) - - Fiction.
    3. Police - - Sweden - - Fiction.
    4. Detective and mystery stories, Swedish - -
    Translations into English.
    5. Large type books.
    I. Title
    839.7'374–dc22

        ISBN 978–0–7531–8384–7 (hb)
        ISBN 978–0–7531–8385–4 (pb)

Printed and bound in Great Britain by
T. J. International Ltd., Padstow, Cornwall

To Rolf Lassgård
with great warmth, gratitude,
and not a little admiration.
He has told me so much
about Wallander that I myself
did not know.

CONTENTS

FOREWORD

It was only after I had written the eighth and final instalment in the series about Kurt Wallander that I thought of the subtitle I had always sought but never found. When everything, or at least most of it, was over, I understood that the subtitle naturally had to be *Novels about the Swedish Anxiety.*

But of course I arrived too late at this insight. And this despite the fact that the books have always been variations on a single theme: "What is happening to the Swedish welfare state in the 1990s? How will democracy survive if the foundation of the welfare state is no longer intact? Is the price of Swedish democracy today too high and no longer worth paying?"

And it is precisely these questions that have also been the subject of the majority of the letters I have received. Many readers have had wise thoughts to share. Indeed, I feel confirmed in my impression that Wallander has in a way served as a kind of mouthpiece for growing insecurity, anger and healthy insights about the relationship between the welfare state and democracy. There have been thick letters and slender postcards from places around the world that I have never heard of, telephone calls that have reached me at odd hours, agitated voices that have spoken to me via email.

Beyond these matters of the welfare state and democracy, I have also been asked other questions. Some of them have regarded inconsistencies that many readers have gleefully discovered. In almost all cases in which readers have brought "errors" to light, they have been correct. (And let me immediately add that new inconsistencies will be discovered even in this volume. Let me simply say that what appears in this volume is what should stand. Let no shadow fall upon any editor. I could not have had a better one than Eva Stenberg.)

But most of the letters have posed the following question: what happened to Wallander before the series began? Everything, to set an exact date, before 8 January 1990. The early winter morning when Wallander is awakened in his bed by a telephone call, the beginning of *Faceless Killers*. I have a great sympathy for the fact that people wonder how it all began. When Wallander appeared on the scene he was forty-two, going on forty-three. But by then he had been a policeman for many years, he had been married and divorced, had a child, and, once upon a time, had left Malmö for Ystad.

Readers have wondered. And naturally I have also sometimes wondered. During these past nine years I have sometimes cleaned out drawers, dug through dusty piles of paper, or searched among the ones and zeros of diskettes.

Several years ago, right after I was done with the fifth book, *Sidetracked*, I realised that I had started to write stories in my head that took place long before the start of the series. Again, this magical date, 8 January 1990.

Now I have gathered these stories. Some have already been published in newspapers. Those I have gone over lightly. Some chronological errors and dead words have been excised. Two of the stories have never been published before.

But I am not publishing these stories now to clean out my desk. I am publishing this volume because it forms an exclamation mark to the period I wrote last year. In the manner of the crab, it can sometimes be good to go backwards. To a beginning. The time before 8 January 1990.

No picture will ever be complete. But I do think these pieces should be part of it.

The rest is, and remains, silence.

Henning Mankell
January 1999

WALLANDER'S FIRST CASE

CHAPTER
ONE

In the beginning, everything was just a fog.

Or perhaps it was like a thick-flowing sea where all was white and silent. The landscape of death. It was also the first thought that came to Kurt Wallander as he slowly began rising back to the surface. That he was already dead. He had reached twenty-one years of age, no more. A young policeman, barely an adult. And then a stranger had rushed up to him with a knife and he had not had time to throw himself out of harm's way.

Afterwards there was only the white fog. And the silence.

Slowly he awakened, slowly he returned to life. The images that whirled around inside his head were unclear. He tried to catch them in flight, as one catches butterflies. But the impressions slipped away and only with the greatest of effort could he reconstruct what had really happened . . .

Wallander was off duty. It was 3 June 1969, and he had just walked Mona down to one of the Denmark ferries, not one of the new ones, the hydrofoils, but one of the old faithfuls, where you still had time for a square meal during the passage to Copenhagen. She was going to meet up with a friend, they were going maybe to the Tivoli, and, more likely, the clothes shops. Wallander had wanted to come along since he was off work, but she had said no. The trip was just for her and her friend. No men allowed.

Now he watched the boat chug out of the harbour. Mona would be back in the evening and he had promised to be there to greet her. If the weather was still as fine as it was now, they would take a walk. And then return to his apartment in Rosengård.

Wallander noticed he was becoming excited at the very thought. He straightened his trousers and then crossed the street and walked into the station. There he bought a packet of cigarettes, John Silver as always, and lit one before he even left the building.

Wallander had no plans for the day. It was a Tuesday and he was free. He had been putting in a lot of overtime, not least because of the frequent, large-scale Vietnam demonstrations both in Lund and Malmö. In Malmö there had been a clash with the police. Wallander had found the whole situation distasteful. He was not sure what he thought of the protestors' demands that the United States get out of Vietnam. He had tried to talk to Mona about it the day before but she had not had any opinion other than that "the protestors are troublemakers". When Wallander, despite everything, insisted on pointing out that it could hardly be right for the world's greatest military power to bomb a poor agricultural nation in Asia to devastation — or "back to the Stone Age", as he had read that some high-ranking American military official had said — she had struck back and said that she certainly had no intention of marrying a communist.

That had knocked the wind out of his sails. They never continued the discussion. And he was going to marry Mona, he was sure of that. The girl with the light brown hair, the pointy nose and the slender chin. Who perhaps was not the most beautiful girl he had ever met. But who nonetheless was the one he wanted.

They had met the previous year. Before then, Wallander had been involved for more than a year with a girl named Helena who worked in a shipping office in the city. Suddenly one day she had simply told him that it was over, that she had found someone else. Wallander had at first been dumbstruck. Thereafter he had spent a whole weekend crying in his apartment. He had been insane with jealousy and had, after he had managed to stop his tears, gone down to the pub at the Central Station and had much too much to drink. Then he had gone home again and continued to cry. Now if he ever walked past the entrance to the pub he shivered. He was never going to set foot in there again.

Then there had been several heavy months when Wallander entreated Helena to change her mind, to come back. But she had flatly refused and at last became so irritated by his persistence that she threatened to go to the police. Then Wallander had beaten a retreat. And strangely enough, it was as if everything was finally over. Helena could have her new man in peace. That had happened on a Friday.

The same evening he had taken a trip across the sound, and on the way back from Copenhagen he wound up sitting next to a girl who was knitting. Her name was Mona.

Wallander walked through the city lost in thought. Wondered what Mona and her friend were doing right now. Then he thought about what had happened the week before. The demonstrations that had got out of hand. Or had he failed to judge the situation correctly? Wallander had been part of a hastily assembled reinforcement group told to stay in the background until needed. It was only when the chaos broke out that they had been called in. Which in turn only served to make the situation more turbulent.

The only person Wallander had actually tried to discuss politics with was his father. His father was sixty years old and had just decided to move out to Österlen. He was a volatile person whose moods Wallander found hard to predict. Not least since his father once became so upset he almost disowned his son. This had happened a few years ago when Wallander came home and told his father he was going to be a policeman. His father was sitting in his studio, which always smelled of oil paints and coffee. He had thrown a brush at Wallander and told him to go away and never come back. He had no intention of tolerating a policeman in the family. A violent quarrel had broken out. But Wallander had stood his ground; he was going to join the police, and all the projectile paintbrushes in the world couldn't change that. Suddenly the quarrelling stopped: his father retreated into acrimonious silence and returned to sit in front of his easel. Then he stubbornly started to outline the shape of a grouse, with the help of a model. He always chose the same motif, a wooded landscape, which he varied sometimes by adding a grouse.

Wallander frowned as he thought of his father. Strictly speaking they had never come to any reconciliation. But now they were on speaking terms again. Wallander had often wondered how his mother, who had died while he was training to be a policeman, could put up with her husband. Wallander's sister, Kristina, had been smart enough to leave home as soon as she was able and now lived in Stockholm.

The time was ten o'clock. Only a faint breeze fanned Malmö's streets. Wallander walked into a cafe next to the NK department store. He ordered a cup of coffee and a sandwich, skimmed through the newspapers *Arbetet* and *Sydsvenskan*. There were letters to the editor in both newspapers from people who either praised or criticised the actions of the police in connection with the protests. Wallander quickly flipped past them. He didn't have the energy to read about it. Soon he was hoping not to have to assume any more duties with the riot police. He was going to be a criminal investigator. He had been clear on that from the start and had never made any secret of it. In only a few months he would work in one of the departments that investigated violent incidents and even more serious crimes.

Suddenly someone was standing in front of him. Wallander was holding his coffee cup in his hand. He looked up. It was a girl with long hair, about seventeen. She was very pale and was staring at him with fury.

Then she leaned forward so her hair fell over her face and pointed to the back of her neck.

"Here," she said. "This is where you hit me."

Wallander put down his cup. He didn't understand anything.

She had straightened back up.

"I don't think I really understand what you mean," Wallander said.

"You're a cop, aren't you?"

"Yes."

"And you were there fighting during the demonstration?"

Wallander finally got it. She had recognised him even though he was not in uniform.

"I didn't hit anybody," he answered.

"Does it really matter who was holding the baton? You were there. Therefore you were fighting against us."

"You did not comply with the regulations regarding public demonstrations," Wallander said and heard how inadequate the words sounded.

"I really hate the police," she said. "I was going to have a cup of coffee here, but now I'm going somewhere else."

Then she was gone. The waitress behind the counter gave Wallander a stern look. As if he had cost her a guest.

Wallander paid and walked out. The sandwich was left half eaten. The incident with the girl had left him considerably shaken. As if he were wearing his uniform after all, not these dark blue pants, light shirt and green jacket.

I have to get away from the streets, he thought. Into an office, into case-review meetings, crime scenes. No more protests for me. Or I'll have to take sick leave.

He started to walk faster. Considered whether or not he should take the bus to Rosengård. But he decided he needed the exercise — and also to be invisible and not bump into anyone he knew.

But naturally he ran into his father outside the People's Park. He was weighed down by one of his paintings, wrapped in brown paper. Wallander, who had been walking with his head down, spotted him too late to make himself invisible. His father was wearing a strange cap and a heavy coat, underneath which he had on some kind of tracksuit and trainers without socks.

Wallander groaned to himself. He looks like a tramp, he thought. Why can't he at least dress properly?

His father put the painting down and took a deep breath.

"Why aren't you in uniform?" he asked, without a greeting. "Aren't you a cop any more?"

"I'm off work today."

"I thought policemen were always on duty. To save us from all evil."

Wallander managed to control his anger.

"Why are you wearing a winter coat?" he asked instead. "It's twenty degrees Celsius."

"That's possible," his father answered, "but I keep myself healthy by sweating as much as I can. You should too."

"You can't wear a winter coat in the summertime."

"Then you'll just have to get sick."

"But I'm never sick."

"Not yet. It'll come."

"Have you even seen what you look like?"

"I don't spend my time looking at myself in the mirror."

"You can't wear a winter cap in June."

"Just try to take it from me if you dare. Then I will report you for assault. I take it you were there and beat up those protesters?"

Not him too, Wallander thought. It's not possible. He's never been interested in politics, even when I have tried to discuss it with him sometimes.

But Wallander was mistaken.

"Every reasonable person must distance himself from that war," his father declared firmly.

"Every person also has to do his job," Wallander said with strained calm.

"You know what I told you. You never should have become a policeman. But you didn't listen. And now see what you are doing. Beating innocent little children over the head with a stick."

"I haven't hit a single person in my entire life," Wallander answered, suddenly full of rage. "And anyway, we don't use sticks, we use batons. Where are you going with that painting?"

"I'm going to swap it for a humidifier."

"Why do you need a humidifier?"

"I'm going to swap it for a new mattress. The one I have now is terrible. It makes my back hurt."

Wallander knew his father was involved in unusual transactions that often involved many stages before the thing he needed finally ended up in his hands.

14

"Do you want me to help you?" Wallander asked.

"I don't need any police protection. You could, however, come over some night and play cards."

"I will," Wallander said, "when I have time."

Playing cards, he thought. It is the last lifeline there is between us.

His father lifted up the painting.

"Why do I never get any grandchildren?" he asked.

But he left without waiting for an answer.

Wallander stood looking after him. Thought it would be a relief when his father moved out to Österlen. So that he would no longer risk running into him by accident.

Wallander lived in an old building in Rosengård. The whole area was constantly under the threat of demolition. But he was happy here, even though Mona had said that if they married they would have to find another place to live. Wallander's apartment consisted of one room, a kitchen and a small bathroom. It was his very first apartment. He had bought the furniture at auctions and various second-hand shops. There were posters on the wall depicting flowers and tropical islands. Since his father sometimes came for a visit, he had also felt compelled to hang one of his landscapes on the wall over the sofa. He had chosen one without a grouse.

But the most important thing in the room was the record player. Wallander did not have many records, and those he did own were almost exclusively opera. On those occasions when he had entertained some of his colleagues, they had always asked him how he could listen to such music. So he had also acquired some other records that could be played when he had guests. For some unknown reason many policemen seemed fond of Roy Orbison.

He ate lunch shortly after one o'clock, drank some coffee, and tidied up the worst of the mess while listening to a recording by Jussi Björling. It was his first record, scratched beyond belief, but he had often thought it was the first thing he would rescue in a fire.

He had just put the record on for a second time when there was a thump on the ceiling. Wallander turned down the volume. The walls in the building were thin. Above him lived a retired woman who had once owned a flower shop. Her name was Linnea Almquist. When she thought he was playing his music too loud she thumped on the ceiling. And he obediently turned down the volume. The window was open, the curtain that Mona had hung up fluttered, and he lay down on the bed. He felt both tired and lazy. He had a right to rest. He started to skim through a copy of *Lektyr*, a men's magazine. He carefully concealed it whenever Mona was coming over. But soon he fell asleep with the magazine on the floor.

He was awakened with a start by a bang. He was unable to determine where it had come from. He got up and walked out into the kitchen to see if anything had fallen to the floor. But everything was in its place. Then he walked back into the room and looked out the window. The courtyard between the buildings was empty. A lone pair of blue worker's overalls was hanging on a line, flapping a little in the breeze.

Wallander returned to his bed. He had been torn from a dream. The girl from the cafe had been there. But the dream had been unclear and disjointed.

He got up and looked at his watch. A quarter to four. He had slept for more than two hours. He sat down at the kitchen table and wrote down everything he needed to buy. Mona had promised to buy something to drink in Copenhagen. He tucked the piece of paper into his pocket and closed the door behind him.

He ended up standing in the dim light of the hallway. The door to his neighbour's apartment was ajar. This surprised Wallander because the man who lived there was extremely private and had even had an extra lock installed this May. Wallander wondered if he should ignore it but decided to knock. The man who lived alone was a retired seaman by the name of Artur Hålén. He was already living in the building when Wallander moved in. They usually said hello to each other and occasionally exchanged a few words if they happened to meet each other on the stairs, but nothing more. Wallander had neither seen nor heard Hålén receive any visitors. In the mornings he listened to the radio, in the evening he turned on the television. But by ten o'clock everything was quiet. A few times Wallander had wondered how much Hålén was conscious of his evening visits, in particular the aroused sounds of the night. But of course he had never asked.

Wallander knocked again. No answer. Then he opened the door and called out. It was quiet. He took some hesitant steps into the hallway. It smelled closed in, a stale old-man smell. Wallander called out again.

17

He must have forgotten to lock up when he went out, Wallander thought. He is about seventy years old, after all. He must be getting forgetful.

Wallander glanced into the kitchen. A crumpled-up football betting form lay on the wax tablecloth next to a coffee cup. Then he drew aside the curtains that led into the room. He winced. Hålén was lying on the floor. His white shirt was stained with blood. A revolver lay next to his hand.

The bang, Wallander thought. What I heard was a shot.

He felt himself start to get sick to his stomach. He had seen dead bodies many times before. People who had drowned or hanged themselves. People who had burned to death or been crushed beyond recognition in traffic accidents. But he had not grown accustomed to it.

He looked around the room. Hålén's apartment was a mirror image of his own. The furnishings gave a meagre impression. Not one plant or ornament. The bed was unmade.

Wallander studied the body for a few more moments. Hålén must have shot himself in the chest. And he was dead. Wallander did not need to check his pulse in order to determine that.

He returned quickly to his own apartment and called the police. Told them who he was, a colleague, filled them in on what had happened. Then he walked out onto the street and waited for the first responders to arrive.

The police and emergency medical technicians arrived at almost the same time. Wallander nodded at them as they got out of their cars. He knew them all.

"What have you found in there?" one of the patrol officers asked. His name was Sven Svensson; he came from Landskrona and was always referred to as "The Thorn" because once, while chasing a burglar, he had fallen into a thicket and been pierced in his lower abdomen by a number of thorns.

"My neighbour," Wallander said. "He's shot himself."

"Hemberg is on his way," The Thorn said. "The crime squad is going to have to go over everything."

Wallander nodded. He knew. Every fatal event, however natural it might seem, had to be investigated.

Hemberg was a man with a certain reputation, not entirely positive. He angered easily and could be unpleasant to his co-workers. But at the same time he was such a virtuoso in his profession that no one really dared contradict him. Wallander noticed that he was starting to get nervous. Had he done anything wrong? If so, Hemberg would immediately let him know. And it was for Detective Inspector Hemberg that Wallander was going to be working as soon as his transfer came through.

Wallander stayed out on the street, waiting. A dark Volvo pulled up to the kerb and Hemberg got out. He was alone. It took several seconds before he recognised Wallander.

"What the hell are you doing here?" Hemberg asked.

"I live here," Wallander answered. "It's my neighbour who's shot himself. I was the one who made the call."

19

Hemberg raised his eyebrows with interest.

"Did you see him?"

"What do you mean, 'see'?"

"Did you see him shoot himself?"

"Of course not."

"Then how do you know it was a suicide?"

"The weapon was lying right next to the body."

"So?"

Wallander didn't know what to say to this.

"You have to learn to pose the right questions," Hemberg said. "If you are to work as a detective. I already have enough people who don't know how to think. I don't want another one."

Then he changed tack and adopted a friendlier tone.

"If you say it was a suicide it probably was. Where is it?"

Wallander pointed to the entrance. They went in.

Wallander attentively followed Hemberg in his work. Watched him crouch down next to the body and discuss the bullet's point of entry with the doctor who had arrived. Studied the position of the weapon, the body, the hand. Then he walked around the apartment, examining the contents in the chest of drawers, the cupboards and the clothes.

After about an hour, he was done. He signalled to Wallander to join him in the kitchen.

"It certainly looks like suicide," Hemberg said while he absently smoothed and read the football betting form on the table.

"I heard a bang," Wallander said. "That must have been the shot."

"You didn't hear anything else?"

Wallander thought it was best to tell the truth.

"I was napping," he said. "The sudden noise woke me up."

"And after that? No sound of anyone running in the stairwell?"

"No."

"Did you know him?"

Wallander told him the little he knew.

"He had no relatives?"

"None that I'm aware of."

"We'll have to look into the matter."

Hemberg sat quietly for a moment.

"There are no family pictures," he went on. "Not on the chest of drawers in there or on the walls. Nothing in the drawers. Only two old sailing books. The only thing of interest that I could find was a colourful beetle in a jar. Larger than a stag beetle. Do you know what that is?"

Wallander did not.

"The largest Swedish beetle," Hemberg said. "But it is nearly extinct."

He put down the betting form.

"There was also no suicide note," he continued. "An old man who has had enough and says goodbye to everything with a bang. According to the doctor he aimed well. Right in the heart."

An officer came into the kitchen with a wallet and handed it to Hemberg, who opened it and took out an ID card issued by the post office.

"Artur Hålén," Hemberg said. "Born in 1898. He had many tattoos. Which is appropriate for a sailor of the old school. Do you know what he did at sea?"

"I think he was a ship's engineer."

"In one of the sailing logs he is registered as an engineer. In an earlier one, simply as a deckhand. He worked in various capacities. Once he became infatuated with a girl named Lucia. That name was tattooed on both his right shoulder and on his chest. One could say he symbolically shot himself straight through this beautiful name."

Hemberg put the ID card and wallet into a bag.

"The medical examiner will have to have the last word," he said. "And we will do a routine examination of both the weapon and the bullet. But it's definitely suicide."

Hemberg threw another glance at the betting form.

"Artur Hålén did not know much about English football," he said. "If he had won on this prediction the jackpot would have been his alone."

Hemberg stood up. At the same time the body was being carried out. The covered stretcher was carefully guided out through the narrow hall.

"It happens more often," Hemberg said thoughtfully. "Old people who take their final exit into their own hands. But not so often with a bullet. And even less often with a revolver."

He was suddenly scrutinising Wallander.

"But of course this has already occurred to you."

Wallander was taken aback.

"What do you mean?"

"That it was strange that he had a revolver. We have gone through the chest of drawers. But there is no licence."

"He must have bought it sometime at sea."

Hemberg shrugged.

"Of course."

Wallander followed Hemberg down onto the street.

"Since you are the neighbour I thought perhaps you could take care of the key," he said. "When the others are done they will leave it with you. Make sure no one who is not supposed to enter goes in there until we are completely sure it is a suicide."

Wallander went back into the building. In the stairwell he bumped into Linnea Almquist, who was on her way out with a bag of rubbish.

"What is all this commotion?" she asked irritably.

"Unfortunately there has been a death," Wallander said politely. "Hålén has passed away."

She was clearly shaken by the news.

"He must have been very lonely," she said slowly. "I tried to get him to come in for a cup of coffee a few times. He excused himself with the fact that he didn't have time. But surely time was the only thing he had?"

"I hardly knew him," Wallander said.

"Was it his heart?"

Wallander nodded.

"Yes," he said. "It was probably his heart."

"We'll have to hope no noisy young people move in," she said, and left.

Wallander returned to Hålén's apartment. It was easier now that the body had been removed. A technician was packing up his bag. The pool of blood had darkened on the linoleum floor. The Thorn was picking at his cuticles.

"Hemberg said that I should take the keys," Wallander said.

The Thorn pointed to a key ring on the chest of drawers.

"I wonder who owns the building," he said. "I have a girlfriend who's looking for a place to live."

"The walls are very thin," Wallander said. "Just so you know."

"Haven't you heard about those new exotic waterbeds?" The Thorn asked. "They don't creak."

It was already a quarter past six when Wallander could finally lock the door to Hålén's apartment. There were still several hours left before he was supposed to meet Mona. He went back to his place and put on some coffee. The wind had picked up. He closed the window and sat down in the kitchen. He had not had any time to buy groceries and now the shop was closed. There was no shop that was open late nearby. It occurred to him that he would have to take Mona out for dinner. His wallet was on the table. There was enough money. Mona liked going out to dinner, but Wallander thought it was throwing away money for no reason.

The coffee pot started to whistle. He poured himself a cup and added three lumps of sugar. Waited for it to cool.

Something was nagging at him.

Where it came from, he didn't know.

But all at once the feeling was very strong.

He did not know what it was, other than that it had to do with Hålén. In his mind he went over what had happened. The bang that woke him, the door that was ajar, the dead body on the floor inside the room. A man who had committed suicide, a man who had been his neighbour.

Nonetheless something didn't add up. Wallander walked into the main room and lay down on the bed. Listened in his memory to the bang. Had he heard anything else? Before or after? Had any sounds penetrated his dreams? He searched but found nothing. Still, he was sure. There was something he had overlooked. He continued to go through his memories. But he remembered only silence. He got up from his bed and walked back out into the kitchen. The coffee had cooled.

I'm imagining things, he thought. I saw it, Hemberg saw it, everyone saw it. An old, lonely man who had had enough.

And yet it was as if he had seen something without realising what he was seeing.

At the same time he had to admit that there was something inherently attractive about this idea. That he may have noticed something that had escaped Hemberg. That would increase his chances of advancing to criminal investigator sooner rather than later.

He checked his watch. He still had time before he had to leave and meet Mona at the Denmark ferry. He put the coffee cup in the sink, grabbed the keys and entered Hålén's apartment. When he reached the main room everything was as it had been when he discovered the body, except that the body itself was now missing. But the room was unchanged. Wallander looked around slowly. How do you do this? he wondered. How do you discover what you see but aren't seeing?

It was something, he was sure of it.

But he couldn't put his finger on it.

He walked into the kitchen and sat down on the chair that Hemberg had used. The betting form lay in front of him. Wallander did not know very much about English football. Actually, he didn't know very much about football, period. If he felt like gambling, he bought a lottery ticket. Nothing else.

The betting form was made out for this coming Saturday, he could see. Hålén had even written out his name and address.

Wallander returned to the room and walked over to the window in order to look at it from another angle. His gaze stopped by the bed. Hålén had been dressed when he took his life. But the bed was unmade. Even though the rest of the apartment was characterised by a meticulous order. Why hadn't he made the bed? Wallander thought. He could hardly have slept with his clothes on, woken up and then shot himself without making his bed. And why leave a completed betting form on the kitchen table?

It did not make sense, but on the other hand it did not necessarily mean anything. Hålén could have very quickly decided to kill himself. Perhaps he had realised the senselessness of making his bed one last time.

Wallander sat down in the room's only armchair. It was old and worn. I'm imagining things, he thought again. The medical examiner will establish that it was a suicide, the forensic investigation will confirm that the weapon and bullet match up and that the shot was fired by Hålén's own hand.

Wallander decided to leave the apartment. It was time to freshen up and change his clothes before leaving to meet Mona. But something kept him there. He walked over to the chest and started pulling open the drawers. He immediately found the two sea logs. Artur Hålén had been a handsome man in his youth. Blond hair, a big wide smile. Wallander had trouble connecting this image with the same man who had lived out his days in Rosengård in peace and quiet. Least of all he felt that these were pictures of someone who would one day come to take his own life. But he knew how wrong his thinking was. People who ended up committing suicide could never be characterised from a given model.

He found the colourful beetle and took it over to the window. On the bottom of the jar he thought he could make out the stamped word "Brazil". A souvenir that Hålén had bought on some trip. Wallander continued to go through the drawers. Keys, coins from various countries, nothing that caught his attention. Halfway under the worn and torn drawer liner he found a brown envelope. Inside was an old photograph, a wedding picture. On the back was the name of the studio and a date: 15 May 1894. The studio was located in Härnösand. There was also the note: *Manda and I the day we got married*. His parents, Wallander thought. Four years later their son was born.

When he was done with the chest of drawers he walked over to the bookcase. To his surprise he found several books in German. They were well thumbed. There were also some books by Vilhelm Moberg, a Spanish cookbook and a few issues of a magazine for people interested in model aeroplanes. Wallander shook his head in bewilderment. Hålén was considerably more complex than he could have imagined. He walked away from the bookcase and checked under the bed. Nothing. He then went on to the cupboard. The clothes were neatly hung; three pairs of shoes, well polished. It is only the unmade bed, Wallander thought again. It doesn't fit.

He was about to shut the cupboard door when the doorbell rang. Wallander flinched. Waited. There was another ring. Wallander had the feeling that he was trespassing on forbidden territory. He kept waiting, but when it rang the third time he went over and opened the door.

Outside there was a man in a grey coat. He looked enquiringly at Wallander.

"Am I mistaken?" he asked. "I am looking for Mr Hålén."

Wallander tried to adopt a formal tone that would sound appropriate.

"May I ask who you are?" he said with unnecessary brusqueness.

The man frowned.

"And if I could ask the same of you?" he asked.

"I am from the police," Wallander said. "Detective Sergeant Kurt Wallander. Would you now be so kind as to answer my question: who are you and what do you want?"

"I sell encyclopedias," the man said meekly. "I was here last week and made a presentation of my books. Artur Hålén asked me to come back today. He has already sent in the contract and the first payment. I was to deliver the first volume and then the gift book that all new clients receive as a welcome bonus."

He took two books out of his briefcase as if to assure Wallander that he was telling the truth.

Wallander had been listening with increasing amazement. The feeling that something didn't add up was strengthened. He stepped aside and nodded for the salesman to come in.

"Has anything happened?" the man asked.

Wallander ushered him into the kitchen without answering and indicated that he should sit down at the table.

Then Wallander realised that he was now going to deliver the news of a death. Something he had always dreaded. But he reminded himself that he was not talking to a relative, only to an encyclopedia salesman.

"Artur Hålén is dead," he said.

The man on the other side of the table did not seem to understand this.

"But I spoke to him earlier today."

"I thought you said you had spoken to him last week?"

"I called him this morning and asked if it would be all right for me to come by this evening."

"What did he say?"

"That it would be fine. Why else would I have come? I am not an intrusive person. People have such bizarre preconceptions about door-to-door salesmen."

It was likely that the man was lying.

"Let's take the whole thing from the top," Wallander said.

"What is it that's happened?" the man interrupted.

"Artur Hålén is dead," Wallander answered. "And that is as much as I can say at this point."

"But if the police are involved then something must have happened. Was he hit by a car?"

"For now that is as much as I can say," Wallander repeated and wondered why he had to overdramatise the situation.

Then he asked the man to tell him the whole story.

"I am Emil Holmberg," the man began. "I am actually a school biology teacher. But I'm trying to sell encyclopedias to save up for a trip to Borneo."

"Borneo?"

"I'm interested in tropical plants."

Wallander nodded for him to continue.

"I walked around the neighbourhood here last week and knocked on people's doors. Artur Hålén showed some interest and asked me to come in. We sat here in the kitchen. I told him about the encyclopedia, what it cost, and showed him a copy of one of the volumes. After about half an hour he signed the contract. Then I

30

called him today and he said that it would be all right for me to come by this evening."

"Which day were you here last week?"

"Tuesday. Between around four and half past five."

Wallander recalled that he had been on duty at that time. But he saw no reason to tell the man that he lived in the building. Especially since he had claimed to be a detective.

"Hålén was the only one who showed any interest," Holmberg continued. "A lady on one of the upper floors started to tell me off for disturbing people. These things happen, but not too often. Next door to here there was no one home, I remember."

"You said that Hålén made his first payment?"

The man opened his briefcase where he kept the books and showed Wallander a receipt. It was dated the Friday from the week before.

Wallander thought it over.

"How long was he supposed to make payments for this encyclopedia?"

"For two years. Until all twenty instalments were paid for."

This makes no sense, Wallander thought, no sense at all. A man who was planning to commit suicide doesn't agree to sign a two-year contract.

"What was your impression of Hålén?" Wallander asked.

"I don't think I know what you mean."

"How was he? Calm? Happy? Did he appear worried?"

"He didn't say very much. But he was genuinely interested in the encyclopedia. I am sure of that much."

Wallander did not have anything else to ask. There was a pencil on the kitchen windowsill. He searched for a piece of paper in his pocket. The only thing he found was his grocery list. He turned it over and asked Holmberg to write down his number.

"We will most likely not be in touch again," he said. "But I'd like to have your telephone number as a precaution."

"Hålén seemed perfectly healthy," Holmberg said. "What is it really that has happened? And what will now happen with the contract?"

"Unless he has relatives that can take it over, I don't think you'll get paid. I can assure you that he is dead."

"But you can't tell me what has happened?"

"I'm afraid not."

"It sounds sinister to me."

Wallander stood up to indicate that their talk was over. Holmberg stood rooted to the spot with his briefcase.

"Would I be able to interest you, Detective Inspector, in an encyclopedia?"

"Detective Sergeant," Wallander said, "and I don't need an encyclopedia right now. At least not at the moment."

Wallander showed Holmberg out to the street. Only when the man had turned the corner on his bike did Wallander go back in and return to Hålén's apartment. Then he sat down at the kitchen table and in his mind walked back over everything that Holmberg had said.

The only reasonable explanation he could come up with was that Hålén had arrived at his decision to kill himself very suddenly. If you could rule out the idea of him being so crazy that he wanted to play a mean trick on an innocent salesman.

Somewhere in the distance a telephone rang. Far too late he realised it was his own. He ran into the apartment. It was Mona.

"I thought you were going to meet me," she said angrily.

Wallander looked at his watch and swore quietly. He should have been down by the boat at least a quarter of an hour ago.

"I got caught up in a criminal investigation," he said apologetically.

"I thought you were off today?"

"Unfortunately they needed me."

"Are there really no other policemen except you? Is this how it's going to be?"

"It was an exception."

"Did you go grocery shopping?"

"No, I ran out of time."

He heard how disappointed she was.

"I'll come get you now," he said, "I'll try to hail a cab. Then we can go to a restaurant somewhere."

"How can I be sure? Maybe you'll get called away again."

"I'll be down there as soon as I can, I promise."

"I'll be on a bench outside. But I'm only waiting for twenty minutes. Then I'm going home."

Wallander hung up and called the cab company. It was busy. It took almost ten minutes for him to get a cab. Between tries, he managed to lock up Hålén's apartment and change his shirt.

He arrived at the ferry terminal after thirty-three minutes. Mona had already left. She lived on Södra Förstadsgatan. Wallander walked up to Gustav Adolf's Square and called from a payphone. There was no answer. Five minutes later he called again. By then she was home.

"If I say twenty minutes, I mean twenty minutes," she said.

"I couldn't get a hold of a cab. The line to the damn cab company was busy."

"I'm tired anyway," she said. "Let's get together another night."

Wallander tried to change her mind, but she was firm. The conversation turned into an argument. Then she hung up. Wallander slammed the receiver into the cradle. A couple of passing patrol officers gave him disapproving looks. They did not appear to recognise him.

Wallander walked over to a hot-dog stand by the square. Then he sat down on a bench to eat and distractedly watched some seagulls fighting over a scrap of bread.

He and Mona did not fight very often but each time it happened it worried him. Inside, he knew it would blow over the next day. Then she would be back to normal. But his reason had no influence on his anxiety. It was there anyway.

When Wallander arrived home he sat down at the kitchen table and tried to concentrate on writing down a systematic account of everything that had happened in the apartment next door. But he didn't feel he was getting anywhere. On top of this he felt unsure of himself. How do you go about conducting an investigation and an analysis of a crime scene? He realised he lacked too many fundamental skills, despite his time at the police academy. After half an hour he angrily threw the pen down. It was all in his imagination. Hålén had shot himself. The betting form and the salesman didn't change anything. He would be better off bemoaning the fact that he had not got to know Hålén. Perhaps it was the man's loneliness that at last became unbearable?

Wallander walked to and fro in the apartment, restless, anxious. Mona had disappointed him. And it had been his fault.

From the street he heard a car drive by. Music was streaming from the open car window. "The House of the Rising Sun". The song had been extremely popular a few years earlier. But what was the name of the group? The Kinks? Wallander could not remember. Then it occurred to him that at this time he normally heard the faint sound of Hålén's TV through the wall. Now everything was quiet.

Wallander sat down on the sofa and put his feet on the coffee table. Thought about his father. The winter coat and hat, the shoes worn without socks. If it hadn't been so late he might have driven out to play cards with him. But he was starting to get tired, even though it was not yet eleven. He turned on the television. As usual there was a public television talk show. It took a while before he understood that the participants were discussing the pros and cons of the approaching era. The age of computers. He turned it off. Stayed put for a while before he undressed and went to bed, yawning the whole time.

Soon he had fallen asleep.

Later he could never figure out what had woken him up. But all of a sudden he was wide awake, listening intently to the dim summer night. Something had awakened him, he was sure of it. Perhaps it was a car with a broken tailpipe driving by? The curtain moved gently in the open window. He closed his eyes again.

Then he heard it, right next to his head.

Someone was in Hålén's apartment. He held his breath and continued to listen. There was a clang, as if someone had moved an object. Shortly thereafter he heard the sound of something dragging on the floor. Someone moving a piece of furniture. Wallander looked at the clock on his bedside table. A quarter to three. He pressed his ear against the wall. He had started to think it was his imagination when he heard another sound. There was no doubt that someone was in there.

He sat up in bed and wondered what he should do. Call his colleagues? If Hålén didn't have any relatives then surely no one had any reason to be in the apartment. But they weren't sure of his family situation. And he may have given a spare key to someone they did not know about.

Wallander got out of bed and pulled on his trousers and shirt. Then he walked barefoot out onto the landing. The door to Hålén's apartment was closed. He had the keys in his hand. Suddenly he wasn't sure what he should do. The most reasonable thing was to ring the doorbell. After all, Hemberg had given him the keys and thus conferred a certain responsibility on him. He pressed the buzzer. Waited. Now it was completely quiet in the apartment. He buzzed again. Still no reaction. At that moment he realised that a person inside the apartment could very easily escape through a window. It was barely two metres to the ground. He swore and ran out onto the street. Hålén had a corner apartment, and Wallander hurried round to the other side. The street was empty. But one of Hålén's windows was wide open.

Wallander went back into the building and unlocked Hålén's door. Before he walked in he called out but received no answer. He turned on the hall light and walked into the main room. The chest drawers were pulled out. Wallander looked around. Someone had been in the apartment and looking for something. He walked over to a window and tried to see if it had been forced open. But he found no marks on it. That meant he could draw two conclusions. The unknown person who had been in the apartment had had access to keys. And he or she had not wanted to be found out.

Wallander turned on the light in the room and started to look around to see if anything that had been there earlier in the day had gone missing. But he was unsure of his memory. The most noticeable things were still there. The beetle from Brazil, the sea logs and the old photograph. But the photograph had been removed from the envelope and was lying on the floor. Wallander crouched down and studied the envelope. Someone had taken the picture out. The only explanation he could think of was that someone had been looking for something that might be found in an envelope.

He got up and continued to look around. The bedclothes were torn from the bed, the cupboard door was open. One of Hålén's two suits had ended up on the floor.

Someone has been searching, Wallander thought. The question is, for what? And did he or she find it before I rang the doorbell?

He walked out to the kitchen. The cabinets were open. A pot had fallen to the floor. Maybe that was what had woken him up? Really, he thought, the answer is obvious. If the person who was in here had found what he was looking for, he would have left. And hardly through the window. Therefore whatever the person was looking for was still here. If it ever had been.

Wallander returned to the room and looked at the dried blood on the floor.

What happened? he thought. Was it really suicide?

He continued to search the apartment. But at ten past four he gave up, returned to his apartment and got back into bed. He set his alarm for seven. He was going to talk to Hemberg first thing in the morning.

A few hours later Wallander had to run to the bus stop in pouring rain. He had had a restless sleep and woken up long before the alarm went off. The thought that he might be able to impress Hemberg with his attentiveness had led him to lie there fantasising about how he would one day be a criminal investigator a cut above the rest. This thought also made him decide to stand his ground with Mona. You could not expect a policeman to be punctual.

It was four minutes to seven when he arrived at the station. He had heard that Hemberg often showed up very early to work and an enquiry to reception revealed this to be correct. Hemberg had been there since six o'clock. Wallander walked up to the section where the crime squad was based. Most of the offices were still empty. He walked straight to Hemberg's door and knocked. When he heard Hemberg's voice he opened it and walked in. Hemberg was sitting in the visitor's chair, cutting his nails. When he saw that it was Wallander he frowned.

"Do we have a scheduled appointment? I don't recall seeing anything like that."

"No. But I have something to report."

Hemberg put the nail scissors next to his pens and sat down at his desk.

"If this is going to take more than five minutes, you can sit down," he said.

Wallander remained standing. Then he told him what had happened. He started with the salesman and went on to the night's events. He could not determine if Hemberg was listening with interest or not. His face revealed nothing.

"That was it," Wallander finished. "I thought I should report this as soon as possible."

Hemberg gestured for Wallander to have a seat. Then he pulled over a pad of paper, chose a pen, and wrote down the name and number of the encyclopedia salesman, Holmberg. Wallander made a mental note to himself about the notepad. Hemberg did not favour loose papers or preformatted report forms.

"The nightly visit appears strange," he then said. "But in the end it does not change anything. Hålén committed suicide. I am convinced of it. When the autopsy and weapons report come in we'll have that confirmed."

"The question is who was there last night."

Hemberg shrugged.

"You have given a possible answer yourself. Someone with keys. Someone looking for something he or she did not want to let slip out of their hands. Rumours spread quickly. People saw the police cars and ambulance. Many people must have known that Hålén was dead after only a couple of hours."

"But it's strange that this person jumped out of the window."

Hemberg smiled.

"He may have thought you were a burglar," he said.

"Who rang the bell?"

"A standard way of seeing if anyone's home."

"At three o'clock in the morning?"

Hemberg threw down the pen and leaned back in his chair.

"You don't seem convinced," he said, without masking the fact that Wallander was beginning to get on his nerves.

Wallander immediately realised that he had gone too far and started his retreat.

"Of course I am," he said. "It's definitely suicide and nothing more."

"Good," Hemberg said. "Then that's settled. It was good of you to report this. I'll send over a couple of guys to deal with the mess. Then we'll wait for the medical examiners and forensic lab. After that we can put Hålén in a folder and forget about him."

Hemberg put his hand on the phone as a signal that the conversation was over and Wallander left the room. He felt like an idiot. An idiot who had run away with himself. What was it he had imagined? That he had tracked down a murder? He walked back to his office and decided that Hemberg was right. Once and for all, forget all thoughts of Hålén. And be a diligent patrolman a little longer.

That evening Mona came out to Rosengård. They had dinner and Wallander said none of his prepared speech. Instead he apologised for being late. Mona accepted this and then spent the night. They lay awake for a long time, talking about July, when they were going on holiday together for two weeks. They had still not decided what they were going to do. Mona worked in a hair salon and did not make much money. Her dream was to be able to open her own place sometime in the future. Wallander also did not have a high salary. To be

41

exact, 1,896 kronor a month. They had no car and they would have to plan carefully to get the money to last.

Wallander had suggested they travel north and hike in the mountains. He had never been further than Stockholm. But Mona wanted to go somewhere where you could swim. They had done the calculation to see if they could afford to go to Mallorca. But that was too expensive. Instead Mona suggested they go to Skagen in Denmark. She had been there a few times with her parents as a child and had never forgotten it. She had also already found out that there were many inexpensive bed and breakfasts that were not yet fully booked. Before they fell asleep they had managed to reach an agreement. They would go to Skagen. The next day Mona would book a room, while Wallander would check the train schedule from Copenhagen.

The following evening, 5 June, Mona went to visit her parents in Staffanstorp. Wallander played poker with his father for several hours. For once his father was in a good mood and did not start criticising Wallander for his choice of profession. When he went on to win almost fifty kronor from his son he became so jolly that he took out a bottle of cognac.

"Sometime I want to go to Italy," he said after they had said cheers. "And once in my life I also want to see the pyramids in Egypt."

"Why?"

His father looked at him for a long time.

"That is an extraordinarily stupid question," he said. "Of course you should see Rome before you die. And the pyramids. It is part of a well-rounded person's general education."

"How many Swedes do you think can afford to go to Egypt?"

His father pretended not to hear his objection.

"But I am not about to die," he added instead. "What I will do is move to Löderup."

"How's the property deal coming along?"

"It's already done."

Wallander stared at him with surprise.

"What do you mean by 'done'?"

"I've already bought and paid for the house. Svindala 12:24 is the address."

"But I haven't even seen it."

"You're not the one who's going to live there. I am."

"Have you even been out there?"

"I've seen a picture of it. That's enough. I make no unnecessary trips. It encroaches on my work."

Wallander groaned inside. He was convinced his father had been duped. Taken advantage of, as he so often had been when he sold his paintings to the dubious characters in their large American cars who had been his clients all these years.

"This is news," Wallander said. "May I ask when you're planning to move?"

"The removal men are coming this Friday."

"You're already moving this week?"

"You heard what I said. Next time we play cards we'll be in the middle of the Skåne mud."

Wallander threw his arms out.

"When will you pack? Everything is a terrible mess."

"I assumed that you wouldn't have any time. So I asked your sister to come down and help me."

"So you're saying that if I hadn't come over tonight I would have found an empty house the next time I came for a visit?"

"Yes, you would have."

Wallander held out his glass for more cognac, which his father parsimoniously only filled halfway.

"I don't even know where it is. Löderup? Is that on this or the far side of Ystad?"

"It's on this side of Simrishamn."

"Can you answer my question?"

"I already have."

His father stood up and put the bottle of cognac away. Then he pointed to the cards.

"One more hand?"

"I have no money left. But I'll try to drop by in the evenings and help you pack. How did you pay for this house?"

"I've already forgotten that."

"You can't have done. Do you have that much money?"

"No. But money doesn't interest me."

Wallander realised he was not going to get a clearer answer than this. It was already half past ten. He needed to get home and sleep. At the same time he had trouble leaving. This was where he had grown up. When he was born they had lived in Klagshamn but he had no real memories of it.

"Who is going to live here now?" he asked.

"I've heard it will be demolished."

"You don't seem to care very much about that. How long have you lived here, anyway?"

"Nineteen years. More than enough."

"I can't accuse you of being sentimental, at any rate. Do you realise that this is my childhood home?"

"A house is a house," his father answered. "Now I've had enough of the city. I want to get out into the countryside. I'll be left in peace there and paint and plan my travels to Egypt and Italy."

Wallander walked all the way back to Rosengård. It was overcast. He realised he was anxious that his father was going to move and that his childhood home was going to be torn down.

I am sentimental, he thought. Perhaps that's why I like opera. The question is, can you be a good police officer if you have a tendency towards sentimentality?

The day after, Wallander called to enquire about train departures for their holiday. Mona had booked a room in a bed and breakfast that sounded cosy. Wallander spent the rest of the day patrolling downtown Malmö. The whole time he thought he saw the girl who had accosted him in the cafe. He longed for the day he could take off his uniform. Everywhere gazes were directed at him, expressing distaste or disdain, especially from people his own age. He was patrolling with an overweight and slow policeman by the name of Svanlund, who spent the whole time talking about the fact that he was going to retire in one year and move to his ancestral farm outside Hudiksvall. Wallander listened absently and mumbled something inconsequential from time to time. Apart from escorting some drunks away from a playground, nothing else happened other than Wallander's feet starting to hurt. It was the first time, even though he had patrolled so often during his working life thus far. He wondered if it was due to his increased desire to become a criminal investigator. When he came home he took out a washbowl and filled it with warm water. A feeling of well-being spread throughout his entire body when he put his feet into the water.

He closed his eyes and started to think about the tempting holiday. He and Mona would have undisturbed time to plan their future. And soon he hoped to be able to hang up his uniform at long last and move up to the floor where Hemberg was.

He nodded off in the chair. The window was open a crack. Someone appeared to be burning rubbish. He picked up a faint smell of smoke. Or perhaps dry twigs. There was a weak crackling sound.

He jerked and opened his eyes. Was there really someone burning rubbish in their garden? There were no free-standing houses with gardens in the neighbourhood.

Then he saw the smoke.

It was filtering in from the hallway. When he ran to the front door he knocked over the bowl of water. The stairwell was full of smoke, but he had no trouble determining the source of the fire.

Hålén's apartment was engulfed in flames.

CHAPTER
TWO

Afterwards Wallander thought that for once he had really managed to act according to the rule book. He had run back into his apartment and called the fire brigade. Then he had returned to the stairwell, run up a floor, and banged on Linnea Almquist's door and made sure that she got out onto the street. She had at first protested but Wallander had insisted, grabbing her by the arm. When they made it out the front door Wallander discovered that he had a large cut on one knee. He had tripped over the bowl when he had gone back into the apartment and had hit his knee on a corner of the table. He only discovered now that it was bleeding.

Extinguishing the blaze had gone quickly since the fire had not really had a chance to establish itself before Wallander had smelled the smoke and alerted the fire brigade. When he approached the fire chief to find out if they had already determined the cause of the blaze, he had been turned away. Furious, he had gone to his apartment and retrieved his police badge. The fire chief's name was Faråker and he was in his sixties, with a ruddy face and a sonorous voice.

"You could have told me you were police," he said.

"I live in this building. I was the one who called in the alarm."

Wallander told him what had happened with Hålén.

"Too many people are dying," Faråker said firmly. Wallander was not completely sure how to take this unexpected comment.

"So this means that the apartment was empty," Wallander said.

"It appears to have been started in the entrance hall," Faråker said. "I'll be damned if it wasn't arson."

Wallander looked quizzically at him.

"How can you know that already?"

"You learn a thing or two as the years go by," Faråker said at the same time that he handed out some instructions.

"You will do this too one day," he continued and started stuffing an old pipe with tobacco.

"If this is arson, the crime division will have to be called in, won't it?" Wallander said.

"They're already on their way."

Wallander joined some colleagues and helped them keep curious onlookers at bay.

"The second one today," one of the officers said. His name was Wennström. "This morning we had a pile of burning timber out near Limhamn."

Wallander wondered briefly if his father had decided to burn the house since he was moving anyway. But he did not pursue this line of thought.

A car pulled up to the kerb. Wallander saw to his surprise that it was Hemberg. He waved Wallander over.

"I heard the dispatch," he said. "Lundin was supposed to take it, but I thought I would take over since I recognised the address."

"The fire chief thinks it's arson."

Hemberg made a face.

"People believe a hell of a lot of things," he said. "I've known Faråker for almost fifteen years. It doesn't matter if it's a burning chimney or car engine. For him everything is a suspected case of arson. Come with me and you may learn something."

Wallander followed him.

"What do you say about this?" Hemberg asked.

"Arson."

Faråker sounded extremely sure. Wallander sensed that there was a deep-seated, mutual antipathy between the two men.

"The man who lives here is dead. Who would have started a fire in there?"

"That's your job to find out. I'm just saying it was arson."

"Can we go in?"

Faråker shouted out to one of the firemen, who gave an all-clear signal. The fire was out and the worst of the smoke gone. They went in. The part of the entrance hall by the front door was scorched. But the flames had never reached further than the curtain that divided the hall from the main room. Faråker pointed to the letter box in the door.

"It might have been started here," he said. "Smouldered first, and then caught fire. There aren't any electrical wires or anything else that could catch fire on their own."

Hemberg crouched down next to the door. Then he sniffed.

"It's possible that you're right for once," he said and stood back up. "It has a smell. Kerosene, maybe."

"If it had been petrol, the fire would have been different."

"So someone put it through the letter box?"

"That's the most likely scenario."

Faråker poked the remains of the hall mat with his foot.

"Hardly paper," he said. "More likely a piece of cloth. Or cotton batting."

Hemberg shook his head gloomily.

"Damn people who start fires in the homes of people who are already dead."

"Your problem," Faråker said. "Not mine."

"We'll have to ask forensics to take a look at this."

For a moment Hemberg appeared concerned. Then he looked at Wallander.

"Any possibility of getting a cup of coffee?"

They walked into Wallander's apartment. Hemberg looked at the overturned bowl and the pool of water on the floor.

"Were you trying to put the fire out yourself?"

"I was taking a footbath."

Hemberg regarded him with interest.

"Footbath?"

"Sometimes my feet hurt."

"Then you must have the wrong kind of shoes," Hemberg said. "I patrolled for more than ten years but my feet never gave me any trouble."

Hemberg sat down at the kitchen table while Wallander prepared the coffee.

"Did you hear anything?" Hemberg asked. "Anyone on the stairs?"

"No."

Wallander thought it was embarrassing to admit he was sleeping this time as well.

"If anyone had been moving around out there, would you have heard them?"

"You can hear the front door slam," Wallander said with deliberate vagueness. "I probably would have heard someone come in. If the person didn't stop the door from slamming."

Wallander set out a packet of plain vanilla wafers. It was the only thing he had to serve with the coffee.

"There's something strange here," Hemberg said. "Everything points to the fact that it was a perfect suicide. Hålén must have had a steady hand. He aimed well. Straight through the heart, no hesitation. The medical examiners aren't done yet, but we don't need to look for a cause of death other than suicide. There is none. The question is rather what this person was looking for. And why someone tried to burn down the apartment. It's probably the same person."

Hemberg nodded to Wallander, indicating that he wanted more coffee.

"Do you have an opinion on this?" Hemberg asked abruptly. "Show me now if you can think."

Wallander was completely unprepared for this.

"The person who was here last night was looking for something," he started. "But probably he didn't find anything."

"Because you interrupted him? Because otherwise he would have left already?"

"Yes."

"What was he looking for?"

"I don't know."

"And now tonight someone sets fire to the apartment. Let us assume it is the same person. What does this mean?"

Wallander pondered this.

"Take your time," Hemberg said. "If you are to make a good detective you have to learn to think methodically, and it is often the same thing as thinking slowly."

"Perhaps he didn't want anyone else to find what he had been looking for?"

"Perhaps," Hemberg said. "Why 'perhaps'?"

"Because there could be another explanation."

"Like what, for example?"

Wallander searched frantically for an alternative without finding one.

"I don't know," he replied. "I can't find another alternative. At least not right now."

Hemberg took a wafer.

"I can't either," he said. "Which means that the explanation may still be in the apartment. Without us having been able to find it. If this had all stopped at the nightly visit, this case would have ended as soon as the results of the weapons examination and autopsy were in. But with this fire, we'll probably have to do another round in there."

"Did Hålén really not have any relatives?" Wallander asked.

Hemberg pushed away his cup and got to his feet.

"Come by my office tomorrow and I'll show you the report."

Wallander hesitated.

"I don't know when I'll get time for that. We have to do a sweep of the Malmö parks tomorrow. Drugs."

"I'll talk to your superior officer," Hemberg said. "We'll work it out."

A little after eight the following day, 7 June, Wallander was reading through all of the case material that Hemberg had collected on Hålén. It was extremely sparse. He had no fortune but also no debt. He appeared to have lived completely within the means of his pension. The only recorded relative was a sister who had died in 1967 in Katrineholm. The parents had passed away earlier.

Wallander read the report in Hemberg's office while Hemberg attended a meeting. He returned shortly after half past eight.

"Have you found anything?" he asked.

"How can a person be so alone?"

"You may ask," Hemberg said, "but it gives us no answers. Let's go over to the apartment."

That morning the forensic technicians were making a thorough examination of Hålén's apartment. The man leading the work was small and thin and said almost nothing. His name was Sjunnesson; he was a legend in Swedish forensics.

"If there's anything here, he'll find it," Hemberg said. "Stay here and learn from him."

Hemberg suddenly received a message and left.

"A man up in Jägersro has hanged himself in a garage," he said when he returned.

Then he left again. When he returned, his hair had been trimmed.

At three o'clock Sjunnesson called the work to a halt.

"There's nothing here," he said. "No hidden money, no drugs. It's clean."

"Then there was someone who imagined there was something here," Hemberg said. "And who was wrong. Now we'll close this case."

Wallander followed Hemberg out onto the street.

"You have to know when it's time to quit," Hemberg said. "That may be the most important thing of all."

Wallander went back to his apartment and called Mona. They agreed to meet later that evening and take a drive. She had borrowed a car from a friend. She would drop by and pick Wallander up at seven.

"Let's go to Helsingborg," she suggested.

"Why?"

"Because I've never been there."

"Me neither," Wallander said. "I'll be ready at seven. And then we'll go to Helsingborg."

But Wallander never made it to Helsingborg that evening. Shortly before six o'clock the phone rang. It was Hemberg.

"Come down here," he said. "I'm in my office."

"Actually I have other plans," Wallander said.

Hemberg interrupted him.

"I thought you were interested in what had happened to your neighbour. Come down here and I'll show you. It won't take long."

Wallander's curiosity was aroused. He called Mona at home but did not get an answer.

I'll make it back in time, he thought. I can't really afford a taxi but that can't be helped. He tore off a piece of paper from a bag and scribbled that he would be back at seven. Then he called for a cab. This time he was able to get through immediately. He attached the note to the door with a drawing pin and left for the police headquarters. Hemberg was sitting in his office with his feet on the table.

He gestured for Wallander to sit down.

"We were wrong," he said. "There was an alternative that we didn't think of. Sjunnesson didn't make a mistake. He told the truth: there wasn't anything in Hålén's apartment. And he was right. But there had been something there."

Wallander did not know what Hemberg was talking about.

"I also admit that I was tricked," Hemberg said. "But Hålén had removed what was in the apartment."

"But he was dead."

Hemberg nodded.

"The medical examiner called," he said. "The autopsy is complete. And he found something very interesting in Hålén's stomach."

Hemberg swung his feet off the desk. Then he took out a little folded piece of cloth from one of the drawers and carefully unwrapped it in front of Wallander.

There were stones inside. Precious stones. Of which type, Wallander was unable to determine.

"I had a jeweller here just before you arrived," Hemberg said. "He made a preliminary examination. These are diamonds. Probably from South African mines. He said they were worth a minor fortune. Hålén had swallowed them."

"He had these in his stomach?"

Hemberg nodded.

"No wonder we didn't find them."

"But why did he swallow them? And when did he do this?"

"The last question is perhaps the most important. The doctor said that he swallowed them only a few hours before he shot himself. Before his intestines and stomach stopped working. Why do you think that might be?"

"He was afraid."

"Exactly."

Hemberg pushed the packet of diamonds away and put his feet back up on the table. Wallander caught a whiff of foot odour.

"Summarise this for me."

"I don't know if I can."

"Try it!"

"Hålén swallowed the diamonds because he was afraid that someone was going to steal them. And then he shot himself. The person who was there that night was looking for them. But I can't explain the blaze."

"Can't you explain it a different way?" Hemberg suggested. "If you tweak Hålén's motive a little. Where does that put you?"

Wallander suddenly realised what Hemberg was getting at.

"Maybe he wasn't afraid," Wallander said. "He had maybe just decided never to be parted from his diamonds."

Hemberg nodded.

"You can draw one more conclusion. That someone knew that Hålén had these diamonds."

"And that Hålén knew that someone knew."

Hemberg nodded, pleased.

"You're coming along," he said. "Even though it's going very slowly."

"But this doesn't explain the fire."

"You still have to ask yourself what is most important," Hemberg said. "Where is the centre? Where is the very kernel? The fire can be a distraction. Or the act of someone who is angry."

"Who?"

Hemberg shrugged.

"It'll be hard for us to find that out. Hålén is dead. How he has managed to get a hold of these diamonds I don't know. If I go to the public prosecutor with this he'll laugh in my face."

"What happens to the diamonds?"

"They go to the General Inheritance Fund. And we can stamp our papers and send in our report about

Hålén's death to go as deep in the basement as possible."

"Does this mean that the fire won't be investigated?"

"Not very thoroughly, I suspect," Hemberg said. "There is no reason to."

Hemberg walked over to a cabinet that stood against one wall. He took a key from his pocket and unlocked it. Then he nodded at Wallander to join him. He pointed at some folders with a ribbon around them that were lying to one side.

"These are my constant companions," Hemberg said. "Three murder cases that are still neither solved nor old enough to have lapsed. I am not the one who is in charge of them. We review these cases once a year. Or if we receive additional information. These are not originals. They are copies. Sometimes I look at them. On occasion I dream about them. Most policemen aren't like this. They do their job and when they go home they forget what they are working on. But then there is another type, like me. Who can never let go of an unsolved case. I even take these folders along with me on holiday. Three cases of murder. A nineteen-year-old girl. 1963. Ann-Louise Franzén. She was found strangled behind some bushes by the highway leading north out of town. Leonard Johansson, also 1963. Only seventeen years old. Someone had crushed his skull with a rock. We found him on the beach south of the city."

"I remember him," Wallander said. "Didn't they suspect that it was a fight over a girl that had spiraled out of control?"

"There was a fight over a girl," Hemberg said. "We interviewed the rival for many years. But we didn't get him. And I don't even think it was him."

Hemberg pointed to the file on the bottom.

"One more girl. Lena Moscho. Twenty years old. 1959. The same year that I came here to Malmö. Her hands had been cut off and buried along a road out to Svedala. It was a dog that found her. She had been raped. She lived with her parents out in Jägersro. An upright sort who was studying to become a physician, of all things. It was in April. She was heading out to buy a newspaper but never returned. It took us five months to find her."

Hemberg shook his head.

"You will discover what type you belong to," he said and closed the cabinet. "The ones who forget or the ones who don't."

"I don't even know if I measure up," Wallander said.

"You want to, at least," Hemberg answered. "And that's a good start."

Hemberg had started to put on his coat. Wallander checked his watch and saw that it was five minutes to seven.

"I have to go," he said.

"I can give you a lift home," Hemberg said, "if you can hold your horses."

"I'm in a bit of a hurry," Wallander said.

Hemberg shrugged.

"Now you know," he said. "Now you know what Hålén had in his stomach."

Wallander was lucky and managed to catch a taxi right outside. When he got to Rosengård it was nine minutes past seven. He hoped that Mona was running late. But when he read the note he had posted on the door he realised that this was not the case.

Is this how it's going to be? she had written.

Wallander took down the note. The drawing pin fell onto the stairs. He didn't bother to retrieve it. In the best-case scenario it would get stuck in Linnea Almquist's shoe.

Is this how it's going to be? Wallander understood Mona's impatience. She did not have the same expectations for her professional life as he did. Her dreams about her own salon were not going to come true for a long time.

When he had gone into the apartment and sat down on the sofa he felt guilty. He should spend more time with Mona. Not simply expect her to be patient every time he was late. To try to call her was pointless. Right now she was driving that borrowed car to Helsingborg.

Suddenly there was an anxiety in him that everything was wrong. Had he really thought about what it would mean to live with Mona? To have a child with her?

He pushed the thoughts away. We'll talk to each other in Skagen, he thought. Then we'll have time. You can't be too late on a beach.

He looked at the clock. Half past seven. He turned on the television. As usual a plane had crashed somewhere. Or was it just a train that had run off the rails? He walked into the kitchen and only half listened to the news. Looked in the fridge for a beer, but only found an opened soda. The desire for something stronger was suddenly very intense. The thought of going into town again and sitting in a bar seemed attractive. But he waved it away since he hardly had any money. Even though it was only the beginning of the month.

Instead he warmed the coffee that was in the pot and thought about Hemberg. Hemberg with his unsolved cases in a cupboard. Was he going to be like that? Or would he learn to switch off work when he came home? I'll have to, for Mona's sake, he thought. She'll go crazy otherwise.

The key ring cut into the chair. He took it up and put it on the table without thinking about it. Then something came into his head, something that had to do with Hålén.

The extra lock. That he had had installed only a short time ago. How to interpret that? It could be a sign of fear. And why had the door been ajar when Wallander found him?

There was too much that didn't add up. Even though Hemberg had declared suicide to be the cause of death, doubt gnawed at Wallander.

He was becoming increasingly certain that there was something hidden in Hålén's death, something they had not even come close to. Suicide or not, there was something more.

Wallander located a pad of paper in a kitchen drawer and sat down to write out the points he was still puzzling over. There was the extra lock. The betting form. Why had the door been ajar? Who had been there that night looking for the diamonds? And why the fire?

Then he tried to remind himself what he had seen in the sailor scrapbooks. Rio de Janeiro, he recalled. But was that the name of a ship or the city? He remembered seeing Gothenburg and Bergen. Then he reminded himself that he had seen the name St Luis. Where was that? He stood up and walked around the room. At the very back of the wardrobe he found his old atlas from school. But suddenly he wasn't sure of the spelling. Was it St Louis or St Luis? The United States or Brazil? As he looked down the list of names in the index he suddenly came to São Luis and was immediately sure that this had been the name.

He went through his list again. Do I see anything that I haven't discovered? he thought. A connection, an explanation, or what Hemberg talked about, a centre?

He found nothing.

The coffee had grown cold. Impatiently he went back to the couch. Now there was one of those public television talk shows on again. This time a number of long-haired people were discussing the new English pop music. He turned it off and put the record player on instead. Immediately Linnea Almquist started to thump on the floor. Mostly he had the desire to turn the volume right up. Instead he turned it off.

At that moment the telephone rang. It was Mona.

"I'm in Helsingborg," she said. "I'm in a telephone kiosk down by the harbour."

"I'm so sorry I came home too late," Wallander said.

"You were called back on duty, I presume?"

"They did actually call for me. From the crime squad. Even though I don't work there yet they called me in."

He was hoping she would be a little impressed but heard that she did not believe him. Silence wandered back and forth between them.

"Can't you come here?" he said.

"I think it's best if we take a break," she said. "At least for a week or so."

Wallander felt himself go cold. Was Mona moving away from him?

"I think it's best," she repeated.

"I thought we were going on holiday together?"

"I thought so too. If you haven't changed your mind."

"Of course I haven't changed my mind."

"You don't need to raise your voice. You can call me in a week. But not before."

He tried to keep her on, but she had already hung up.

Wallander spent the rest of the evening with a sense of panic growing inside. There was nothing he feared as much as abandonment. It was only with the utmost effort that he managed to stop himself from calling Mona when it was past midnight. He lay down only to get back up again. The light summer sky was suddenly threatening. He fried a couple of eggs that he didn't eat.

Only when it was approaching five o'clock did he manage to doze off. But almost immediately he was up again.

A thought in his mind.

The betting form.

Hålén must have turned these in somewhere. Probably at the same place every week. Since he mostly kept to the neighbourhood, it must be in one of the little newsagents that were close by.

Exactly what finding the right shop would yield, he wasn't sure. In all likelihood, nothing.

Nonetheless he decided to pursue his thought. It at least had the benefit that it kept his panic about Mona at bay.

He fell into a restless slumber for several hours.

The next day was Sunday. Wallander spent that day doing nothing much at all.

On Monday, 9 June, he did something he had not done before. He called in sick, citing stomach flu as the cause. Mona had been sick the week before. To his surprise, he felt no guilt.

It was overcast but there was no precipitation when he left his building shortly after nine in the morning. It was windy and had become colder. Summer had still not arrived in earnest.

There were two small newsagents nearby that handled bets. One was very close by, on a side street. As Wallander walked through the door it occurred to him that he should have brought a picture of Hålén with him. The man behind the counter was Hungarian. Even though he had lived here since 1956 he spoke Swedish very badly. But he recognised Wallander, who often bought cigarettes from him. He did so now as well, two packs.

"Do you take bets?" Wallander asked.

"I thought you only bought lottery tickets?"

"Did Artur Hålén place his bets with you?"

"Who is that?"

"The man who died in the fire recently."

"Has there been a fire?"

Wallander explained. But the man behind the counter shook his head when Wallander described Hålén.

"He did not come here. He must have gone to someone else."

Wallander paid and thanked him. It had started to rain lightly. He hurried his pace. The whole time he was thinking about Mona. The next newsagent had not had anything to do with Hålén either. Wallander went and stood under the cover of an overhanging balcony and asked himself what he was doing. Hemberg would think I was crazy, he thought.

Then he walked on. The next newsagent was almost a kilometre away. Wallander regretted not having worn a raincoat. When he reached the newsagent, which was right next to a grocery, he had to wait behind someone else. The person behind the counter was a woman about Wallander's age. She was beautiful. Wallander did not take his eyes off her as she searched for an old issue of a specialised motorcycle magazine that the customer ahead of him wanted. It was very hard for Wallander not to immediately fall in love with a beautiful woman who came his way. Then and only then could he force all thoughts of Mona and associated anxiety into submission. Even though he had already bought two packs of cigarettes he bought one more. At the same time he was trying to work out if the woman in front of him was someone who would show disapproval if he said he was a policeman. Or if she belonged to the majority of the population who despite everything still believed that most policemen were in fact needed and honourably occupied. He took a chance on the latter.

"I have some questions for you too," he said as he paid for his cigarettes. "I am Detective Inspector Kurt Wallander."

"Oh my," the woman answered. Her dialect was different.

"You aren't from around here?" he asked.

"Was that what you wanted to ask?"

"No."

"I'm from Lenhovda."

Wallander did not know where that was. He guessed it was in Blekinge. But he did not say this. Instead he continued to the matter of Hålén and the betting forms. She had heard about the fire. Wallander described Hålén's appearance. She thought for a moment.

"Maybe," she said. "Did he speak slowly? Kind of quietly?"

Wallander thought about it and nodded. That could describe Hålén's manner of speaking.

"I think he played a small game," Wallander said. "Only thirty-two rows or so."

She reflected on this, then nodded.

"Yes," she said. "He came here. Once a week. One week thirty-two rows, the next sixty-four."

"Do you remember what he wore?"

"A blue coat," she said immediately.

Wallander recalled that almost every time he had seen Hålén he had been wearing a blue jacket with a zip.

There was nothing wrong with her memory. Nor with her curiosity.

"Had he done something?"

"Not that we know."

"I heard it was suicide."

"Indeed it was. But the fire was arson."

I shouldn't have said that, Wallander thought. We don't know that for sure yet.

"He always had exact change," she said. "Why do you want to know if he placed his bets here?"

"Routine questioning," Wallander answered. "Can you remember anything else about him?"

Her answer caught him by surprise.

"He used to borrow the telephone," she said.

The telephone was on a little shelf next to the table where the betting forms were kept.

"Was that a frequent occurrence?"

"It happened every time. First he placed the bet and paid. Then he made his call, came back to the counter and paid for it."

She bit her lip.

"There was something strange about those phone calls. I remember thinking about it one time."

"What was it?"

"He always waited until another customer came into the shop before he dialled the number and started to talk. He never called when he and I were the only ones in the shop."

"He didn't want you to overhear."

She shrugged.

"Maybe he just wanted his privacy. Isn't that normal?"

"Did you ever hear what he talked about?"

"You can listen even when you're attending a customer."

Her curiosity is a big help, Wallander thought.

"What did he say?"

"Not very much," she answered. "The conversations were always very brief. He gave times, I think. Not much more."

"Times?"

"I had the feeling he was arranging a time with someone. He often looked at his watch while he was talking."

Wallander thought for a moment.

"Did he usually come here on the same day of the week?"

"Every Wednesday afternoon. Between two and three, I think. Or perhaps a little later."

"Did he buy anything else?"

"No."

"How can you remember all this so precisely? You must have a large number of customers."

"I don't know," she said. "But I think you remember more than you realise. If someone starts to ask you it just comes back up."

Wallander looked at her hands. She wore no rings. He briefly considered asking her out but then dismissed the thought, horrified.

It was as if Mona had overheard his thoughts.

"Is there anything else you remember?"

"No," she said, "but I'm sure he was talking to a woman."

That surprised Wallander.

"How can you be sure of that?"

"You can hear it," she said firmly.

"You mean that Hålén was calling to set up a time to meet with a woman?"

"What would be strange about that? He was old, of course, but that doesn't matter."

Wallander nodded. Of course she was right. And if she was right he had found out something valuable. There had been a woman in Hålén's life after all.

"Good," he said. "Do you remember anything else?"

Before she answered, a customer walked in. Wallander waited. There were two little girls who took a great deal of care in selecting two bags of sweets, which they then paid for with an endless series of five-öre pieces.

"That woman may have had a name that started with A," she said. "He always spoke very quietly. I said that earlier. But her name may have been Anna. Or a double name. Something with A."

"Are you sure of this?"

"No," she said. "But I think so."

Wallander only had one more question.

"Did he always come in alone?"

"Yes, always."

"You've been a great help," he said.

"May I ask why you need this information?"

"Unfortunately not," Wallander said. "We ask questions, but we can't always tell you why."

"Maybe I should join the police," she said. "I'm not planning to work in this shop for the rest of my life."

Wallander leaned over the counter and wrote down his telephone number on a small notepad next to the cash register.

"Call me sometime," he said. "We can get together and I can tell you what it's like to be a police officer. Anyway, I live right round the corner."

"Wallander," she said. "Is that what it is?"

"Kurt Wallander."

"My name is Maria. But don't get any ideas. I already have a boyfriend."

"I won't," Wallander said and smiled.

Then he left.

A boyfriend can always be overcome, he thought as he stepped into the street. And stopped short. What would happen if she really called him? If she called while Mona was over? He asked himself what he had done. At the same time he couldn't help but feel a certain satisfaction.

Mona deserved it. That he gave his phone number to someone named Maria who was very beautiful.

As if Wallander was being punished for the mere thought of sinning, the rain started to pour down at that moment. He was drenched by the time he got home. He laid the wet cigarette packets on the kitchen table and stripped off all his clothes. Maria should have been here now to towel me off, he thought. And Mona can cut hair and take her damn coffee break.

He put on his dressing gown and wrote down in his notepad what Maria had said. So Hålén had called a woman every Wednesday. A woman whose name started with the letter A. In all likelihood it was her first name. The question now was simply what this meant, other than that the image of the lonely old man had been shattered.

Wallander sat at the kitchen table and read through what he had written the day before. Suddenly he was struck by a thought. There should be a sailors' register somewhere. Someone who could tell him about Hålén's many years at sea, which vessels he had worked on.

I know someone who could help me, Wallander thought. Helena. She works for a shipping company. At the very least she can tell me where I can look. If she doesn't hang up on me when I call.

It was not yet eleven. Wallander could see through the kitchen window that the downpour was over. Helena didn't normally take her lunch break until half past twelve. That meant that he would be able to get hold of her before she left.

He got dressed and took the bus down to the Central Station. The shipping company that Helena worked for was in the harbour district. He walked in through the gates. The receptionist nodded at him in recognition.

"Is Helena in?" he asked.

"She's on the phone. But you can go on up. You know where her office is."

It was not without a feeling of dread that Wallander made his ascent to the first floor. Helena could get angry. But he tried to calm himself, thinking that at first she would simply be surprised. That could give him the time he needed to say that he was here purely on business. It was not her ex-boyfriend Kurt Wallander who was here, it was the police officer by the same name, the would-be criminal investigator.

The words "Helena Aronsson, Assistant Clerk", were printed on the door. Wallander drew a deep breath and knocked. He heard her voice and walked in. She had finished her phone call and was sitting at the typewriter. He had been right. She was clearly surprised, not angry.

"You," she said. "What are you doing here?"

"I'm here on police business," Wallander said. "I thought you might be able to help me."

She had stood up and was already looking like she was going to ask him to leave.

"I mean it," Wallander said. "It's nothing personal, not at all."

She was still on her guard.

"What would I be able to help you with?"

"May I sit down?"

"Only if it won't take long."

The same power language as Hemberg, Wallander thought. You're supposed to stand there and feel subordinate, while the person with power remains seated. But he sat down and wondered how he could once have been so in love with the woman on the other side of the desk. Now he could not remember her being anything other than stiff and dismissive.

"I'm fine," she said. "So there's no need for you to ask."

"I'm fine too."

"What do you want?"

Wallander sighed internally over her rude tone but told her what had happened.

"You work in the shipping industry," he finished. "You would know how I could find out what Hålén really did at sea. Which companies he worked for, which ships."

"I work with freight," Helena said. "We rent vessels or cargo space for Kockums and Volvo. That's all."

"There must be someone who knows."

"Can't the police find this out some other way?"

Wallander had anticipated this question and had thus prepared an answer.

"This case is being handled a little on the side," he said, "for reasons that I can't go into."

He could see that she only partly believed him. But she seemed amused.

"I could ask some of my colleagues," she said. "We have an old sea captain. But what do I get in return? If I help you?"

"What would you like?" he asked in return, in as friendly a tone as he could muster.

She shook her head.

"Nothing."

Wallander stood up.

"I have the same phone number as before," he said.

"Mine is different," Helena said. "And you're not getting it."

When Wallander was back out on the street he noticed that he was damp with sweat. The meeting with Helena had been more stressful than he had wanted to admit. He ended up standing still, wondering what to do next. If he had had more money he would have gone to Copenhagen. But he had to remember that he had taken a sick day. Someone could call him. He shouldn't stay away from home too long. And also he was finding it increasingly difficult to justify the fact that he was spending so much time on his dead neighbour. He went to a cafe across from the Denmark ferries and had the daily special. But before he ordered he checked to see how much money he had. He would have to go to the bank tomorrow. He still had a thousand kronor there. That would last him for the rest of the month. He ate stew and drank some water.

By one o'clock he was back out on the pavement. New storms were moving in from the south-west. He decided to go home. But when he saw a bus that was going to his father's suburb he took that instead. If nothing else he could spend a few hours helping his father pack.

There was indescribable chaos in the house. His father was reading an old newspaper, a torn straw hat on his head. He looked up at Wallander in surprise.

"Have you finished?" he asked.

"Finished with what?"

"Have you come to your senses and finished being a cop?"

"I'm off today," Wallander said. "And there's no use bringing up the subject again. We're never going to see eye to eye."

"I've found a paper from 1949," he said. "There's a great deal of interest in it."

"Do you really have time to read newspapers that are more than twenty years old?"

"I never had time to read it at the time," his father said. "Among other things, because I had a two-year-old son who did nothing but scream all day. That's why I'm reading it now."

"I was planning to help you pack."

His father pointed to a table stacked with china.

"That stuff needs to be packed in boxes," he said. "But it has to be done correctly. Nothing can break. If I find a broken plate you'll have to replace it."

His father returned to his paper. Wallander hung up his coat and started to pack the china. Plates that he remembered from his childhood. He found a cup with a chip in it that he could remember particularly clearly. His father turned a page in the background.

"How does it feel?" Wallander asked.

"How does what feel?"

"To be moving."

"Good. Change is nice."

"And you still haven't seen the house?"

"No, but I'm sure it'll be fine."

My father is either crazy or else he's becoming senile, Wallander thought. And there's nothing I can do about it.

"I thought Kristina was coming," he said.

"She's out shopping."

"I'd like to see her. How is she doing?"

"Fine. And she's met an excellent fellow."

"Did she bring him?"

"No. But he sounds good in all respects. He'll probably see to it that I get grandchildren soon."

"What's his name? What does he do? Do I have to drag all this out of you?"

"His name is Jens and he's a dialysis researcher."

"What's that?"

"Kidneys. If you've heard of them. He's a researcher. And in addition he likes to hunt small game. Sounds like an excellent man."

At that precise moment Wallander dropped a plate. It cracked in two. His father did not look up from the paper.

"That'll cost you," he said.

Wallander had had enough. He took his coat and left without a word. I will never go out to Österlen, he thought. I will never set foot in his home again. I don't understand how I have put up with that man all these years. But now I've had enough.

Without realising it he had started to speak aloud. A cyclist, who was huddled up against the wind, stared at him.

Wallander went home. The door to Hålén's apartment was open. He walked in. A lone technician was gathering up the remains of some ashes.

"I thought you were done?" Wallander said, surprised.

"Sjunnesson is thorough," the technician answered.

There was no continuation of the conversation. Wallander went back out onto the stairwell and unlocked his own door. At the same time Linnea Almquist walked into the building.

"How terrible," she said. "The poor man. And so alone."

"Apparently he had a lady friend," Wallander said.

"I find that hard to believe," Linnea Almquist said. "I would have noticed that."

"I'm sure you would have," Wallander said. "But he may not have been in the habit of seeing her here."

"One should not speak ill of the dead," she said and started up the stairs.

Wallander wondered how it could be considered speaking ill of the dead to suggest that there may have been a woman in an otherwise lonely existence.

Once he was in his apartment, Wallander could no longer push aside thoughts of Mona. He should call her. Or would she call him of her own accord in the evening? In order to shake off his anxiety, Wallander started to gather up and throw out old newspapers. Then he started in on the bathroom. He did not have to do much before he realised that there was much more old, ingrained dirt than he could have imagined. He kept going at it for over three hours before he felt satisfied with the result. It was five o'clock. He put some potatoes on to boil and chopped some onions.

The phone rang. He thought at once it had to be Mona, and his heart started to beat faster.

But it was another woman's voice. She said her name, Maria, but it took a few seconds before he realised it was the girl from the newsagent.

"I hope I'm not disturbing you," she said. "I lost the piece of paper you gave me. And you're not in the phone book. I could have called directory assistance, I suppose. But I called the police instead."

Wallander flinched.

"What did you say?"

"That I was looking for an officer by the name of Kurt Wallander. And that I had important information. At first they didn't want to give me your home phone number. But I didn't give in."

"So you asked for Detective Inspector Wallander?"

"I asked for Kurt Wallander. What does it matter?"

"It doesn't," Wallander said and felt relieved. Gossip moved quickly at the station. It could have brought about complications and spawned an unnecessary funny story about Wallander walking around claiming to be a detective inspector. That was not how he envisioned starting his career as a criminal investigator.

"I asked if I was disturbing you," she repeated.

"Not at all."

"I was thinking," she said. "About Hålén and his betting forms. He never won, by the way."

"How do you know?"

"I would entertain myself by checking to see how he had bet. Not just him. And he was very ill-informed when it came to English football."

Exactly what Hemberg said, Wallander thought. There can be no more doubt in that regard.

"But then I was thinking about the phone calls," she went on. "And then I thought of the fact that a couple of times he also called someone other than that woman."

Wallander increased his concentration.

"Who?"

"He called the cab company."

"How do you know that?"

"I heard him place an order for a car. He gave his address as the building right next to the shop."

Wallander thought about it.

"How often did he order a cab?"

"Three or four times. Always after first calling the other number."

"You didn't happen to hear where he was going?"

"He didn't mention it."

"Your memory isn't half bad," Wallander said admiringly. "But you don't remember when he made those calls?"

"It must have been on a Wednesday."

"When did it happen last?"

The answer came quickly and confidently.

"Last week."

"Are you sure of that?"

"Of course I'm sure. He called a cab last Wednesday, the twenty-eighth of May, for your information."

"Good," Wallander said. "Very good."

"Is that of any help?"

"I'm certain it is."

"And you're still not planning to tell me what it is that has happened?"

"I couldn't," Wallander said. "Even if I wanted to."

"Will you tell me later?"

Wallander promised. Then he hung up and thought about what she had told him. What did it mean? Hålén had a woman somewhere. After calling her, he ordered a taxi.

Wallander checked the potatoes. They were not yet soft. Then he reminded himself that he actually had a good friend who drove a cab in Malmö. They had been schoolmates since year one and had kept in touch over the years. His name was Lars Andersson and Wallander recalled that he had written his number on the inside of the telephone directory.

He found the number and dialled it. A woman answered, Andersson's wife Elin. Wallander had met her a few times.

"I'm looking for Lars," he said.

"He's out driving," she said. "But he's on a day shift. He'll be back in about an hour."

Wallander asked her to tell her husband he had called.

"How are the children?" she asked.

"I have no children," Wallander said, amazed.

"Then I must have misunderstood," she answered. "I thought Lars said that you had two sons."

"Unfortunately, no," Wallander said. "I'm not even married."

"That never stopped anyone."

Wallander returned to the potatoes and onions. Then he composed a meal using some of the leftovers that had accumulated in the fridge. Mona had still not called. It had started to rain again. He could hear accordion music from somewhere. He asked himself what the hell he was doing. His neighbour Hålén had committed suicide, after first swallowing some precious stones. Someone had tried to retrieve them and had subsequently set fire to the apartment in a rage. There were plenty of lunatics around, also greedy people. But it was no crime to commit suicide. Nor to be greedy per se.

It was half past six. Lars Andersson had not called. Wallander decided to wait until seven o'clock. Then he would try again.

The call from Andersson came at five minutes to seven.

"Business always picks up when it's raining. I heard that you had called?"

"I'm working on a case," Wallander said. "And I was thinking that you could perhaps help me. It's a matter of tracking down a driver who had a client last Wednesday. Around three o'clock. A pickup from an address here in Rosengård. A man by the name of Hålén."

"What's happened?"

"Nothing that I can talk about right now," Wallander said and felt his discomfort grow every time he avoided giving an answer.

"I can probably find out," Andersson said. "The Malmö call centre is very organised. Can you give me the details? And where should I call to? The police headquarters?"

"It's best if you call me. I'm leading this thing."

"From home?"

"Right now I am."

"I'll see what I can do."

"How long do you think it will take?"

"With a little luck, not very long."

"I'll be home," Wallander said.

He gave Andersson all the details he had. When the call was over he had a cup of coffee. Still no call from Mona. Then he thought of his sister. Wondered what excuse his father would give for him having left the house so abruptly. If he even bothered to say that his son had been there. Kristina often took her father's side. Wallander suspected it had to do with cowardice, that she was afraid of their father and his unpredictable temper.

Then he watched the news. The auto industry was doing well. There was an economic boom in Sweden. After that they showed footage from a dog show. He turned down the volume. The rain continued. He thought he heard thunder somewhere in the distance. Or else it was a Metropolitan plane coming in for landing at Bulltofta.

It was ten minutes past nine when Andersson called back.

"It's as I expected," he said. "The Malmö taxi call centre is extremely well organised."

Wallander had already pulled over a pen and paper.

"The drive went out to Arlöv," he said. "There is no record of another name. The driver's name was Norberg. But I can probably hunt him down and ask him if he remembers what the client looked like."

"There's no chance that it could have been another trip?"

"No one else ordered a taxi to that address on Wednesday."

"And the car went out to Arlöv?"

"More specifically, to Smedsgatan 9. That's right next to a sugar mill. An old neighbourhood with rows of terraced houses."

"No rented apartments then," Wallander said. "Only a family must live there. Or a single person, I suppose."

"You would think so."

Wallander made a note of it.

"You've done good," he said.

"I may have even more for you," Andersson replied. "Even if you never asked me for it. There is also a record of a cab ride from Smedsgatan. Specifically, Thursday morning at four o'clock. The driver's name was Orre. But you won't be able to get hold of him right now. He's on holiday in Mallorca."

Can taxi drivers afford to do that? Wallander thought. Is that because they make money under the table? But of course he mentioned nothing of these speculations to Andersson.

"It could be important."

"Do you still not have a car?"

"Not yet."

"Are you planning to go there?"

"Yes."

"You can use a police car, of course, can't you?"

"Of course."

"Because otherwise I could take you. I'm not doing anything in particular. It's a long time since we had a chat."

Wallander decided to take him up on his offer and Lars Andersson promised to pick him up in half an hour. During that time Wallander called directory assistance and asked who was registered on telephone service at Smedsgatan 9. He received the answer that there was service there but that the number was private.

It was raining harder. Wallander put on his rubber boots and a raincoat. He stood at the kitchen window and saw Andersson slow down in front of his building. The car had no sign on the roof. It was his private car.

A crazy expedition in crazy weather, Wallander thought as he locked the front door. But rather this than pacing around the apartment waiting for Mona to call. And if she does it'll serve her right. That I don't answer.

Lars Andersson immediately started to bring up old school memories. Half of it Wallander no longer had any recollection of. He often thought Andersson tiring because he constantly returned to their school years, as if they represented the best time of his life so far. For Wallander, school had been a grey drudge, where only geography and history enlivened him somewhat. But he still liked the man who sat behind the wheel. His parents had run a bakery out in Limhamn. For a while, the boys had been in frequent contact. And Lars Andersson was someone Wallander had always been able to count on. Someone who took their friendship seriously.

They left Malmö behind and were soon in Arlöv.

"Do you often get requests out here?" Wallander asked.

"It happens. Mostly on the weekends. People who have been drinking in Malmö or Copenhagen and who are on their way home."

"Has anything bad ever happened to you?"

Lars Andersson glanced over at him.

"What do you mean?"

"Muggings, threats. I don't know."

"Never. I've had a guy who tried to slip away without paying. But I caught up with him."

They were now in the centre of Arlöv. Lars Andersson drove straight to the address.

"Here it is," he said and pointed through the wet windscreen. "Smedsgatan 9."

Wallander cranked down his window and squinted out into the rain. Number 9 was the last of a row of six town houses. There was a light on in one window. Someone must be home.

"Aren't you going to go in?" Lars Andersson asked with surprise.

"It's a matter of surveillance," Wallander answered vaguely. "If you drive up a little I'll get out and take a look around."

"Do you want me to come along?"

"That won't be necessary."

Wallander got out of the car and pulled up the hood of his raincoat. What do I do now? he wondered. Ring the doorbell and ask if it is possible that Mr Hålén was here last Wednesday between three in the afternoon and four in the morning? Is it a matter of adultery? What do I say if a man answers the door?

Wallander felt silly. This is senseless and childish and a waste of time, he thought. The only thing that I have managed to prove is that Smedsgatan 9 is actually an address in Arlöv.

Nonetheless, he couldn't help crossing the street. There was a mailbox next to the gate. Wallander tried to read the name on it. He had cigarettes and a box of matches in his pocket. With some difficulty he was able to light one of the matches and read the name before his flame was extinguished by the rain.

"Alexandra Batista," he read. So Maria in the newsagent had been right, it was the first name that started with A. Hålén had called a woman named Alexandra. The question now was if she lived there alone or with family. He looked over the fence to see if there were any children's bicycles or other items that would indicate a family's presence. But he saw nothing like that.

He walked round the house. On the other side there was an undeveloped piece of property. Several old rusty drums had been placed behind a dilapidated fence. That was all. The house was dark from the back. Light was only coming from the kitchen window facing the street. Despite a rising feeling of being involved in something absolutely unjustified and senseless, Wallander decided to complete his investigation. He stepped over the low fence and ran across the lawn to the house. If anyone sees me they will call the police, he thought.

And I will get caught. And then the rest of my police career goes up in smoke.

He decided to give up. He could find the telephone number for the Batista family tomorrow. If it was a woman who answered he could ask a few questions. If it was a man he could hang up.

The rain was letting up. Wallander dried off his face. He was about to go back the same way that he had come when he discovered that the door to the balcony was open. Maybe they have a cat, he thought. That needs free passage at night.

At the same time he had a feeling that something wasn't right. He could not put his finger on what it was. But he was not able to dismiss it. Carefully he walked over to the door and listened. The rain had stopped almost completely now. In the distance he heard the sound of a tractor trailer die away and disappear. From inside the house he heard nothing. Wallander left the balcony door and walked over to the front of the house again.

The light was still shining in the window, which was open a little. He pressed up against the wall and strained to hear something. Everything was still, quiet. Then he gently raised himself on tiptoe and peered in through the window.

He jumped. Inside, there was a woman sitting in a chair, staring straight at him. He ran out to the street. At any moment someone was going to come running out onto the front steps and call for help. Or else there would be police cars. He hurried over to the car where Andersson was waiting and jumped into the front seat.

"Has anything happened?"

"Just drive," Wallander said.

"Where to?"

"Away from here. Back to Malmö."

"Was anyone home?"

"Don't ask. Start the engine and drive. That's all."

Lars Andersson did as Wallander asked. They came out onto the main road towards Malmö. Wallander thought about the woman who had stared at him.

The feeling was there again. Something wasn't right.

"Turn into the next car park, would you?"

Lars Andersson continued to do as he was told. They stopped. Wallander sat without saying anything.

"You don't think it's best that I be told what's going on?" Andersson asked gingerly.

Wallander didn't answer. There was something about that woman's face. Something he couldn't pinpoint.

"Go back," he said.

"To Arlöv?"

Wallander could hear that Andersson was starting to resist.

"I'll explain later," Wallander said. "Drive back to the same address. If you have the taxi meter you can turn it on."

"I don't charge my friends, damn it!" Andersson said angrily.

They drove back to Arlöv in silence. There was no longer any rain.

Wallander got out of the car. No police cars, no reaction. Nothing. Only the lone light in the kitchen window.

Wallander carefully opened the gate. He walked back to the window. Before he heaved himself up to look he drew some deep breaths.

If things were as he suspected it would be very unpleasant.

He stood on tiptoe and gripped the windowsill. The woman was still sitting in the chair, staring straight at him with the same expression.

Wallander walked round the back of the house and opened the balcony door. In the light from the street he glimpsed a table lamp. He turned it on, then he removed his boots and walked out into the kitchen.

The woman was sitting there in the chair. But she was not looking at Wallander. She was staring at the window.

Around her neck was a bicycle chain, tightened with the help of a hammer handle.

Wallander felt his heart thumping in his chest.

Then he located the telephone, which was out in the hall, and he called the police station in Malmö.

It was already a quarter to eleven.

Wallander asked to speak to Hemberg. He was told that Hemberg had left the police station at around six o'clock. Wallander asked for his home number and called him immediately.

Hemberg picked up. Wallander could hear that he had been sleeping and had been awakened by the call.

Wallander explained the situation.

That there was a dead woman sitting in a chair in a town house in Arlöv.

CHAPTER
THREE

Hemberg came out to Arlöv a little after midnight. At that point the forensic investigation was already under way. Wallander had sent Andersson home in his car without giving him a better explanation of what had happened. Then he had stood by the gate and waited for the first police car to arrive. He had spoken with a detective inspector by the name of Stefansson, who was his own age.

"Did you know her?" he asked.

"No," Wallander answered.

"Then what are you doing here?"

"I'll explain that to Hemberg," Wallander said.

Stefansson regarded him sceptically but did not ask any further questions.

Hemberg started by walking around the kitchen. He stood in the doorway for a long time, simply looking at the dead woman. Wallander saw how his gaze travelled around the room. After standing there for a length of time he turned to Stefansson, who appeared to have great respect for him.

"Do we know who she is?" Hemberg asked.

They went into the living room. Stefansson had opened a handbag and spread some identifying documentation on the table.

"Alexandra Batista-Lundström," he answered. "A Swedish citizen, but born in Brazil in 1922. It seems she came over right after the war. If I have understood this correctly, she was married to a man named Lundström. There are divorce papers here from 1957. But at that point she already had citizenship. She gave up the Swedish surname later on. She has a post office savings account under the name of Batista. No Lundström."

"Did she have any children?"

Stefansson shook his head.

"It doesn't seem like anyone else lived here with her. We've talked to one of the neighbours. Apparently she has lived here since the place was built."

Hemberg nodded and then turned to Wallander.

"Let's go up a floor," he said, "and let the technicians work undisturbed."

Stefansson was on his way to join them, but Hemberg held him back. There were three rooms upstairs. The woman's bedroom, a room that was basically empty except for a linen cupboard, and a guest room. Hemberg sat down on the bed in the guest room and indicated to Wallander that he should sit in the chair in the corner.

"I really only have one question," Hemberg began. "What do you think it is?"

"You're of course wondering what I was doing here."

"I would probably put it more forcefully," Hemberg said. "How the hell did you end up here?"

"It's a long story," Wallander said.

"Make it short," Hemberg replied. "But leave nothing out."

Wallander told him. About the betting forms, the telephone calls, the taxicabs. Hemberg listened with his eyes stubbornly directed at the floor. When Wallander finished, he sat for a while without saying anything.

"Since you've found a murder victim, I naturally have to praise you for it," he started. "There also seems to be nothing wrong with your determination. Nor has your thinking been completely wrong. But apart from these things, it goes without saying that your actions have been completely unjustifiable. There is no room in police work for anything resembling independent and secret surveillance, with detectives assigning themselves their own work. I say this only once."

Wallander nodded. He understood.

"Do you have anything else to tell me? Apart from what led you here to Arlöv?"

Wallander told him about his visit to Helena at the shipping company.

"Nothing more?"

"Nothing."

Wallander was prepared for a lecture. But Hemberg simply got up from the bed and nodded for him to follow suit.

On the stairs he stopped and turned round.

"I looked for you today," he said. "To tell you the results of the weapons inspection. There was nothing unexpected in the report. But they said you had called in sick?"

"I had a stomach ache this morning. Stomach flu."

Hemberg gave him an ironic look.

"That was quick," he said. "But since you seem to have got better you can stay here tonight. You may learn something. Don't touch anything, don't say anything. Just make mental notes."

At half past three the woman's body was taken away. Sjunnesson had arrived shortly after one. Wallander wondered why he didn't seem at all tired even though it was the middle of the night. Hemberg, Stefansson and another detective had methodically searched the apartment, opened drawers and cupboards, and found a number of things that they put out on the table. Wallander had also listened to a conversation between Hemberg and a medical examiner called Jörne. There was no doubt that the woman had been strangled. In his initial examination Jörne had also found signs that she had been struck on the head from behind. Hemberg explained that what he most needed to know was how long she had been dead.

"She has probably been sitting in that chair for a couple of days," Jörne answered.

"How many?"

"I won't hazard a guess. You'll have to wait until the autopsy is complete."

When the conversation with Jörne was over, Hemberg turned to Wallander.

"You understand, of course, why I asked him this," he said.

"You want to know if she died before Hålén?"

Hemberg nodded.

"In that case it would give us a reasonable explanation for why a person had taken his own life. It is not unusual for murderers to commit suicide."

Hemberg sat down on the couch in the living room. Stefansson was standing out in the hall, talking to the police photographer.

"One thing we can nonetheless see quite clearly," Hemberg said after a pause. "The woman was killed as she sat in the chair. Someone hit her on the head. There are traces of blood on the floor and on the wax tablecloth. Then she was strangled. That gives us several possible points of departure."

Hemberg looked at Wallander.

He's testing me, Wallander thought. He wants to know if I measure up.

"It must mean that the woman knew the person who killed her."

"Correct. And more?"

Wallander searched his mind. Were there any other conclusions to be drawn? He shook his head.

"You have to use your eyes," Hemberg said. "Was there something on the table? One cup? Several cups? How was she dressed? It is one thing that she knew the person who killed her. Let us for the sake of simplicity assume it was a man. But how well did she know him?"

Wallander understood. It bothered him that he had initially missed what Hemberg had been getting at.

"She was wearing a nightgown and robe," he said. "That's not something you wear with just anyone."

"How did her bed look?"

"It was unmade."

"Conclusion?"

"Alexandra Batista may have had a relationship with the man who killed her."

"More?"

"There were no cups on the table, but there were some unwashed glasses next to the stove."

"We will examine them," Hemberg said. "What did they drink? Are there fingerprints? Empty glasses have many exciting things to tell us."

He rose heavily from the couch. Wallander suddenly realised that he was tired.

"So we actually know a great deal," Hemberg continued. "Since there are no signs of an intruder we will work with the hypothesis that the murder was committed under the auspices of a personal connection."

"That still doesn't explain the fire at Hålén's place," Wallander said.

Hemberg studied him critically.

"You're getting ahead of yourself," he said. "We are going to move forward calmly and methodically. We know some things with a great deal of certainty. We proceed from these things. What we do not know, or what we cannot be sure of, will have to wait. You cannot solve a puzzle if half of the pieces are still in the box."

They had reached the hall. Stefansson had finished his conversation with the photographer and was now talking on the phone.

"How did you get here?" Hemberg asked.

"Taxi."

"You can come back with me."

During the trip back to Malmö Hemberg did not say anything. They drove through fog and a drizzling rain. Hemberg dropped Wallander off outside his building in Rosengård.

"Get in touch with me later on today," Hemberg said. "If you've recovered from your stomach flu, that is."

Wallander let himself into his apartment. It was already morning. The fog had begun to dissipate. He didn't bother taking his clothes off. Instead, he lay down on top of the bed. He was soon asleep.

The doorbell jerked him awake. He sleepily stumbled out into the hall and opened the door. His sister, Kristina, was standing there.

"Am I disturbing you?"

Wallander shook his head and let her in.

"I've been working all night," he said. "What time is it?"

"Seven. I'm going out to Löderup with Dad today. But I thought I would look in on you first."

Wallander asked her to put some coffee on while he had a wash and changed his clothes. He bathed his face in cold water for a long time. By the time he came back out to the kitchen he had chased the long night out of his body. Kristina smiled at him.

"You are actually one of the few men I know who doesn't have long hair," she said.

"It doesn't suit me," Wallander answered. "But God knows I've tried. I can't have a beard either. I look ridiculous. Mona threatened to leave me when she saw it."

"How is she doing?"

"Fine."

Wallander briefly considered telling her what had happened. About the silence that now lay between them.

Earlier, when they had both lived at home, he and Kristina had had a close and trusting relationship. Even so, Wallander decided to say nothing. After she had moved to Stockholm the contact between them had become vague and more irregular.

Wallander sat down at the table and asked how things were with her.

"Good."

"Dad said you had met someone who works with kidneys."

"He's an engineer and he works at developing a new kind of dialysis machine."

"I'm not sure I know what that is," Wallander said. "But it sounds very advanced."

Then he realised that she had come for a particular reason. He could see it in her face.

"I don't know why," he said, "but I can tell that you want something in particular."

"I don't understand how you can treat Dad this way."

Wallander was taken aback.

"What do you mean?"

"What do you think? You don't help him pack. You don't even want to see his house in Löderup and when you bump into him on the street you pretend you don't know him."

Wallander shook his head.

"Did he say that?"

"Yes. And he's very upset."

"None of this is true."

"I haven't seen you since I got here. He's moving today."

"Didn't he tell you that I came by? And that he basically threw me out?"

"He hasn't said anything like that."

"You shouldn't believe everything he says. At least not about me."

"So it isn't true?"

"Nothing is true. He didn't even tell me he had bought the house. He hasn't wanted to show it to me, hasn't even told me what it cost. When I was helping him pack I dropped an old plate and all hell broke loose. And actually I do stop and talk to him when I see him on the street. Even though he often looks like a crazy person."

Wallander could tell she wasn't quite convinced. That irritated him. But even more upsetting was the fact that she was sitting here scolding him. That reminded him of his mother. Or Mona. Or Helena, for that matter. He couldn't stand these meddling women who tried to tell him what to do.

"You don't believe me," Wallander said, "but you should. Don't forget that you live in Stockholm and that I have the old man in my face all the time. That makes a big difference."

The telephone rang. It was twenty minutes past seven. Wallander answered. It was Helena.

"I called you last night," she said.

"I worked all night."

"Since no one answered I thought I must have the wrong number, so I called Mona to check."

Wallander almost dropped the receiver.

"You did what?"

"I called and asked Mona for your telephone number."

Wallander had no illusions about what the consequences of this would be. If Helena had called Mona that meant Mona's jealousy would flare up with full force. It would not improve their relationship.

"Are you still there?" she asked.

"Yes," Wallander said, "but right now my sister is here."

"I'm at work. You can call me."

Wallander hung up and went back to the kitchen. Kristina looked curiously at him.

"Are you ill?"

"No," he said. "But I probably should go in to work now."

They said goodbye in the hall.

"You should believe me," Wallander said. "You can't always rely on what he tells you. Let him know I'll be out to see him as soon as I have time. If I'm welcome, that is, and if someone can tell me where this house is."

"At the edge of Löderup," Kristina said. "First you go past a country stall, then down a road bordered with willows. When that ends the house is on the left, with a stone wall to the road. It has a black roof and is very nice."

"When did you go there?"

"The first load went yesterday."

"Do you know what he paid for it?"

"He won't say."

Kristina left. Wallander waved at her through the kitchen window. He forced away his anger over what his father had said about him. What Helena had said was more serious. Wallander called her. When he was told she was on the line with another caller he banged the receiver back on the hook. He rarely lost control, but now he noticed that he was close. He called again. Still busy. Mona is going to end our relationship, he thought. She thinks I've started courting Helena again. It won't matter what I say. She's not going to believe me anyway. He called again. This time he got an answer.

"What did you want?"

Her voice was cold when she replied.

"Do you have to sound so unpleasant? I was actually trying to help you."

"Was it really necessary to call Mona?"

"She knows I'm not interested in you any more."

"She does? You don't know Mona."

"I'm not going to apologise for trying to find your telephone number."

"What did you want?"

"I've received some information from Captain Verke. Do you remember? I said that we had an old sea captain here."

Wallander remembered.

"I have some paper copies in front of me. Lists of sailors and engineers who have worked for Swedish shipping lines for the past ten years. As you can imagine, this includes quite a number of people. By the way, are you sure that the man you mentioned had only served on Swedish-registered vessels?"

"I'm not sure of anything," Wallander said.

"You can pick up the lists from here," she said. "When you have time. But I'll be in meetings all afternoon."

Wallander promised to come by in the morning. Then he hung up and thought that what he should do now was call Mona and explain the situation. But he let it be. He simply didn't dare.

It was ten minutes to eight. He started to put on his coat.

The thought of patrolling for a whole day increased his despondence.

He was just about to leave the apartment when the telephone rang again. Mona, he thought. Now she's calling to tell me to go to hell. He drew a deep breath and lifted the receiver.

It was Hemberg.

"How are you doing with that stomach flu?"

"I was just on my way in to the station."

"Good. But come up and report to me. I have talked with Lohman. You are after all a witness who we need to talk to more. That means no patrolling today. And to top it off, you won't have to participate in raids on drug-infested neighbourhoods."

"I'm on my way," Wallander said.

"Come by at ten o'clock. I thought you could sit in on a meeting we have scheduled about the murder in Arlöv."

The conversation was over. Wallander checked his watch. He would have time to pick up the papers waiting for him at the shipping office. On the kitchen wall he had a schedule for the buses to and from Rosengård. If he hurried, he wouldn't have to wait.

When he walked out the front door, Mona was there. He had not expected that. As little as he expected what happened next. She walked right over to him and slapped him on the left cheek. Then she twirled round and walked away.

Wallander was so shocked he did not even manage to react. His cheek burned and a man who was unlocking his car door stared at him with curiosity.

Mona was already gone. Slowly he started walking to the bus stop. He had a knot in his stomach now. It had never occurred to him that she would react so violently.

The bus arrived. Wallander made his way down towards the Central Station. The fog had gone. But it was overcast. The morning drizzle continued unabated. He sat in the bus and his head was completely empty. The events of last night no longer existed. The woman who had been sitting dead in her chair was part of a dream. The only thing that was real was that Mona had hit him and then walked away. Without a word, without hesitation.

I have to talk to her, he thought. Not now, while she is still upset. But later, tonight.

He got off the bus. His cheek still stung. The slap had been forceful. He checked his reflection in a shop window. The redness on his cheek was noticeable.

He lingered, confused about his course of action. Thought that he should talk to Lars Andersson as soon as possible. Thank him for his help and explain what had happened.

Then he thought about a house in Löderup he had never seen. And his childhood home, which no longer belonged to his family.

He started to walk. Nothing was made better by his standing unmoving on a pavement in downtown Malmö.

Wallander picked up the large envelope that Helena had left with the office receptionist.

"I need to talk to her," he said to the receptionist.

"She's busy" was the answer. "She just asked me to give you this."

Wallander realised Helena was probably angry about the morning's conversation and did not want to see him. He didn't have great difficulties relating to this.

It wasn't more than five minutes past nine when Wallander arrived at the police station. He walked to his office and to his relief found that no one was waiting for him. Once again he thought through everything that had happened this morning. If he called the hair salon where Mona worked she would say she didn't have time to talk. He would have to wait until tonight.

He opened the envelope and was amazed at how long the lists of names from various shipping companies that Helena had managed to dig up were.

He looked for Artur Hålén's name, but it wasn't there. The closest names he saw were a seaman by the name of Håle who had mostly sailed for the Gränges shipping line, and a chief engineer on the Johnson line by the name of Hallén. Wallander pushed aside the pile of paper. If the records he had in front of him were complete that meant that Hålén had not worked on any ships registered in the Swedish merchant fleet. Then it would be nearly impossible to find him. Wallander suddenly did not know any longer what he was hoping to find. An explanation of what?

It had taken him almost three-quarters of an hour to go through the lists. He got to his feet and walked up to the next floor. He bumped into his boss, Inspector Lohman, in the corridor.

"Weren't you supposed to be with Hemberg today?"

"I'm on my way."

"What were you doing out in Arlöv, anyway?"

"It's a long story; that's what the meeting with Hemberg is about."

Lohman shook his head and hurried on. Wallander felt relief at not having to go to the dreary and depressing drug-infested neighbourhoods that his colleagues were going to have to deal with that day.

Hemberg was sitting in his office, sorting through some papers. As usual he had his feet up on the desk. He looked up when Wallander appeared in the doorway.

"What happened to you?" Hemberg asked and pointed to his cheek.

"I bumped into a doorpost," Wallander said.

"Just what abused wives say when they don't want to turn in their husbands," Hemberg said breezily and sat up.

Wallander felt found out. It was getting harder and harder for him to determine what Hemberg was really thinking. Hemberg seemed to have a double-edged language, one that made the listener constantly search for the meaning behind the words.

"We're still waiting for definitive results from Jörne," Hemberg said. "That takes time. As long as we can't pinpoint exactly when the woman died we also cannot proceed with the theory that Hålén killed her and then went home and shot himself out of regret or fear."

Hemberg stood with his papers tucked under his arm. Wallander followed him to a conference room further down the corridor. There were already several detectives there, among them Stefansson, who regarded Wallander with animosity. Sjunnesson was picking his teeth and did not look at anyone. There were also two other men who Wallander recognised. One was called Hörner and the other Mattsson. Hemberg sat down at the short end of the table and pointed out a chair to Wallander.

"Is the patrol squad helping us out now?" Stefansson said. "Don't they have enough to do with all those damn protestors?"

"The patrol squad has nothing to do with this," Hemberg said. "But Wallander found that lady out in Arlöv. It's as simple as that."

Only Stefansson seemed to object to Wallander's presence. The others nodded kindly. Wallander

105

imagined that more than anything they were happy to have an additional hand. Sjunnesson put down the toothpick with which he had been picking his teeth. Apparently this was the sign that Hemberg could begin. Wallander noted the methodical care that characterised the investigative unit's proceedings. They worked from the existing facts, but they also took time — Hemberg, above all — to feel their way in exploring various directions. Why had Alexandra Batista been murdered? What could the connection to Hålén be? Were there any other leads?

"The precious stones in Hålén's stomach," Hemberg said towards the end of the meeting. "I have received an evaluation from a jeweller of about 150,000 kronor. A lot of money, in other words. People in this country have been murdered for much less."

"Someone hit a taxi driver on the head with an iron pipe a couple of years ago," Sjunnesson said. "He had twenty-two kronor in his wallet."

Hemberg looked around the table.

"The neighbours?" he asked. "Have they seen anything? Heard anything?"

Mattsson glanced through his notes.

"No observations," he said. "Batista lived an isolated life. Rarely went out except to buy groceries. Had no visitors."

"Someone must have seen Hålén come by?" Hemberg objected.

"Apparently not. And the nearest neighbours gave the impression of being regular Swedish citizens. That is to say, extremely nosy."

"When did someone see her last?"

"There were differing opinions on this. But of what I have been able to document, one can draw the conclusion that it was several days ago. What's not clear is if it was two or three days ago."

"Do we know what she lived on?"

Then it was Hörner's turn.

"She seems to have had a small annuity," he said. "In part with unclear origins. A bank in Portugal that in turn has affiliated branches in Brazil. It always takes a damn long time with banks. But she didn't work. If you look at the contents of her cupboards, fridge and pantry, her life did not cost much."

"But the house?"

"No loans. Paid for in cash by her former husband."

"Where is he?"

"In a grave," Stefansson said. "He died a couple of years ago. Was buried in Karlskoga. I spoke to his widow. He had remarried. That was unfortunately somewhat embarrassing. I realised too late that she had no idea that there had once been an Alexandra Batista in his life. But he did not appear to have had any children with Batista."

"That's how it can be," Hemberg said, and turned to Sjunnesson.

"We're in the process," he said. "Different fingerprints on the glasses. Seems to have been red wine in them. Spanish, I think. We're trying to match this to an empty bottle that was in the kitchen. We're checking to see if we have the prints in the register. Then of course we'll also compare them to Hålén's."

"He may also be in Interpol's registers," Hemberg pointed out. "It can take a while until we hear back from them."

"We can assume she let him in," Sjunnesson continued. "There were no signs of forced entry on the windows or doors. He can also have had his own key, for that matter. But there were none that fitted. The balcony door was open, as our friend Wallander has informed us. Since Batista had neither a dog nor a cat, one could imagine that it was open to let in the night air. Which in turn should mean that Batista did not fear or expect that anything would happen. Or else the perpetrator exited that way. The back of the house is more protected from prying eyes."

"Any other evidence?" Hemberg said.

"Nothing out of the ordinary."

Hemberg pushed away the papers that were spread out in front of him.

"Then all we can do is keep going," he said. "The medical examiner will have to hurry up. The best possible outcome is if Hålén can be bound to the crime. Personally, that is what I believe. But we will have to keep talking to neighbours and digging around in background material."

Then Hemberg turned to Wallander.

"Do you have anything to add? You found her, after all."

Wallander shook his head and noticed that his mouth was dry.

"Nothing?"

"I didn't notice anything that you haven't already commented on."

Hemberg drummed his fingers against the tabletop.

"Then we have no need to sit here any longer," he said. "Does anyone know what the lunch is today?"

"Herring," Hörner said. "It's usually good."

Hemberg asked Wallander to join him for lunch. But he declined. His appetite was gone. He felt that he needed to be alone to think. He went to his office to get his coat. He could see through the window that it had stopped raining. Just as he was about to leave his office, one of his colleagues from the patrol squad came in and threw his police cap on a table.

"Shit," he said, and sat down heavily in a chair.

His name was Jörgen Berglund and he came from a farm outside Landskrona. Wallander sometimes had trouble understanding his dialect.

"We've cleaned up two blocks," he said. "In one of them we found some runaway thirteen-year-old girls who had been missing for weeks. One of them smelled so bad we had to hold our noses. Another one bit Persson on the leg when we were going to lift them out. What is happening in this country, anyway? And why weren't you there?"

"I was called in by Hemberg," Wallander said. As to the other question, about what was happening in Sweden, he had no answer.

He took his coat and left. In the reception area he was stopped by one of the girls who worked in the call centre.

"You have a message," she said and she handed him a note through the window. There was a phone number on it.

"What is this?" he asked.

"Someone called and said he was a distant relative to you. He wasn't sure you would even remember him."

"Didn't he say what his name was?"

"No, but he seemed old."

Wallander studied the telephone number. There was an area code: 0411. This can't be true, he thought. My father calls and introduces himself as a distant relative. One I may not even remember.

"Where is Löderup?" he asked.

"I think that's the Ystad police district."

"I'm not asking about the police district. Which area code is it?"

"It's Ystad."

Wallander tucked the note in his pocket and left. If he had had a car he would have driven straight out to Löderup and asked his father what he had meant by calling like that. When he had got an answer, he would let him have it. Say that from this point on all contact between them would be severed. No more poker evenings, no phone calls. Wallander would promise to come to the funeral, which he hoped was not too far off. But that was all.

Wallander walked along Fiskehamnsgatan. Then he swung onto Slottsgatan and continued into Kungsparken. I have two problems, he thought. The biggest and most important one is Mona. The other is my father. I have to solve both problems as soon as possible.

110

He sat down on a bench and watched some grey sparrows bathing in a puddle of water. A drunk man was sleeping behind some bushes. I should really lift him up, Wallander thought. Put him down on this bench or even make sure he gets picked up and can sleep it off somewhere. But right now I don't care about him. He can stay where he is.

He rose from the bench and kept going. Left Kungsparken and came out on Regementsgatan. He still wasn't feeling hungry. Even so, he stopped at a hot-dog stand on Gustav Adolf's Square and bought a grilled hot dog on a bun. Then he returned to the station.

It was half past one. Hemberg was unavailable. What he should do with himself, he didn't know. He should really talk to Lohman about what he was expected to do during the afternoon. But he didn't. Instead he pulled out the lists that Helena had given him. Again he browsed through the names. Tried to see the faces, imagine their lives. Sailors and engineers. Their birth information was noted in the margins. Wallander put the lists down again. From the corridor he heard something that sounded like a taunting laugh.

Wallander tried to think about Hålén. His neighbour. Who had turned in betting sheets, put in an extra lock and thereafter shot himself. Everything pointed to Hemberg's theory holding water. For some reason Hålén had killed Alexandra Batista and then taken his own life.

That's where it came to a stop for Wallander. Hemberg's theory was logical and straightforward.

Nonetheless Wallander thought it was hollow. The outside coordinates matched up. But the content? It was still very murky. Not least, this idea did not fit very well with the impression Wallander had had of his neighbour. Wallander had never found anything passionate or violent in him.

Of course even the most retiring person was capable of exploding in anger and violence under certain circumstances. But did it actually make sense to think that Hålén had taken the life of the woman he most likely had a relationship with?

Something is missing, Wallander thought. Inside this shell there is nothing.

He tried to think more deeply but didn't get anywhere. Absently he gazed at the lists on the table. Without being able to say where the thought came from, he suddenly started to look through all of the birth information in the margins. How old had Hålén been? He recalled that he was born in 1898. But which date? Wallander called reception and asked to be put through to Stefansson. He picked up at once.

"This is Wallander. I'm wondering if you have Hålén's birthdate available?"

"Are you planning to wish him a happy birthday?"

He doesn't like me, Wallander thought. But in time I'll show him that I am a much better investigator than he is.

"Hemberg asked me to look into something," Wallander lied.

Stefansson put down the receiver. Wallander could hear him riffling through papers.

112

"It's 17 September 1898," Stefansson said. "Anything else?"

"That's all," Wallander said and hung up.

Then he pulled over the lists again.

On the third page he found what he had not been consciously aware of looking for. An engineer who was born on 17 September 1898. Anders Hansson. Same initials as Artur Hålén, Wallander thought.

He went through the rest of the entries to assure himself that there were no others who were born on the same day. He found a sailor who was born on 19 September 1901. That was the closest thing. Wallander took out the phone book and looked up the number of his local pastor's office. Since Wallander and Hålén had lived in the same building, they must also be registered in the same parish. He dialled the number and waited. A woman answered. Wallander thought he might as well continue to introduce himself as a detective.

"My name is Wallander and I'm with the Malmö police," he started. "This is in regard to a violent death that occurred a few days ago. I'm from the homicide unit."

He gave Hålén's name, address and birthdate.

"What is it you want to know?" the woman asked.

"If there is any information about Hålén possibly having a different name earlier in his life."

"You mean such as changing his last name?"

Damn it, Wallander thought. People don't change their first names. Only their last names.

"Let me check," the woman said.

113

This was wrong, Wallander realised. I react before I've thought my ideas through enough.

He wondered if he should just hang up. But the woman would wonder about that, think the call had been cut off, and might call for him at the station. He waited. It took a long time before she returned.

"His death was just in the process of being recorded," she said. "That's why it took a while. But you were right."

Wallander sat up.

"His name was Hansson before. He changed his name in 1962."

Right, Wallander thought. But wrong anyway.

"The first name," he said. "What was it?"

"Anders."

"It should have been Artur."

The answer came as a surprise.

"It was. He must have had parents who loved names, or who couldn't agree. His name was Anders Erik Artur Hansson."

Wallander held his breath.

"Thank you so much for your help."

When the call was over, Wallander felt a strong urge to contact Hemberg. But he stayed where he was. The question was how much his discovery was worth. I'll follow up on this myself, he decided. If it doesn't lead anywhere, no one has to know about it.

Wallander pulled over his notepad and started to make a summary. What did he really know? Artur Hålén had changed his name seven years ago. Linnea

Almquist had said at some point that Hålén had moved in at the start of the 1960s. That could fit.

Wallander ended up sitting with the pen in his hand. Then he called back the pastor's office. The same woman answered.

"I forgot to ask you something," Wallander excused himself. "I need to know when Hålén moved to Rosengård."

"You mean Hansson," the woman said. "I'll go see."

This time she was much faster.

"He is registered as newly moved on 1 January 1962."

"Where did he live before?"

"I don't know."

"I thought that information was available?"

"He was registered as being out of the country. There is no information about where."

Wallander nodded into the receiver.

"Then I think that is all. I promise not to disturb you again."

He returned to his notes. Hansson moves to Malmö from some unknown foreign location in 1962 and changes his name at the same time. A few years later he starts a relationship with a woman in Arlöv. If they had known each other earlier, I don't know. After several more years she is murdered and Hålén commits suicide. It's not clear in what order this occurs. But Hålén kills himself. After first filling out a betting form and putting an extra lock on his door. And after swallowing a number of precious stones.

Wallander made a face. He still wasn't finding a direction from which to proceed. Why does a person change his name? he thought. To make himself invisible? To make himself impossible to find? So that no one will know who he is or who he has been?

Who you are or who you have been?

Wallander thought about this. No one had known Hålén. He had been a loner. There could, however, be people who had known a man by the name of Anders Hansson. The question was how he could find them.

At that moment he was reminded of something that had happened the preceding year that might help him find a solution. A fight had broken out between some drunks down by the ferry terminal. Wallander was one of the officers who responded to the dispatch and helped to break up the fight. One of the parties involved was a Danish sailor by the name of Holger Jespersen. Wallander had had the impression that he had unwillingly been dragged into the fight and said as much to his superiors. He had also insisted that Jespersen had not done anything and the man had been allowed to go free while the others were brought in. Later on Wallander had forgotten all about it.

But a few weeks later Jespersen had suddenly turned up outside his door in Rosengård and given him a bottle of Danish aquavit as thanks for his help. Wallander had never managed to establish how Jespersen had found him. But he had invited him in. Jespersen had problems with alcohol, but only from time to time. Usually he worked on various ships as an engineer. He was a good storyteller and seemed to know every northern sailor from the past fifty years. Jespersen had told him that he usually spent his evenings in a bar in Nyhavn. When he was sober he always drank coffee. Otherwise beer. But always in the same place. If he was not somewhere out at sea.

Now Wallander came to think of him. Jespersen knows, he thought. Or else he can give me some advice.

Wallander had already made his decision. If he was lucky, Jespersen would be in Copenhagen and hopefully not in the middle of one of his drinking binges. It was not yet three o'clock. Wallander would spend the rest of the day going to Copenhagen and back. No one seemed to miss his presence at the station. But before he set off across the sound he had a telephone call to make. It was as if his decision to go to Copenhagen had given him the necessary courage. He dialled the number to the hair salon where Mona worked.

The woman who answered the phone was called Karin and was the owner. Wallander had met her on several occasions. He found her intrusive and nosy. But Mona thought she was a good boss. He told her who he was and asked her to give a message to Mona.

"You can talk to her yourself," Karin said. "I have a woman under a dryer here."

"I'm in a case meeting," Wallander said and tried to sound busy. "Just tell her that I'll be in touch by ten o'clock tonight."

Karin promised to forward the message.

Afterwards Wallander noticed that he had started sweating during the short conversation. But he was still happy that he had accomplished it.

Then he left the station and just managed to catch the hydrofoil that left at three o'clock. Earlier in the year he had often gone to Copenhagen. First alone, and then with Mona. He liked the city, which was so much bigger than Malmö. Sometimes he also went to Det Kongelige Theatre when there was an opera performance he wanted to see.

He didn't much care for the hydrofoils. The trip went too fast. The old ferries gave him a stronger feeling that there was actually some distance between Sweden and Denmark; that he was travelling abroad when he crossed the sound. He looked out the window as he drank his coffee. One day they will probably build a bridge here, he thought. But I probably won't have to live to see that day.

When Wallander arrived in Copenhagen it had started to drizzle again. The boat docked in Nyhavn. Jespersen had told him where his regular pub was and it was not without a feeling of excitement that Wallander stepped into the semi-darkness. It was a quarter to four. He looked around the dim interior. There were a few customers scattered about, sitting at tables, drinking beer.

A radio was turned on somewhere. Or was it a record player? A Danish woman's voice was singing something that seemed very sentimental. Wallander didn't see Jespersen at any of the tables. The bartender was working on a crossword puzzle in a newspaper spread out over the counter. He looked up when Wallander approached.

"A beer," Wallander said.

118

The man gave him a Tuborg.

"I'm looking for Jespersen," Wallander said.

"Holger? He won't be in for another hour or so."

"He's not out at sea, then?"

The bartender smiled.

"If he was, he would hardly be coming in in an hour, would he? He usually comes in around five."

Wallander sat down at a table and waited. The sentimental female voice had now been replaced by an equally schmaltzy male voice. If Jespersen came in around five, Wallander would have no trouble being back in Malmö before he was set to call Mona. Now he tried to think out what he was going to say. He would not even acknowledge the slap. He would tell her why he had contacted Helena. He would not give up until she believed what he said.

A man at one of the tables had fallen asleep. The bartender was still hunched over his crossword. Time was passing slowly. Now and again the door opened and let in a glimpse of daylight. Someone came in and a few others left. Wallander checked his watch. Ten to five. Still no Jespersen. He became hungry and was given some slices of sausage on a plate. And another Tuborg. Wallander had the feeling that the bartender was puzzling over the same word as he had been when Wallander had arrived at the bar an hour ago.

It was five o'clock. Still no Jespersen. He's not coming, Wallander thought. Today of all days he's slipped and started drinking again.

Two women walked in through the door. One of them ordered a schnapps and sat down at a table. The other one went behind the counter. The bartender left his newspaper and started to go through the bottles lined up on the shelves. Apparently the woman worked there. It was now twenty minutes past five. The door opened and Jespersen entered, dressed in a denim jacket and a cap. He walked straight to the counter and said hello. The bartender immediately poured him a cup of coffee and pointed to Wallander's table. Jespersen took his cup and smiled when he saw Wallander.

"This is unexpected," he said in broken Swedish. "A Swedish police servant in Copenhagen."

"Not a servant," Wallander said. "Constable. Or criminal investigator."

"Isn't that the same thing?"

Jespersen chuckled and dropped four lumps of sugar into his coffee.

"In any case, it's nice to get a visitor," he said. "I know everyone who comes here. I know what they're going to drink and what they're going to say. And they know the same about me. Sometimes I wonder why I don't go someplace else. But I don't think I dare."

"Why not?"

"Maybe someone will say something I don't want to hear."

Wallander wasn't sure he understood everything that Jespersen was saying. For one thing, his Swedo-Danish was unclear, for another his pronouncements were somewhat vague.

"I came here to see you," Wallander said. "I thought you might be able to help me."

"With any other police servant I would have told you to go to hell," Jespersen answered jovially. "But with you it's different. What is it you want to know?"

Wallander filled him in on what had happened.

"A sailor, called both Anders Hansson and Artur Hålén," he finished. "Who also worked as an engineer."

"Which line?"

"Sahlén."

Jespersen slowly shook his head.

"I would have heard about someone who changed his name," he said. "That isn't an everyday occurrence."

Wallander tried to describe Hålén's appearance. At the same time he was thinking of the photographs he had seen in the sailor's books. A man who changed. Maybe Hålén also deliberately altered his appearance when he changed his name?

"Can you add anything else?" Jespersen said. "He was a sailor and an engineer. Which in itself is an unusual combination. Which ports did he sail to? Which type of vessel?"

"I think he went to Brazil a number of times," Wallander said hesitantly. "Rio de Janeiro, of course. But also a place called São Luis."

"Northern Brazil," Jespersen said. "I've been there once. Had shore leave there and stayed in an elegant hotel called Casa Grande."

"I don't think I have anything more to tell," Wallander said.

Jespersen studied him while he dropped a few more sugar cubes into his coffee.

"Someone who knew him? Is that what you want to know? Someone who knew Anders Hansson? Or Artur Hålén?"

Wallander nodded.

"Then we won't get any further right now," Jespersen said. "I'll check around. Both here and in Malmö. Now I think we should go have a bite to eat."

Wallander looked at his watch. Half past five. There was no need to hurry. If he took the hydrofoil back to Malmö at half past eight he would still get home in time to call Mona. And he was hungry anyway. The sausage slices had not been enough.

"Mussels," Jespersen said and stood up. "We're going to Anne-Birte's to have a bite."

Wallander paid for his drinks. Since Jespersen had already gone out to the street, Wallander had to pay for him as well.

Anne-Birte's establishment was located in the lower part of Nyhavn. Since it was early, they had no problems getting a table. Mussels were not really what Wallander most wanted to have, but that was Jespersen's choice and so mussels it was. Wallander kept drinking beer while Jespersen had switched to an intensely yellow lemon drink, Citronvand.

"I'm not touching the drink right now," he said. "But I will in a few weeks."

Wallander ate and listened to Jespersen's many well-told stories from his years at sea. Shortly before half past eight they were ready to leave.

For a while, Wallander worried that he wouldn't have enough money to pay the bill since Jespersen appeared

122

to take for granted that Wallander would pay. But in the end Wallander had enough to cover it.

They parted outside the restaurant.

"I'll look into this," Jespersen said. "I'll be in touch."

Wallander walked down to the ferries and stood in line. They cast off at exactly nine o'clock. Wallander closed his eyes and dozed off almost immediately.

He was awakened by the fact that everything had grown very quiet around him. The roar of the ship's engines had stopped. He looked around in bewilderment. They were about halfway between Denmark and Sweden. Then an announcement from the captain came over the ship's PA system. The ship had sustained engine damage and would have to be towed back to Copenhagen. Wallander leaped up out of his seat and asked one of the stewardesses if there was a telephone aboard. He received an answer in the negative.

"When will we get to Copenhagen?" he asked.

"That will unfortunately take several hours. But we will be offering a range of sandwiches and beverages in the meantime."

"I don't want a sandwich," Wallander said. "I want a telephone."

But no one could help him. He turned to a ship's mate who answered curtly that the radio phones could not be used for personal calls when the vessel was in a state of emergency.

Wallander sat back down in his seat.

She won't believe me, he thought. A hydrofoil that breaks down. That will be the last straw for her. Then our relationship will break down as well, for good.

★   ★   ★

Wallander reached Malmö at half past two in the morning. They had not arrived in Copenhagen until shortly after midnight. At that point he had already abandoned all thoughts of calling her. When he landed in Malmö there was a downpour. Since he did not have enough money to take a taxi he had to walk all the way back to Rosengård. He had only just stepped inside the door when he suddenly became violently ill. After vomiting, he developed a fever.

The mussels, he thought. Don't tell me I'm really getting the stomach flu now.

Wallander spent the rest of the night in a constant series of trips between the bedroom and the bathroom. He had the energy to remind himself that he had actually never called in to say he was over his illness. Therefore he was still on sick leave. At dawn he finally managed to catch a few hours of sleep. But at nine he started running to the toilet again. The thought of calling Mona while shitting and vomiting was beyond him. In the best-case scenario she would realise that something had happened to him, that he was sick. But the telephone didn't ring. No one tried to reach him all day.

Late that evening he started to feel somewhat better. But he was so weak that he didn't manage to make himself anything except a cup of tea. Before he fell asleep again he wondered how Jespersen was feeling. He hoped he was as sick since he was the one who had suggested the mussels.

The next morning he tried to have a boiled egg. But this only resulted in him having to rush to the toilet again. He spent the rest of the day in bed and felt that his stomach was slowly starting to get back to normal.

Shortly before five, the phone rang. It was Hemberg.

"I've been looking for you," he said.

"I'm sick in bed," Wallander said.

"The stomach flu?"

"More precisely, mussels."

"Surely no sensible person eats mussels?"

"I did, unfortunately. And was duly punished."

Hemberg changed the subject.

"I'm calling to tell you that Jörne is finished," he said. "It wasn't what we thought. Hålén killed himself before Alexandra Batista was strangled. This means, in other words, that we have to turn this investigation in another direction. There is an unknown perpetrator."

"Maybe it's a coincidence," Wallander said.

"That Batista dies and Hålén shoots himself? With precious stones in his stomach? You can try to convince someone else of that. What is missing is the link in this chain of events. For the sake of simplicity we can say that a drama of two people has suddenly been changed into a triangle."

Wallander wanted to tell Hemberg about Hålén's change of name but felt another urge to vomit coming on. He excused himself.

"If you feel better tomorrow, then come up and see me," Hemberg said. "Remember to drink a lot. Liquids are the only thing that help."

After very hastily concluding the conversation and making yet another trip to the bathroom, Wallander returned to his bed. He spent that evening and night

125

somewhere in the no-man's-land between sleep, wakefulness and half-sleep. His stomach had calmed itself now, but he was still very tired. He dreamed about Mona and thought about what Hemberg had said. But he did not have the energy to get worked up, could not bring himself to think in earnest.

He felt better in the morning. He toasted some bread and brewed a weak cup of coffee. His stomach did not react. He let fresh air into the apartment, which had started to smell bad. The rain clouds had gone away and it was warm. At lunchtime Wallander called the hair salon. Again it was Karin who answered.

"Could you tell Mona I'll call her tonight?" he said. "I've been sick."

"I'll let her know."

Wallander could not determine if there was a tinge of sarcasm in her voice. He didn't think Mona talked much about her personal life. At least he hoped she didn't.

Around one o'clock Wallander got ready to go down to the police station. But to make sure, he called and asked if Hemberg was in. After several fruitless attempts to get hold of him or at least information about where he might be, Wallander gave up. He decided to go grocery shopping and then spend the rest of the afternoon preparing for the conversation with Mona, which was not going to be an easy matter.

He made soup for dinner and then lay down on the couch and watched TV. A little after seven the door rang. Mona, he thought. She has realised that something is wrong and she's come over.

But when he opened the door, Jespersen was standing there.

"You and your damn mussels," Wallander said angrily. "I've been ill for two days."

Jespersen looked enquiringly at him.

"I didn't notice anything," he said. "I'm sure there was nothing wrong with the mussels."

Wallander decided it was meaningless to keep talking about the dinner. He let Jespersen in. They sat down in the kitchen.

"Something smells funny in here."

"It usually does when someone has spent almost forty hours on the toilet."

Jespersen shook his head.

"It must have been something else," he said. "Not Anne-Birte's mussels."

"You're here," Wallander said. "That means you have something to tell me."

"A little coffee would be nice," Jespersen said.

"I'm all out, sorry. And anyway, I didn't know you were coming."

Jespersen nodded. He didn't take offence.

"Mussels can certainly give you a stomach ache," he said, "but if I'm not completely mistaken, it's something else that's worrying you."

Wallander was amazed. Jespersen saw right into him, right into the centre of pain that was Mona.

"You may be right," he said. "But that's not something I want to talk about."

Jespersen held up his hands.

"You're here. That means you have something to tell me," Wallander repeated.

"Have I ever told you what respect I have for your president, Mr Palme?"

"He's not a president, he's not even prime minister yet. But you hardly came all the way here to tell me that."

"Nonetheless, it should be said," Jespersen insisted. "But you are right that other reasons have brought me here. If you live in Copenhagen, only an errand will bring you to Malmö. If you know what I mean."

Wallander nodded impatiently. Jespersen could be very long-winded. Except when he was telling his tales from his life at sea. Then he was a master.

"I talked a little with some friends in Copenhagen," Jespersen said. "That gave me nothing. Then I went over to Malmö and things went better. I spoke with an old electrician who sailed the seven seas for a thousand years. Ljungström is his name. Lives in a retirement home nowadays. Except I've forgotten the name of the place. He could hardly stand on his two legs. But his memory is clear."

"What did he say?"

"Nothing. But he suggested that I chat a little with a man out in Frihamnen. And when I found him and asked him about Hansson and Hålén he said, 'Those two are in constant demand.'"

"What did he mean by that?"

"What do you think? You're a policeman and should be able to understand what regular folks don't."

"What did he say again, exactly?"

"That 'those two are in constant demand'."

Wallander understood.

"There must have been someone else who had been asking about them, or him, to be precise."

"Yes."

"Who?"

"He didn't know the name. But he claimed it was a man who seemed a little unstable. How can I put this? Unshaven and badly dressed. And drunk."

"When did this happen?"

"About a month ago."

About the same time that Hålén had the extra lock put in, Wallander thought.

"He didn't know the man's name? Can I speak with this fellow in Frihamnen myself? He must have had a name?"

"He didn't want to talk to a cop."

"Why not?"

Jespersen shrugged.

"You know how things can be at the docks. Crates of alcohol that break open, some bags of coffee that go missing."

Wallander had heard about such things.

"But I kept asking around," Jespersen said. "And if I'm not mistaken I think there are some slightly scruffy individuals who have a habit of meeting up to share a bottle or two in that park in the middle of town that I've forgotten the name of. Something that starts with P?"

"Pildamms Park?"

"That's the one. And the man who asked about Hålén, or maybe it was Hansson, had a sagging eyelid."

"Which eye?"

"I don't think it'll be hard to see if you find him."

"And he asked about Hålén or Hansson about a month ago? And he hangs out in Pildamms Park?"

"I thought maybe we could look him up before I head back," Jespersen said. "And maybe we'll find a cafe on the way?"

Wallander checked his watch. It was half past seven.

"I can't do it tonight. I'm busy."

"Then I'm going back to Copenhagen. I'm going to have a word with Anne-Birte about her mussels."

"It could have been something else," Wallander said.

"Just what I'll say to Anne-Birte."

They had walked out into the hall.

"Thanks for coming," Wallander said. "And thanks for your help."

"Thank you," Jespersen said. "If you hadn't been there I would have got nothing but trouble and fines that time the guys started to fight."

"I'll see you around," Wallander said. "But no more mussels next time."

"No more mussels," Jespersen said and left.

Wallander went back into the kitchen and wrote down everything he had just heard. Someone had been asking about Hålén or Hansson. This had taken place about a month ago. At around the same time that Hålén had an extra lock put in. The man looking for Hålén had a sagging eyelid. Seemed in one way or

130

another to be drifting along. And was possibly hanging out in Pildamms Park.

Wallander put the pen down. I'm going to talk to Hemberg about this too, he thought. Right now this is actually a real lead.

Then Wallander thought that he should of course have asked Jespersen to find out if there was anyone in his circle who had heard of a woman named Alexandra Batista.

He was irritated at his sloppiness. I didn't think it all the way through, he said to himself. I make unnecessary errors.

It was already a quarter to eight. Wallander walked to and fro in the apartment. He was nervous, but his stomach was fine now. He thought about calling his father at the new telephone number in Löderup, but chances were they would start quarrelling. It was enough to deal with Mona. In order to get the time to pass he took a walk around the block. Summer had arrived. The evening was warm. He wondered what would happen with their planned trip to Skagen.

At half past eight he walked back into his apartment. Sat down at the kitchen table with his watch laid out in front of him. I'm acting like a child, he thought. But right now I don't know what to do in order to act any different.

He called at nine o'clock. Mona picked up almost immediately.

"Before you hang up, I would like to explain myself," Wallander started.

"Who said I was going to hang up?"

This threw him off guard. He had prepared himself carefully, knew what he was going to say. Instead she was the one who talked.

"I actually do believe that you have an explanation," she said. "But right now that doesn't interest me. I think we should meet and talk in person."

"Now?"

"Not tonight. But tomorrow. Can you do that?"

"Yes, I can do that."

"Then I'll come to your place. But not until nine o'clock. It's my mother's birthday. I promised to stop by."

"I can cook dinner."

"That won't be necessary."

Wallander started over again from the beginning with his prepared explanations. But she interrupted him.

"Let's talk tomorrow. Not now, not on the phone."

The conversation was over in less than a minute. Nothing had turned out the way Wallander had expected. It had been a conversation that he had hardly dared to dream about. Even if there had also been something that he could interpret as ominous.

The thought of staying in for the rest of the evening made him restless. It was only a quarter past nine. Nothing prevents me from taking a walk through Pildamms Park, he thought. Maybe I'll even bump into a man with a sagging eyelid.

Wallander took out a hundred kronor in small notes which he kept tucked between the pages of a book in his bookcase. He put the notes in his pocket, picked up his coat and walked out. There was no wind and it was still warm. While he walked to the bus stop he hummed a melody from an opera. *Rigoletto*. He saw the bus come and started to run.

When he reached Pildamms Park he began to wonder if it had been such a good idea. It was a large park. In addition, he was actually looking for a suspected murderer. The regulations against officers acting on their own rang in his ears. But I can take a walk, he thought. I have no uniform, no one knows that I'm a policeman. I'm just a single man who's out walking his invisible dog.

Wallander started to walk down one of the park paths. A group of young people were sitting under one of the trees. Someone was playing guitar. Wallander saw a few bottles of wine. He wondered how many laws they were breaking at this moment. Lohman would surely have moved in quickly. But Wallander simply walked on by. A few years ago he could have been one of the people sitting under the tree. But now he was a policeman and should instead arrest a person drinking wine in a public place. He shook his head at the thought. He could hardly wait until he got to work in criminal investigations. It wasn't for this that he had joined the police. To seize young people who were playing guitar and drinking wine on one of the first warm evenings of the summer. It was to get the really big criminals. The ones who committed violent crimes or large-scale theft, or smuggled drugs.

He walked on into the park. Traffic roared in the distance. Two young people walked by, wrapped tightly around each other. Wallander thought about Mona. It would probably work out. Soon they would take their trip to Skagen, and he would never again be late for a date.

Wallander stopped. Some people were sitting and drinking alcohol on a bench not far ahead. One of them was pulling on the leash of a German shepherd who wouldn't lie still. Wallander approached them slowly. They didn't appear to pay him any attention. Wallander couldn't see that any of them had a sagging eyelid. But suddenly one of the men stood up on swaying legs in front of Wallander. He was very burly. The muscles swelled out under his shirt, which was unbuttoned over his stomach.

"I need a tenner," he said.

Wallander had at first intended to say no. Ten kronor was a lot of money. Then he changed his mind.

"I'm looking for a friend of mine," he said. "A guy with a sagging eyelid."

Wallander had not expected a hit. But to his amazement, he received an unexpected reply.

"Rune's not here. The devil only knows where he's got to."

"That's the one," Wallander said. "Rune."

"Who the hell are you?" the swaying man said.

"My name is Kurt," Wallander said. "I'm an old friend."

"I've never seen you before."

Wallander gave him a ten.

"Tell him if you see him," Wallander said. "Tell him Kurt was here. Do you happen to know Rune's last name, by the way?"

"I don't even know if he has a last name. Rune is Rune."

"Where does he live, then?"

The man stopped swaying for a moment.

"I thought you said you were friends? Then you should know where he lives."

"He moves around a lot."

The man turned to the others who were sitting on the bench.

"Do any of you know where Rune lives?"

The conversation that followed was extremely confused. At first it took a long time to establish which Rune they were talking about. Then many suggestions were offered to where this Rune might live. If he even had a home. Wallander waited. The German shepherd next to the bench barked the whole time.

The man with the muscles returned.

"We don't know where Rune lives," he said. "But we'll tell him that Kurt was here."

Wallander nodded and swiftly walked away. Of course, he might be wrong. There was more than one person with a sagging eyelid. But still, he was sure he was on the right track. It occurred to him that he should immediately contact Hemberg and suggest that the park be put under surveillance. Maybe the police already had a man with a sagging eyelid on their records?

But then Wallander felt doubtful. He was proceeding too fast again. First he should have a thorough conversation with Hemberg. He should tell him about the name change and what Jespersen had said. Then it

135

would be up to Hemberg to decide if this was a lead or not.

Wallander would wait to talk to Hemberg the following day.

Wallander left the park and took the bus home.

He was still tired from the stomach flu and fell asleep before midnight.

The following day Wallander woke up refreshed at seven o'clock. After noting that his stomach was completely restored to normal he had a cup of coffee. Then he dialled the number he had been given by the girl in reception.

His father answered after many rings.

"Is that you?" his father said brusquely. "I couldn't find the telephone in all this mess."

"Why did you call the police station and introduce yourself as a distant relative? Can't you damn well say that you're my father?"

"I don't want anything to do with the police," his father answered. "Why don't you come to see me?"

"I don't even know where you live. Kristina only explained it vaguely."

"You're too lazy to figure it out. That's your whole problem."

Wallander realised the conversation had already taken a wrong turn. The best thing he could do now would be to end it as soon as possible.

"I'll be out in a few days," he said. "I'll call first and get directions. How are you liking it?"

"Fine."

"Is that it? 'Fine'?"

"Things are in a bit of disarray. But once I get that sorted out it will be excellent. I have a wonderful studio in an old barn."

"I'll be there," Wallander said.

"I won't believe it until you stand here," his father said. "You can't really trust the police."

Wallander finished and hung up. He could live for twenty more years, he thought desperately. And I'm going to have him over me the whole time. I'll never escape him. I may as well face that now. And if he's bad-tempered now it will only get worse as he gets older.

Wallander ate some sandwiches with a newly regained appetite and then took the bus in to the station. He knocked on Hemberg's half-open door shortly after eight. He heard a grunt in reply and walked in. For once Hemberg did not have his feet on the table. He was standing at the window, flipping through a morning paper. As Wallander walked in, Hemberg scrutinised him with an amused expression.

"Mussels," he said. "You should watch out for them. They suck up everything that's in the water."

"It could have been something else," Wallander said evasively.

Hemberg set the newspaper down and took his seat.

"I need to talk to you," Wallander said. "And it will take longer than five minutes."

Hemberg nodded at his visitor's chair.

Wallander told him of his discovery, that Hålén had changed his name a few years earlier. He noticed that

Hemberg immediately became more attentive. Wallander went on and told him about his conversation with Jespersen, last night's visit, and the walk in Pildamms Park.

"A man named Rune," he concluded. "Who doesn't have a last name. And has a droopy eyelid."

Hemberg considered everything he had said in silence.

"No person lacks a last name," he said thereafter. "And there can't be that many people with droopy eyelids in a city like Malmö."

Then he frowned.

"I've already told you once not to act on your own. And you should have contacted me or someone else last night. We would have picked up the people you met in the park. With some thorough questioning and some time to sober up, people tend to remember more. Did you, for example, write down any of these men's names?"

"I didn't say I was from the police. I said I was a friend of Rune's."

Hemberg shook his head.

"You can't do that kind of stuff," he said. "We act openly unless there are compelling reasons to the contrary."

"He wanted money," Wallander said, defending himself. "Otherwise I would simply have walked on by."

Hemberg looked narrowly at him.

"What were you doing in Pildamms Park?"

"Taking a walk."

"You were not undertaking your own investigation?"

"I needed some exercise after my illness."

Hemberg's face expressed strong disbelief.

"It was, in other words, pure coincidence that made you choose Pildamms Park?"

Wallander did not reply. Hemberg got up out of his chair.

"I'll put some men on this development. Right now we need to proceed on the widest possible front. I think I had fixed on it being Hålén who killed Batista, but you get it wrong sometimes. Then all you can do is strike it and start over."

Wallander left Hemberg's room and walked down to the lower floor. He was hoping to be able to avoid Lohman but it was as if his boss had been waiting for him. Lohman walked out of a conference room, a cup of coffee in his hand.

"I had just started to wonder where you were," he said.

"I've been ill," Wallander said.

"And yet people reported seeing you in the building."

"I'm fine again now," Wallander said. "It was the stomach flu. Mussels."

"You've been assigned to foot patrol," Lohman said. "Talk to Håkansson."

Wallander walked to the room where the patrol squad received their assignments. Håkansson, who was large and fat and always sweating, was sitting at a table and leafing through a magazine. He looked up when Wallander walked in.

"Central city," he said. "Wittberg is leaving at nine. End at three. Go with him."

Wallander nodded and walked to the changing room. He took his uniform out of his locker and changed. Just as he finished, Wittberg walked in. He was thirty-years old and always talked about his dreams of one day driving a racing car.

They left the station at a quarter past nine.

"Things are always calmer when it's warm," Wittberg said. "No unnecessary intervention on our part, then perhaps the day will turn out calm."

And the day did indeed turn out to be calm. By the time Wallander hung up his uniform, shortly after three, they had not made a single intervention, except for stopping a cyclist who was riding on the wrong side of the street.

Wallander got home at four o'clock. He had stopped at the shop on the way home, just in case Mona changed her mind and was hungry when she came by after all.

By half past four he had showered and changed his clothes. There were still four and a half hours until Mona would come. Nothing prevents me from taking another walk in Pildamms Park, Wallander thought. Especially if I'm out with my invisible dog.

He hesitated. Hemberg had given him express orders.

But he went anyway. At half past five he walked down the same path as before. The young people who had been playing guitar and drinking wine were gone.

140

The bench where the drunk men had been sitting was also empty. Wallander decided to keep going for another quarter of an hour. Then he would go home. He walked down a hill and paused, watching some ducks swimming around in the large pond. He heard birds singing nearby. The trees gave off a strong scent of early summer. An older couple walked past. Wallander heard them talking about someone's "poor sister". Whose sister it was and why she was the object of pity, he never found out.

He was just about to walk back the same way he had come when he discovered two people sitting in the shade of a tree. If they were drunk, he couldn't tell. One of the men stood up. His walk was unsteady. His friend still sitting under the tree had nodded off. His chin rested against his chest. Wallander walked closer but did not recognise him from the night before. The man was poorly dressed and there was an empty vodka bottle between his feet.

Wallander crouched down to try to see his face. At the same time he heard the crunch of steps on the gravel path behind him. When he turned round there were two girls standing there. He recognised one of them without being able to say from where.

"It's one of those damn cops," the girl said. "Who hit me at the demonstration."

Then Wallander realised who it was: the girl who had verbally assaulted him at the cafe the week before.

Wallander rose to his feet. At that same moment he saw from the other girl's face that something was happening behind his back. He quickly turned round.

The man who had been leaning against the tree had not been asleep. Now he was standing. And he had a knife in his hand.

After that everything happened very quickly. Later Wallander would only remember that the girls had screamed and run away. Wallander had lifted his arms to shield himself, but it was too late. He had not managed to block the thrust. The knife struck him in the middle of his chest. A warm darkness washed over him.

Even before he sank down onto the gravel path his memory had stopped registering what was happening.

After that everything had been a fog. Or perhaps a thickly flowing sea in which everything was white and still.

Wallander lay sunken in deep unconsciousness for four days. He underwent two complicated operations. The knife had grazed his heart. But he survived. And slowly he returned from the fog. When at last, on the morning of the fifth day, he opened his eyes, he did not know what had happened or where he was.

But next to his bed there was a face he recognised.

A face that meant everything. Mona's face.

And she was smiling.

EPILOGUE

One day at the start of September, when Wallander received the goahead from his doctor that he could start work a week later, he called up Hemberg. Later that afternoon Hemberg came out to his apartment in Rosengård. They bumped into each other in the stairwell. Wallander had just taken out the rubbish.

"It was here where it all started," Hemberg said, nodding at Hålén's door.

"No one else has moved in yet," Wallander said. "The furniture is still there. The fire damage hasn't been repaired. Every time I walk in or out I still think it smells like smoke."

They sat in Wallander's kitchen drinking coffee. The September day was unusually brisk. Hemberg was wearing a thick sweater under his coat.

"Autumn came early this year," he said.

"I went out to visit my father yesterday," Wallander said. "He's moved from the city to Löderup. It's beautiful out there in the middle of the plains."

"How one can voluntarily make one's home out there in the middle of all that mud exceeds my powers of comprehension," Hemberg said dismissively. "Then comes winter. And one is trapped by the snow."

"He seems to like it," Wallander said. "And I don't think he cares very much about the weather. He just works on his paintings from morning till night."

"I didn't know your father was an artist."

"He paints the same motif again and again," Wallander said. "A landscape. With or without a grouse."

He stood up. Hemberg followed him to the main room, where the painting hung.

"One of my neighbours has one of those," Hemberg said. "They appear to be popular."

They returned to the kitchen.

"You made all the mistakes you can make," Hemberg said. "But I've already told you that. You don't undertake investigative work alone, you don't intervene without backup. You were only a centimetre or so from death. I hope you've learned something. At least how *not* to act."

Wallander did not answer. Hemberg was right, of course.

"But you were stubborn," Hemberg continued. "It was you who discovered that Hålén had changed his name. We would of course also have discovered this eventually. We would also have found Rune Blom. But you thought logically, and you thought correctly."

"I called you out of curiosity," Wallander said. "There's still a lot I don't know."

Hemberg told him. Rune Blom had confessed, and he could also be tied to the murder of Alexandra Batista through the forensic evidence.

144

"The whole thing started in 1954," Hemberg said. "Blom has been very detailed. He and Hålén, or Hansson as he was called back then, had been on the same crew on a ship bound for Brazil. In São Luis they had come into possession of the precious stones. He claims that they bought them for a negligible price from a drunk Brazilian who didn't know their true worth. They probably didn't either. If they stole them or actually purchased them, we'll probably never know. They had decided to split their bounty. But then it so happened that Blom ended up in a Brazilian prison, for manslaughter. And then Hålén took advantage of the situation, since he had the stones. He changed his name and quit sailing after a few years and hid out here in Malmö. Met Batista and counted on the fact that Blom would spend the rest of his life in a Brazilian prison. But Blom was later released and started to look for Hålén. Somehow Hålén found out that Blom had turned up in Malmö. He got scared and put an extra lock on the door. But continued seeing Batista. Blom was spying on him. Blom claims that Hålén committed suicide on the day that Blom found out where he lived. Apparently this was enough to frighten him so much that he went home and shot himself. You may wonder about that. Why didn't he give the stones to Blom? Why swallow them and then shoot himself? What's the point of being so greedy that you prefer dying instead of giving away something that has a little monetary value?"

Hemberg sipped his coffee and looked thoughtfully out the window. It was raining.

"You know the rest," he continued. "Blom did not find any stones. He suspected that Batista must have them. Since he introduced himself as a friend of Hålén, she let him in without suspecting anything. And Blom took her life. He had a violent nature. He had shown that before. From time to time when he was drinking he proved himself capable of extreme brutality. There are a number of cases of assault in his past. On top of the manslaughter charge in Brazil. This time Batista bore the brunt."

"Why did he take the trouble to go back and set the apartment on fire? Wasn't he taking a risk?"

"He hasn't given any explanation other than the fact that he became enraged that the stones were missing. I think it's true. Blom is an unpleasant person. But perhaps he was afraid that his name was somewhere in the apartment on some piece of paper. He probably hadn't had time to check around exhaustively before you surprised him. But of course he was taking a risk. He could have been discovered."

Wallander nodded. Now he had the whole picture.

"It's really just a case of a horrible little murder, and a greedy man who shoots himself," Hemberg said. "When you become a criminal investigator you'll come across this many times. Never in the same way. But with more or less the same basic motive."

"That was what I was going to ask you about," Wallander said. "I realise that I have made many mistakes."

"Don't worry about that," Hemberg said curtly. "You'll start with us the first of October, but not before."

146

Wallander had heard correctly. He exulted inside. But he didn't show it, only nodded.

Hemberg stayed a little while longer. Then he left and went off in the rain. Wallander stood at the window and watched him drive away in his car. He absently fingered the scar on his chest.

Suddenly he thought of something he had read. In what context, he did not know.

There is a time to live, and a time to die.

I made it, he thought. I was lucky.

Then he decided never to forget these words.

There is a time to live, and a time to die.

These words would become his personal incantation from now on.

The rain spattered against the windowpane.

Mona arrived shortly after eight.

That evening they talked for a long time about finally making the planned trip to Skagen next summer.

THE MAN WITH
THE MASK

Wallander checked his watch. It was a quarter to five. He was sitting in his office at the Malmö police headquarters. It was Christmas Eve, 1975. The two other colleagues he shared the office with, Stefansson and Hörner, were off. He was leaving in less than an hour himself. He got up and walked to the window. It was raining. It would not be a white Christmas this year either. He stared absently out through the window, which had started to fog up. Then he yawned. His jaw popped. He carefully closed his mouth. Sometimes when he yawned wide he got a cramp in a muscle under his chin.

He went back and sat down at his desk. There were some papers on it that he didn't need to worry about right now. He leaned back in his chair and thought with pleasure about the holiday time that awaited. Almost a whole week. He was not returning to duty until New Year's Eve. He put his feet up on the desk, took out a cigarette and lit it. He started coughing immediately. He had decided to quit. Not as a New Year's resolution. He knew himself too well to think he would be able to succeed. He needed a long time to prepare. But one day he would wake up and know that it was the last day he would light a cigarette.

He looked at the time again. He could really leave now. It had been an unusually calm December. The Malmö crime squad had no cases of violent crime under investigation at the moment. The family conflicts that normally took place during the holidays would happen on someone else's watch.

Wallander took his feet down from the desk and called home to Mona. She answered at once.

"It's me."

"Don't tell me you're going to be late."

The irritation came out of nowhere. He didn't manage to conceal it.

"I'm actually just calling to say that I'm leaving now. But maybe that's a mistake?"

"Why are you so upset?"

"I sound upset?"

"You heard me."

"I hear what you're saying. But can you hear me? That I was actually calling to tell you I was on my way home. If you don't have anything against that."

"Just drive carefully."

The call ended. Wallander sat there with the telephone receiver in his hand. Then he banged it hard onto the hook.

We can't even talk on the phone any more, he thought angrily. Mona starts to nag at the smallest provocation. And she probably says the same thing about me.

He sat back in the chair and watched the smoke rising towards the ceiling. He noticed that he was trying to avoid thinking about Mona and himself. And about the quarrels that were getting more frequent. But he couldn't. Increasingly, he found himself thinking the thought he most wanted to avoid. That it was their daughter of five years, Linda, who held their relationship together. But he chased it away. The thought of living without Mona and Linda was unbearable.

He also thought about the fact that he had not yet turned thirty. He knew he had the necessary qualifications to become a good policeman. If he wanted, he would be able to make a noteworthy career within the force. The six years he had spent in the crime squad and his quick advancement to criminal investigator had convinced him of this, even if he also often felt inadequate. But was this really what he wanted? Mona had often tried to convince him to apply to one of the private security firms that were becoming more common in Sweden. She clipped out job announcements and told him he would make considerably more money in the private sector. His work schedule would become more predictable. But he knew that deep inside she was pleading with him to switch professions because she was afraid. Afraid that something would happen to him again.

He walked back over to the window. Looked out over Malmö through the fogged-up glass.

It was his last year in this city. This summer he would start a job in Ystad. They had already moved there and had lived in a centrally located apartment since September. Mariagatan. They had actually never hesitated over the decision, despite the fact that it

153

would hardly advance his career to move to a small town. Mona wanted Linda to grow up in a smaller city than Malmö. Wallander felt a desire for change. And the fact that his father lived in Österlen as of a few years back was yet another reason for them to move to Ystad. But even more important was the fact that Mona had been able to buy a hair salon for a good price.

He had visited the police headquarters in Ystad on several occasions and had got to know the people who would soon be his co-workers. Above all, he had developed an appreciation for a middle-aged policeman by the name of Rydberg.

Before meeting him Wallander had heard persistent rumours about Rydberg, that he was abrupt and dismissive. But from the first moment his impression had been different. It could not be disputed that Rydberg was a man who did things his own way. But Wallander had been impressed with his ability to accurately describe and analyse a crime under investigation with just a few words.

He walked back to the desk and put out his cigarette. It was a quarter past five. He could go now. He took his coat, which was hanging on the wall. He would drive home slowly and carefully.

Maybe he had sounded upset and unfriendly on the phone without knowing it? He was tired. He needed this time off. Mona would probably understand when he got the opportunity to explain himself.

He put on his coat and felt in his pocket for the keys to his Peugeot.

On the wall next to the door was a little shaving mirror. Wallander looked at his face. He felt satisfied with what he saw. He would soon turn twenty-seven, but in the mirror he saw a face that could have been five years younger.

At that moment, the door opened. It was Hemberg, his immediate supervisor since he'd joined the squad. Wallander often found it easy to work with him. The few times there were any problems were almost always due to Hemberg's violent temper.

Wallander knew that Hemberg was going to be on duty over both the Christmas and New Year holidays. As a bachelor, Hemberg was giving up his holiday to fill in for another supervising officer who had a family with many children.

"I was just wondering if you were still here," Hemberg said.

"I was about to leave," Wallander answered. "I was thinking of slipping away half an hour early."

"That's fine by me," Hemberg said.

But Wallander had immediately understood that Hemberg had come into his office with a specific purpose.

"You want something," he said.

Hemberg shrugged his shoulders.

"You've just moved to Ystad," he began. "It hit me that you might be able to make a little stop on the way. I don't have much manpower right now. And this is probably nothing anyway."

Wallander waited impatiently for the continuation.

155

"A woman has called here several times this afternoon. She has a little grocery shop by the furniture warehouse right before the last roundabout to Jägersro. Next to the OK gas station."

Wallander knew where that was. Hemberg glanced down at a piece of paper in his hand.

"Her name is Elma Hagman and she is most likely fairly old. She says that a strange individual has been hanging around outside the shop all afternoon."

Wallander waited in vain for more.

"Is that it?"

Hemberg made a wide gesture with his arms.

"It appears so. She called again quite recently. That was when I thought of you."

"So you want me to stop and talk to her?"

Hemberg cast an eye at the clock.

"She was going to close up at six. You'll just make it. But I expect she's imagining things. If nothing else, you can reassure her. And wish her a merry Christmas."

Wallander thought quickly. It would take him at most ten minutes to stop by the shop and make sure that everything was as it should be.

"I'll talk to her," he said. "I am still on duty, after all."

Hemberg nodded.

"Merry Christmas," he added. "I'll see you New Year's Eve."

"I hope things are calm tonight," Wallander replied.

"The conflicts start at night," Hemberg said gloomily. "We can only hope they don't turn too violent. And that not too many excited children are disappointed."

They parted in the hallway. Wallander hurried down to his car, which he had parked in front of the building today. It was raining hard now. He pushed a cassette into the car stereo and turned up the volume. The city around him glittered with illuminated signs and street decorations. Jussi Björling's voice filled the car. He relished the thought of all the time off that awaited him.

He had almost forgotten what Hemberg had asked of him when he approached the last roundabout before the exit towards Ystad. He was abruptly forced to brake and change lanes. Then he turned by the furniture warehouse, which was closed. But the lights were on in the grocery shop just past the workshop. Wallander pulled up and got out. He left the keys in the car. He closed the door so carelessly that the interior light stayed on. But he let it be. His business here would be over and done with in a couple of minutes.

The rain was still very intense. He looked around quickly. No one could be seen. The roar of traffic that reached him was faint. He wondered briefly how a grocery shop of the old kind could survive in an area that consisted almost exclusively of warehouses and small industry. Without finding an answer he hurried through the rain and opened the door.

As soon as he came into the shop he knew that something was not as it should be.

Something was wrong, seriously wrong.

What it was that caused this immediate reaction, he could not say. He remained standing just inside the door. The shop was empty. Not a single person. And it was quiet.

Too quiet, he thought.

Too quiet and peaceful. And where was Elma Hagman?

He walked carefully towards the counter. Leaned over it and checked the floor. Nothing. The cash register was closed. The silence around him was deafening. It occurred to him that he really should leave the shop. Since he didn't have a radio in the car, he needed a telephone. He should call for reinforcements. There should be at least two policemen here: one was not enough for an emergency response.

But he dismissed the idea that something was wrong. He could not be controlled forever by his feelings.

"Is anyone here?" he called out. "Mrs Hagman?"

No answer.

He walked round the counter. There was a door behind it that was closed. He knocked. Still no answer. He slowly depressed the handle. It was unlocked. He gently pushed the door open.

Then everything happened at once, very quickly. A woman was lying face down in the inner room. He registered that a chair was knocked over and that blood had run out from her face, which was turned away. He winced, although he had been prepared for something. The silence had been too substantial.

Even as he turned round he also knew there was someone behind him. As he completed his turn, he steeled himself, catching sight of a shadow that was coming towards his face at great speed. Then everything went dark.

When he opened his eyes he knew at once where he was. His head ached and he felt nauseous. He was sitting on the floor, behind the counter. He could not have been unconscious for long. Something dark had come towards him, a shadow that had struck him hard in the head. That was the last image in his memory. And it was very clear. He tried to get up but realised that he was tied up. A rope around his legs and arms bound him to something behind him that he couldn't see.

There was also something familiar about the rope. Then he realised that it was his own tow rope, which he always kept in the boot of his car.

At once his memory flooded back. He had discovered a dead woman in the office. A woman who could hardly be anyone other than Elma Hagman. Someone had subsequently hit him on the back of the head. And now he was bound with his own rope. He looked around, listening. There had to be someone nearby. Someone he had every reason to fear. The nausea came in waves. He tried to stretch the rope. Could he free himself? He strained his ears the whole time. It was still as quiet as before, but the silence had a different quality. It was not the one he had encountered when he entered the shop. He pulled on the rope. His arms and legs were not bound so tightly, but they were twisted in a way that did not allow him to make full use of his strength.

Now he also realised how afraid he was. Someone had murdered Elma Hagman and then struck him over the head and bound him. What was it Hemberg had said? *An Elma Hagman has called and reported that a strange individual has been hanging around outside the shop.* It turned out she had been right. Wallander tried to think calmly. Mona knew that he was on his way home. When he did not show up she would get worried and call the Malmö office. Hemberg would then immediately think of the fact that he had been on his way to Elma Hagman's shop. Then it would not take many minutes for the patrol cars to show up.

Wallander listened. Everything was quiet. He stretched to see if the cash register had now been opened. This could hardly be anything other than a robbery-homicide. If the cash register was open there would be every likelihood that the robber had taken off. He stretched as much as he could, but it was still impossible to see if the drawer was pulled out or not. Nonetheless, he was growing convinced of the fact that he was now alone in the shop with the dead owner.

The man who had murdered her and struck Wallander must have fled. The chances were also great that his car was gone, since he had left the keys in the ignition.

Wallander continued to struggle with the rope. After stretching out his arms and legs as far as they would go, he started to sense that he should concentrate on his left leg. If he kept pushing with his leg, he could stretch out the line and perhaps free himself. This would in turn mean that he would be able to twist his body and examine the manner in which he was attached to the wall.

He had broken out in a sweat. If it was due to his exertions or the crawling fear, he did not know. Six years earlier, when he had still been a very young and gullible police officer, he had been stabbed. Everything had happened so fast that he had not had time to react, to protect himself. The blade of the knife had entered his chest right next to his heart. That time the fear had come afterwards. But now it was here from the beginning. He tried to convince himself that nothing more would happen. Sooner or later he would be able to free himself. Sooner or later they would start looking for him.

He rested from his efforts for a moment. The whole situation suddenly came over him with full force. An old woman had been murdered on Christmas Eve in her own shop, shortly before closing. There was something frighteningly surreal about this act of brutality. These things simply didn't happen in Sweden. Least of all on Christmas Eve.

He started to tug on the rope again. It went slowly but he thought it was already chafing less. He managed to turn his arm with great difficulty so he could read his watch. Nine minutes past six. It would not be long now before Mona would start to wonder. A half-hour more and she would start to worry. By seven-thirty at the latest she would be calling Malmö.

Wallander was interrupted in his thoughts. He had picked up a sound somewhere close by. He held his breath and listened. Then he heard it again. A scraping sound. He had heard it before. It was the outer door. The same sound that he had heard when he himself walked into the store. Someone was on his way in, someone who was walking very quietly.

Then he saw the man.

He was standing next to the counter, looking down at him.

He was wearing a black hood pulled over his head, a thick coat and gloves on his hands. He was of average height and appeared thin. He was standing absolutely motionless. Wallander tried to pick out his eyes, but the light from the neon tubes in the ceiling were no help and he saw no face. Only two small holes were cut out for the eyes.

The man held a metal pipe in his hands. Or perhaps it was the end of a wrench.

He stood without moving.

Wallander felt fear and helplessness. The only thing he could do was to scream. But it would be useless. No one was around. No one would hear him.

The man in the hood continued to stare at him.

Then he swiftly turned and disappeared from view.

Wallander felt his heart thumping inside his chest. He strained to hear something. The door? But he heard nothing. The man must still be inside the shop.

Wallander thought frantically. Why didn't he go? Why did he linger? What was he waiting for?

162

He came from outside, Wallander thought. *Then he returns to the shop. He comes over to check that I'm still tied up where he left me.*

There is only one explanation. He's waiting for someone. Someone who should already be here.

He tried to finish this line of thought. He listened the whole time.

A man with a hood and gloves is out to commit a burglary without being recognised. He has selected Elma Hagman's remote shop. Why he has killed her is incomprehensible. She cannot have offered any resistance. He also does not give the impression of being nervous or under the influence of drugs.

The crime is over, but still he lingers. He does not flee. Despite the fact that he most likely was not expecting to have killed someone. Or that anyone else would come by the shop just before it closes on Christmas Eve. And yet he stays. Why?

Wallander realised that there was something that did not add up. This was not an average burglary he had walked in on. Why was the man staying? Had he become paralysed? He knew it was important to find an answer to this question. But the pieces did not fit together.

There was also another circumstance that Wallander knew was significant.

The man in the hood did not know he was a policeman.

He had no reason to believe anything other than that Wallander was a late customer who had come into the shop. If this was an advantage or a disadvantage, Wallander could not decide.

He continued working his left leg, keeping an eye on the sides of the counter as well as he could. The man with the hood was there somewhere in the background. And he moved soundlessly. The rope had started to give a little. The sweat ran down Wallander's chest. With a violent effort he managed to free his leg. He sat still. Then he gently turned round. The rope had been pulled through a piece of hardware supporting a wall-mounted shelf. Wallander realised that he would not be able to free himself without tearing the shelf down. On the other hand he could now use his free leg to help release the other leg from the rope. He glanced at his watch. Only seven minutes had gone by since he had last checked it. Mona had probably not yet called Malmö. The question was if she had even started to worry. Wallander struggled on. Now there was no going back. If the man with the hood reappeared he would immediately realise that Wallander was about to free himself and at the same time Wallander had no way of defending himself.

He worked as quickly and silently as he could. Both legs were free now, shortly thereafter his left arm too. Now only the right arm remained. Then he could get up. What he would do then he did not know. He was not carrying a weapon. He would have to use his hands if he was attacked. But he had the feeling that the man in the mask was neither particularly big nor strong. In addition, he would be unprepared. The element of surprise was the only weapon Wallander had. Nothing else. And he was going to leave the shop as quickly as possible. He would not drag the fight out any longer than necessary. On his own he could not achieve anything. He had to get in touch with Hemberg at the station as soon as possible.

His right hand was now free. The rope lay at his side. Wallander noticed that he had already started to feel stiff in his joints. He carefully got to his knees and peeked out from behind one corner of the counter.

The man in the hood stood with his back to Wallander.

Wallander could now see him in full for the first time. His earlier impression was correct: the man was very thin. He was wearing dark jeans and white trainers.

He was standing completely still. The distance was not more than three metres. Wallander would be able to throw himself at him and deliver a blow to the neck. That should give him enough time to make it out of the shop.

But still he hesitated.

At that moment he caught sight of the iron pipe. It was lying on a shelf next to the man.

Wallander did not hesitate any longer. Without a weapon the man in the hood would not be able to defend himself.

Slowly he got to his feet. The man did not react. Wallander was now standing upright.

At that precise moment the man suddenly turned round. Wallander lunged forward. The man stepped aside swiftly. Wallander banged into a shelf stocked mainly with bread and rusks. But he did not fall over, he managed to keep his balance. He twisted round in order to grab the man. But he cut his movement short and drew back.

The man in the hood had a gun in his hand.

He was aiming it steadily at Wallander's chest.

Then he slowly raised his arm until the weapon pointed straight at Wallander's forehead.

For one dizzying moment Wallander thought he was going to die. Once he had survived a stabbing. But the pistol that was now directed at his forehead was not going to miss. He would die. On Christmas Eve. In a grocery shop on the outskirts of Malmö. A completely meaningless death, which Mona and Linda would have to live with for the rest of their lives.

He shut his eyes involuntarily. Maybe in order not to have to see. Or to make himself invisible. But he opened his eyes again. The gun was still directed at his forehead.

Wallander could hear his own breathing. Each time he exhaled it sounded like a groan. But the man who was pointing the gun at him was breathing without a sound. He appeared to be completely unaffected by the situation. Wallander still could not see into the two holes cut into the hood. Where his eyes were.

Thoughts whirled in his head. Why was the man staying in the shop? What was he waiting for? And why did he not say anything?

Wallander stared at the gun, at the hood with the two dark holes.

"Don't shoot," he said and heard that his voice was unsteady and stammering.

The man did not react.

Wallander held out his hands. He had no weapon, he had no intention of resisting.

"I was just doing some shopping," Wallander said. Then he pointed at one of the shelves. He was careful to make sure that his hand gestures were not too quick.

"I was on my way home," he continued. "They're waiting for me. I have a daughter who is five years old."

The man did not answer. Wallander could not perceive any reaction at all.

He tried to think. Was he making a mistake by presenting himself as simply a late customer? Maybe he should have told the truth instead. That he was a policeman and that he had been alerted because Elma Hagman had called and said that an unknown man was hanging around her shop.

He did not know. Thoughts spun in his head. But they always returned to the same point of departure.

Why doesn't he leave? What is he waiting for?

Suddenly the man with the hood took a step back. The gun was aimed at Wallander's head the whole time. With his foot he pulled over a little stool. Then he pointed at it with his gun, which he then immediately pointed at Wallander again.

Wallander realised he was supposed to sit down. As long as he doesn't tie me up again, he thought. If there's gunfire when Hemberg arrives, I don't want to be tied up.

He walked forward slowly and sat down on the stool. The man had pulled back a few steps. When Wallander had sat down the man tucked the gun inside his belt.

He knows that I have seen the dead woman, Wallander thought. He was here in these rooms without me discovering him. But that's why he's keeping me here. He doesn't dare let me go. That's why he tied me up.

Wallander considered throwing himself at the robber and then leaving the shop. But there was the weapon. And the front door to the shop was most likely locked at this point.

He dismissed the idea. The man gave the impression of being in complete control of the situation.

He hasn't said anything so far, Wallander thought. It is always easier to get a sense of a person when you have heard his voice. But the man standing here is mute.

Wallander made a slow movement with his head. As if he had started to get a stiff neck. But it was in order to be able to glance at his watch.

Twenty-five minutes to seven. By now Mona would have started to wonder. Perhaps she was even worried. But I can't count on the fact that she has already called. It is too early. She is much too accustomed to me being late.

"I don't know why you want to keep me here," Wallander said. "I don't know why you don't let me go."

No reply. The man twitched but said nothing.

168

His fear had died down for several minutes. But now it returned in full force.

The man must be crazy in some way, Wallander thought. He robs a store on Christmas Eve and kills an old woman. He ties me up and threatens me with a pistol.

And he doesn't leave. That above all. He stays here.

The telephone next to the cash register started to ring. Wallander was startled, but the man in the hood appeared unmoved. He did not seem to hear it.

The ringing continued. The man did not move. Wallander tried to imagine who it could be. Someone who wondered why Elma Hagman had not come home? That was most likely. She should have closed up her shop by now. It was Christmas. Somewhere her family was waiting for her.

Anger welled up inside him. It was so strong that it swept away his fear. How could you kill an old woman so brutally? What was happening to Sweden?

They often talked about it at the station, over lunch or while drinking coffee. Or while commenting on a case they were handling.

What was happening? An underground fissure had suddenly surfaced in Swedish society. Radical seismographers had registered it. But where had it come from? The fact that criminal activity was always changing was nothing noteworthy in itself. As one of Wallander's colleagues had once put it: "In the past, people stole hand-cranked record players. You didn't steal car stereos, for the simple reason that they didn't exist."

But the emerging fissure was of a different order. It brought an increase in violence. A brutality that did not ask if it was necessary or not.

And now Wallander found himself caught in it. On Christmas Eve. Before him stood a man wearing a hood and with a gun in his belt. A dead woman lay a few metres behind him.

There was no logic in all of this. If you looked hard enough, there was often a factor that was comprehensible. But not this time. You didn't bludgeon a woman with an iron pipe in a remotely located shop if it wasn't absolutely necessary. If she hadn't offered violent resistance.

Above all, you did not linger at the scene with a hood over your face, waiting.

The telephone rang again. Wallander was now convinced that someone was expecting Elma Hagman. Someone who was starting to become concerned.

He tried to imagine what the man in the hood was thinking.

But the man remained quiet and unmoving. His arms hung by his sides.

The ringing stopped. In one of the neon tubes the light started to flicker.

Wallander noticed suddenly that he was thinking about Linda. He saw himself standing in the doorway to the apartment in Mariagatan, happily anticipating her running to meet him.

The whole situation is insane, he thought. I should not be sitting here on a stool. With a big bruise on the back of my neck, nauseous and afraid.

170

The only things people should wear on their heads at this time of year are Santa Claus hats. Nothing else.

He twisted his head again. It was nineteen minutes to seven. Now Mona would call and ask for him. And she would not give up. She was stubborn. In the end the call would be routed to Hemberg, who would send out a dispatch. In all likelihood he would check up on it personally. When something was thought to have happened to a police officer, there were always resources. Then even the commanding officers did not hesitate to immediately rush out into the field.

The nausea returned. On top of this he felt he would need to use the toilet soon.

At the same time he felt that he could no longer remain ignorant. There was only one way to go. He knew that. He had to start talking to the man in the black mask.

"I'm in civilian dress," he started. "But I'm a policeman. The best thing you can do is give up. Give up your weapon. It won't be long before there will be a lot of police cars outside. The best thing you can do is give up now. So things won't get any worse than they already are."

Wallander had been speaking slowly and clearly. He had forced his voice to appear firm.

The man did not react.

"Put the gun on the counter," Wallander said. "You can stay or leave. But put the gun on the counter."

Still no reaction.

Wallander started to wonder if the man was mute. Or was he so confused that he did not hear what Wallander said?

"I have my badge in my inside pocket," Wallander continued. "So you can see that I am a police officer. I am unarmed. But you probably already know that."

And then at last came a reaction. From nowhere. A sound like clicking. Wallander thought that the man must have smacked his lips. Or clicked his tongue against the roof of his mouth.

That was all. And he continued to stand without moving.

Perhaps as much as a minute went by.

Then he suddenly lifted one hand. Gripped the top of the mask and pulled it off.

Wallander stared at the man's face. He was looking straight into a pair of dark and tired eyes.

Later, Wallander would ask himself many times what he had really expected. How had he imagined the face under the mask? The only thing he was absolutely sure of was that he had never expected the face that he finally saw.

The man standing in front of him was a black man. Not brown, not copper-coloured, not a mestizo. Just that: black.

And he was young. Hardly more than twenty.

Different thoughts went through Wallander's head. He realised that the man probably had not understood him when he had been speaking Swedish. Wallander repeated what he had just said in his poor English. And now he could see that the man understood. Wallander spoke very slowly. And told him the facts. That he was a policeman. That the shop would soon be surrounded by patrol cars. That the best thing he could do would be to give himself up.

The man shook his head, almost imperceptibly. Wallander thought he gave an impression of great fatigue. It was visible now that the mask was removed.

I can't forget that he has brutally murdered an old woman, Wallander reminded himself. He knocked me down and tied me up. He pointed a gun at my head.

What had he really learned about how to behave in a situation like this? Retain his calm, not make any sudden movements or confrontational speeches. Speak calmly, an even stream of words. Patience and kindness. Try to start a conversation. Not lose control of oneself. Above all, not that. To lose control of oneself was to lose control, full stop.

Wallander thought a good start might be to talk about himself. So he said his name. That he had been on his way home to his wife and daughter to celebrate Christmas. He noticed that the man was listening now.

Wallander asked him if he could understand.

The man nodded. But he still said nothing.

Wallander looked at the time. By now Mona had surely called. Hemberg might already be on his way.

He decided to tell the man this.

The man listened. Wallander had the impression that he already expected to hear the approaching sirens.

Wallander paused. He tried to smile.

"What is your name?" he asked. "Everyone has a name."

"Oliver."

173

His voice was unsteady. Despondent, Wallander thought. He is not waiting for someone to come. He is waiting for someone to explain to him what he has done.

"Do you live here in Sweden?"

Oliver nodded.

"Are you a Swedish citizen?"

Wallander immediately realised the superfluousness of this question.

"No."

"Where do you come from?"

He did not answer. Wallander waited. He was sure that the answer would come. There was much that he wanted to know before Hemberg and the police cars arrived outside. But he could not hurry this up. The step towards the moment where this man raised his gun and shot him was not necessarily so great.

The ache in the back of his head had increased. But Wallander tried to think it away.

"Everyone comes from somewhere," he said. "And Africa is large. I read about Africa when I was at school. Geography was my best subject. I read about the deserts and rivers. And the drums, beating in the night."

Oliver listened attentively. Wallander had the feeling that he was already now somewhat less on his guard.

"Gambia," Wallander said. "Swedes go there on holiday. Even some of my colleagues. Is that where you come from?"

"I come from South Africa."

The answer came quickly and decidedly. Almost harshly.

Wallander was very poorly informed about what exactly was going on in South Africa. He did not know more than that the apartheid system and its racial laws were now more severe than ever before. But the resistance had also increased. He had read in newspapers about bombs exploding in Johannesburg and Cape Town.

He also knew that some South Africans had received asylum in Sweden. Not least those who had openly taken part in the black resistance and risked being sentenced to death by hanging if they remained.

He made a quick summary in his head. A young South African by the name of Oliver has killed Elma Hagman. That was what he knew. Neither more nor less.

No one would believe me, Wallander thought. This simply doesn't happen. Not in Sweden, and not on Christmas Eve.

"She started to scream," Oliver said.

"She must have been frightened. A man who enters the store with a mask on is frightening," Wallander said. "Especially if he has a gun or an iron pipe in his hand."

"She should not have screamed," Oliver said.

"You should not have killed her," Wallander answered. "She would probably have given you the money anyway."

Oliver pulled the gun out of his belt. It happened so fast that Wallander never had time to react. Again he saw the gun pointed at his head.

175

"She should not have screamed," Oliver said, and now his voice was unsteady with distress and fear.

"I can kill you," he added. "Yes," Wallander said. "You can. But why would you do that?"

"She should not have screamed."

Wallander now realised that he had been completely wrong. The South African was not in the least controlled and calm. He was at a breaking point. What exactly was on the point of breaking, Wallander did not know. But now he seriously started to fear what would happen when Hemberg arrived. It could become an all-out massacre.

I have to disarm him, Wallander thought. Nothing else is important. First I have to get him to tuck that gun back into his belt. This man is fully capable of starting to shoot wildly around him. Hemberg is probably on his way right now. And he doesn't sense anything. Even if he fears that something has happened, he isn't expecting this. As little as I did. It could be an all-out catastrophe.

"How long have you been here?" he asked.

"Three months."

"Not longer?"

"I came from West Germany," Oliver said. "From Frankfurt. I could not stay there."

"Why?"

Oliver did not answer. Wallander sensed that it was perhaps not the first time that Oliver had put a mask over his head and robbed a store in a remote location. He could be on the run from the West German authorities.

And in turn this would mean that he was in Sweden illegally.

"What was it that happened?" Wallander asked. "Not in Frankfurt but in South Africa. Why did you have to leave?"

Oliver took a step closer to Wallander.

"What do you know about South Africa?"

"Not much. Only that the blacks are treated very badly."

Wallander almost bit his tongue. Were you allowed to say "blacks", or was that discrimination?

"My father was killed by the police. They beat him to death with a hammer and chopped off one of his hands. It is preserved in a jar of alcohol somewhere. Maybe in Sanderton. Maybe somewhere else in Johannesburg's white suburbs. As a souvenir. And the only thing he had done was join the ANC. The only thing he had done was speak to his co-workers. About resistance and freedom."

Wallander did not doubt that Oliver was telling the truth. His voice was calm now, in the midst of all this uproar. There was no room for lies.

"The police started looking for me too," Oliver continued. "I hid. Every night I slept in a new bed. At last I went to Namibia and from there to Europe. To Frankfurt. And then here. But I am still running. In reality I don't exist."

Oliver grew silent. Wallander listened for sounds of approaching cars.

"You need money," he said. "You found this shop. She started to scream and you killed her."

177

"They killed my father with a hammer. And one of his hands is preserved in alcohol in a glass jar."

He's confused, Wallander thought. Helpless and disorientated. He doesn't know what he's doing.

"I am a policeman," Wallander said. "But I have never hit anyone on the head with a hammer. As you hit me."

"I did not know you were police."

"Right now that is lucky for you. They have started looking for me. They know I am here. Together we have to try to resolve this situation."

Oliver shook his head.

"If anyone tries to take me I will shoot."

"That will make nothing better."

"Nothing can get worse either."

Suddenly Wallander saw how he should continue this strained conversation.

"What do you think your father would have said about what you have done?"

This travelled like a shiver through Oliver's body. Wallander realised that the youth had never thought about this before. Or else he had thought it too many times.

"I promise that you won't be beaten," Wallander said. "I guarantee it. But you have committed the gravest crime there is. You have killed a person. The only thing you can do now is give up."

Oliver never had time to answer. The sound of approaching cars was suddenly very clear. They braked abruptly. Car doors opened and slammed shut again.

Hell, Wallander thought. I needed more time. He slowly stretched out his hand.

"Give me the gun," he said. "Nothing will happen. No one will hit you."

There was a banging on the door. Wallander heard Hemberg's voice. Dazed, Oliver looked from Wallander to the door.

"The gun," Wallander said. "Give it to me."

Hemberg called out and asked if Wallander was there.

"Wait!" Wallander called back. Then he repeated himself in English.

"Is everything all right?" Hemberg's voice was anxious.

Nothing is all right, Wallander thought. This is a nightmare.

"Yes," he said. "Wait. Do nothing."

Again he repeated these words in English.

"Give me the gun. Give it to me now."

Oliver suddenly pointed it to the ceiling and fired. The noise was deafening.

Then he turned the weapon to the door. Wallander shouted a warning to Hemberg to keep clear at the same time as he threw himself onto Oliver. They tumbled to the floor and took a magazine rack with them. All of Wallander's consciousness was focused on trying to get hold of the weapon. Oliver clawed him in the face and screamed words in a language that Wallander did not understand. When Wallander felt how Oliver was trying to tear his ear off he became furious. He freed one hand and tried to hit Oliver in the face with his fist. The gun had slid to the side and lay on the floor among the strewn newspapers. Wallander was just about to grab it when Oliver struck him with a kick right in the stomach. Wallander lost his breath while watching Oliver lunging after the weapon. He couldn't do anything. The kick had paralysed him. Oliver sat on the floor in the newspaper pile and pointed the gun at him.

For the second time that evening Wallander closed his eyes in the face of the unavoidable. Now he would die. There was no longer anything he could do. Outside the shop several sirens approached and agitated voices shouted questions about what was going on.

I am dying, Wallander thought. That is all.

The shot was deafening. Wallander was thrown back. He fought to get his breath back.

Then he realised he had not been hit. He opened his eyes.

Oliver lay stretched out on the floor in front of him.

He had shot himself in the head. The gun lay next to him.

Hell, Wallander thought. Why did he do that?

At that moment the door was kicked in. Wallander caught sight of Hemberg. Then he looked down at his hands. They shook. His whole body was shaking.

Wallander had been given a cup of coffee and been patched up. He had given Hemberg a brief summary of the events.

"I had no idea about this," Hemberg said later. "And I was the one who asked you to stop by on your way home."

"How were you supposed to know?" Wallander said. "How could anyone be expected to imagine something like this?"

Hemberg appeared to consider what Wallander had said.

"Something is happening," he said finally. "Anxiety is streaming in across our borders."

"We create it just as much ourselves," Wallander answered. "Even if Oliver here was an unhappy and restless young man from South Africa."

Hemberg flinched, as if Wallander had said something inappropriate.

"Restless?" he said finally. "I don't like the fact that foreign criminals are pouring in across our borders."

"What you just said is not true," Wallander said.

Then there was silence. Neither Hemberg nor Wallander had the energy to continue the conversation. They both knew they would not be able to agree.

Even here there is a crack, Wallander thought. Just now I was caught in one. Now I am standing in another that is growing wider between me and Hemberg.

"Why did he stay in here, anyway?" Hemberg said.

"Where should he have gone?"

Neither of them had anything to add.

"It was your wife who called," Hemberg said after a while. "She was wondering why you hadn't shown up. You had apparently called and said you were on your way?"

Wallander thought back to that telephone call. The brief quarrel. But he did not feel anything other than emptiness and fatigue. He chased the thoughts away.

181

"You should probably call home," Hemberg said gently.

Wallander looked at him.

"What should I say?"

"That you've been delayed. But if I were you I wouldn't tell her everything in detail. I would wait to do that until I got home."

"Aren't you unmarried?"

Hemberg smiled.

"I can still imagine what it's like to have someone waiting for you at home."

Wallander nodded. Then he got up heavily from the chair. His body ached. The nausea came and went in waves.

He made his way past Sjunnesson and the other forensic technicians at work.

When he came out of the building he sat completely still and pulled the chilly air into his lungs. Then he kept going to one of the patrol cars. He got into the front seat and looked at the radio dispatcher and then at his watch. Ten minutes past eight.

Christmas Eve, 1975.

Through the wet windscreen he discovered a telephone booth next to the gas station. He stepped out of the car and walked over. It was most likely out of order. But he still wanted to try it.

A man with a dog on a leash was standing in the rain, looking at the patrol cars and the lit-up shop.

"What has happened?" he asked.

He regarded Wallander's scraped-up face with a furrowed brow.

182

"Nothing," Wallander said. "An accident."

The man with the dog realised that what Wallander said wasn't true. But he asked no further questions.

"Merry Christmas" was all he said.

"And to you too," Wallander answered.

Then he called Mona.

It was raining more heavily.

The wind had picked up.

A gusty wind from the north.

THE MAN ON
THE BEACH

On the afternoon of Sunday, 26 April 1987, Detective Chief Inspector Kurt Wallander sat in his office in the Ystad police station, absent-mindedly clipping some hair from one of his nostrils. It was shortly after five o'clock. He had just put down a file containing documentation of a gang smuggling stolen luxury cars over to Poland. The investigation had already celebrated its tenth birthday, admittedly with various breaks as the years passed by. It had begun not long after Wallander had first started work in Ystad. He had often wondered if it would still be under way on that far distant day when he started to draw his pension.

Just for once, his desk was neat and tidy. It had been a chaotic mess for a long time, and he had used the bad weather as an excuse to do some work because he was on his own. A few days earlier Mona and Linda had left for a couple of weeks in the Canaries. It had come as a complete surprise to Wallander. He had no idea how Mona had managed to scrape together the money, and Linda hadn't breathed a word either. Despite the opposition of her parents, she had recently insisted on leaving grammar school. Now she seemed to be constantly irritated, tired and confused. He had driven them to Sturup airport early in the morning, and on the way back home to Ystad he had decided that, in fact, he quite liked the idea of a couple of weeks on his own. His and Mona's marriage was heading for the rocks. Neither of them knew what was wrong. On the other hand, it had been obvious over this last year that Linda was the one holding their relationship together. What would happen now that she had left school and was starting to make her own way in life?

He stood up and walked over to the window. The wind was pulling and tugging at the trees on the other side of the street. It was drizzling. Four degrees Celsius, the thermometer said. No sign of spring yet.

He put on his jacket and left the room. He nodded to the weekend receptionist, who was talking on the phone. He went to his car and drove down towards the centre of town. He inserted a Maria Callas cassette into the player on the dashboard as he wondered what to buy for the evening meal.

Should he buy anything at all, in fact? Was he even hungry? He was annoyed by his indecision. But he had no desire to fall into his old bad habit of eating at some hamburger bar. Mona kept telling him that he was getting fat. And she was right. One morning only a few months ago, he had examined his face in the bathroom mirror and realised that his youth was definitely a thing of the past. He would soon be forty, but he looked older. In the old days he had always looked younger than he really was.

Irritated by the thought, he turned into the Malmö road and stopped at one of the supermarkets. He had just locked his car door when his mobile phone rang from inside. At first he thought he would ignore it.

Whatever it was, somebody else could look after it. He had enough problems of his own just now. But he changed his mind, opened the door and reached for the phone.

"Is that Wallander?" It was his colleague Hansson.

"Yes."

"Where are you?"

"I was just going to buy some groceries."

"Leave that for now. Come here instead. I'm at the hospital. I'll meet you at the entrance."

"What's happened?"

"It's hard to explain over the phone. It'll be better if you come here."

End of call. Wallander knew that Hansson wouldn't have phoned if it hadn't been serious. It only took him a few minutes to drive to the hospital. Hansson came to meet him outside the main entrance. He was obviously feeling the cold. Wallander tried to work out from his expression what had happened.

"What's going on?" Wallander asked.

"There's a taxi driver by the name of Stenberg in there," said Hansson. "He's drinking coffee. He's very upset."

Wallander followed Hansson through the glass doors, still wondering what had happened.

The hospital cafeteria was to the right. They walked past an old man in a wheelchair who was slowly chewing on an apple. Wallander recognised Stenberg, who was alone at a table. He had met the man before, but couldn't put his finger on when or where. Stenberg was in his fifties, on the portly side and almost completely bald. His nose was bent, suggesting he had been a boxer in his younger days.

"Maybe you recognise Inspector Wallander?" Hansson said.

Stenberg nodded and started to get up to shake hands.

"No, don't stand up," said Wallander. "Tell me what's happened instead."

Stenberg's eyes were constantly on the move. Wallander could see that the man was very upset, or even scared. He couldn't yet tell which.

"I got a call to take some guy from Svarte back to Ystad," Stenberg said. "The fare was supposed to wait by the main road. Alexandersson, his name was. Sure enough, there he was when I drove up. He got into the back seat and asked me to take him back to town. As far as the square. I could see in the rear-view mirror that he had his eyes closed. I thought he was having a snooze. We came to Ystad and I drove to the square and told him we were there. He didn't react at all. I got out of the car, opened the back door and tapped him on the shoulder. No reaction. I thought he must be ill, so I drove him to the emergency room. They said he was dead."

Wallander frowned.

"Dead?"

"They tried to revive him," Hansson said. "But it was too late. He was dead."

Wallander thought.

"It takes about fifteen minutes to drive from Svarte to Ystad," he said to Stenberg. "Did he look ill when you picked him up?"

"If he'd been ill I'd have noticed," said Stenberg. "Besides, he'd have asked to be taken to the hospital, surely?"

"You didn't notice any injury?"

"Not a thing. He was wearing a suit and a light blue overcoat."

"Was he carrying anything? A suitcase or something?"

"No, nothing. I thought I'd better call the police. Although I expect the hospital will have to do that in any case."

Stenberg's answers were immediate, without hesitation. Wallander turned to Hansson.

"Do we know who he is?"

Hansson took out his notebook.

"Göran Alexandersson," Hansson said. "Forty-nine years of age. Runs his own business, electronics. Lives in Stockholm. He had quite a lot of money in his wallet. And several credit cards."

"Odd," Wallander said. "I assume it must have been a heart attack. What do the doctors say?"

"That only an autopsy will give the definite cause of death."

Wallander nodded and stood up.

"You can contact whoever's in charge of his estate and claim your fare," he said to Stenberg. "We'll be in touch if we have any more questions."

"It was a nasty experience," said Stenberg firmly. "But I certainly wouldn't ask his next of kin to pay me for driving a corpse to the hospital."

Stenberg left.

"I'd like to take a look at him," said Wallander. "You don't need to come if you don't want to."

"I'd rather not," said Hansson. "I'll try to get in touch with his next of kin."

"What was he doing in Ystad?" wondered Wallander. "That's something we should find out."

Wallander only stayed with the body for a short time, in a room in the emergency unit. The dead man's expression gave nothing away. Wallander searched his clothes. Like his shoes, they were of high quality. If it transpired that a crime had been committed, the forensic team would need to take a closer look at the clothes. He found nothing in the man's wallet that Hansson hadn't already mentioned. Then he went to talk to one of the doctors.

"It appears to be death from natural causes," said the doctor. "No sign of any violence, no injuries."

"Who on earth could have killed him while he was in the back seat of a taxicab?" asked Wallander. "But let me have the post-mortem results as soon as you can, please."

"We'll transfer him to the medico-legal unit in Lund now," the doctor said. "Unless the police have anything against that?"

"No," said Wallander. "Why should we?"

He drove back to the police station and went to see Hansson, who was just winding up a telephone call. As he waited for him to finish, Wallander miserably felt his stomach, which was hanging out over his belt.

"I've just spoken to Alexandersson's office in Stockholm," Hansson said as he put down the phone.

"To his secretary and his number two. They were shocked, of course. But they were able to tell us that Alexandersson had been divorced for the last ten years."

"Did he have any children?"

"One son."

"We'd better find him, then."

"That won't be possible," Hansson said.

"Why not?"

"Because he's dead."

Wallander could sometimes get very annoyed by Hansson's roundabout way of coming to the point. This was one of those occasions.

"Dead? What do you mean, dead? Do I have to drag every detail out of you?"

Hansson checked his notes.

"His only child, a son, died nearly seven years ago. Apparently it was some sort of accident. I couldn't quite grasp what they meant."

"Did the son have a name?"

"Bengt."

"Did you ask what Göran Alexandersson was doing in Ystad? Or Svarte?"

"He'd told them he was going on holiday for a week. He'd be staying at the King Charles Hotel. He arrived four days ago."

"Right, let's go there," Wallander said.

They spent over an hour going through Alexandersson's room but found nothing of interest. Only an empty suitcase, some clothes neatly hung in the cupboard and a spare pair of shoes.

"Not a single sheet of paper," said Wallander thoughtfully. "No book, nothing."

Then he called the front desk and asked if Alexandersson had received or made any telephone calls or had had any visitors. The receptionist's reply was crystal clear: nobody had called room 211, nobody had been to visit.

"He's staying here in Ystad," Wallander said, "but he calls a taxi from Svarte. Question: How did he get there in the first place?"

"I'll call the taxi companies," said Hansson.

They drove back to the police station. Wallander stood at his office window, absent-mindedly contemplating the water tower on the other side of the street. He found himself thinking about Mona and Linda. They were probably in some restaurant or other, having dinner. But what were they talking about? No doubt what Linda was going to do next. He tried to imagine their conversation, but all he could hear was the humming from the radiators. He sat down to write a preliminary report while Hansson was calling the Ystad taxi companies. Before starting, he went to the break room and helped himself to some biscuits that somebody had abandoned. It was nearly eight by the time Hansson knocked on his door and came in.

"He took a cab out to Svarte three times in the four days he'd been here in Ystad," Hansson said. "He was dropped off on the edge of the village each time. He went out early in the morning, and he ordered a taxi to take him back in the afternoon."

Wallander was miles away but nodded in acknowledgement.

"That's not against the law," he said. "Perhaps he had a mistress there?"

Wallander stood up and walked over to the window. The wind was building up.

"Let's search for him in the computer records," he said after a few moments' thought. "I get the impression we'll draw a blank. But let's do it anyway. Then we'll have a good look at the post-mortem report."

"I bet it was a heart attack," said Hansson, rising to leave.

"No doubt you're right," said Wallander.

Wallander drove home and opened a can of sausages. Göran Alexandersson was already fading out of his consciousness. After eating his simple meal, he fell asleep in front of the television.

The following day, Wallander's colleague Martinsson searched through all available criminal registers for the name Göran Alexandersson. There was nothing. Martinsson was the youngest member of the investigation team, and the one most willing to embrace new technology.

Wallander devoted the day to the stolen luxury cars being driven around Poland. In the evening he went to see his father in Löderup and played cards for a few hours. They ended up arguing over who owed whom and how much. As Wallander drove home, he wondered if he would grow to be like his father as he got older. Or had he already started ageing that way? Argumentative, complaining and miserable? He should ask somebody. Perhaps somebody other than Mona.

On the morning of 28 April, Wallander's phone rang. It was the medico-legal department in Lund.

"I'm calling in connection with a person by the name of Göran Alexandersson," said the doctor at the other end of the line. He was called Jörne and Wallander knew him from his time in Malmö.

"What was it?" Wallander asked. "Cerebral haemorrhage or a heart attack?"

"Neither," said the doctor. "Either he committed suicide or he was murdered."

Wallander pricked up his ears.

"Murdered? What do you mean by that?"

"Exactly what I say," said Jörne.

"But that's impossible. He can't have been murdered in the back seat of a taxi. Stenberg, the driver of the cab, isn't the type who goes around killing people. But surely he can't have committed suicide either?"

"I can't tell you how it happened," said Jörne dismissively. "But what I can tell you with absolute certainty is that he died from a poison that got into his system somehow, either something he'd eaten or something he'd drunk. That seems to me to suggest murder. But of course, it's your business to establish that."

Wallander made no comment.

"I'll fax the papers over to you," said Jörne. "Are you still there?"

"Yes," Wallander said. "I'm still here."

He thanked Jörne, replaced the receiver and thought about what he'd just been told. Then he asked Hansson over the intercom to come to his office right away. Wallander took one of his notepads and wrote two words.

Göran Alexandersson.

Outside the police station, the wind was getting stronger. Some gusts were already gale strength.

The squally wind continued blowing all over Skåne. Wallander sat in his office and contemplated the fact that he had no idea what had happened to the man who had died in the back seat of a taxi some days earlier. At 9.30 he went to one of the conference rooms and closed the door behind him. Hansson and Rydberg were already sitting at the table. Wallander was surprised to see Rydberg. He'd been off sick with back pains and given no indication that he was returning to work.

"How are you?" Wallander asked.

"I'm here," said Rydberg evasively. "What's all this nonsense about a man being murdered in the back seat of a taxi?"

"Let's start at the beginning," Wallander said.

He looked around. Somebody was missing.

"Where's Martinsson?"

"He called in to say he had tonsillitis," said Rydberg. "Maybe Svedberg can stand in for him?"

"We'll see if we need him," said Wallander, picking up his papers. The fax had arrived from Lund.

Then he looked at his colleagues.

"What started off looking like a straightforward case could turn out to be much more problematic than I'd thought. A man died in the back seat of a taxi. The medico-legal people in Lund have established that he was poisoned. What we don't know yet is how long before his death the poison got into his system. Lund promises to let us know that in a few days."

"Murder or suicide?" Rydberg wondered.

"Murder," said Wallander without hesitation. "I find it hard to imagine a suicide taking poison and then calling for a taxi."

"Could he have taken the poison by mistake?" Hansson asked.

"Hardly likely," said Wallander. "According to the doctors it's a very unusual mixture of poisons."

"What do they mean by that?" Hansson asked.

"It's something that can only be made by a specialist — a doctor, a chemist or a biologist, for instance."

Silence.

"So, we need to regard this as a murder case," Wallander said. "What do we know about this man, Göran Alexandersson?"

Hansson leafed through his notebook.

"He was a businessman," he said. "He owned two electronics shops in Stockholm. One in Västberga, the other in Nortull. He lived alone in an apartment in Åsögatan. He doesn't seem to have had any family. His divorced wife lives in France. His son died seven years ago. The employees I've spoken to all describe him in exactly the same way."

"How?" asked Wallander.

"They say he was nice."

"Nice?"

"That was the word they all used. Nice."

Wallander nodded.

"Anything else?"

"He appears to have led a pretty humdrum existence. His secretary guessed that he probably collected stamps. Catalogues kept arriving at the office. He doesn't seem to have had any close friends. At least, none that his colleagues knew about."

Nobody said anything.

"We'd better ask Stockholm to help us with his apartment," Wallander said when the silence had started to feel oppressive. "And we must get in touch with his ex-wife. I'll concentrate on trying to find out what he was doing down here in Skåne, in Ystad and Svarte. Who did he meet? We can get together again this afternoon and see how far we've got."

"One thing puzzles me," said Rydberg. "Can a person be murdered without knowing anything about it?"

Wallander nodded.

"That's an interesting idea," he said. "Somebody gives Göran Alexandersson some poison that doesn't have any effect until an hour later. I'll ask Jörne to answer that one."

"If he can," muttered Rydberg. "I wouldn't count on it."

The meeting was over. They went their different ways after dividing up the various tasks. Wallander stood at the window of his office, coffee cup in hand, and tried to make up his mind where to start.

Half an hour later he was in his car, on the way to Svarte. The wind was slowly dropping. The sun shone through the parting clouds. For the first time that year Wallander had the feeling that perhaps spring really was on the way at last. He stopped when he came to the edge of Svarte and got out of the car. Göran Alexandersson came here, he thought. He came in the morning and returned to Ystad in the afternoon. On the fourth occasion, he was poisoned and died in the back seat of a taxi.

Wallander started walking towards the village. Many of the houses on the beach side of the road were summer cottages and were boarded up for the winter.

He walked through the whole village and only saw two people. The desolation made him feel depressed. He turned round and walked quickly back to his car.

He had already started the engine when he noticed an elderly lady working on a flower bed in a garden next to where the car was parked. He switched off the ignition and got out. When he closed the door, the woman turned to look at him. Wallander walked over to her fence, raising his hand in greeting.

"I hope I'm not disturbing you," he said.

"Nobody disturbs anybody here," said the woman, giving him an inquisitive look.

"My name's Kurt Wallander and I'm a police officer from Ystad," he said.

"I recognise you," she said. "Have I seen you on TV? Some current affairs debate, maybe?"

"I don't think so," Wallander said. "But my picture has been in the papers now and again, I'm afraid."

"My name's Agnes Ehn," said the woman, reaching out her hand.

"Do you live here year-round?" Wallander asked.

"No, just the summer half of the year. I usually move out here at the beginning of April and stay till October. I spend the winter in Halmstad. I'm a retired schoolteacher. My husband died a few years ago."

"It's pretty here," said Wallander. "Pretty, and quiet. Everybody knows everybody else."

"I don't know about that," she said. "Sometimes you don't even know your next-door neighbour."

"Did you happen to see a man by himself who came here to Svarte by taxi several times this last week? And was then picked up by a taxi again in the afternoon?"

Her reply surprised him.

"He used the telephone in my house to call for the taxi," she said. "Three days in a row, in fact. Assuming it's the same man."

"Did he say his name?"

"He was very polite."

"Did he introduce himself?"

"You can be polite without saying what your name is."

"And he asked to use your phone?"

"Yes."

"Did he say anything else?"

"Has something happened to him?"

Wallander thought he might as well tell her the truth.

"He's dead."

"That's awful. What happened?"

"We don't know. All we know at the moment is that he's dead. Do you know what he did here in Svarte? Did he say who he'd come to see? Where did he go? Was there anybody with him? Anything at all you can remember is important."

She surprised him again with her precise reply.

"He walked down to the beach," she said. "There's a path leading to the beach on the other side of the house. He took that. Then he walked along the sands in a westerly direction. He didn't come back until the afternoon."

"He walked along the beach? Was he alone?"

"I can't tell you that. The beach curves away. He might have met somebody further away, where I can't see."

"Did he have anything with him? A briefcase or a package, for instance?"

She shook her head.

"Did he seem worried at all?"

"Not as far as I could tell."

"But he borrowed your telephone?"

"Yes."

"Did you notice anything worth mentioning?"

"He seemed to be a very nice, friendly man. He insisted on paying for all the telephone calls."

Wallander nodded.

"You've been a big help," he said, giving her his business card. "If you remember anything else, please call me at the number on the card."

"It's a tragedy," she said. "Such a pleasant man."

Wallander went round to the other side of the house and walked down the path to the beach. He went as far as the water's edge. The beach was deserted. When he turned back he saw that Agnes Ehn was watching him.

He must have met somebody, Wallander thought. There's no other plausible explanation. The only question is, who?

He drove back to the police station. Rydberg stopped him in the corridor and told him he had managed to track Alexandersson's ex-wife to a house on the Riviera.

"But nobody answered the telephone," he said. "I'll try again later."

"Good," said Wallander. "Let me know when you get hold of her."

"Martinsson came in," said Rydberg. "It was almost impossible to understand a word he said. I told him to go home again."

"You did the right thing," Wallander said.

He went to his office, closed the door behind him and pulled over the notepad on which he had written Göran Alexandersson's name. Who? he wondered. Who did you meet on the beach? I must find out.

By one o'clock Wallander felt hungry. He put on his jacket and was about to leave when Hansson knocked on his door. It was obvious he had something important to say.

"I've got something that might be important," Hansson said.

"What?"

"As you'll recall, Alexandersson had a son who died seven years ago. It looks very much like he was murdered. But as far as I can see, nobody's ever been charged with it."

Wallander looked long and hard at Hansson.

"Good," he said eventually. "Now we've got something to go on. Even if I can't put my finger on what it is."

The hunger he'd been feeling just moments ago had disappeared.

Shortly after two in the afternoon on 28 April, Rydberg knocked on Wallander's half-open door.

"I've made contact with Alexandersson's ex-wife," he said as he came into the room. He made a face as he sat down on the visitor's chair.

"How's your back?" Wallander asked.

"I don't know," said Rydberg. "There's something funny going on."

"Perhaps you came back to work too soon?"

"Lying at home staring at the ceiling wouldn't do it any good."

That put an end to any discussion about Rydberg's back. Wallander knew it was a waste of time trying to persuade him to go home and rest.

"What did she have to say?" he asked instead.

"She was shocked, naturally enough. It must have been a minute before she was able to say anything at all."

"That will be an expensive call for the Swedish state," said Wallander. "But then what? After that minute had passed."

"She asked what had happened, of course. I gave her the facts. She had trouble understanding what I was talking about."

"That's hardly surprising," said Wallander.

"Anyway, I found out that they weren't in touch with each other. According to the wife, they divorced because their married life was so boring."

Wallander frowned.

"What exactly did she mean?"

"I suspect that's a more common reason for divorce than people realise," said Rydberg. "I think it would be awful, having to live with a boring person."

Wallander thought that over. He wondered if Mona had the same view of him. What did he think himself?

"I asked her if she could think of anybody who might want to murder him, but she couldn't. Then I asked her if she could explain what he was doing in Skåne, but she didn't know that either. That was all."

"Didn't you ask her about that son of hers who died? The one Hansson says was murdered?"

"Of course I did. But she didn't want to talk about it."

"Isn't that a bit odd?"

"That's exactly what I thought."

"I think you'll have to talk to her again," Wallander said.

Rydberg nodded and left the room. Wallander thought he would have to find an opportunity to talk to Mona and ask her if boredom was the biggest problem in their marriage. His train of thought was interrupted by the phone ringing. It was Ebba in reception, telling him that the Stockholm police wanted to talk to him. He pulled over his notepad and listened. An officer by the name of Rendel was put through to him. Wallander had never had any contact with him before.

"We went to take a look at that apartment in Åsögatan," Rendel said.

"Did you find anything?"

"How could we find anything when we'd no idea what we were looking for?"

Wallander could hear that Rendel was under pressure.

"What was the apartment like?" Wallander asked, as nicely as he could.

"Clean and neat," said Rendel. "Everything in its place. A bit fussy. I had the impression of a bachelor pad."

"That's what it was, in fact," Wallander said.

"We checked his mail," said Rendel. "He seems to have been away for a week at most."

"That's correct," said Wallander.

"He had an answering machine, but there was nothing on it. Nobody had tried to call him."

"What was the message he'd recorded?" Wallander asked.

"Just the usual."

"Well, at least we know that," said Wallander. "Thanks for your help. We'll come back to you if we need anything else."

He hung up and saw from the clock that it was time for the investigative team's afternoon meeting. When he got to the conference room, Hansson and Rydberg were already there.

"I've just been speaking to Stockholm," Wallander said as he sat down. "They found nothing of interest in the apartment in Åsögatan."

"I called the wife again," said Rydberg. "She was still unwilling to talk about her son, but when I told her we could make her come back home to assist us with our inquiries, she thawed a little. The boy was evidently beaten up in a street in the centre of Stockholm. It must have been a totally pointless attack. He wasn't even robbed."

"I've dug up some documentation about that attack," said Hansson. "It hasn't yet been written off, but nobody's done anything about it for at least the last five years."

"Are there any suspects?" Wallander wondered.

Hansson shook his head.

"None at all. There's absolutely nothing. No witnesses, nothing."

Wallander pushed his notepad to one side.

"Just as little as we've got to go on here at the moment," he said.

Nobody spoke. Wallander realised he would have to say something.

"You'll have to speak to the people working in his shops," he said. "Call Rendel from the Stockholm police and ask him for some assistance. We'll meet again tomorrow."

They divided up the tasks that had to be done, and Wallander went back to his office. He thought he should call his father out in Löderup and apologise for the previous night. But he didn't. He couldn't get what had happened to Göran Alexandersson out of his mind. The whole situation was so preposterous that it should be explicable on those grounds alone. He knew from experience that all murders, and most other crimes as well, had something logical about them, somewhere. It was just a matter of turning over the right stones in the correct order and following up possible connections between them.

Wallander left the police station shortly before five and took the coastal road to Svarte. This time he parked further into the village. He took a pair of wellingtons out of the boot, put them on, then walked down to the beach. In the distance he could see a cargo ship steaming westward.

He started walking along the beach, examining the houses on his right side. There seemed to be somebody living in every third house. He kept on walking until he had left Svarte behind. Then he returned. He suddenly realised that he was hoping Mona would appear from nowhere, walking towards him. He thought back to the time they had gone to Skagen. That had been the best part of their life together. They had so much to talk about, things they never had time to do.

He shook off these unpleasant thoughts and forced himself to concentrate on Göran Alexandersson. As he walked along the sand he tried to make a summary of the case so far.

What did they know? That Alexandersson lived by himself, that he owned two electronics shops, that he was forty-nine years old, and that he had travelled to Ystad and stayed at the King Charles Hotel. He had told his staff he was going on holiday. While at the hotel he had received no telephone calls or visitors. Nor had he used the phone in his room himself.

Every morning he had taken a taxi out to Svarte, where he had spent the day walking up and down the beach. In the afternoon, he had returned to Ystad after borrowing Agnes Ehn's telephone. On the fourth day, he had entered the back seat of a taxi and died.

Wallander stopped and looked around. The beach was still deserted. Alexandersson is visible nearly all the time, he thought, but somewhere along the sand he disappears. Then he comes back again, and a few minutes later, he's dead.

He must have met somebody here, Wallander thought. Or rather, he must have arranged to meet somebody. You don't bump into a poisoner by accident.

Wallander started walking again. He eyed the houses along the beach. The following day they would start knocking on doors here. Somebody must have seen Alexandersson walking on the beach, somebody might have seen him meeting somebody else.

Wallander saw that he was no longer alone on the beach. An elderly man was coming towards him. He had a black Labrador trotting decorously along by his side. Wallander paused and looked at the dog. Lately he had been wondering if he should suggest to Mona that they buy a dog. But he hadn't done so because he so often found himself working unsociable hours. In all probability a dog would mean more guilt rather than more company.

The man raised his cap as he approached Wallander.

"Are we going to have any spring this year, do you think?" the man asked.

Wallander noticed that he didn't speak with a local accent.

"I expect it will show up eventually, as usual," Wallander replied.

The man was about to continue on his way when Wallander spoke again.

"I take it you go walking along the beach every day?" he asked.

The man pointed at one of the houses.

"I've been living here ever since I retired," he said.

"My name's Wallander and I'm a police officer in Ystad. Did you happen to see a man of about fifty walking along the sand here by himself in recent days?"

The man's eyes were blue and bright. His white hair stuck out from under his cap.

"No," he said, with a smile. "Who would want to come walking here? I'm the only person who walks along this beach. Now, in May, when it gets a bit warmer, it will be a different story."

"Are you absolutely sure?" Wallander asked.

"I walk the dog three times every day," said the man. "And I haven't seen any man wandering around here by himself. Until you appeared, that is."

Wallander smiled.

"Don't let me disturb you any longer," he said.

Wallander resumed walking. When he stopped and turned round, the man with the dog had disappeared.

Where the thought — or rather, the feeling — came from, he never managed to figure out. Nevertheless, from that moment on, he was quite certain. There had been something about the man's expression, a faint, almost imperceptible movement of his eyes, when Wallander asked him if he had seen a solitary man walking along the beach. He knows something, Wallander thought. But what?

Wallander looked around once more. The beach was deserted.

He stood there motionless for several minutes.

Then he went back to his car and drove home.

Wednesday, 29 April, was the first day of spring in Skåne that year. Wallander woke up early, as usual. He was sweaty and knew he had had a nightmare but couldn't remember what it was about. Perhaps he had dreamed yet again about being chased by bulls? Or that Mona had left him? He took a shower, had a cup of coffee and leafed absentmindedly through the *Ystad Chronicle*.

He was in his office by six-thirty. The sun was shining from a clear blue sky. Wallander hoped that Martinsson had recovered and could take over the register searches from Hansson. That usually produced better and faster results. If Martinsson was well again, Wallander could take Hansson with him to Svarte and start knocking on doors. But perhaps the most important thing just now was to try to create as accurate a picture as possible of Göran Alexandersson. Martinsson was much more thorough than Hansson when it came to contact with people who might be able to provide information. Wallander also made up his mind that they should make a serious effort to find out what had really happened when Alexandersson's son had been beaten to death.

When the clock struck seven, Wallander tried to get hold of Jörne, who had done the autopsy on Alexandersson, but in vain. He realised he was being impatient. The case of the dead man in the back seat of Stenberg's taxi was making him uneasy.

It was 7.58 when they assembled in the conference room. Rydberg reported that Martinsson still had a fever and a very sore throat. Wallander thought how typical it was that Martinsson should succumb to something like this when he was so obsessed by germs in general.

"OK, in that case it'll be you and me knocking on doors in Svarte today," he said. "You, Hansson, stay here and keep digging away. I'd like to know more about Alexandersson's son, Bengt, and how he died. Ask Rendel for help."

"Do we know any more about that poison yet?" asked Rydberg.

"I tried to find out this morning," Wallander said, "but I haven't heard anything yet and I can't get a response from anybody."

The meeting was very short. Wallander asked for an enlargement of the photograph on Alexandersson's driver's licence, plus several copies. Then he went to see Björk, the chief of police. On the whole, he thought Björk was good at his job and let everybody get on with their own work. Occasionally, however, the chief would suddenly become proactive and ask for a rundown on the latest situation in an investigation.

"How's it going with that gang exporting the luxury cars?" Björk asked, dropping his hands onto his desk as a sign that he wanted a concise answer.

"Badly," said Wallander, truthfully.

"Are any arrests imminent?"

"No, none," Wallander told him. "If I were to go to one of the prosecutors with the evidence I have available, they'd throw me out immediately."

"We mustn't give up, though," said Björk.

"Of course not," said Wallander. "I'll keep working away. As soon as we've solved this case of the man who died in the back seat of a taxi."

"Hansson told me about that," said Björk. "It all sounds very strange."

"It *is* strange," said Wallander.

"Can that man really have been murdered?"

"The doctors tell us he was," Wallander said. "We'll be knocking on doors today out at Svarte. Somebody must have seen him."

"Keep me informed," said Björk, standing up as a signal that the conversation was at an end.

They drove to Svarte in Wallander's car.

"Skåne is beautiful," said Rydberg, apropos of nothing.

"On a day like this, at least," said Wallander. "But let's face it, it can be pretty awful in the autumn. When the mud's higher than your doorstep. Or when it seeps in under your skin."

"Who's thinking about autumn now?" said Rydberg. "Why worry about the bad weather in advance? It'll come eventually, like it or not."

Wallander didn't respond. He was too busy passing a tractor.

"Let's start with the houses along the beach to the west of the village," he said. "We can go in different directions and work our way towards the middle. Try to find out who lives in the empty houses as well."

"What are you hoping to find?" Rydberg asked.

"The solution," he replied, without beating around the bush. "Somebody must have seen him out there on the beach. Somebody must have seen him meeting some other person."

Wallander parked the car. He let Rydberg start with the house where Agnes Ehn lived. Meanwhile Wallander tried to contact Jörne from his mobile phone. No luck this time either. He drove a bit further west, then parked the car and started working his way east. The first house was an old, well-cared-for traditional Skåne cottage. He opened the gate, went down the path and rang the doorbell. When there was

214

no reply, he rang again, and was just about to leave when the door was opened by a woman in her thirties, dressed in stained overalls.

"I don't like being interrupted," she said, glaring at Wallander.

"Sometimes it's necessary, I'm afraid," he said, showing her his ID.

"What do you want?" she asked.

"You may find my question a little strange," Wallander said, "but I want to know if you've seen a man aged about fifty wearing a light blue overcoat walking along the beach in the last few days."

She raised her eyebrows and looked at Wallander with a smile.

"I paint with the curtains drawn," she said. "I haven't seen anything at all."

"You're an artist," said Wallander. "I thought you needed light."

"I don't. But that's not a jailable offence, is it?"

"So you haven't seen anything at all?"

"No, nothing — that's what I just said, isn't it?"

"Is there anybody else here in the house who might have seen something?"

"I have a cat who likes to lie on a windowsill behind the curtains. You can ask him if you like."

Wallander could feel himself getting annoyed.

"It's sometimes necessary for police officers to ask questions, you know. Don't think I'm doing this for fun. I won't disturb you any longer."

The woman shut the door. He heard her turning several locks. He moved on to the next property. It was a relatively recently built two-storey house. There was a little fountain in the garden. When he rang the bell a dog started barking. He waited.

The dog stopped barking and the door opened. He was facing the old man he had met on the beach the previous day. Wallander had the immediate impression that the man was not surprised to see him. He had been expecting him, and was on his guard.

"You again," said the man.

"Yes," Wallander said. "I'm knocking on the doors of people who live in houses along the beach."

"I told you yesterday that I hadn't seen anything."

Wallander nodded.

"People sometimes remember things afterwards," he said.

The man stepped aside and let Wallander into the house. The Labrador sniffed him inquisitively.

"Do you live here year-round?" asked Wallander.

"Yes," said the man. "I was a doctor in Nynäshamn for twenty years. When I retired we moved here, my wife and I."

"Maybe she saw something?" Wallander said. "Assuming she's here?"

"She's ill," said the man. "She hasn't seen anything."

Wallander produced a notebook from his pocket.

"Can I have your name?" he asked.

"I'm Martin Stenholm," the man said. "My wife's name is Kajsa."

Wallander noted down the names and put the book back in his pocket.

"I won't disturb you any more," he said.

"No problem," said Stenholm.

"I might come back in a few days' time and speak to your wife," he said. "Sometimes it's better for people to say for themselves what they've seen or haven't seen."

"I don't think there would be much point," said Stenholm. "My wife is very ill. She has cancer and is dying."

"I understand," Wallander said. "In that case I won't come back and intrude."

Stenholm opened the door for him.

"Is your wife also a doctor?" Wallander asked.

"No," said the man. "She was a lawyer."

Wallander walked down the path to the road, then on to three more houses, none of which produced any information. He caught sight of Rydberg and could tell he had almost finished his quota of doors. Wallander went to get his car and waited for Rydberg outside Agnes Ehn's house. When Rydberg arrived, he had no positive information. Nobody had seen Göran Alexandersson on the beach

"I always thought people were curious," Rydberg said. "Especially in the country, and especially where strangers are concerned."

They drove back to Ystad. Wallander didn't say a word. When they got back to the police station he asked Rydberg to find Hansson and bring him to Wallander's office. He then phoned the medico-legal unit in Lund and this time managed to get hold of Jörne. Hansson and Rydberg had arrived by the time he had finished the call. Wallander looked questioningly at Hansson.

"Any news?" he asked.

"Nothing that changes the picture we already have of Alexandersson," Hansson said.

"I've just spoken to Jörne," said Wallander. "The poison that killed Alexandersson could very well have been administered without him noticing it. It's not possible to say precisely how fast it works. Jörne guessed it would be at least half an hour. When death does come, it happens very quickly."

"So we're right in our suppositions so far," said Hansson. "Does this poison have a name?"

Wallander read out the complicated chemical description he had written down on his notepad.

Then he told them about the conversation he'd had with Martin Stenholm in Svarte.

"I don't know why," he said, "but I can't help feeling we'll find the solution to our problem in that doctor's house."

"A doctor knows about poisons," Rydberg said. "That's always a start."

"You're right, of course," said Wallander. "But there's something else too. I can't put my finger on it, though."

"Why don't I run a search through the registers?" asked Hansson. "It's too bad Martinsson is sick. He's the best at that sort of thing."

Wallander nodded. Then an idea struck him.

"Do one for his wife as well. Kajsa Stenholm."

The investigation was put on hold for the Valpurgis Night holiday and the weekend. Wallander spent a large part of his free time at his father's house. He spent one afternoon repainting the kitchen. He also called

Rydberg, for no other reason than the fact that Rydberg was as solitary as he was. But when Wallander called, Rydberg turned out to be drunk, and the conversation was a very short one.

On Monday, 4 May, he was back at the police station early. While he waited to hear if Hansson had found anything of interest in the registers, he resumed his work on the gang smuggling stolen cars into Poland. It wasn't until eleven the next morning that Hansson eventually showed up.

"I can't find a thing about Martin Stenholm," he said. "It looks as if he's never done a dishonest thing in his whole life."

Wallander wasn't in the least surprised. He had been aware from the start that they could be heading into a cul-de-sac.

"What about his wife?"

Hansson shook his head.

"Even less," said Hansson. "She was a prosecutor in Nynäshamn for many years."

Hansson put a file full of papers on Wallander's desk.

"I'll go and talk to the taxi drivers again," he said. "Perhaps they saw something without realising it."

When Hansson had left, Wallander opened the file. It took him an hour to work his way carefully through all the documents. For once Hansson hadn't overlooked anything. Even so, Wallander was convinced that Alexandersson's death had something to do with the old doctor. He knew without knowing, as so many times before. He didn't trust his intuition, it was true,

219

but he couldn't deny that it had served him well many times in the past. He called Rydberg, who came to his office immediately. Wallander handed him the file.

"I'd like you to read through this," he said. "Neither Hansson nor I can see anything of interest, but I'm sure we're missing something."

"We can forget Hansson," Rydberg said, making no attempt to disguise the fact that his respect for his colleague was limited.

Late that afternoon Rydberg returned the file, shaking his head. He hadn't found anything either.

"We'll have to start again from the beginning," said Wallander. "Let's meet here in my office tomorrow morning and decide where we go from here."

An hour later Wallander left the police station and drove to Svarte. Once again he took a long walk along the beach. He didn't see another soul. Then he sat in his car and read one more time through the material Hansson had given him. What is it that I'm missing? he asked himself. There is a link between this doctor and Göran Alexandersson. It's just me who can't see what it is.

He drove back to Ystad and took the file home with him to Mariagatan. They had lived in the same three-room apartment ever since they moved to Ystad twelve years earlier.

He tried to relax, but the file gave him no peace. As midnight approached, he sat down at the kitchen table and went through it one more time. Although he was very tired, he did in fact find one detail that caught his attention. He knew it might well have no significance.

Nevertheless, he decided to look into it early the following morning.

He slept badly that night.

He was back at the police station by 7 a.m. Ystad was enveloped in drizzle. Wallander knew the man he was looking for was just as much of an early bird as he was. He went to the part of the building that housed the prosecutors and knocked on Per Åkeson's door. As usual, the room was in chaos. Åkeson and Wallander had worked together for many years and had great faith in each other's judgement. Åkeson pushed his glasses up on top of his head and looked at Wallander.

"Are you here already?" he said. "So early? That must mean you have something important to tell me."

"I don't know if it's important," Wallander said, "but I need your help."

Wallander moved several bundles of paper from the visitor's chair to the floor and sat down. Then he summarised briefly the circumstances of Göran Alexandersson's death.

"It sounds very strange," said Åkeson when Wallander had finished.

"Strange things do happen now and then," Wallander said. "You know that as well as I do."

"I don't think you've come here at seven in the morning just to tell me this. I hope you're not going to suggest we should arrest that doctor?"

"I need your help with his wife," Wallander said. "Kajsa Stenholm. A former colleague of yours. She worked in Nynäshamn for many years. But she had several temporary assignments too. Seven years ago she was filling in for somebody in Stockholm. It happened to be at the same time as Alexandersson's son's murder. I need your help to find out if there is a connection between those two events."

Wallander leafed through his papers before continuing.

"The son was called Bengt," he said eventually. "Bengt Alexandersson. He was eighteen when he was killed."

Åkeson leaned his chair back and looked at Wallander with a furrowed brow.

"What do you think might have happened?" he asked.

"I don't know," said Wallander, "but I want to find out if there could be some sort of link. If Kajsa Stenholm was somehow involved in the investigation into the death of Bengt Alexandersson."

"I take it you want to know as soon as possible?"

Wallander nodded.

"You should know by now that my patience is more or less non-existent," he said, rising to his feet.

"I'll see what I can do," said Åkeson. "But don't expect heaven and earth to be moved."

When Wallander passed through reception on his way back to his office, he asked Ebba to send Rydberg and Hansson in to see him as soon as they came in.

"How are you nowadays?" Ebba asked. "Are you getting a good night's sleep?"

"I sometimes feel I'm sleeping too much," said Wallander evasively. Ebba was reception's stalwart and kept a maternal watch on everybody's state of health. Wallander sometimes had to fend off her concern in as friendly a way as possible.

Hansson came to Wallander's office at about a quarter past eight, and Rydberg followed soon afterwards. Wallander summarised briefly what he had found in what were already being called "Hansson's papers".

"We'll have to wait and see what Åkeson comes up with," said Wallander. "Maybe it's just a meaningless guess on my part. But on the other hand, if it does turn out that Kajsa Stenholm was assigned to Stockholm when Bengt Alexandersson was murdered and that she was involved in the investigation, we've found the link we've been looking for."

"Didn't you say she was on her deathbed?" wondered Rydberg.

"That's what her husband claimed," Wallander said. "I haven't actually met her."

"With all due respect for your ability to find your way through complicated criminal investigations, this seems pretty vague to me," said Hansson. "Let's suppose that you're right. That Kajsa Stenholm was in fact involved in the investigation into the killing of young Alexandersson. So what? Are you suggesting that a woman dying of cancer murdered a man who showed up out of her past?"

"It *is* very vague," Wallander admitted. "Let's wait and see what Åkeson comes up with."

When Wallander was alone in his office again, he sat around for some time in a state of indecision. He wondered what Mona and Linda were doing at the moment. And what they were talking about. At about nine-thirty he went to get a cup of coffee, and another one an hour or so later. He had just returned to his office when the telephone rang. It was Åkeson.

"It went quicker than I'd expected," he said. "Do you have a pen handy?"

"I'm all set," Wallander said.

"Between 10 March and 9 October 1980, Kajsa Stenholm was working as a prosecutor in the city of Stockholm," Åkeson said. "With some help from an efficient registry clerk at the county court, I found the answer to your second question, about whether Kajsa Stenholm was involved in the Bengt Alexandersson case."

He fell silent. Wallander could feel the tension rising.

"It seems you were right," said Åkeson. "She was in charge of the preliminary investigation, and she was also the one who eventually put it aside. When the killer wasn't found."

"Thank you for your help," said Wallander. "I'll look into this. I'll be in touch in due course."

He hung up and walked over to the window. The glass was misted over. It was raining more heavily now. There's only one thing to do, he thought. I must get inside the house and find out what actually happened. He decided to take only Rydberg with him. He called him and Hansson on the intercom, and when they were in his office he told them what Åkeson had found out.

"Well, I'll be damned!" said Hansson.

"I thought you and I should take a drive out there," Wallander said to Rydberg. "Three would be one too many."

Hansson nodded; he understood.

They drove to Svarte in Wallander's car. Neither spoke. Wallander parked about a hundred metres short of Stenholm's property.

"What do you want me to do?" asked Rydberg as they walked through the rain.

"Be there," Wallander said. "That's all."

It suddenly struck Wallander that this was the first time Rydberg had ever assisted him, rather than the other way round. Rydberg had never formally lorded it over his colleague; it didn't suit his temperament to be a boss, and they had always worked in tandem. But during the years Wallander had been in Ystad, it was Rydberg who had been his teacher. Everything he knew today about the work of a police officer was mainly due to Rydberg.

They went through the gate and up to the front door. Wallander rang the bell. As if they had been expected, the door was opened almost immediately by the elderly doctor. Wallander thought in passing that it was odd the Labrador hadn't appeared.

"I hope we're not disturbing you," Wallander said, "but we have a few more questions that can't wait, unfortunately."

"What about?"

Wallander noticed that all the friendliness the man had shown before was gone. He seemed scared and irritated.

"About that man on the beach," Wallander said.

225

"I've already told you I've never seen him."

"We'd also like to talk to your wife."

"I've told you she's fatally ill. What could she have seen? She's in bed. I don't understand why you can't leave us in peace!"

"Then we won't disturb you any more," said Wallander. "Not just now, at least. But I have no doubt we'll be back. And then you'll have to let us in."

He took Rydberg's arm and steered him towards the gate. The door closed behind them.

"Why did you give in so easily?" Rydberg asked.

"Something you taught me," Wallander said. "That it does no harm to let people stew for a while. Besides, I need a warrant from Åkeson to search the house."

"Is he really the one who killed Alexandersson?" asked Rydberg.

"Yes," said Wallander. "I'm certain of it. He's the one. But I still don't understand how it all fits together."

That afternoon Wallander received the authorisation he needed. He decided to wait until the next morning. But just in case, he persuaded Björk to have a guard placed on the house until then.

When Wallander woke up as dawn was breaking the next morning, 7 May, and opened the curtains, Ystad was covered in fog. Before taking a shower he did something he had forgotten to do the previous night: he looked up Stenholm in the telephone directory. There was no mention of a Martin or Kajsa Stenholm. He phoned directory assistance and ascertained that the number was unlisted. He nodded to himself, as if that was exactly what he had expected.

As he drank his morning cup of coffee, he asked himself if he should take Rydberg with him or drive out to Svarte on his own. It wasn't until he was behind the wheel that he decided to go himself. The fog was thick along the coast road.

Wallander drove very slowly. It was nearly eight when he pulled up outside the Stenholm house. He walked through the gate and rang the doorbell. It wasn't until the third ring that the door opened. When Stenholm saw that it was Wallander, he tried to slam it shut again, but Wallander managed to put his foot in the way.

"What right do you have to break in here?" the old man shouted in a shrill voice.

"I'm not breaking in," Wallander said. "I have a search warrant. You might as well accept that. Can we sit down somewhere?"

Stenholm suddenly seemed resigned. Wallander followed him into a room full of books. Wallander sat down in a leather armchair, and Stenholm sat opposite him.

"Do you really have nothing to say to me?" Wallander asked.

"I haven't seen anybody wandering up and down the beach. Nor has my wife, who's seriously ill. She's in bed upstairs."

Wallander decided to come right to the point. There was no reason to beat around the bush any longer.

"Your wife was a public prosecutor," he said. "For most of 1980 she was assigned to Stockholm. Among a lot of other things, she was in charge of a preliminary investigation into the circumstances surrounding the death of an eighteen-year-old named Bengt Alexandersson. She was also responsible for putting the case aside some months later. Do you recall those events?"

"Of course not," said Stenholm. "It has always been our habit not to talk shop at home. She said nothing about the people she was prosecuting, I said nothing about my patients."

"The man who was walking on the beach here was the father of Bengt Alexandersson," said Wallander. "He was poisoned and died in the back seat of a taxi. Does that seem like a mere coincidence?"

Stenholm made no reply. And then the penny suddenly dropped for Wallander.

"When you retired you moved down from Nynäshamn to Skåne," he said slowly. "To a place in the middle of nowhere like Svarte. You're not even in the telephone book because your number's unlisted. Needless to say, that could be because you want to be left in peace and quiet, to live out your old age in anonymity. But there could be another explanation. You might have moved out here as discreetly as possible in order to escape from something or somebody. Perhaps to get away from a man who can't understand why a prosecutor didn't put more effort into solving the pointless murder of his only child. You moved, but he tracked you down. I don't suppose we'll ever know how he managed that. But one day, there he is on the beach. You meet him while you're out walking your dog. Naturally, it's a big shock. He repeats his accusations,

228

maybe he even makes threats. Your wife is seriously ill upstairs. I have no doubt that's the case. The man on the beach keeps on coming back, day after day. He won't let you shake him off. You see no way of getting rid of him. No way out at all. Then you invite him into your house. Presumably you promise him that he can talk to your wife. You give him some poison, possibly in a cup of coffee. Then you suddenly change your mind and tell him to come back the next day. Your wife is in great pain, or perhaps she's asleep. But you know he'll never come back. The problem is solved. Göran Alexandersson will die of something that looks like a heart attack. Nobody has ever seen you together, nobody knows about the link between you. Is that what happened?"

Stenholm sat motionless in his chair.

Wallander waited. He could see through the window that the fog was still very thick. Then the man raised his head.

"My wife never did anything wrong," he said. "But times changed, crimes multiplied and became more serious. Overworked police officers and courts couldn't cope with it. You should know that, you're a policeman yourself. That's why it was so unjust for Alexandersson to blame my wife when the murder of his son was never solved. He persecuted us and threatened us and terrorised us for seven years. And he did it in such a way that we could never actually pin anything on him."

Stenholm fell silent. Then he stood up.

"Let's go up to my wife. She can tell you about it herself."

"That's not necessary any more," Wallander said.

"For me it's necessary," said Stenholm.

They went upstairs. Kajsa Stenholm was lying in a sickbed in a large, bright, airy room. The Labrador was lying on the floor beside the bed.

"She's not asleep," said Stenholm. "Go up to her and ask her whatever you want."

Wallander approached the bed. Her face was so thin, her skin was stretched tight over her cranium. Wallander realised she was dead. He turned round quickly. The old man was standing in the doorway. He was holding a pistol, aimed at Wallander.

"I knew you'd come back," he said. "That's why it's just as well she died."

"Put the gun down," Wallander said.

Stenholm shook his head. Wallander could feel himself stiffening with fear.

Then everything happened very fast. Suddenly Stenholm pointed the gun at his own head and pulled the trigger. The shot echoed through the room. The man was thrown halfway through the door. Blood had spurted all over the walls. Wallander felt as if he were about to faint. Then he staggered out of the door and down the stairs. He called the police station. Ebba answered.

"Hansson or Rydberg," he said. "As fast as possible."

It was Rydberg who came to the phone.

"It's all over," said Wallander. "I want an emergency team sent to the house in Svarte. I've got two dead bodies here."

"Did you kill them? What's happened?" Rydberg asked. "Are you hurt? Why the hell did you go there on your own?"

"I don't know," Wallander said. "Get a move on. I'm not hurt."

Wallander went outside to wait. The beach was covered in fog. He thought about what the old doctor had said. About crimes becoming more frequent and more serious. Wallander had often thought that as well. He sometimes thought he was a police officer from another age. Even though he was only forty. Maybe a new kind of police officer was needed nowadays.

He waited in the fog for them to arrive from Ystad. He was deeply upset. Yet again, against his will, he had found himself involved in a tragedy. He wondered how long he would be able to keep going.

When the emergency services arrived and Rydberg got out of his car, it seemed to him that Wallander was a black shadow in the white fog.

"What happened?" Rydberg asked.

"We've solved the case of the man who died in the back seat of Stenberg's taxi," Wallander said.

He could see that Rydberg was waiting for something more, but there would be nothing more.

"That's all," he said. "That's all we've done, in fact."

Then Wallander turned on his heel and walked down to the beach. Soon he had disappeared into the fog.

THE DEATH OF THE PHOTOGRAPHER

Every year, in early spring, he had a recurring dream. That he could fly. The dream always unfolded in the same way. He was walking up a dimly lit staircase. Suddenly the ceiling opened and he discovered that the stairs led him to a treetop. The landscape spread out under his feet. He lifted up his arms and let himself fall. He ruled the world.

At that moment he always woke up. The dream always left him right there. Although he had had the same dream for many years, he had not yet experienced actually floating away from the top of the tree.

The dream kept coming back. And it always cheated him.

He was thinking of this as he walked through central Ystad. The dream had come to him one night a week ago. And as always, it left him right as he was going to fly away. Now it would probably not return for a long time.

It was an evening in the middle of April, 1988. The warmth of spring had not yet manifested itself with any seriousness. As he walked through the town he regretted not having put on a warmer sweater. He also still had a lingering cold. It was shortly after eight o'clock. The streets were empty of people. Somewhere in the distance he heard a car drive off with a screech. Then the engine noise died away. He always followed the same route. From Lavendelvägen, where he lived, he followed Tennisgatan. At Margareta Park he turned left and then followed Skottegatan down to the centre. Then he took another left, crossed Kristianstad Road, and soon arrived at St Gertrude's Square, where he had his photography studio. If he had been a young photographer who was just in the process of establishing himself in Ystad, it would not have been the optimal location. But he had run his studio for more than twenty-five years. He had a stable list of clients. They knew where to find him. They came to him to be photographed for their weddings. Then they liked to return with the first child. Or for different occasions that they knew they would want to remember. The first time he had taken the wedding pictures for a client's child, he realised he was getting old. He had not thought so much about it before but suddenly he had turned fifty. And that was now six years ago.

He stopped at a shop window and studied his face in the reflection. Life was what it was. He couldn't really complain. If he were allowed his health for ten or fifteen years more, then . . .

He abandoned his thoughts about the passage of time and walked on. There was a gusty wind and he pulled his coat more tightly around him. He was walking neither quickly nor slowly. There was no urgency. Two evenings a week he went down to his studio after dinner. These were the holy moments of his life. Two evenings when he could be completely alone with his own pictures in the room at the back of the studio.

He reached his destination. Before unlocking the door to the shop he studied the display window with a mixture of disapproval and irritation. He should have changed the display a long time ago. Even if he didn't attract new clients, he should be able to follow the rule he made more than twenty years ago. Once a month he changed the photographs on display. Now almost two months had gone by. When he had employed an assistant, he had had more time to devote to the shop window. But he had let the last one go almost four years ago. It had become too expensive. And it wasn't more work than he could manage on his own.

He unlocked the door and walked in. The shop lay in darkness. He had a cleaning woman who came in three days a week. She had her own key and usually came in at around five in the morning. Since it had rained earlier that morning, the floor was dirty. He didn't like dirt. Therefore he did not turn on the light and instead walked straight through his studio and into the innermost room, where he developed his pictures. He closed the door and turned on the light. Hung up his coat. Turned on the radio that he kept on a little shelf. He always kept it tuned to a station he could expect to play classical music. Then he filled the coffee-maker and washed out a cup. A feeling of well-being started to spread through his body. The innermost room behind his studio was his cathedral. His holy room. He didn't let anyone other than his cleaning woman in here. Here he found himself in the centre of the world. Here he was alone. An absolute ruler.

While he waited for the coffee to brew, he thought about what awaited him. He always decided in advance what work he would do on a given evening. He was a methodical man who never left anything to chance.

This evening, it was the Swedish prime minister's turn. Actually it had surprised him that he had not spent an evening on him yet. But at least he had been able to prepare. For more than a week he had scoured the daily papers for the picture he was going to use. He had found it in one of the evening papers and known at once that it was the right one. It filled all of his requirements. He had photographed a copy of it a few days ago. Now it was locked in one of his desk drawers. He poured out the coffee and hummed along with the music. A piano sonata by Beethoven was playing. He preferred Bach to Beethoven. And Mozart best of all. But the piano sonata was beautiful. He could not deny it.

He sat down at the desk, adjusted the lamp and unlocked the drawers on the left. The photograph of the prime minister was inside. He had enlarged the image, as he usually did, to a size somewhat larger than a standard sheet of paper. He laid it out on the table, sipped his coffee and studied the face. Where should he start, where should he begin the distortion? The man in the picture was smiling and looking to the left. There was a touch of anxiety or uncertainty in his gaze. He decided to begin with the eyes. They could be made to look cross-eyed. And smaller. If he angled the enlarger, the face would also become thinner. He could try to place the paper in an arc in the enlarger and see what effect that had. Then he could cut and paste and excise the mouth. Or perhaps sew it up. Politicians talked too much.

He finished his coffee. The clock on the wall showed a quarter to nine. Some noisy teenagers walked by on the street outside and disturbed the music for a moment.

He put the coffee cup away. Then he started the painstaking but enjoyable work of retouching. He could slowly see the face changing.

It took him more than two hours. You could still see that it was the prime minister's face. But what had happened to it? He got up out of his chair and hung the picture on the wall. Directed the light on it. The music on the radio was different now. Stravinsky's *Rite of Spring*. The dramatic music was fitting as he regarded his work. The face was no longer the same.

Now the most important part remained. The most enjoyable. Now he would reduce the picture. Make it small and insignificant. He put it on the glass plate and focused the light. Made it smaller and smaller. The details pulled together. But remained sharp. Only when the face started to blur did he stop.

He was done.

It was almost half past eleven when he had the finished product in front of him on the desk. The prime minister's distorted face was no bigger than a passport picture. Once again he had shrunk a power-hungry individual down to more suitable proportions. Of large men he made small men. In his world there was no one who was bigger than himself. He remade their faces, made them smaller, more ridiculous, into small and unimportant insects.

He took out the album he kept in his desk and flipped through it until he got to the first empty page. There he pasted in the picture he had just manipulated. He wrote in the day's date with a fountain pen.

He leaned back in his chair. Yet another picture had been produced. It had been a successful evening. The result had been good. And nothing had disturbed him. No restless thoughts had flown around in his head. It had been an evening in the cathedral when everything breathed peace and quiet.

He put the album back and locked the cabinet. Stravinsky's *Rite of Spring* had been followed by Handel. Sometimes he was irritated by the programme director's inability to make softer transitions.

At that moment he had the feeling that something wasn't right. He stood still and listened. Everything was quiet. He thought that he had imagined it. He turned off the coffee-maker and started turning off the lights. Then he stopped again. Something wasn't right. He heard a sound from the studio. Suddenly he was afraid. Had someone broken into the store? He walked carefully over to the door and listened. Everything was quiet. I'm imagining things, he thought with irritation. Who would break into a photographer's studio where there are not even any cameras for sale? At least cameras can be stolen.

240

He listened again. Nothing. He took his coat from the peg and put it on. The clock on the wall said nineteen minutes before midnight. Everything was normal. Now he was ready to lock up his cathedral and go home.

He looked around one more time before he turned off the last light. Then he opened the door. The studio lay in darkness. He turned on the light. It was as he had thought. There was no one there. He turned the light off again and walked out towards the shop.

Then everything happened very quickly.

Suddenly someone came at him from the shadows. Someone who had been hiding behind one of the backdrops he used for his studio portraits. He could not see who it was. Since the shadow was blocking the exit there was only one thing left for him to do. Flee into the back room and lock the door. He also had a phone in there. He could call for help.

He turned round. But he never made it to the door. The shadow was quicker. Something struck him in the back of the head, something that made the world explode in a white light, then become total darkness.

He was dead before he hit the ground.

The time was seventeen minutes to midnight.

The cleaning woman's name was Hilda Waldén. She arrived at Simon Lamberg's studio shortly after five o'clock, when she began her morning round. She leaned her bike next to the entrance and locked it carefully with a chain. It was drizzling and had grown colder, and she shivered as she searched for the right key. Spring was taking its time. She opened the door and stepped inside. The floor was dirty after the latest rain shower. She put her handbag on the counter next to the cash register and put her coat on the chair next to the little newspaper table.

There was a cupboard in the studio where she kept her cleaning coat as well as her equipment. Lamberg would have to buy her a new vacuum cleaner soon. This one was getting too weak.

She saw him as soon as she walked into the studio. She immediately understood that he was dead. The blood had run out around his body.

Then she ran out onto the street. A retired bank director who had been ordered to take regular walks by his doctor anxiously asked her what had happened, after he managed to calm her down somewhat.

She was shaking all over, and he ran to a telephone booth on the nearest street corner and dialled emergency.

It was twenty minutes past five.

A drizzling rain, with a gusty wind from the south-west.

It was Martinsson who called and woke up Wallander. It was three minutes past six. Wallander knew from long experience that when the phone rang this early something serious must have happened. Normally he was awake before six. But this morning he was sleeping and he woke up with a start when the telephone rang. The main reason he wasn't already awake was that he had bitten off part of his tooth the night before and had been in pain during the night. He had only fallen asleep around four after having been up several times to take pills for the pain. Before he picked up the receiver he noted that the pain was still there.

"Did I wake you?" Martinsson asked.

"Yes," Wallander said and was surprised that he answered truthfully for once. "You did, actually. What's happened?"

"The night shift called me at home. Sometime around half past five they received an unclear emergency call about a supposed murder by St Gertrude's Square. A patrol unit was dispatched."

"And?"

"And it turned out to be correct, unfortunately."

Wallander sat up in bed. The call must have come in half an hour ago.

"Have you been down there?"

"How would I have had time to do that? I was getting dressed when the phone rang. I thought it was best to call you myself immediately."

Wallander nodded mutely on the other end.

"Do we know who it is?" he then asked.

"It seems to be the photographer whose studio is at the square. But right now I've forgotten the name."

"Lamberg?" Wallander said, furrowing his brow.

"Yes, that was his name. Simon Lamberg. If I've understood correctly, it was the cleaning lady who discovered him."

"Where?"

"What do you mean?"

"Was he found dead inside the shop or outside?"

"Inside."

Wallander thought about this while he looked at his alarm clock next to the bed. Seven minutes past six.

"Should we say we'll meet in a quarter of an hour?" he then said.

"Yes," Martinsson replied. "The patrol unit down there said it was very unpleasant."

"Murder scenes tend to be," Wallander said. "I think I have never in my life been at a crime scene that you would have been able to describe as pleasant."

They ended the conversation.

Wallander remained sitting up in the bed. The news Martinsson had given him had disturbed him. If he was right, Wallander knew very well who had been murdered. Simon Lamberg had photographed Wallander on several occasions. Memories of various times he had visited the photo studio went through his head. When he and Mona had married at the end of May in 1970, it was Lamberg who had photographed them. That had not taken place in his studio, however, but down by the beach right next to the Saltsjöbadens Hotel. It was Mona who had insisted on this. Wallander remembered how he felt it was an unnecessary amount of trouble. That their wedding had even taken place in Ystad was due to the fact that Mona's old confirmation minister was now posted there. Wallander had thought they should get married in Malmö, in a civil service. But Mona had not agreed. That they should have to stand on a cold and blustery beach on top of all this trouble and let themselves be photographed had not amused him. For Wallander it was a wasted effort for a romantic product that was not particularly successful. Lamberg had also taken their daughter Linda's picture on more than one occasion.

Wallander got up out of bed, decided he would have to skip the shower and put on his clothes. Then he walked into the bathroom and opened his mouth wide. How many times he had done this during the night he couldn't say. Each time he opened his mouth he hoped the tooth would have become whole again.

The tooth he had bitten in half was on the left side of his lower jaw. When he pulled on the corner of his mouth with his finger he could clearly see that half of the tooth was gone. He gently brushed his teeth. When he reached the damaged tooth it hurt a great deal.

He left the bathroom and walked into the kitchen. Dishes were piled up. He glanced out through the kitchen window. The wind was blowing hard and it was drizzling outside. The street light was swaying in the wind. The thermometer showed four degrees above zero. He made an irritated face. Spring was delayed. Just as he was about to leave the apartment he changed his mind and walked back into the living room. Their wedding picture was in the bookcase.

Lamberg took no picture when we separated, Wallander thought. Nothing of that has been preserved, thankfully. In his thoughts he went back over what had happened. Suddenly one day about a month ago Mona had said she wanted them to separate for a while. She needed time to think about how she wanted things to be. Wallander had been caught off guard, even though deep down he had not been surprised. They had grown apart, had less and less to talk about, and less and less pleasure in their sex life, and in the end Linda had been the only unifying link.

Wallander had fought it. He had pleaded and threatened but Mona had been firm. She was going to move back to Malmö. Linda wanted to move with her. The bigger city lured her. And that was what had happened. Wallander still hoped they would one day be able to start over again together. But he did not know if this hope would be worth anything.

He shook off these thoughts, put the photograph back on the shelf, left the apartment and wondered what had happened. What kind of man was Lamberg? Even though he had been photographed by him four or five times, he had no real memory of him as a person. Right now this surprised him. Lamberg was essentially anonymous. Wallander even had trouble conjuring up his face.

It took him only a few minutes to drive to St Gertrude's Square. Two patrol cars were parked outside the studio. A group of onlookers had gathered outside. Several police officers were in the process of cordoning off the area around the entrance. Martinsson arrived at the same time. Wallander observed that he was unshaven for once.

They walked up to the restricted area. Nodded to the police officer from the night shift.

"It's not a pleasant sight," he said. "The body is sprawled out on the floor. There's a lot of blood."

Wallander cut him short with a nod of his head.

"And is it certain that this is the photographer, Lamberg?"

"The cleaning lady was sure."

"She's probably not doing so well right now," Wallander said. "Drive her up to the station. Give her some coffee. We'll be there as soon as we can."

They walked up to the door, which was open.

"I called Nyberg," Martinsson said. "The technicians are on their way."

They stepped into the shop and removed their shoes. Everything was very quiet. Wallander went in first, Martinsson right behind him. They walked past the counter and into the studio. Things looked terrible in there. The man lay face down on a large sheet of paper, the kind that photographers used as backdrops for taking their pictures. The paper was white. The blood formed a sharp contour around the dead man's head.

Wallander approached him with care. Then he bent down.

The cleaning lady had been right. It was indeed Simon Lamberg. Wallander recognised him. The face was twisted so that half was visible. The eyes were open.

Wallander tried to interpret the facial expression. Was there something more than pain and surprise? He did not discover anything else that he could determine with any certainty.

"There can hardly be any doubt about the cause of death," he said and pointed.

There was blunt trauma to the back of the head. Martinsson crouched down next to the body.

"The whole back of the head has been crushed," he said with evident discomfort.

Wallander glanced at him. On some other occasions when they had inspected a crime scene, Martinsson had become violently ill, but right now he appeared to have any nausea under control.

They stood up. Wallander looked around. He could not discover any disarray. No signs that the murder had been preceded by a struggle. He did not see anything that could be the murder weapon. He walked past the dead man and opened a door at the far end of the room. Turned on a light. Lamberg must have had his office in here and it was also here that he apparently developed his negatives. Nothing had been touched in this room either, it seemed. The drawers of the desk were closed, the cabinet locked.

"It doesn't look like burglary," Martinsson said.

"We don't know that yet," Wallander said. "Was Lamberg married?"

"The cleaning lady appeared to think so. Said they lived on Lavendelvägen."

Wallander knew where that was.

"Has the wife been informed?"

"I doubt it."

"Then we'll have to start with that. Svedberg can do it."

Martinsson looked at Wallander in amazement.

"Shouldn't you do it?"

"Svedberg will do as good a job as me. Call him. Tell him not to forget to take a minister."

248

It was a quarter to seven. Martinsson walked out into the shop area and called. Wallander stayed in the studio and looked around. He tried to imagine what had happened. This was made more difficult by not having a time frame. He thought that he must first speak to the cleaning lady. Before then he would not be able to draw any conclusions whatsoever.

Martinsson came back into the room.

"Svedberg is on his way to the station," he said.

"So are we," Wallander said. "I want to talk to the cleaning lady. Is there no time frame?"

"It's been difficult to talk to her. She's only now beginning to get herself under control."

Nyberg appeared behind Martinsson's back. They nodded to each other. Nyberg was an experienced and skilled, if bad-tempered, forensic technician. On many occasions Wallander had had only him to thank for being able to solve a complicated crime.

Nyberg made a face when he spotted the body.

"The photographer himself," he said.

"Simon Lamberg," Wallander said.

"I had some passport pictures taken here a few years ago," Nyberg said. "I certainly didn't imagine that anyone would end up bashing the guy's head in."

"He ran this place for many years," Wallander said. "He's not someone who has always been here, but it's something close to that."

Nyberg had taken off his coat.

"What do we know?" he asked.

"His cleaning lady discovered the body sometime after five. That is actually all we know."

"So we know nothing," Nyberg said.

Martinsson and Wallander left the studio. Nyberg should be able to work in peace with his colleagues. Wallander knew the work would be done thoroughly.

They went up to the station. Wallander paused in reception and asked Ebba, who had just arrived, to call and make an appointment for him at the dentist's. He gave her the name.

"Are you in pain?" she asked.

"Yes," Wallander said. "I'm going to talk to the cleaning lady who discovered the photographer Lamberg's body. That may take an hour. After that I would like to get to the dentist as quickly as possible."

"Lamberg?" Ebba repeated in shock. "What happened?"

"He's been murdered."

Ebba sank down her chair.

"I've been to him many times," she said sadly. "He's taken pictures of all my grandchildren. One after the other."

Wallander nodded but did not say anything.

Then he walked along the corridor to his office.

Everyone seems to have been to Lamberg, he thought. All of us have stood in front of his camera. I wonder if everyone's impression of him is as vague as mine.

It was now five minutes past seven.

A few minutes later Hilda Waldén was shown in. She had very little to say. Wallander realised at once that it was not simply because she was distraught. The reason was that she did not know Lamberg at all, even though she had been cleaning his studio for more than ten years.

When she walked into Wallander's office, followed by Hansson, he had shaken her hand and kindly asked her to sit down. She was in her sixties and had a thin face. Wallander had the impression that she had worked hard all her life. Hansson left the room and Wallander pulled out a pad of paper from the stacks in his drawers. He started by expressing his condolences over what had happened. He could understand her being upset. But his questions could not wait. A terrible crime had been committed. Now they had to identify the perpetrator and the motive as quickly as possible.

"Let's take this from the beginning," he said. "You cleaned Simon Lamberg's studio?"

She answered in a very low voice. Wallander had to lean over the table to hear her reply.

"I have been cleaning there for twelve years and seven months. Three mornings a week. Monday, Wednesday and Friday."

"When did you get to the shop this morning?"

"At my usual time. A little after five. I clean four shops in the mornings. I usually take Lamberg's first."

"I assume you have your own key?"

She looked surprised at him.

"How else would I be able to get in? Lamberg did not open until ten."

Wallander nodded and continued.

"Did you walk in from the street?"

"There is no other entrance."

Wallander made a note.

"And the door was locked?"

"Yes."

"The lock had not been tampered with in any way?"

"Not that I noticed."

"What happened after that?"

"I went in. Put down my handbag and took off my coat."

"Did you notice anything that was not as it should be?"

He saw that she was really trying to think and remember.

"Everything was normal. It rained yesterday morning. The floor was unusually muddy. I went to get my buckets and rags."

She stopped abruptly.

"Was that when you saw him?"

She nodded mutely. For a second Wallander was afraid she was going to cry. But she drew a deep breath and collected herself.

"What time was it when you discovered him?"

"Nine minutes past five."

He looked surprised at her.

"How can you know that so precisely?"

"There was a wall clock in the studio. I looked at it immediately. Perhaps in order not to have to look at him lying there dead. Perhaps in order to fix the exact time of the worst moment in my entire life."

Wallander nodded. He thought he understood.

"What did you do next?"

"I ran out into the street. I may have screamed, I don't know. But there was a man. He called the police from a telephone booth nearby."

Wallander put down his pen for a moment. Now he had a list of Hilda Waldén's actions and times. He had no doubt about its veracity.

"Can you tell me why Lamberg was in the shop so early in the morning?"

Her answer came quickly and firmly. Wallander realised she must have been thinking about it before he asked.

"Sometimes he went down to the studio at night. He stayed until midnight. It must have happened before then."

"How do you know he went down there at night? If you clean in the morning?"

"A few years ago I left my purse in the pocket of the cleaning coat. I went down there at night to get it. He was there then. He told me he usually came in two evenings a week."

"To work?"

"I think he mostly sat in that back office and shuffled papers. The radio was on."

Wallander nodded thoughtfully. She was probably right. The murder had not happened that morning but the evening before.

He looked at her.

"Do you have any idea who could have done this?"

"No."

"Did he have any enemies?"

"I didn't know him. I don't know if he had any friends or enemies. I just cleaned there."

Wallander held onto the thread.

"But you worked there for more than ten years. You must have learned about him? His habits. Or weaknesses."

Her answer came just as firmly.

"I did not know him at all. He was extremely reserved."

"You must be able to describe him in some way."

His answer was unexpected.

"Can you describe a person who is so anonymous he blends into the wall?"

"No indeed," Wallander said. "I see your point."

He pushed the notepad aside.

"Did you notice anything unusual recently?"

"I only met him once a month. When I picked up my pay cheque. But there was nothing unusual then."

"When did you see him last?"

"Two weeks ago."

"And he seemed the same as always?"

"Yes."

"He wasn't anxious? Nervous?"

"No."

"You didn't notice anything in the shop either? Something that had changed?"

"Nothing."

She is an excellent witness, Wallander thought. Her answers are firm. She has good powers of observation. I have no need to doubt her memory.

He had nothing more to ask her. The conversation had taken less than twenty minutes. He called Hansson, who promised to make sure that Hilda Waldén was taken home.

When he was alone again he walked over to the window and stared out into the rain. He wondered absently when spring was going to come. And how it would feel to experience it without Mona. Then he noticed that his tooth had started to ache again. He checked the time. It was still too early. He did not think his dentist would be in his office yet. At the same time he wondered how things had gone for Svedberg. To convey the news of a death in the family was one of the most feared tasks. Especially when you had to report an unexpected and brutal killing. But he was sure Svedberg could manage it. He was a good officer. Perhaps without exceptional talent, but diligent and with a fastidiously organised desk. In some ways he was among the best officers Wallander had ever worked with. And Svedberg had always been extremely loyal to Wallander.

He left the window, went out to the break room, and got a cup of coffee. While he walked back down the corridor he tried to understand what could have happened.

Simon Lamberg was a photographer, approaching sixty. A man with regular habits whose way of conducting his business was beyond reproach, photographing confirmations, weddings and children of various ages. According to his cleaning lady he came into the studio two evenings a week. At these times he sat in his inner office and shuffled papers around, listened to music. If the cleaning lady's information was correct he usually left around midnight.

Wallander came back to his office. He took up his former position at the window with the cup of coffee in his hand and stared out into the rain.

Why did Lamberg spend those evenings sitting in the studio? Something about the situation stirred Wallander's curiosity.

He checked his watch. At that moment Ebba called. She had reached his dentist. Wallander could be seen at once.

He decided not to wait. If he was going to lead a murder investigation he couldn't walk around with a toothache. He went over to Martinsson's office.

"I broke a tooth yesterday," he said. "I'm going to the dentist. But I'm assuming I'll be back within the hour. Let's have a meeting then. Has Svedberg come back?"

"Not that I know."

"Try Nyberg and see if he can make it in an hour or so. Then we'll be able to get his initial impression."

Martinsson yawned and stretched.

"Who can possibly have had anything to gain by killing an old photographer?" he said. "There doesn't appear to have been any burglary."

"Old?" Wallander objected. "He was fifty-six. But other than that I agree with you."

"He was attacked inside the shop. How did the perpetrator enter?"

"Either with a key or else Lamberg let him in."

256

"Lamberg was struck from behind."

"Which can have many different explanations. And we have none of them."

Wallander left the station and walked down to the dentist, who had his practice by the Main Square, right next to the electronics shop. As a child, Wallander had always been afraid of the dentist visits he had been dragged to. As an adult the fear had suddenly left him. Now he simply wanted to be free from the pain as quickly as possible. But he realised the broken tooth was a sign of ageing. He was only forty years old. But the deterioration had already started to set in.

Wallander was shown in at once and took his place in the dentist's chair. The dentist was young and worked quickly, with ease. He was done in about half an hour. The pain changed into a dull throbbing.

"It will soon be gone," the dentist said. "But you should come back here so that we can remove that tartar. I don't think you brush as well as you should."

"Probably not," Wallander said.

He made an appointment to come back in two weeks and returned to the station. At ten o'clock he gathered his colleagues in the conference room. Svedberg had returned, and Nyberg was also present. Wallander sat at his usual place at the head of the table. Then he looked around. He wondered briefly how many times he had sat here, gathering himself to launch into yet another criminal investigation. He had noticed that it took more effort over the years. But he also knew that there was nothing else to do but throw oneself into it. They had a brutal murder to solve. It could not wait.

"Does anyone know where Rydberg is?" he asked.

"Backache," Martinsson replied.

"Too bad," Wallander said. "We could have used him here now."

He turned to Nyberg, and nodded at him to start.

"It is of course too early to say," Nyberg said, "but there are no indications of burglary. No marks on any doors, nothing that appears to have been stolen, at least not at first glance. The whole thing is very strange."

Wallander had not expected Nyberg to have made any decisive observations at this stage. But he had still wanted him to be present.

He turned to Svedberg.

"As expected, Elisabeth Lamberg got a terrible shock. Apparently they have separate bedrooms. She doesn't normally notice when he comes home if he's out at night. They had dinner at about half past six that night. Shortly before eight he left for the studio. She went to bed a little after eleven and fell asleep at once. She doesn't understand who could have murdered him. She dismissed the idea that he had any enemies."

Wallander nodded.

"Then this is what we know," he said. "We have a dead photographer. But that is also all that we know."

Everyone knew what this meant. Now the laborious investigations would proceed.

Where this would lead them they had no idea.

The case review that morning, the first in the hunt for the single or multiple perpetrators who for unknown reasons were responsible for the murder of the photographer Simon Lamberg, was of short duration. There were countless routine methods for proceeding that they always followed. They had to wait for the report from the medical examiner's office in Lund, as well as the results of the forensic investigation of the crime scene that Nyberg and his men were conducting. They would now make a study of Simon Lamberg and chart out the life that he had lived. They would also question neighbours and look for others who might have witnessed something. There was naturally also hope that even in these early stages information would come in that would make it possible to clear up the murder in the course of a few days. But Wallander already had an instinctive feeling that they stood on the brink of a complicated case. They had very little — or rather, nothing — to go on.

He noticed as he sat in the conference room that he was anxious. The ache in his tooth was now gone. But instead he had this new worry in his stomach.

Björk came into the room and sat down to listen to Wallander's attempt to make a preliminary review of the events and timeline. No one had any questions when it was over. They assigned the most important tasks and then broke up the meeting. Wallander would speak with Lamberg's widow later in the day. First he wanted to do a more thorough inspection of the crime scene. Nyberg said he could let Wallander into the studio and the inner room in a couple of hours.

Björk and Wallander lingered in the conference room after the others had filed out.

"You don't believe this was a burglar who was caught red-handed and got out of control?" Björk asked.

"No," Wallander answered. "But I could very well be wrong. We cannot rule out any possibilities. But I wonder what a burglar thought he would be able to get in Lamberg's studio."

"Cameras?"

"He didn't sell any photographic equipment. He only took pictures. The only items he had for sale were frames and albums. I think a burglar hardly makes an effort for that."

"What does that leave? A private motive?"

"I don't know. But according to Svedberg, the widow, Elisabeth Lamberg, was apparently adamant that he had no enemies."

"But there is also no indication that it was a crazed madman?"

Wallander shook his head.

"There are no indications of anything," he said, "but we can make three reflections even at this stage. How did the perpetrator enter the studio? There are no marks on the door or windows. Lamberg had most likely not left the door unlocked. According to Elisabeth Lamberg he was always careful about locking."

"That leaves two possibilities. Either he had a key. Or else Simon Lamberg let him in."

Wallander nodded. Björk had understood. He went on.

"The second observation is that the blow that killed Lamberg was delivered with violent force to the back of the head. That can be a sign of determination. Or rage. Or both. And a great capacity for strength. At the moment of his death, Simon Lamberg had turned his back on the killer. Which in turn could mean two things. That he had not expected anything bad. Or he had tried to flee."

"If he had let in the person who killed him, that would explain why he turned his back."

"We can probably take yet another step," Wallander said. "Would he have let someone in that late at night who he didn't have a good relationship with?"

"Anything else?"

"According to the cleaning lady, Lamberg was in the habit of going to his studio two evenings a week. The days could vary. But there is a possibility that the perpetrator was aware of this. It is conceivable that we are looking for someone who knew Lamberg's habits, at least in part."

They left the conference room and ended up standing in the hallway.

"That means that there are at least some possible avenues for investigation," Björk said. "It's not a complete void."

Wallander made a face.

"Almost," he said. "It's as close to a void as it can be. We could have used Rydberg."

"I'm worried about his back problems," Björk said. "Sometimes I have the feeling it's something else."

Wallander stared at him with surprise.

"What would that be?"

"He may have another illness. Back pain doesn't have to come from just muscles or bone."

Wallander knew that Björk had a brother-in-law who was a doctor. And since Björk from time to time considered himself to be suffering from any number of severe illnesses, Wallander assumed he was now transferring his concerns onto Rydberg.

"Rydberg always gets better after a week or so," Wallander said.

They parted ways. Wallander returned to his room. Since the news of the murder had now spread, Ebba was able to give him the message that several reporters had called and asked when they would be able to get information. Without consulting anyone, Wallander announced that he would be available to answer questions at three o'clock.

Afterwards he devoted an hour to writing a summary of the case for himself. He had just finished when Nyberg called to say that Wallander could now start investigating the back room. Nyberg had still not made any noteworthy discoveries. Nor could the medical examiner state anything other than that Lamberg had been killed by a violent blow to the back of the head. Wallander asked if they could say something about the kind of weapon that had been used at this stage. But it was too early for an answer. Wallander ended the conversation and his thoughts returned to Rydberg. His teacher and mentor, the most skilled detective he had ever met. He had taught Wallander how important it was to turn and twist one's arguments and approach a problem from an unexpected angle.

262

I could have used him right now, Wallander thought. Maybe I should call him at home tonight.

He walked to the break room and drank yet another cup of coffee. Carefully munched on a rusk. The pain in his tooth did not return.

Since he felt tired from his interrupted sleep the night before, he took a walk down to St Gertrude's Square. The drizzling rain continued. He wondered when spring was coming. Our collective Swedish impatience in April is very high, he thought. Spring never seems to come at the right time. Winter always comes too early and spring too late.

Several people were gathered outside Lamberg's shop. Wallander knew some of them or at least had seen their faces before. He nodded and said hello. But he did not answer any questions. He stepped over the police tape and walked into the shop. Nyberg was standing with a Thermos mug in his hand, arguing with one of his technicians. He did not stop when Wallander walked in. Only when he had finished saying his piece did he turn to Wallander. He pointed towards the studio. The body had been removed. There was only the large bloodstain on the white background paper. An artificial trail of plastic had been laid out.

"Walk there," Nyberg instructed. "We found a lot of footprints in the studio."

Wallander pulled plastic booties over his shoes, slipped some rubber gloves into his pocket, and carefully walked into the room that had served as a combination office and developing room.

Wallander remembered how he, when he was very young, perhaps fourteen or fifteen years old, had nourished a passionate dream of becoming a photographer. But he did not aspire to have his own studio; he was going to be a press photographer. At all great events he would be there on the front lines and he would take his pictures while others took pictures of him.

As he stepped into the inner room he wondered where that dream had gone. It had suddenly just left him. Today he owned a simple Instamatic that he rarely used. Several years later he wanted to become an opera singer. Nothing had come of that either.

He removed his coat and looked around the room. From the studio he could hear that Nyberg had started arguing again. Wallander heard vaguely that it was about a sloppy measurement of the distance between two footprints. He walked over to the radio and turned it on. Classical music. Lamberg walked down to the studio sometimes in the evenings, Hilda Waldén had said. To work and to listen to music. Classical music. So far so good. He sat down at the desk. Everything was carefully arranged. He lifted the green writing pad. Nothing. Then he stood up and walked out to see Nyberg and ask if they had found any keys. They had. Wallander put on his rubber gloves and walked back. He searched for the right key to open the desk cabinet. In the top drawer there were various tax documents and other correspondence with Lamberg's accountant. Wallander gingerly leafed through the papers. He was not looking for anything in particular. Therefore anything could turn out to be important.

He went drawer by drawer methodically. Nothing caught his eye. So far Simon Lamberg's life was a well-organised one, without secrets, without surprises. But he was still only scraping the surface. He bent down and and pulled out the lowest drawer. There was just a photo album inside. The cover and binding were made of a luxurious leather. Wallander put it on the desk in front of him and turned to the front page. He studied the single snapshot with a furrowed brow. It was no larger than a passport photograph. Wallander had noticed a magnifying glass in one of the other drawers he had searched. Now he located it again, turned on one of the two desk lamps, and studied the image more closely.

It was a picture of the American president, Ronald Reagan. But it was deformed, the face had been distorted. It was still Ronald Reagan. And yet not. The wrinkled old man had been turned into a horrifying monster. Right next to the picture there was a date written in ink: 10 August 1984.

Wallander turned the page hesitantly. The same thing. A single snap-shot glued onto the middle of the page. This time it featured one of Sweden's former prime ministers. The same deformed, misshapen face. A date written in ink.

Without studying each picture in detail, Wallander slowly made his way through the album. On every page a single shot. Misshapen, deformed. Men — they were exclusively men — remade into revolting monsters.

Swedish as well as foreign. Mainly politicians but also some businessmen, an author and a few others that Wallander did not recognise.

He tried to understand what the images communicated. Why did Simon Lamberg have this uncommon photo album? Why had he distorted the pictures? Was it in order to work on this album that he had spent his evenings at the studio alone? Wallander had increased his concentration. Behind Simon Lamberg's well-ordered facade there was obviously something else. At least a man who deliberately destroyed the faces of well-known people.

He turned another page. Winced. An acute discomfort radiated through his body.

He had difficulty believing it was true.

At that moment Svedberg came into the room.

"Look at this," Wallander said slowly.

Then he pointed at the picture. Svedberg bent over his shoulder.

"That's you," he said with amazement.

"Yes," Wallander answered. "It's me. Or at least maybe."

He looked at it again. It was a photograph from a newspaper. It was him, and yet it wasn't. He looked like an unusually abominable individual.

Wallander could not think of a time when he had been so shaken. The distorted and grotesque depiction of his face nauseated him. He had certainly been the object of verbal assaults from criminals he had arrested, but the thought that someone had spent hours producing this hate-picture of him was frightening.

Svedberg registered his reaction and went to get Nyberg. Together they went through the album. The last picture was from the day before, when the Swedish prime minister had had his face destroyed. The date was written in next to it.

"The person who did this has to be sick," Nyberg said.

"There's no doubt that it is Simon Lamberg who has spent his evenings on these photographs," Wallander said. "What I am naturally wondering is why I've been included in this macabre collection. The only person from Ystad, no less. Among men of state and presidents. I won't deny that I find it very disturbing."

"And what is the purpose?" Svedberg asked.

No one had any reasonable answer to offer.

Wallander felt he had to leave the studio. He asked Svedberg to take over an examination of the room. For his part, he would soon have to give the press the information they were waiting for. By the time he was back out on the street, his nausea was clearing up. He stepped over the police tape and went straight to the police station. It was still drizzling. Even though the nausea had passed, he felt ill at ease.

Simon Lamberg spends his evenings in his studio, listening to music. At the same time he distorts the faces of various prominent heads of state. And a detective inspector from Ystad. Wallander tried furiously to find an explanation, without success. That a man could lead a double life, concealing insanity under a surface appearance of complete normality, was nothing unique. You could find many examples of this in the annals of criminal history. But why was Wallander himself in the album? What did he have in common with the other individuals represented there? Why was he the exception?

He walked straight into his office and closed the door. When he sat down in his chair, he realised that he was concerned. Simon Lamberg was dead. Someone had crushed the back of his head with violent force. They did not know why. And in his desk they had found a secret photo album with grotesque contents.

He was wrenched out of his thoughts by a knock on the door. It was Hansson.

"Lamberg is dead," he said, as if delivering a piece of news. "He took pictures of me when I was confirmed, many years ago."

"You've been confirmed?" Wallander asked, surprised. "I thought you would be the person least likely to care about the higher powers."

"And I don't," he answered happily, while carefully picking at his ear. "But I very much wanted to get a watch and my first real suit."

He pointed over his shoulder back out into the corridor.

"Reporters," he said. "I thought I'd better tag along and listen and learn what's happened."

"I can tell you that now," Wallander said. "Someone bashed in the back of Lamberg's head last night, between eight and midnight. It doesn't seem to be a case of burglary. That's about all we know."

"Not much," Hansson said.

"No," Wallander answered, and stood up. "It could hardly be any less."

The meeting with the press was largely improvised, and short. Wallander gave a sketch of what was known and brief answers to individual questions. The whole thing was over in half an hour. The time had become half past three. Wallander noticed that he was hungry. But the picture in Simon Lamberg's album remained on his mind the whole time, worrying him. The question gnawed at him: why had he been chosen to have his face shrunken and deformed? He sensed that this was the work of an insane person. But still, why him?

At a quarter to four he decided that it was time to go to Lavendelvägen, where the Lambergs lived. When he left the station, the rain had stopped. The wind, however, had picked up. He wondered if he should try to get hold of Svedberg and bring him along. But he let this stay as a thought. What he most of all wanted was to meet with Elisabeth Lamberg alone. There was a great deal that he wanted to talk to her about. But one of the questions was more important than the others.

He found his way up to Lavendelvägen and got out of the car. The house lay within a garden that he could see was well tended, despite the empty flower beds. He rang the doorbell. It was opened almost immediately by a woman in her fifties. Wallander stretched out his hand and said hello. The woman seemed guarded.

"I'm not Elisabeth Lamberg," she said. "I'm a friend. My name is Karin Fahlman."

She let him into the hall.

"Elisabeth is resting in the bedroom," she said. "I take it this conversation can't wait?"

"No, unfortunately. When it comes to apprehending whoever committed this crime, it's important not to lose any time."

Karin Fahlman nodded and showed him into the living room. Then she left without a sound.

Wallander looked around the room. The first thing that struck him was how quiet it was. No clocks. No sounds from the street penetrated inside. Through a window he saw some children playing, but he could not hear them even though it was obvious they were shouting and screaming. He walked over and inspected the window. It was double-glazed and appeared to be a particular model that was extremely sound-proof. He walked around the room. It was tastefully furnished, neither tacky nor overdone. A mixture of old and new. Copies of old woodcuts. A whole wall covered with books.

He did not hear her enter the room. But suddenly she was there, right behind him. He gave an involuntary start. She was very pale, almost as if her face bore a thin layer of white make-up. She had dark and straight short hair. Wallander thought she had probably been very beautiful at one time.

"I'm sorry to have to disturb you," he said and stretched out his hand.

"I know who you are," she said. "And I do understand that you have to come here."

"I can start by expressing my condolences."

"Thank you."

Wallander could see that she was doing her utmost to remain collected. He wondered how long she would be able to do this before she lost control.

They sat down. Wallander caught sight of Karin Fahlman in a nearby room. He assumed she was sitting there in order to listen to their conversation. For a moment he thought about how to begin. But he was interrupted in his thinking by Elisabeth Lamberg posing the first question.

"Do you know anything about who killed my husband?"

"We have no direct leads to follow. But there isn't much to support it being a burglary. This means either your husband must have let the person in or the person had keys."

She shook her head energetically, as if she violently opposed what Wallander had just said.

"Simon was always very careful. He would not have let in an unknown person, least of all at night."

"But for someone he knew?"

"Who would that have been?"

"I don't know. Everyone has friends."

"Simon went to Lund once a month. There was an association for amateur astronomers there. He was on the board. That was the only social outlet he had, as far as I know."

Wallander realised that Svedberg had missed a very important question.

"Do you have any children?"

"A daughter. Matilda."

271

Something in the way she answered put Wallander on his guard. The faint change in tone had not escaped him. As if the question bothered her. He went on hesitantly.

"How old is she?"

"Twenty-four."

"She no longer lives at home?"

Elisabeth Lamberg looked him straight in the eye as she answered.

"When Matilda was born she was seriously handicapped. We had her home for four years. Then it didn't work any more. Now she lives in an institution. She needs help with absolutely everything."

Wallander was taken aback. Exactly what he had been expecting, he couldn't say, but it was hardly the answer he had received.

She continued to look him right in the eye.

"It was not my decision. It was Simon who wanted it. Not me. He made the decision."

For one moment Wallander felt as if he were staring straight down into a bottomless pit. Her pain was that strong.

Wallander sat quietly for a long time before he went on.

"Can you think of anyone who would have had any reason to kill your husband?"

Her answers continued to astonish him.

"After that happened, I didn't know him any more."

"Even though it was twenty years ago?"

"Some things never heal."

"But you were still married?"

272

"We lived under the same roof. That was all."

Wallander thought about it before continuing.

"So you have no idea who the murderer could be?"

"No."

"Nor can you think of a motive?"

"No."

Wallander now tackled the most important question head-on.

"When I arrived you said you knew me. Can you remember if your husband ever talked about me?"

She raised her eyebrows.

"Why would he have done that?"

"I don't know. But that's the question."

"We never talked much to each other. But I cannot think of an occasion when we talked about you."

Wallander proceeded to his next point.

"We found an album in the studio. There were a great number of photographs of heads of state and other well-known people in it. For some reason my picture appeared among them. Do you know of this album?"

"No."

"Are you sure?"

"Yes."

"The photographs were distorted. All of these people, including me, were made to look like monsters. Your husband must have spent many hours achieving these effects. But you claim to know nothing about this?"

"No. It sounds very strange. Incredible."

273

Wallander saw that she was telling the truth. She really did not know much about her husband, since for twenty years she had not wished to know anything.

Wallander got up out of his chair. He knew he would be back with more questions. But right now he had nothing more to say.

She followed him to the front door.

"My husband probably had many secrets," she said out of the blue. "But I didn't share them."

"If you didn't, then who would have?"

"I don't know," she said, almost pleading. "But someone must have."

"What kind of secrets?"

"I've already said that I don't know. But Simon was full of secret rooms. I neither wanted nor was able to look into them."

Wallander nodded.

He ended up sitting in the car. It had started raining again.

What had she meant by that? Simon was a man "full of secret rooms". As if the inner office in the shop was only one? As if there were more? That they had not yet found?

He drove slowly back to the station. The anxiety that he had felt earlier became stronger.

The rest of the afternoon and evening they continued to spend working on what little material they had. Wallander went home at around ten o'clock. The squad would be meeting up the following morning at eight.

Back in his apartment, he heated up a can of beans, which was the only thing he could find in the way of food. He fell asleep a little after eleven.

The telephone call came at four minutes to midnight. Wallander lifted the receiver while still half asleep. It was a man who claimed to be out for a late-night walk. He introduced himself as the man who had taken care of Hilda Waldén that morning.

"I just saw someone slip into Lamberg's studio," he whispered.

Wallander sat up in bed.

"Are you sure of that? And it was not a police officer?"

"A shadow slipped in through the door," he said. "My heart is bad. But there is nothing wrong with my eyes."

The connection broke off, most likely due to a problem with the line. Wallander sat with the receiver in his hand. It was unusual for him to be called by someone other than the police, especially at night. His name was of course not printed in the telephone directory. But someone must have given the man Wallander's number during the morning chaos.

Then he got out of bed and quickly put on his clothes.

It was just past midnight.

Wallander arrived at the square where the studio was located a few minutes later. He had walked, or half run, since it was only a short distance from Mariagatan, where he lived. Nonetheless he was out of breath. When he arrived, he spotted a man standing a little way off in the distance. He hurried over to him, greeted him and took him to a place where they still had a view of the entrance but would not be as visible. The man was in his seventies and introduced himself as Lars Backman. He was a retired director of Handels Bank. He still referred to it by its former name, Svenska Handelsbanken.

"I live right next to here, on Ågatan," he said. "I am always out walking early in the morning and late at night. Doctor's orders."

"Tell me what happened."

"I saw a man slip in through the door to the studio."

"A man? On the phone you called him a shadow."

"I suppose I automatically thought it was a man. But of course it could have been a woman."

"And you haven't seen anyone leave the shop?"

"I've been keeping my eye on it. No one has left."

Wallander nodded. He ran over to the telephone booth and called Nyberg, who answered after the third ring. Wallander had the feeling that he had been asleep. But he didn't ask, he simply explained quickly what had happened. He extracted the most important piece of information, which was that Nyberg had keys to the shop. In addition, he had not left them at the police station but had them with him at home. He had been planning to return to the studio early the next morning in order to wrap up the forensic investigation. Wallander asked him to come as quickly as possible, then ended the call. Deliberated over whether he should contact Hansson or any of the others. All too often Wallander violated the rule that a detective who finds himself in a situation beyond his immediate control should never be alone. But Wallander hesitated. Nyberg counted as backup. Once he arrived they would decide how to proceed. Lars Backman was still there. Wallander asked him kindly to leave the square. Another officer was on his way and they needed to be left alone. Backman did not appear to be displeased at this dismissal. He simply nodded and left.

Wallander started to feel cold. He was only wearing a shirt under his coat. The wind had intensified. The cloud cover was breaking up. It was probably only a couple of degrees above freezing. He watched the entrance to the shop. Could Backman have been mistaken? He didn't think so. He tried to figure out if there was a light on inside. But it was impossible to tell. A car went by, then another. Then he spotted Nyberg on the other side of the square and went to meet him. They leaned against the side of a house in order to escape the wind. Wallander kept an eye on the shop entrance the entire time. He quickly told Nyberg what had happened. Nyberg stared back at him in amazement.

"Did you think we were going to go in alone?"

"First I just wanted you to come down here, since you have the keys. And apparently there's no back door."

"No."

"So the only way to get in or out is through this door to the street?"

"Yes."

"Then we'll alert one of the night patrol squads," Wallander said. "Then we'll open the door and order him to come out."

Wallander went and called the station, while maintaining continuous surveillance of the door. He was assured that a night squad would arrive in a couple of minutes. They walked over to the shop. It was now twenty-five minutes to one. The streets were deserted.

Then the door to the studio was opened. A man came out. His face was concealed by the shadows. The three of them caught sight of each other at the same time and came to a halt. Wallander was just about to call out to the man to stay where he was when the man turned round and started to run down North Änggatan at breakneck speed. Wallander shouted to Nyberg to wait for the night squad. Then he followed the suspect, who was moving very quickly. Wallander was unable to gain on him, even though he was running as fast as he could. The man turned right on Vassgatan and continued on towards Folk Park. Wallander wondered why the night squad hadn't shown up. There was now a great chance that he would lose sight of the fleeing suspect. The man turned right again and disappeared up Aulingatan. Wallander tripped on some loose flagstones on the pavement and fell. He hit one knee hard on the ground and ripped a hole in his trousers. There was a shooting pain in his knee as he continued running. The distance between himself and the man kept growing. Where were Nyberg and the night squad? He cursed silently. His heart was thumping like a hammer in his chest. The man reached Giödde's Alley and turned out of sight. When Wallander reached the corner he thought he should probably stop and wait for Nyberg. But he kept going.

The man was waiting round the corner. A violent blow struck Wallander right in the face. Everything grew dark.

When Wallander came to he did not know where he was. He stared straight up at the stars. The ground underneath him was cold. When he reached out around him, his hands groped asphalt. Then he remembered what had happened. He sat up. His left cheek was aching where he had been struck. With his tongue he could feel that a tooth had been broken. The same tooth he had just had fixed. He got to his feet with some effort. His knee was sore, his head throbbed. Then he looked around. As he expected, the suspect was nowhere to be seen. He limped over to Aulingatan, back towards Surbrunn Road. Everything had happened so fast that he had not had time to register what the man's face looked like. He had turned that corner and then the world had exploded.

The patrol car came from Ågatan. Wallander walked out into the middle of the street in order to be seen. Wallander knew the officer who was driving. His name was Peters and he had been in Ystad as long as Wallander himself. Nyberg jumped out of the car.

"What happened?"

"He ran down Giödde's Alley and knocked me down. I don't think we'll find him. But we could always try."

"You're going to the hospital," Nyberg said. "First things first."

Wallander felt his cheek. His hand grew wet with blood. He was suddenly overcome with dizziness. Nyberg took his arm and helped him into the car.

Wallander was allowed to leave the hospital at four in the morning. By then Svedberg and Hansson had arrived. Various night squads had criss-crossed the city in the hunt for the man who had knocked him down. But since there was only a vague description, a mid-length coat that could have been black or navy blue, the effort had predictably been in vain. Wallander was patched up. The broken tooth would have to be attended to later in the day. Wallander's cheek had swollen up. The blood had come from a wound near his hairline.

When they left the hospital, Wallander insisted on going directly to the studio. Both Hansson and Svedberg protested and said he needed to rest first. But Wallander ignored their objections. Nyberg was already on the scene when they arrived. They turned on all of the available lights and gathered in the studio.

"I haven't been able to identify anything as missing or altered," Nyberg said.

Wallander knew that Nyberg had a tremendous memory for details. But he realised at the same time that the man could have been searching for something that might not have been particularly noticeable. Above all, they had no way of knowing why the man had sought out the studio in the middle of the night.

"What about fingerprints?" Wallander asked. "Footprints?"

Nyberg pointed to the floor where several areas had been taped and marked as restricted.

"I have checked the door handles. But I suspect the man was wearing gloves."

"And the front door?"

"No marks. We can safely assume he had access to keys. I was the one who locked up last night."

Wallander looked at his colleagues.

"Shouldn't there have been surveillance posted here?"

"It was my call," Hansson said. "I didn't see any reason for it, particularly given our current staffing issues."

Wallander knew that Hansson was right. He wouldn't have ordered surveillance either if he had been in charge.

"We can only speculate as to who the man was," he went on. "And what he was after in here. Even if there was no visible police presence, he must have realised that it was possible we were keeping the place under surveillance. But I want someone to talk to Lars Backman, who not only called me at midnight but also took care of Hilda Waldén yesterday morning. He seems like a good resource. He may have noticed something that he didn't think of at once."

"It's four o'clock in the morning," Svedberg pointed out. "Do you want me to call him right now?"

"He is probably awake," Wallander said. "Yesterday morning he was out already at 5a.m. He is both an early riser and a night owl."

Svedberg nodded and left. There was no reason for Wallander to keep the others.

"We'll have to review the case thoroughly tomorrow," he said when Svedberg had walked out the front door. "The best thing you can do is get a few hours of sleep. For my part, I'm going to stay here for a while."

"Do you think that's wise?" Hansson asked. "After what you've been through?"

"I don't know if it's wise or not. But that's what I'm doing."

Nyberg handed him the keys. When Hansson and Nyberg had left, Wallander locked the door. Even though he was exhausted and his cheek ached, his attention was sharp. He listened to the silence. Nothing appeared changed. He went into the inner room, did the same thing, scrutinising it. Nothing jumped out at him. But the man had come here for a reason. And he had been in a hurry. He could not wait. There could only be one explanation. There was something in the studio that he needed to get. Wallander sat down at the desk. There were no marks on the lock. He opened the cabinet, pulled out drawer after drawer. The album was the same as when he had last seen it. Nothing appeared to be missing. Wallander tried to calculate how long the man had been in the shop. The telephone call from Backman had come at four minutes to midnight. Wallander had arrived here at ten past twelve. His conversation with Backman and his call to Nyberg had not been longer than a couple of minutes apiece. At that point it was a quarter past twelve. Nyberg arrived at half past twelve. The unknown man was in the studio for forty minutes. When he left, he had been taken by surprise. That meant he had not been fleeing. He had left the studio because he was done.

Done with what?

Wallander looked around the room again, this time even more methodically. Somewhere something must have changed. He simply wasn't seeing it. Something was gone. Or added, returned? He walked out into the studio and repeated his initial examination, finally even in the shop portion.

Nothing. He returned to the inner room again. Something told him that was where he should search. In Simon Lamberg's secret room. He sat in the chair, allowing his gaze to wander around the walls, over the desk and bookcases. Then he stood up and walked over to the developing equipment. Turned on the red light. Everything was as he remembered. The faint smell of chemicals. The empty plastic tubs, the enlarger.

He walked back to the desk, pensive. Remained standing. Where the impulse came from he wasn't sure. But he walked over to the shelf where the radio was and turned it on.

The music was deafening.

He stared at the radio. The volume was at the same level as before.

But the music was not classical. It was loud rock music.

Wallander was convinced that neither Nyberg nor any of the other technicians would have switched the radio station. They did not alter anything unless it was absolutely necessary for their work.

Wallander took a handkerchief out of his pocket and turned off the radio. There was only one possibility.

The unknown man had turned the dial to a different frequency.

He had changed stations.

The question was simply: why?

The squad was finally able to start the meeting at ten o'clock in the morning. The delay was due to the fact that Wallander had not been able to get back from the dentist's before then. Now he was hurrying back for the meeting, his tooth provisionally repaired, with a swollen cheek and a large bandage at his hairline. He was seriously beginning to feel the effects of his lack of sleep. But more serious was the anxiety gnawing at him.

It had now been one day since Hilda Waldén had discovered the dead photographer. Wallander began the meeting by summing up the state of their investigation. He then told them in detail what had happened during the night.

"The changed radio station is strange," Svedberg said. "Can there have been anything inside the radio itself?"

"We've examined it," Nyberg answered. "In order to remove the cover you have to loosen eight screws. This has not been done. The radio has never been opened since it was assembled at the factory. The finish still covers the screw heads."

"There is a lot that's strange," Wallander said. "Something we shouldn't forget is the album with the distorted images. His widow tells us that Simon

284

Lamberg was a man who had many secrets. Right now we should be concentrating on creating a better picture of who he really was. Clearly, the surface does not match up with what was underneath. The polite, quiet and fastidious photographer must in reality have been someone quite different."

"The question is just who would know more about him," Martinsson said. "If, as seems to be the case, he doesn't have any friends. No one seems to have known him."

"We have the amateur astronomers in Lund," Wallander said. "We have to get in touch with them, of course. Former assistants who worked for him. You can't live your whole life in a town like Ystad without anybody knowing you. And we've barely begun our conversations with Elisabeth Lamberg. In other words, we have a lot to dig into. Everything has to be pursued simultaneously."

"I spoke to Backman," Svedberg said. "You were right about him being up. When I arrived at his apartment his wife was also up and dressed. It felt like the middle of the day, even though it was only four in the morning. Unfortunately he could not give any kind of description of the man who knocked you down. Nothing apart from the man's coat being mid-length and most likely navy blue."

"Couldn't he even say anything about the man's height? Was he short or tall? What colour was his hair?"

"It all happened very fast. Backman only wanted to say what he felt sure about."

"We know at least one thing about the man who attacked me," Wallander said. "That he ran much faster than I did. My impression was that he was of average height and fairly strong. He was also in much better shape than I am. My sense — even if it's somewhat vague — is that he may have been around my age. But this is really just a guess."

They were still waiting for the first preliminary report from the medical examiner in Lund. Nyberg and the forensic laboratory in Linköping were in contact. Many fingerprints needed to be run through the various databases.

They all had a lot to do. Wallander therefore wanted to draw the meeting to a close as quickly as possible. It was eleven when they stood up. Wallander hadn't done more than walk into his office when the phone rang. It was Ebba from reception.

"You have a visitor," she said. "A man named Gunnar Larsson. He wants to talk to you about Lamberg."

Wallander had just decided to make another trip out to see Elisabeth Lamberg.

"Can't anyone else deal with him?"

"He wanted to speak to you specifically."

"Who is he?"

"He used to work for Lamberg."

Wallander immediately changed his mind. The conversation with the widow would have to wait.

"I'll come out and get him," Wallander said and got to his feet.

Gunnar Larsson was in his thirties. They went back to Wallander's office. Larsson declined the offer of a cup of coffee.

"I'm glad that you thought of coming in yourself," Wallander began. "Your name would have come up sooner or later. But this saves us some time."

Wallander had flipped open one of his notebooks.

"I worked for Lamberg for six years," Gunnar Larsson said. "He let me go about four years ago. I don't think he's employed anyone else since then."

"Why did he let you go?"

"He claimed that he could no longer afford to keep someone on. I think that was the truth. I think I had actually been expecting it. Lamberg didn't have more business than he could handle on his own. Since he didn't sell cameras or accessories, his profits were not great. And when times are bad people don't go and get their picture taken as often."

"But you worked there for six years. That means you must have got to know him pretty well?"

"Both yes and no."

"Let's start with the former."

"He was always polite and friendly. To everyone: me and the customers alike. He had boundless patience with children. And he was very orderly."

Wallander was suddenly struck by a thought.

"Would you say that Simon Lamberg was a good photographer?"

"There wasn't anything original about him. The pictures he took were conventional, since that's what people want. Photos that look like any other. And he was good at that. He never cut corners. He wasn't original, since he didn't have to be. I doubt that he cherished any artistic ambitions. At least I never saw any hint of it."

Wallander nodded.

"I get the impression of a kindly but relatively colourless person. Is that right?"

"Yes."

"Let us then proceed to why you feel you didn't know him."

"He was probably the most reserved person I've ever known in my life."

"In what way?"

"He never talked about himself. Or his feelings. I cannot recall a single instance where he described his own experience of anything. But in the beginning I tried to have regular conversations with him."

"About what?"

"About anything. But I soon stopped."

"Didn't he ever comment on current events?"

"I think he was very conservative."

"Why do you think that?"

Gunnar Larsson shrugged.

"I just do. But on the other hand I doubt that he ever read the papers."

I think you're wrong there, Wallander thought. He did read newspapers. And he probably knew a great deal about international affairs. He kept his opinions in a photo album of a kind that the world has probably never seen before.

"There was another thing I found strange," Gunnar Larsson went on. "During the six years that I worked for him, I never met his wife. Not that I was ever invited to their house, of course. To get a sense of where they lived, I walked past their house one Sunday."

"So you never met their daughter?"

Perplexed, Gunnar Larsson looked at Wallander.

"They had children?"

"You didn't know this?"

"No."

"They had a daughter. Matilda."

Wallander chose not to add that she was severely handicapped. But evidently Gunnar Larsson had no idea that she even existed.

Wallander put his pen down.

"What did you think when you heard what had happened?"

"That it was utterly incomprehensible."

"Do you think you could ever have imagined anything happening to him?"

"I still can't imagine it. Who could have had a reason to kill him?"

"That's what we're trying to ascertain."

Wallander noticed that Gunnar Larsson appeared uncomfortable. It was as if he was unable to decide what to say next.

"You're thinking about something," Wallander guessed. "Am I right?"

"There were some rumours," Gunnar Larsson said hesitantly. "Rumours that Simon Lamberg gambled."

"Gambled how?"

"Gambled to win money. Someone had seen him at the Jägersro racetrack."

"Why would that start rumours? It's not unusual to go to Jägersro on occasion."

"People also said he turned up regularly at illegal gambling clubs. Both in Malmö and Copenhagen."

Wallander frowned.

"How did you hear this?"

"There are a lot of rumours floating around a small town like Ystad."

Wallander knew all too well how true this was.

"There were rumours that he had heavy debts."

"Did he?"

"Not during the time that I worked there. I could see that from his bookkeeping."

"He may of course have taken out private loans. He could have ended up in the hands of a loan shark."

"In that case I wouldn't know about it."

Wallander thought for a moment.

"Rumours always start somewhere," he said.

"It was a long time ago," Gunnar Larsson said. "Where or when I heard those rumours I really can't remember."

"Did you know about the photo album he kept locked in his desk?"

"I never saw what he had in his desk."

Wallander felt sure that the man sitting across from him was telling the truth.

"Did you have your own keys when you worked for Lamberg?"

"Yes."

"What happened to those when you were let go?"

"I gave them back."

Wallander nodded. He wasn't going to get any further. The more people he talked to, the more mysterious Simon Lamberg in all his colourlessness appeared. He made a note of Gunnar Larsson's phone number and address. The conversation came to a close and Wallander walked him out to the reception area. Then he went and got a cup of coffee and returned to his office. He unplugged the phone. He could not recall when he had last felt at such a loss. In which direction should they turn for their solution? Everything seemed to consist of loose threads. Even though he tried to avoid it, the image of his own face, distorted and pasted in a photo album, returned again and again.

The loose threads did not connect anywhere.

He checked the time. Almost twelve. He was hungry. The wind outside the window appeared to be blowing stronger. He plugged his phone back in. It rang immediately. It was Nyberg, who wanted to let him know that the forensic investigation was complete and that they had not found anything out of the ordinary. Now Wallander was free to look through the other rooms as well.

Wallander sat at his desk and tried to come up with a review of the events. In his mind he was conducting a conversation with Rydberg, and he cursed the fact that his colleague was absent. What do I do now? How do I go further? We're grasping at nothing, as if we were stumbling around in a circle.

291

He read through what he had written. Tried to coax a secret out of the brief account. But there was nothing. Irritated, he tossed the notepad aside.

It was now a quarter to one. The best thing he could do would be to go and get a bite to eat. Later in the afternoon he would need to have another conversation with Elisabeth Lamberg.

He realised he was too impatient. Despite everything that had happened, only one day had gone by since Simon Lamberg was murdered.

In his mind, Rydberg agreed with him. Wallander knew that he didn't have enough patience.

He put on his coat and got ready to leave.

The door opened. It was Martinsson.

He could tell from his face that something important had happened.

Martinsson paused in the doorway. Wallander regarded him with anticipation.

"We never found the man who attacked you last night," Martinsson said. "But someone saw him."

Martinsson pointed to a map of Ystad that hung on Wallander's wall.

"He knocked you down at the corner of Aulingatan and Giödde's Alley. Then he most likely fled along Herrestadsgatan and turned north. Shortly after you were attacked, he was observed in a garden close by, on Timmermansgatan."

"What do you mean, 'observed'?"

Martinsson took out his little notebook from his pocket and turned the pages.

"It was a young family by the name of Simovic. The wife was awake, since she was nursing her three-month-old baby. At some point she looked out into the garden and caught sight of a person lurking in the shadows. She immediately woke her husband. But when he got to the window, the person was gone. He said she was just imagining things. She was apparently convinced by this, and when her child fell asleep she went back to bed. It was only today, when she was out in the garden, that she remembered what had happened. She went over to the spot where she thought she had seen someone that night. I should also mention that she had heard that Lamberg had been murdered. Ystad is small enough that even the Simovics had a family portrait taken in his studio."

"But she can't possibly have heard about our night-time chase," Wallander objected. "We haven't gone public with that."

"Yes, that's right," Martinsson said. "That's why we should be thankful she even contacted us."

"Was she able to offer a useful description?"

"She only saw a shadow at best."

Wallander looked curiously at Martinsson.

"Then these observations aren't really of much use to us, are they?"

"No," Martinsson said, "if it weren't for the fact that she found something on the ground. Which she came by and dropped off a little while ago. And that is lying on my desk at this very moment."

Wallander followed Martinsson to the latter's office.

"This? Was this what she found?"

"A hymn book. From the Church of Sweden."

Wallander tried to think it through.

"What compelled Mrs Simovic to bring it in?"

"A murder had been committed. She had observed someone moving around in a suspicious manner in her garden at night. At first she had allowed herself to be convinced by her husband that it was only her imagination. But then she found the hymn book."

Wallander slowly shook his head.

"This isn't necessarily the same man," he said.

"And yet I would claim that there's a lot that says it is. How many people sneak around in other people's gardens at night in Ystad? In addition, the night patrol units were out and looking. I've talked with one officer who was out last night. They were out on Timmermansgatan several times. A garden was therefore a good place to hide."

Wallander knew that Martinsson was right.

"A hymn book," he said. "Who the hell carries around a hymn book in the middle of the night?"

"And drops it in someone's garden after having attacked a police officer," Martinsson added.

"Let Nyberg take care of the book," Wallander said. "And make sure to thank the Simovics for their help."

He thought of something else as he was on his way out of Martinsson's office.

"Who is in charge of the office pool?"

"Hansson. But it doesn't seem to have gained any serious momentum yet."

"It may never," Wallander replied doubtfully.

Wallander walked down to the bakery-cafe by the bus terminal and had a couple of sandwiches. The hymn book was as mysterious a discovery as anything else that had so far been associated with the ongoing investigation of the photographer's death. Wallander realised how lost he really was. They were searching blindly for anything concrete to go on.

After lunch Wallander drove to Lavendelvägen. Again it was Karin Fahlman who opened the door. But this time Elisabeth Lamberg was not resting. She was sitting in the living room when Wallander came in. Again he was struck by her pallor. He had the feeling it came from somewhere inside and also had roots far back in time and was not simply a reaction to her husband's murder.

Wallander sat down across from her. She scrutinised him.

"We are no closer to solving this case," Wallander began.

"I know you're doing the best you can," she said.

Wallander briefly wondered what she really meant. Was it a disguised criticism of their work? Or did she mean it honestly?

"This is the second time that I've come to see you," he said, "but I think we can safely assume it will not be the last. New questions turn up all the time."

"I'll try to answer to the best of my ability."

"This time I haven't simply come to ask questions," Wallander continued. "I also need to be able to look through your husband's belongings."

She nodded but said nothing.

295

Wallander decided to take the bull by the horns.

"Did your husband have any debts?"

"Not as far as I know. The house is paid for. He never made any new investments in the studio without knowing that he could pay off the loans quickly."

"Could he have taken out any loans that you would not have known about?"

"Of course he could have. I've already explained this to you. We lived under the same roof, but we had separate lives. And he was very secretive."

Wallander grabbed hold of the last thing she said.

"In what way was he secretive? I still haven't fully understood this."

Her eyes bored into him.

"What is a secretive person? Perhaps it would be more precise to say that he was a closed person. One never knew if he really meant what he said. Or was thinking something completely different. I could be standing right next to him and have the feeling that he was somewhere far, far away. I could never determine if he really meant it when he smiled. I could never be sure of who he really was."

"It must have been a trying situation," Wallander said. "But it could hardly always have been like that?"

"He changed a great deal. It started back when Matilda was born."

"Twenty-four years ago?"

"Perhaps not immediately. Let me say twenty years ago. At first I thought it was grief. Over Matilda's fate. Then I didn't know any more. Before it grew worse."

"Worse?"

"About seven years ago."

"What happened then?"

"I honestly don't know."

Wallander stopped and backed up a little.

"So if I understand this correctly, something happened seven years ago? Something that changed him dramatically?"

"Yes."

"And you don't have any idea what this might have been?"

"Maybe. Every spring he would let his assistant take care of his business for about fourteen days. Then he would go on a bus trip somewhere down on the Continent."

"But you didn't accompany him?"

"He wanted to go on his own. And I had no particular desire to go. If I wanted to get away, I would travel with my friends. To different places."

"So what happened?"

"That time the destination was Austria. And when he came home he was completely changed. Seemed both upbeat and sad at the same time. When I tried to ask him about it he had one of the few outbursts of temper I ever experienced from him."

Wallander had started making notes.

"When exactly did this happen?"

"Nineteen eighty-one. In February or March. The bus trip was arranged from Stockholm, but Simon got on in Malmö."

"You don't happen to recall the name of the travel agency?"

"I think it was Markresor. He almost always went with them."

After writing down this name, Wallander tucked the notebook into his pocket.

"Now I'd like to have a look around," he said. "Above all, I'd like to see his room."

"He had two. A bedroom and an office."

Both were located on the basement level. Wallander only cast a cursory glance at the bedroom and opened the wardrobe. She was standing behind him, watching what he did. Then they continued on to Lamberg's expansive office. The walls were covered with bookcases. There was an extensive record collection, a well-used armchair and a large desk.

Wallander suddenly thought of something.

"Was your husband religious?" he asked.

"No," she said, surprised. "I can't imagine that he was."

Wallander's gaze wandered along the spines of the books. There were literary works in many languages but also non-fiction on various subjects. Several rows of books were devoted to astronomy. Wallander sat down at the desk. Nyberg had given him the keys. He unlocked the first drawer. Lamberg's wife sat down in the reading chair.

"If you don't want to be disturbed, I'm happy to leave," she said.

"That's not necessary," Wallander answered.

It took him a couple of hours to comb through the office. She sat in the armchair the whole time and followed him with her eyes. He did not find anything that brought him or the investigation forward.

Something had happened on a trip to Austria about seven years ago, he thought. The question is simply: what?

It was close to five-thirty when he gave up. Simon Lamberg's life appeared to have been hermetically sealed. No matter how hard he looked he could not find an entrance. They walked up to the ground floor again. Karin Fahlman was moving around in the background. Everything was quiet, just as before.

"Did you find what you were looking for?" Elisabeth Lamberg asked.

"I don't know what I'm looking for, other than a clue that could give us an idea about a motive and about who may have killed your husband. I have not found such a thing yet."

Wallander said goodbye and drove back to the police station. The wind was still gusty. He was cold and wondered, for what seemed like the hundredth time, when spring was going to arrive.

He met up with the public prosecutor, Per Åkeson, outside the station. They walked into reception together. He gave Åkeson a quick overview of the case.

"So you have no direct leads to go on right now?" he said when Wallander was done.

"No," Wallander answered. "There is nothing yet that points in a particular direction. The needle of the compass is spinning wildly."

Åkeson walked back out through the front doors. Wallander bumped into Svedberg in the corridor. He was just the person Wallander wanted to see. They went into Wallander's office and Svedberg sat down in the rickety visitor's chair. One of the armrests was threatening to come off.

"You should get a new chair," he said.

"Do you think there's money for that?"

Wallander had his notebook out in front of him.

"There are two things I want to ask you," he said. "First, that you try to find out if there's a travel agency in Stockholm by the name of Markresor. Simon Lamberg went on a two-week trip with them to Austria in February or March of 1981. Find out what you can about this bus trip. And if you could dig up a passenger list after all these years that would be ideal."

"Why is this important?"

"Something happened on that trip. His widow was very sure of that. Simon Lamberg was not the same when he returned."

Svedberg made a note of this request.

"One more thing," Wallander said. "We should find out where this daughter, Matilda, is. She lives in an institution for the severely handicapped. But we don't know where."

"You didn't ask about this?"

"I didn't think of it, actually. That blow last night might have been harder than I thought."

"I'll find out about it," Svedberg said and stood up.

He almost collided in the doorway with Hansson, who was on his way in.

300

"I think I've found something," Hansson said. "I've been searching for something in my mind. Simon Lamberg never had any run-ins with the law, of course, but I still thought I remembered him from somewhere."

Wallander and Svedberg waited eagerly. They both knew that Hansson from time to time had a good memory.

"I just thought of what it was," he went on. "About a year ago Lamberg wrote some letters of complaint to the police. He addressed them to Björk, even though almost none of his criticisms had anything to do with the Ystad police. Among other things he was unhappy about how we dealt with various cases of violent crime. One was about Kajsa Stenholm, who failed with that case in Stockholm that culminated down here last spring, after Bengt Alexandersson was killed. You were in charge of that one. I thought that might explain why your face was included in his bizarre photo album."

Wallander nodded. Hansson could be right. But it didn't get them anywhere.

The feeling of being at a complete loss was very strong.

They simply had nothing concrete to go on.

The perpetrator was still only a fleeting shadow.

The weather changed on the third day of the investigation. When Wallander woke up fully rested at half past five, the sun shone through the window. The thermometer outside the kitchen window said it was seven degrees above zero Celsius. Perhaps spring had finally arrived.

Wallander studied his face in the bathroom mirror. His left cheek was swollen and blue. When he gently tried to remove the bandage at his hairline, the wound immediately started to bleed. He searched around for a fresh Band-Aid and put it on. Then he felt the temporary crown on his tooth. He still had not become accustomed to it. He showered and put on his clothes. The mountain of dirty laundry drove him grumpily down to the laundry room to sign up for a time while the coffee was brewing. He could not comprehend how so much laundry could accumulate in such a short time. Normally Mona managed the laundry. He felt a tug inside when he thought of her. Then he sat down at the kitchen table and read the paper. Lamberg's murder was given a lot of space. Björk had spoken to the press, and Wallander nodded approvingly. He had expressed himself well. Spelled out the facts, no speculation.

At a quarter past six, Wallander left the apartment and drove up to the station. Since everyone on the squad had a lot to do, they had decided to meet at the end of the day. The systematic mapping of Simon Lamberg, his habits, finances, social circle and past required time. Wallander had decided to investigate whether there was any basis to the rumours that Gunnar Larsson had talked about. That Simon Lamberg had been a man who had moved in the illegal world of gambling. He decided to draw on an old contact. He was planning to drive to Malmö and look up a man he hadn't seen for four years. But he knew where he was most likely to be found. He walked out to reception, went through the telephone messages, and decided there was nothing important. Then he went to Martinsson, who was an early riser. He was sitting in front of the computer, engaged in a search.

"How's it going?" Wallander asked.

Martinsson shook his head.

"Simon Lamberg must have been the closest to an umblemished citizen that you can get," he said. "Not a speck, not even a parking ticket. Nothing."

"There were rumours that he gambled," Wallander said. "Illegally, no less, and that he had accumulated unregulated debt. I was planning to spend the morning looking into it. I'm driving up to Malmö."

"What weather we have," Martinsson said, without looking up from the screen.

"Yes," Wallander said. "I think it gives us grounds for hope."

Wallander drove to Malmö. The temperature had risen by a few degrees. He enjoyed the thought of the transformation the landscape would now undergo. But not many minutes went by before his thoughts returned to the murder case that was his responsibility. They still lacked direction. They had no apparent motive. Simon Lamberg's death was incomprehensible. A photographer who had lived a quiet life. Who had undergone the tragedy of having a severely handicapped daughter. Who also to all intents and purposes lived separated from his wife. Nothing in all of this indicated, however, that anyone would have felt the need to crush his head with a furious blow.

To top it off, something had occurred on a bus trip to Austria seven years ago. Something that had significantly altered Lamberg.

Wallander surveyed the landscape as he drove. He wondered what it was in this picture of Lamberg that he had not seen through. There was something blurry about his whole figure. His life, his character, were strangely ephemeral.

Wallander arrived in Malmö shortly before eight o'clock. He drove straight to the parking garage behind the Savoy Hotel, then used the back entrance to the hotel. He headed for the dining room.

The man he was looking for was sitting by himself at a table at the very back of the room. He was absorbed in the morning paper. Wallander walked up to the table. The man started and looked up.

"Kurt Wallander," he said. "Are you so hungry that you have to come all the way to Malmö to eat breakfast?"

"Your logic is off as usual," Wallander answered, and sat down.

He poured himself a cup of coffee as he thought about the first time he had met Peter Linder, the man on the other side of the table. It had been more than ten years ago, in the mid-1970s. Wallander had just started working in Ystad. They had made a raid on an illegal gambling club that had sprung up on a remotely located farm outside Hedeskoga. It had been clear to everyone that Peter Linder had been the man behind this business. The large profits had gone to him. But at the subsequent trial Linder had been acquitted. A band of lawyers had been able to put a hole in the prosecutor's case, and Linder had left the court a free man. No one had been able to get at the money he had made, since no one had been able to figure out where it was. A few days after the verdict, he had unexpectedly turned up at the police station and asked to speak to Wallander. He had complained of the treatment he had received at the hands of the Swedish legal system. Wallander had been furious.

"Everyone knows that you were behind it," he had said.

"Of course it was me," Peter Linder replied. "But the prosecutor didn't manage to prove it well enough to determine my guilt. This does not mean, however, that I have to abandon my right to complain of mistreatment."

Peter Linder's impudence had rendered Wallander speechless. For the next couple of years he was absent from Wallander's life. But one day an anonymous letter arrived to Wallander with a tip about another gambling club in Ystad. This time they managed to arrest and sentence several of the men involved. Wallander had known the whole time that it was Peter Linder who had written the anonymous letter. Since for some reason he had mentioned to Wallander at that first meeting that he "always ate dinner at the Savoy", Wallander had looked him up there. With a smile, he had denied having written the letter. But both of them had known better.

"I'm reading in the paper that photographers live dangerously in Ystad," Peter Linder said.

"No more dangerously than in other places."

"And gambling clubs?"

"I think we're free of those for the moment."

Peter Linder smiled. His eyes were very blue.

"Perhaps I should consider re-establishing myself in the Ystad region. What do you think?"

"You know what I think," Wallander said. "And if you come back, we'll put you away."

Peter Linder shook his head. He smiled. This irritated Wallander, but he didn't show it.

"I actually came here to talk to you about the photographer who was killed."

"I only ever go to a royal photographer who is here in Malmö. He took pictures of Sofiero Castle during the old king's time. An excellent photographer."

"You only need to answer my questions," Wallander broke in.

"Is this an interrogation?"

"No. But I'm dumb enough to think you might be able to help me. And even dumber to think that you'd be prepared to do it."

Peter Linder spread his arms out in a gesture of invitation.

"Simon Lamberg," Wallander went on, "the photographer. There were rumours about him, that he was a gambler who bet large. Moreover, in an illegal setting. Both here and in Copenhagen. Also, unregulated loans. A man deeply entrenched in debt. All according to the rumours."

"In order for a rumour to be interesting, at least fifty per cent of it must be true," Peter Linder said philosophically. "Is it?"

306

"I was hoping you would be able to answer that. Have you heard of him?"

Peter Linder considered the question.

"No," he said after a moment. "And even if only half of those rumours were true, I would have known who he was."

"Is it possible that you might have missed him for some reason?"

"No," Peter Linder said. "That's inconceivable."

"You are all-knowing, in other words."

"When it comes to the illegal gambling world in southern Sweden, I know everything. I also know something about classical philosophy and Moorish architecture. Beyond this, I know almost nothing."

Wallander did not protest. He knew that Peter Linder had achieved an astonishingly rapid rise in the academic world. Then one day, without warning, he had wandered out of the academy and in a short time established himself as a gambling-club owner.

Wallander finished his coffee.

"If you hear anything, I would be grateful for one of your anonymous letters," he said.

"I'll put out some feelers in Copenhagen," Peter Linder replied, "but I doubt I'll find anything to offer you."

Wallander nodded. He quickly rose to his feet. He could not bring himself to go so far as to shake Peter Linder's hand.

Wallander was back at the station by ten o'clock. A couple of officers were outside, drinking coffee in the spring warmth. Wallander checked Svedberg's office. He was not there. Same with Hansson. Only Martinsson was still diligently working in front of his computer screen.

"How did it go in Malmö?" he asked.

"Unfortunately, the rumours aren't true," Wallander answered.

"Unfortunately?"

"It would have given us a motive. Gambling debts, hired guns. Everything we need."

"Svedberg managed to find out through the business register that the company Markresor no longer exists. They merged with another company five years ago. And that company went under last year. He thought it would be impossible to get any old lists of passengers. But he thought it might be possible to trace the bus driver. If he's still alive."

"Where is he?"

"I don't know."

"Where are Hansson and Svedberg?"

"Svedberg is rooting around in Lamberg's finances. Hansson is talking to the neighbours. Nyberg is scolding a technician who misplaced a footprint."

"Is it really possible to misplace a footprint?"

"It's possible to lose a hymn book in a garden."

Martinsson is right, Wallander thought. Anything can be lost.

"Have we received any information from the public?" he asked.

"Nothing, apart from the Simovic family and the hymn book. As well as a few things that can be written off immediately. But there could be more. People normally take their time."

"And Backman the bank director?"

"Reliable. But he hasn't seen more than we already know."

"And the cleaning lady? Hilda Waldén?"

"Nothing more there either."

Wallander leaned against the door frame.

"Who the hell killed him? What kind of a motive could there have been?"

"Who changes a radio station?" Martinsson said. "And who runs around town at night with a hymn book in his pocket?"

The questions remained unanswered for the moment. Wallander went to his office. He felt restless and anxious. The meeting with Peter Linder had ruled out finding an answer to the murder in the illegal gambling world. What was left? Wallander sat down at his desk and tried to write out a new overview of the case. It took him over an hour. He read through what he had written. More and more he was leaning towards the possibility that the man had been let into the shop. It was most likely someone Lamberg knew and trusted. Someone who his widow in all likelihood did not know. He was interrupted in his thoughts by Svedberg knocking on the door.

"Guess where I've been," he said.

Wallander shook his head. He was not in the mood for guessing.

"Matilda Lamberg is cared for at a facility right outside Rydsgärd," he said. "Since it was so close I thought I might as well go out there."

"So you've met Matilda?"

Svedberg immediately became sombre.

"It was terrible," he said. "She is incapable of doing anything."

"You don't have to tell me more," Wallander said. "I think I get the picture."

"Something strange happened," Svedberg continued. "I spoke to the director. A kind-hearted woman who is one of these quiet heroes of the world. I asked her how often Simon Lamberg came to visit."

"What did she say?"

"He had never been there. Not once in all these years."

Wallander said nothing, feeling disturbed.

"Elisabeth Lamberg comes once a week, usually on a Saturday. But that wasn't what was strange."

"Then what was it?"

"The director said that there's another woman who comes to visit. On an irregular basis, but she does turn up on occasion. No one knows her name, no one knows who she is."

Wallander frowned.

An unknown woman.

Suddenly he had a strong feeling. He didn't know where it had come from, but he was convinced. They had finally turned up a clue.

"Good," he said. "Very good. Try to round people up for a meeting."

Wallander had the investigative team assembled at half past eleven. They came in from all over and everyone appeared brimming with the new energy that the fine weather had brought. Just before the meeting, Wallander had received a preliminary report from the medical examiner. It could be presumed that Simon Lamberg had died sometime before midnight. The blow to the back of his head had been delivered with tremendous force and had killed him immediately. In the wound they had recovered tiny slivers of metal that were easily recognisable as brass veneer, so it was now possible to make some assumptions about the murder weapon. A brass statuette or some such thing. Wallander had immediately called Hilda Waldén and asked if there had been any brass objects in the studio. She said no, which was the answer Wallander had wanted. The man who had come to kill Simon Lamberg had brought the murder weapon. This in turn meant that the murder had been planned. It was not something that had arisen from a heated argument or some other sudden impulse.

This was received as an important statement by the investigative squad. They now knew they were looking for a perpetrator who had acted with deliberation. They did not, however, know why he had returned to the scene of the crime. He had most likely left something behind. But Wallander could not let go of the feeling that there may have been another reason, one that they had not yet discovered.

"What would that be?" Hansson asked. "If he hadn't forgotten something? Did he come there to plant something?"

"Which in turn may indicate a degree of forgetfulness," Martinsson said.

They proceeded through the facts slowly and methodically. Most of the case was still very unclear. They were waiting for many answers or had not yet managed to put the information they did have in order. But Wallander wanted everything on the table even now. He knew from experience that detectives on an investigative squad needed to get access to information at the same time. One of his own worst policing sins was that he often kept information to himself. As the years went by he had managed to get a little better in this regard.

"We have a fair number of fingers and shoes," Nyberg said when Wallander as usual turned to him first. "We also have a good thumb on the hymn book. I don't know yet if it matches any of the prints we recovered in the studio."

"Is there anything to say about the hymn book?" Wallander asked.

"It gives the impression of frequent use. But there is no name in it. Nor is there a stamp of any kind to indicate that it belongs to a particular parish or church."

Wallander nodded and looked at Hansson.

"We aren't quite done with the neighbours yet," he began. "But no one that we've talked to has reported hearing or seeing anything unusual. No nightly tumult inside the studio. Nothing out on the street. No one could remember seeing anyone behaving in an unusual manner outside the studio either that night or on any earlier occasion. Everyone has assured us that Simon Lamberg was a pleasant person, although reserved."

"Have any calls come in?"

"Calls are constantly coming in. But there's nothing of any immediate interest."

Wallander asked about the letters that Lamberg had written in which he complained about police performance.

"They're archived in some central location in Stockholm and are being retrieved. There was only one that marginally touched on our district."

"I have trouble evaluating that album," Wallander said. "If it's of any significance or not. It may of course be because I'm included in it. At first I found it disturbing. Now I just don't know any more."

"Other people sit at the kitchen table and write scathing missives to various political leaders," Martinsson said. "Simon Lamberg was a photographer. He didn't write. Symbolically, the darkroom was his kitchen table."

"You may be right. Hopefully, we'll come back to this when we know more."

"Lamberg was a complicated person," Svedberg said. "Pleasant and reserved. But also something else. We just can't articulate what this something else might be."

"No, not yet," Wallander said. "But a picture of him will eventually take shape. It always does."

For his part, Wallander told them about his trip to Malmö and the conversation with Peter Linder.

"I think we can discard the rumours about Lamberg as a gambler," he concluded. "It doesn't seem to have been anything other than just that: rumours."

"I don't see how you can put stock in anything that man says," Martinsson objected.

"He's smart enough to know when he should tell the truth," Wallander said. "He's smart enough not to lie when he doesn't need to."

Then it was Svedberg's turn. He talked about the Stockholm travel agency that was no longer in existence, but he declared firmly that they would be able to locate the driver who had worked on the trip to Austria in March 1981.

"Markresor used a bus company in Alvesta," he said. "And that company is still there. I've checked that."

"Can it really be of any importance?" Hansson asked.

"Maybe," Wallander said. "Or maybe not. But Elisabeth Lamberg was adamant. Her husband was a changed man when he returned."

"Maybe he fell in love," Hansson suggested. "Isn't that what happens on charter trips?"

"For example, something like that," Wallander said and suddenly wondered if that had happened to Mona in the Canary Islands last year.

He turned back to Svedberg.

"Find out about the driver. That may give us something."

Svedberg then told them about his visit to Matilda Lamberg. The mood turned melancholy when they learned that Simon Lamberg had never visited his daughter. The fact that an unknown woman had turned up from time to time was met with less interest. Wallander, however, was convinced that this could be a lead. He had no thoughts about how she fitted into the picture. But he was not planning to drop her until he knew who she was.

Finally they discussed the public image of Simon Lamberg. With every step, the impression of a man living a well-ordered life was reinforced. There were no blemishes either on his finances or elsewhere in his exemplary existence. Wallander reminded the group that someone needed to pay a visit soon to the association of amateur astronomers in Lund that Lamberg had been a member of. Hansson took on this task.

Martinsson was busy with his computer searches. He could only confirm his earlier observations that Simon Lamberg had never had anything to do with the police.

It was past one o'clock. Wallander brought the meeting to a close.

"This is where we are right now," he said. "We still have no motive or any clear indication of who the perpetrator can be. The most important thing, however, is that we are now sure that the killing was planned. The perpetrator had his weapon with him. That means that we can disregard all earlier speculations that it was a burglary gone wrong."

Everyone got up and went his own way. Wallander had decided to go out to the care facility where Matilda Lamberg lived. He was already dreading what would confront him. Sickness, suffering and lifelong handicaps were things he had never dealt with very well. But he wanted to know more about the unknown woman. He left Ystad and took Svartevägen out towards Rydsgård.

The sea glittered temptingly on his left. He rolled down the window and drove slowly.

Suddenly he started to think about Linda, his eighteen-year-old daughter. Right now she was in Stockholm. She wavered between various ideas about what work she should pursue. Furniture refurbisher or physical therapist, or even actress. She and a friend rented an apartment in Kungsholmen. Wallander was not completely clear how she supported herself, but he did know that she waited tables at various restaurants from time to time. When she wasn't in Stockholm, she was with Mona in Malmö. And then she came often but irregularly to Ystad and visited him.

He could tell he was getting worried. At the same time there was so much in her character that he himself lacked. Deep down he had no doubt she would manage to find her own way through life. But the worry was there nonetheless. He couldn't do anything about it.

Wallander stopped in Rydsgård and ate a late lunch at the inn. Pork chops. At the table behind him, some farmers were loudly discussing the pros and cons of a new type of manure-spreading device. Wallander ate, trying to focus completely on his food. It was something that Rydberg had taught him. When he ate, he should think only of what was on his plate. Afterwards it felt as if his head had been aired out, like a house that is opened up after having been shut for a long time.

The care facility was near Rynge. Wallander followed Svedberg's directions and had no trouble finding it. He turned into the car park and stepped out of his car. The

316

facility consisted of a mixture of old and new buildings. He went in through the main entrance. From somewhere a shrill laughter could be heard. A woman was in the middle of watering flowers. Wallander walked over to her and asked to speak to the director.

"That would be me," the woman said and smiled. "My name is Margareta Johansson. And I already know who you are, I've seen you so often in the papers."

She continued watering the flowers. Wallander tried not to pay any attention to her comment about him.

"Sometimes it must be terrible to be a policeman," she went on.

"I can agree with that," Wallander answered. "But I don't think I would want to live in this country if there were no police."

"That's probably true," she said and put down the watering can. "I take it you're here about Matilda Lamberg?"

"Not for her sake, of course. It's about the woman who visits her. The one who isn't her mother."

Margareta Johansson looked at him. A swift wave of concern passed over her face.

"Does this have anything to do with the father's murder?"

"It's not very likely, but I have been wondering who she is."

Margareta Johansson pointed at a half-open door leading to an office.

"We can sit in there."

She asked if Wallander wanted any coffee, and he declined.

"Matilda doesn't get many visitors," she said. "When I came here fourteen years ago, she had already been here six years. Only her mother came to see her. Perhaps another relative on some rare occasion. Matilda doesn't really notice if she has a visitor. She is blind, with poor hearing, and she doesn't react much to what goes on around her. But we still wish that those who reside here for many years, perhaps their whole lives, receive visits. Perhaps simply to give a feeling that they do in fact belong? In the larger context."

"When did this woman begin her visits?"

Margareta Johansson thought back.

"Seven or eight years ago."

"How often does she come?"

"It has always been very irregular. Sometimes half a year has gone by between visits."

"And she has never given her name?"

"Never. Only that she is here to see Matilda."

"I assume you have informed Elisabeth Lamberg about this?"

"Yes."

"How did she react?"

"With surprise. She has also enquired as to who the woman is, and has asked us to call and tell her as soon as she arrives. The problem is simply that the woman's visits have always been very brief. Elisabeth Lamberg has never managed to get here before the woman has left."

"How does the woman get here?"

"By car."

"That she has driven herself?"

318

"I have never actually thought about that. Perhaps there has been someone else in the car that no one has noticed."

"I assume that there isn't anyone who might have noticed what type of car it was? Or even made a note of the number plate?"

Margareta Johansson shook her head.

"Could you describe the woman to me?"

"She is between forty and fifty years old. Slender, not particularly tall. Simply but tastefully dressed. Short, blonde hair. No make-up."

Wallander jotted this down.

"Is there anything else you've noticed about her?"

"No."

Wallander stood up.

"Don't you want to meet Matilda?" she asked.

"I don't think I have the time," Wallander said evasively. "But most likely I'll be back here again. And I want you to notify the Ystad police if that woman returns. When was she here last?"

"A few months ago."

She followed him outside. A nurse's assistant walked by pushing a wheelchair. Wallander caught sight of a shrunken boy under a blanket.

"Everyone feels better in the spring," Margareta Johansson said. "We can see it even in our patients, who are often completely sealed in their own worlds."

Wallander said goodbye and walked over to his car. He had just started the engine when the telephone rang in Margareta Johansson's office. She called out that it was Svedberg. Wallander walked back in and took the receiver.

"I've tracked down the driver," Svedberg said. "It was easier than I had dared hope. His name is Anton Eklund."

"Good," Wallander said.

"It gets better. Guess what he told me? That he has the habit of keeping the passenger lists of all his trips. And that he has pictures from this particular one."

"Taken by Simon Lamberg?"

"How did you know?"

"I did what you told me. I guessed."

"To top it off, he lives in Trelleborg. He's retired these days. But we have a standing invitation to look him up."

"We should absolutely take him up on that. As soon as possible."

But first Wallander had another visit to think about. One that couldn't be put off.

From Rynge he was planning to drive straight to Elisabeth Lamberg's house.

He had a question he wanted an immediate answer to.

She was out in the garden when he pulled up. She was bent over the flower beds. Her grief over her recent loss was apparently neither deep nor long-lasting; as he listened over the fence, he thought he could hear her humming. As Wallander opened the gate, she heard him and straightened up. She held a little shovel in her hand and squinted in the sunlight.

320

"I'm sorry I had to come back and bother you again so soon," Wallander said. "But I have an urgent question."

She put the shovel down in a basket next to her.

"Should we go in?"

"It's not necessary."

She pointed to some deckchairs that were nearby. They sat down.

"I've talked to the director of the nursing home where Matilda is," Wallander began. "I went there."

"Did you see Matilda?"

"Unfortunately, I had very little time."

He didn't want to tell her the truth. That it was almost impossible for him to confront the seriously handicapped.

"We talked about the unknown woman who comes to visit her."

Elisabeth Lamberg had put on a pair of dark glasses. He could not see her eyes.

"When we spoke about Matilda last time, you never mentioned anything about this woman. That surprises me. It makes me curious. Above all, it strikes me as strange."

"I didn't think it was important."

Wallander hesitated over how hard or direct to be. After all, her husband was brutally murdered a couple of days ago.

"It's not the case, then, that you know who the woman is? And that you for some reason don't want to talk about her?"

She took off her sunglasses and looked at him.

"I have no idea who she is. I've tried to find out, but I haven't been successful."

"What have you done in order to find out about her?"

"The only thing I could do, which is to ask the staff to call me as soon as she appears. Which they have. But I've never made it out there in time."

"You could of course have asked the staff not to let her in? Or given orders that she was not allowed to visit Matilda without providing a name?"

Elisabeth Lamberg looked confused.

"She did give her name, the first time she was there. Didn't the director tell you that?"

"No."

"She introduced herself as Siv Stigberg, and she said she lived in Lund, but I haven't been able to find anyone by that name there. I've looked into it. I've looked through telephone directories for the entire country. There is a Siv Stigberg in Kramfors, and another in Motala. I've even been in touch with both of them. Neither one understood what I was talking about."

"She gave a false name? That must have been why Margareta Johansson didn't say anything."

"Yes. That's the only reason I can imagine."

Wallander reflected on this. He now believed that she was telling the truth.

"The whole thing is remarkable. I still don't understand why you didn't tell me this from the start."

"I realise now that I should have."

"You must have really wondered who she was, why she was paying these visits."

"Of course. That was why I instructed the director to let her keep visiting Matilda. I was hoping to make it in time one day."

"What does she do when she's there?"

"She only stays a short while. Looks at Matilda, but never says anything. Even though Matilda can hear when someone talks to her."

"Did you ever ask your husband about her?"

Her voice was filled with bitterness when she answered.

"Why should I have done that? He wasn't interested in Matilda. She didn't exist."

Wallander got up out of the deckchair.

"Nonetheless, I have an answer to my question," he said.

He went straight to the station. The feeling of urgency was suddenly very strong. It was already late afternoon. Svedberg was in his office.

"Now we go to Trelleborg," Wallander said from the doorway. "Do you have the driver's address?"

"Anton Eklund lives in an apartment in the middle of town."

"It's probably best if you call and ask if he's home."

Svedberg looked up the number. Eklund picked up almost immediately.

"We can come any time," Svedberg said when he had finished the brief conversation.

They took his car, which was better than Wallander's. Svedberg drove quickly and confidently. Wallander travelled west along Strandvägen for the second time that day. He told Svedberg about his visits to the nursing home and Elisabeth Lamberg.

"I can't escape the feeling that this woman is important," he said. "And that she definitely has something to do with Simon Lamberg."

They continued on in silence. Wallander enjoyed the view, some-what distractedly. He also dozed off for a moment. His cheek no longer hurt, although it was still discoloured. His tongue had also started to get used to the temporary crown.

Svedberg only needed to ask for directions once in order to find Eklund's address in Trelleborg. It was a red-brick apartment building in the centre of town. Eklund was on the ground floor. He had spotted them and was waiting with an open door. He was a large man with abundant grey hair. When he shook Wallander's hand, he squeezed so hard it almost hurt. He invited them into the small apartment. Coffee had been set out. Wallander immediately assumed that Eklund lived on his own. The apartment was tidy but nonetheless projected the impression of a single man living alone. He had this idea confirmed as soon as he sat down.

"I've been on my own for the past three years," he said. "My wife died. That was when I moved here. We only had one year together in retirement. One morning she lay dead in the bed."

Neither of the detectives said anything. There was nothing to say. Eklund picked up the plate of pastries. Wallander chose a piece of Bundt cake.

"You were the driver on a charter bus trip to Austria in 1981," he started. "Markresor were the organisers. You left from Norra Bantorget in Stockholm, with Austria as your final destination."

"We were going to Salzburg and Vienna. Thirty-two passengers, one travel director and me. The bus was a Scania, completely new."

"I thought that bus trips to the Continent went out of vogue after the 1960s," Svedberg said.

"They did," Eklund said. "But they came back. Markresor — Ground Travel — may seem like a silly name for a travel agency, but they were on the right track. There turned out to be a lot of people who absolutely did not want to go up in the air and be tossed to some distant holiday destination. There were people who really wanted to experience travelling. And for that you have to stay on the ground."

"I've heard that you kept the passenger lists," Wallander said.

"It became an obsession," Eklund said. "I look through them sometimes. I don't remember most of them. Some names bring out memories. Most of them good, some that you'd rather forget."

He got up and reached for a plastic sleeve on a shelf. He held it out to Wallander. It contained a list of thirty-two names. He picked out the name Lamberg almost immediately. He went slowly through the rest of the names, none of which had appeared in the context of the investigation before. More than half of the passengers came from the middle of Sweden. There was also a couple from Härnösand, a woman from Luleå, as

325

well as seven individuals from southern Sweden. From Halmstad, Eslöv and Lund. Wallander passed the list to Svedberg.

"You said you had pictures from the trip? That Lamberg had taken?"

"Because of his profession, he was appointed our official photographer. He took almost all of the shots. Those who wanted copies wrote their names on a list. Everyone received what they had ordered. He kept his promises."

Eklund lifted a newspaper. Under it there was an envelope with photographs.

"Lamberg gave me all of these free of charge. He had chosen them himself. I wasn't the one who picked them out."

Wallander slowly looked through the stack of pictures. There were nineteen in all. He already sensed that Lamberg would not appear in any of them, since he had been behind the camera. But in the second-to-last one he appeared in a group shot. On the back someone had written that the photo had been taken in a rest area between Salzburg and Vienna. Even Eklund was in it. Wallander assumed that Lamberg had used a timer. He went through the stack one more time. Studied details and faces. Suddenly he noticed a woman's face that appeared again and again. She always stared straight into the camera. And smiled. When Wallander looked at her features, he had the feeling that there was something familiar about it, without being able to put his finger on what it was.

He asked Svedberg to take a look at them.

"What do you remember of Lamberg from that trip?"

"To begin with I didn't notice him very much. But then there was plenty of drama."

Svedberg looked up quickly.

"What do you mean?" Wallander asked.

"Maybe one shouldn't talk about these kinds of things," Eklund said hesitantly. "He's dead now. But he got together with one of the ladies on the trip. And it was not an uncomplicated matter."

"Why not?"

"Because she was married. And her husband was there."

Wallander let this sink in.

"There was something else," Eklund said, "that probably didn't help matters much."

"What was that?"

"She was a minister's wife. He was a man of the Church."

Eklund pointed him out in one of the pictures. The hymn book flashed through Wallander's head. He realised he was sweating. He glanced at Svedberg. He had the feeling his colleague was having the same associations.

Wallander grabbed the stack of photographs, taking out one where the unknown woman was smiling at the camera.

"Is this her?" he asked.

Eklund looked at it and nodded.

"It is. Can you imagine? A minister's wife from a parish outside Lund."

Wallander looked at Svedberg again.

"How did the whole thing end?"

"I don't know. And I'm not even sure if the minister discovered what was going on behind his back. To me he seemed very unaware of worldly things. But the whole situation on the trip was very uncomfortable."

Wallander looked at the image of the woman. Suddenly he knew who she was.

"What is the name of this family?"

"Wislander. Anders and Louise."

Svedberg studied the passenger list and wrote down their address.

"We need to borrow these photos for a while," Wallander said. "You'll get them back of course."

Eklund nodded.

"I hope I haven't said too much," he said.

"Quite the opposite. You've been a big help."

They said goodbye, thanked him for the coffee and walked out onto the street.

"This woman fits the description of the woman who visits Matilda Lamberg," Wallander said. "I want to confirm that it is her, as soon as possible. Why she visits Matilda, I don't know. But that will have to be a later question."

They hurried to the car and left Trelleborg. Before they left, however, Wallander called Ystad from a phone booth and, after considerable effort, managed to get hold of Martinsson. Wallander quickly explained what had happened and asked Martinsson to find out if Anders Wislander was still minister of a parish outside Lund.

They would come in to the station as soon as they had been to Rynge.

"Do you think she could be the one?" Svedberg asked later.

Wallander sat silent for a long time before answering.

"No," he said finally. "But it could be him."

Svedberg glanced at him.

"A minister?"

Wallander nodded.

"Why not? Ministers are ministers, but also human. Of course it's possible. And aren't there any number of brass objects in a church?"

They stopped only briefly in Rynge. The director immediately identified the unknown woman in the picture Wallander showed her. Then they continued on to the station in Ystad and went straight into Martinsson's office. Hansson was also there.

"Anders Wislander is still a minister outside Lund," Martinsson said. "But right now he's on sick leave."

"Why?" Wallander asked.

"Because of personal tragedy."

Wallander looked searchingly at him.

"What happened?"

"His wife died about a month ago."

The room fell silent.

Wallander held his breath. He didn't know anything for sure, and yet he was now convinced they were on the right track. They would find the solution to the case, at least in part, with the minister Anders Wislander in Lund. He sensed a context unfolding.

329

Wallander and his colleagues went into the conference room. Nyberg had also appeared from somewhere. During the meeting, Wallander was very firm in his approach. They were to focus completely on Anders Wislander and his dead wife. That evening they tried to find out as much as possible about the couple. Wallander had ordered everyone to proceed with caution, to be as discreet as possible. When Hansson had suggested that they should contact Wislander that evening, Wallander had summarily dismissed it. That could wait until the following day. The task at hand was to take care of as much groundwork as possible.

This was not to say there was very much they could actually clarify. Rather, their task was to sift through what they already knew and introduce Anders and Louise Wislander as a grid over the known circumstances of Simon Lamberg's death.

They could, after all, establish a great deal. Svedberg managed, with the help of a reporter, to locate the obituary of Louise Wislander in *Sydsvenska Dagbladet*. From this they learned that she had been forty-seven at the time of her death. "After drawn-out and patient suffering," the obituary said. They went back and forth on what this phrase meant. She could hardly have committed suicide. Perhaps it had been cancer. In a death announcement they noted two children among the grieving. They discussed at length whether they should notify their colleagues in Lund. Wallander hesitated, but decided against it. It was still too early.

A little after eight, Wallander asked Nyberg to do something that did not ordinarily fall under his responsibilities. But Wallander turned to him, because he felt he needed to keep the others close by. Nyberg was assigned the task of finding out if Wislander's home address was a free-standing house or an apartment. Nyberg left. They sat down to conduct a fresh review. A pizza had been ordered from somewhere. While they ate, Wallander tried to come up with an interpretation where Anders Wislander was the perpetrator.

There were many objections. The professed love affair between Simon Lamberg and Louise Wislander lay several years back in time. In addition, she was deceased. Why would Anders Wislander react at this late stage? Was there even anything that indicated that he had this capacity for violence? Wallander realised that all of these objections were major. He wavered, but did not relinquish his conviction that they were nonetheless close to the answer.

"The only thing we have left is to talk to Wislander," he said. "And we'll do that tomorrow. Then we'll see."

Nyberg returned. He informed Wallander that Wislander lived in a free-standing house owned by the Church of Sweden. Since he was on leave, Wallander assumed they would find him at home. Before they broke up for the evening, Wallander decided to take Martinsson with him the next day. They did not need to be more than two.

He drove home through the spring warmth around midnight. He took the street past St Gertrude's Square. Everything was very still. A wave of melancholy and fatigue washed over him. For a moment, the world appeared to consist entirely of sickness and death. And an emptiness left by Mona. But then he thought about spring having arrived at last. He shook off his distress. They were going to speak to Wislander tomorrow. Then they would know if they were closer to a solution or not.

He stayed up for a long time. He had the urge to call both Linda and Mona. Around one o'clock he boiled a couple of eggs that he ate standing in front of the sink. Before he went to bed he studied his face in the bathroom mirror. His cheek was still discoloured. He also saw that he needed a haircut.

He slept badly and got up at five o'clock. While he waited for Martinsson to arrive he sorted through the mountain of laundry and vacuumed the apartment. He had several cups of coffee, standing at the kitchen window, once again reviewing all the circumstances of Simon Lamberg's death.

At eight o'clock he walked down to the street and waited. It was going to be yet another beautiful spring day. Martinsson was punctual as usual. Wallander got into the car. They drove towards Lund.

"I slept badly for once," Martinsson said. "I don't usually. But it was as if I had a premonition."

"A premonition about what?"

"I don't know."

"It's probably just spring."

Martinsson glanced over at him.

"What do you mean, 'just spring'?"

Wallander didn't reply, just muttered something under his breath.

332

They arrived in Lund shortly before nine-thirty. As usual, Martinsson had driven jerkily and with poor concentration. But apparently he had memorised the directions. He had no trouble finding the street where Wislander lived. They drove past number 19 and parked the car out of sight.

"Let's go," Wallander said. "Let me do all the talking."

The house was large. Wallander guessed that it dated to the beginning of the century. As they walked in through the gate he noticed that the garden needed attention. He saw that Martinsson had noticed the same thing. Wallander rang the doorbell, wondering what awaited them. He rang again. No one opened. More rings. Same response: nothing. Wallander made a quick decision.

"Wait here. Not by the house, out in the street. His church isn't far from here. I'll take your car."

Wallander had written down the name of the church. Svedberg had pointed it out on a map last night. It took him five minutes to get there. The church looked abandoned. At first he thought he was mistaken. Anders Wislander wasn't there. But when he tried the church doors, they were unlocked. He stepped into the dim vestibule and pulled the door shut behind him. It was very quiet. No sound from the outside penetrated the thick walls. Wallander walked into the main church space. It was well lit in there. The sun streamed in through the tinted stained-glass windows.

Wallander saw that someone was sitting in the front row, closest to the altar. He walked slowly down the aisle. A man was sitting there, hunched over, as if in prayer. Only when Wallander had reached the front did he look up. Wallander recognised him. It was Anders Wislander. The face was the same as in the only one of Lamberg's photographs in which he appeared. He was unshaven and his eyes were moist. Wallander immediately started to feel ill at ease. He now regretted having left Martinsson behind.

"Anders Wislander?" he asked.

The man stared back at him earnestly.

"Who are you?"

"My name is Kurt Wallander and I'm with the police. I'd like to talk to you."

Wislander's voice suddenly became shrill and impatient when he answered.

"I am grieving. You are disturbing me. Leave me in peace."

Wallander felt his discomfort grow. The man in the pew appeared close to a breaking point.

"I know that your wife is dead," he said. "That's what I want to talk to you about."

Wislander stood up from his seat so forcefully that Wallander shrank back. Now he was certain that Wislander was unbalanced.

"You disturb me and do not leave although I ask you. Therefore I must listen to what you have to say," he said. "We can go into the sacristy."

Wislander showed the way and turned left when he reached the altar. Wallander observed from his back that he appeared unusually strong. This could have been the man he had tried to catch up with and who had knocked him down.

There was a little table and a couple of chairs in the sacristy. Wislander sat down and pointed at the other chair. Wallander pulled it out from under the table, wondering how he should begin. Wislander stared at him with his moist eyes. Wallander glanced around the room. On another table there were two large candelabra. Wallander studied them without first knowing what it was that had caught his attention. Then he saw that one was different from the other. One of the arms of one candelabrum was missing. And it was made of brass. He looked at Wislander, and realised that the man was aware of what Wallander had seen. Nonetheless the attack took him by surprise. Wislander threw himself at Wallander with something like a roar. His fingers dug into his neck and his strength, or his insanity, was great. Wallander struggled against him while Wislander shouted things incomprehensibly, something about Simon Lamberg, that the photographer had to die. Then Wislander, in his delirium, started in on a diatribe about the riders of the Apocalypse. Wallander struggled to free himself. Finally, with enormous effort, he managed to do so. But then Wislander was on him again, like an animal fighting for its life. During their wrestling match, they reached the table with the candelabra. Wallander managed to grab one and strike Wislander in the face. Wislander immediately collapsed. For a moment, Wallander believed he had killed him. The same way that Lamberg had died. But then he saw that Wislander was breathing.

Wallander sank down on a chair and tried to catch his breath. He noticed that his face was scratched up. The repaired tooth had broken for the third time.

Wislander lay on the floor. Slowly he started to regain consciousness. At the same moment Wallander heard the church door open.

He left the sacristy to meet Martinsson, who had got worried and called a taxi from the house of one of the neighbours.

Everything had happened very fast, but Wallander knew it was now over. He had also recognised Wislander as the man who had attacked him. He had recognised him without ever really having seen his face. But it was him, there was no doubt about that.

A couple of days later Wallander had a meeting with his colleagues in the conference room. It was the afternoon. A window was open. The spring warmth appeared to have arrived for good. Wallander had completed his questioning of Anders Wislander, at least for the moment. The man was now in such poor psychological shape that a physician had advised Wallander to stop. But the picture was complete. Wallander had called this meeting in order to provide them with an overview of what had happened.

"It is dark and sombre and tragic," he began. "But Simon Lamberg and Louise Wislander continued to meet in secret after that bus trip. And Louise's husband knew nothing of it. Until recently, shortly before she died. She had a tumour on her liver. On her deathbed she confessed her infidelity. Wislander had then been overcome by something that can only be described as insanity. In part, grief over his wife's death, in part rage and anguish over her betrayal. He started stalking Lamberg. In his mind, Lamberg was also guilty of his wife's death. He took sick leave and spent almost all his time here in Ystad. He kept the studio under surveillance, staying at one of the small hotels in town. He followed the cleaning lady, Hilda Waldén. One Saturday, he broke into her apartment, took the keys, and had them copied. Before she returned, he replaced the originals. Then he entered the studio and killed Lamberg with the candelabrum. After that, in his confusion, he still believed that Lamberg was alive. He actually returned in order to kill him a second time. He dropped the hymn book when he was hiding in the garden. The fact that he turned on the radio and changed the setting is a bizarre detail. He had apparently started imagining that he would be able to hear God's voice through the radio. That God would forgive him for the sin he had committed. But all he managed to find was a station that broadcast rock music. The photographs were Lamberg's work through and through. They had nothing to do with the death He nourished a contempt for politicians and other powerful men. In addition, he was displeased with the work of the police. He was a curmudgeon. A little man who tried to control his world by deforming faces. But this solves our case. I can't help pitying Wislander. His world collapsed. He didn't have the strength to bear it."

The room was silent.

"Why did Louise visit Lamberg's handicapped daughter?" Hansson asked.

"I've been asking myself that," Wallander answered. "Perhaps her love affair had religious undertones. Perhaps the two of them were involved in praying for Matilda? Did Louise then go to the nursing home in order to check the effect of her prayers? Perhaps she regarded Matilda as the victim of her parents' earlier sinful life? We'll never know. As little as we'll ever know what bound these two singular people together. There are always secret rooms that we don't manage to find a way into. And perhaps that's for the best."

"One can take a step further," Rydberg said, "if you think about Wislander. Perhaps his rage actually stemmed from the fact that Lamberg had seduced his wife from a religious perspective. Not erotically. One has reason to question if it was only the usual jealousy that played a role in this case."

Again, there was silence. Then they went on to discuss Lamberg's pictures.

"He must have been crazy in his own way," Hansson said. "To spend his spare time distorting images of well-known people."

"Perhaps the explanation is quite different," Rydberg suggested. "Perhaps there are people in today's society that feel so powerless they no longer partake in what we call democratic society. Instead they devote themselves to rites. If this is the case, our nation is in trouble."

"I hadn't considered that possibility," Wallander said. "But you could be right. And in that case I agree with you. Then the foundation has really started to crack."

338

The meeting came to an end. Wallander felt tired and despondent, despite the beautiful weather. And he missed Mona.

Then he checked the time. A quarter past four.

He had to go back to the dentist.

How many times it had been, he no longer knew.

THE PYRAMID

PROLOGUE

The aeroplane flew in over Sweden at a low altitude just west of Mossby Beach. The fog was thick out at sea but growing lighter closer to shore. Contours of the shoreline and the first few houses rushed towards the pilot. But he had already made this trip many times. He was flying by instruments alone. As soon as he crossed the Swedish border and identified Mossby Beach and the lights along the road to Trelleborg, he made a sharp turn north-east and then another turn east. The plane, a Piper Cherokee, was obedient. He positioned himself along a route that had been carefully planned. An air corridor cut an invisible path over an area in Skåne where the houses were few and far between. It was a little before five o'clock on the morning of 11 December 1989. Around him there was an almost solid darkness. Every time he flew at night he thought about his first few years, when he had worked as a co-pilot for a Greek company that had transported tobacco at night and in secret from what had then been Southern Rhodesia, restricted by political sanctions. That had been in 1966 and 1967. More than twenty years ago. But the memory never left him. That was when he had

343

learned that a skilled pilot can fly even at night, with a minimum of aids, and in complete radio silence.

The plane was now flying so low that the pilot did not dare to take it any lower. He began to wonder if he would have to turn back without completing his mission. That happened sometimes. Safety always came first and visibility was still bad. But suddenly, right before the pilot would have been forced to make his decision, the fog lifted. He checked the time. In two minutes he would see the lights where he was supposed to make his drop. He turned round and shouted out to the man who was sitting on the only chair left in the cabin.

"Two minutes!"

The man behind him in the darkness directed a torch into his own face and nodded.

The pilot peered out into the darkness. One minute to go now, he thought. And that was when he saw the spotlights that formed a square of two hundred metres per side. He shouted to the man to make himself ready. Then he prepared for a left turn and approached the lighted square from the west. He felt the cold wind and light shaking of the fuselage as the man behind him opened the cabin door. Then he put his hand on the switch that glowed red in the back of the cabin. He had decreased his speed as much as possible. Then he threw the switch, the light changed to green, and he knew that the man back there was pushing out the rubber-clad cistern. The cold wind stopped when the door shut. At that point, the pilot had already changed his course to the south-east. He smiled to himself. The cistern had

344

landed now, somewhere between the spotlights. Someone was there to collect it. The lights would be turned off and loaded onto a truck, and then the darkness would become as compact and impenetrable as before. A perfect operation, he thought. The nineteenth in a row.

He checked his watch. In nine minutes they would pass over the coast and leave Sweden again. After another ten minutes he would rise another several hundred metres. He had a Thermos with coffee next to his seat. He would drink it as they crossed the sea. At eight o'clock he would set his plane down on his private landing strip outside Kiel, and then get into his car and already be on his way to Hamburg, where he lived.

The aeroplane lurched once. And then again. The pilot checked his instrument panel. Everything seemed normal. The headwind was not particularly strong, nor was there any turbulence. Then the plane lurched a third time, more strongly. The pilot worked the rudder, but the plane rolled onto its left side. He tried to correct it without success. The instruments were still normal. But his extensive experience told him that something wasn't right. He could not straighten the plane up. Although he was increasing his speed, the plane was losing altitude. He tried to think with complete calm. What could have happened? He always examined a plane before he took off. When he had arrived at the hangar at one o'clock in the morning, he had spent over half an hour examining it, going through all the lists that the mechanic provided, and then he had followed all the directions on the checklist before take-off.

He was unable to straighten the plane. The twisting continued. Now he knew the situation was serious. He increased his speed even more and tried to compensate with the rudder. The man in the back shouted and asked what was wrong. The pilot didn't reply. He had no answer. If he didn't manage to steady the plane they would crash in a few minutes. Right before they reached the sea. He was working with a pounding heart now. But nothing helped. Then came a brief moment of rage and hopelessness. Then he continued to pull on the levers and push the foot pedals until everything was over.

The aeroplane struck the ground with vehement force at nineteen minutes past five on the morning of the eleventh of December, 1989. It immediately burst into flame. But the two men on board did not notice their bodies catching fire. They had died — torn into pieces — at the moment of impact.

The fog had come rolling in from the sea. It was four degrees above zero and there was almost no breeze.

CHAPTER
ONE

Wallander woke up shortly after six o'clock on the morning of the eleventh of December. At the same moment that he opened his eyes, his alarm clock went off. He turned it off and lay staring out into the dark. Stretched his arms and legs, spread his fingers and toes. That had become a habit, to feel if the night had left him with any aches. He swallowed in order to check if any infection had sneaked into his respiratory system. He wondered sometimes if he was slowly becoming a hypochondriac. But this morning everything seemed in order, and for once he was completely rested. He had gone to bed early the night before, at ten o'clock, and had fallen asleep immediately. And once he fell asleep, he slept. But if he ended up lying there awake it could take many hours for him to eventually find some rest.

He got out of bed and walked into the kitchen. The thermometer read six degrees above zero. Since he knew it showed the wrong temperature, he was able to calculate that he would greet the world at four degrees this day. He looked up at the sky. Ribbons of fog wafted by above the rooftops. No snow had fallen in Skåne yet this winter. But it is coming, he thought. Sooner or later, the snowstorms arrive.

He made coffee and some sandwiches. As usual, his fridge was basically empty. Prior to going to bed he had written a shopping list that now lay on the kitchen table. While he was waiting for the coffee, he went to the bathroom. When he returned to the kitchen, he added toilet paper to the list. And a new brush for the toilet. He skimmed the *Ystad Allehanda* that he had picked up from the hall while he ate breakfast. He only paused when he reached the back page with the advertisements. Somewhere in the back of his mind there was a vague longing for a house in the country. Where he could walk straight outside in the morning and piss on the grass. Where he could have a dog, and maybe — this dream was the most remote — a dovecote. There were several houses for sale, but none that interested him. Then he saw that some Labrador puppies were for sale in Rydsgård. I can't start at the wrong end, he thought. First a house, then a dog. Not the other way round. Otherwise I'll have nothing but problems, the work hours that I keep, as long as I don't live with anyone who could help out. It was now two months since Mona had definitively left him. Deep inside he still refused to accept what had happened. At the same time he didn't know what to do to get her to come back.

He was ready to leave at seven o'clock. He selected the sweater he usually wore when it was zero to eight degrees Celsius. He had sweaters for various temperatures and was very selective about what he wore. He hated being cold in the damp Skåne winter and he was annoyed the minute he started to sweat. He thought it

348

affected his ability to think. Then he decided to walk to the station. He needed to move. When he stepped outside he felt a faint breeze from the sea. The walk from Mariagatan took him ten minutes.

While he walked he thought about the day ahead. If nothing in particular had occurred during the day, which was his constant prayer, he would question a suspected drug dealer who had been brought in yesterday. There were also constant piles on his desk with current investigations that he should do something about. Looking into the export to Poland of stolen luxury cars was one of the most thankless of his ongoing assignments.

He walked in through the glass doors of the station and nodded at Ebba sitting at the reception desk. He saw that she had permed her hair.

"Beautiful as always," he said.

"I do what I can," she replied. "But you should watch out so you don't start putting on weight. Divorced men often do."

Wallander nodded. He knew she was right. After the divorce from Mona he had started to eat more irregularly and poorly. Every day he told himself he would break his bad habits, without any success so far. He walked to his office, hung up his coat and sat down at his desk.

The telephone rang at that moment. He lifted the receiver. It was Martinsson. Wallander was not surprised. The two of them were the homicide division's earliest risers.

"I think we have to drive out to Mossby," Martinsson said.

"What's happened?"

"A plane has crashed."

Wallander felt a pang in his chest. His first thought was that it must be a commercial airliner coming in for landing or taking off from Sturup. Then it meant a catastrophe, perhaps with many fatalities.

"A small sport plane," Martinsson went on.

Wallander exhaled, while cursing Martinsson for not being able to provide him with a clear sense of the situation from the start.

"The call came in a while ago," Martinsson said. "The fire brigade is already on the scene. Apparently the plane was in flames."

Wallander nodded into the receiver.

"I'm on my way," he said. "Who else do we have in the field?"

"No one, as far as I know. But the patrol units are there, of course."

"Then you and I will go first."

They met in the reception area. Just as they were about to leave, Rydberg walked in. He had rheumatism and looked pale. Wallander quickly told him what had happened.

"You two go on ahead," Rydberg replied. "I have to go to the toilet before I do anything else."

Martinsson and Wallander left the station and walked over to Martinsson's car.

"He looked ill," Martinsson said.

"He is ill," Wallander said. "Rheumatism. And then there's something else. Something with his urinary system, I think."

They took the coastal road going west.

"Give me the details," Wallander said while he stared out at the sea. Ragged clouds were still drifting across the water.

"There are no details," Martinsson said. "The plane crashed some time around half past five. It was a farmer who called. Apparently the crash site is just north of Mossby, out in a field."

"Do we know how many were in the plane?"

"No."

"Sturup must have issued a dispatch about a missing plane. If the plane crashed in Mossby, the pilot must have had radio contact with the control tower in Sturup."

"That was my thought too," Martinsson said. "That's why I contacted the control tower just before I called you."

"What did they say?"

"They aren't missing any planes."

Wallander looked at Martinsson.

"What does that mean?"

"I don't know," Martinsson said. "It should be an impossibility, to fly in Swedish airspace without an assigned flight path and continuous radio contact with various towers."

"Sturup received no emergency transmission? The pilot must have radioed if he ran into problems.

Doesn't it usually take at least a couple of seconds before a plane hits the ground?"

"I don't know," Martinsson answered. "I don't know more than what I've told you."

Wallander shook his head. Then he wondered what lay in store for him. He had seen a plane accident before, also a small plane. The pilot had been alone. The plane had crashed north of Ystad and the pilot had literally been torn to pieces, but the plane had not burned.

Wallander was filled with dread at the prospect of what awaited him. The day's morning prayer had been in vain.

When they got to Mossby Beach, Martinsson turned to the right and pointed. Wallander had already seen the pillar of smoke that rose to the sky.

They arrived a few minutes later. The plane had come down in the middle of a muddy field, about one hundred metres from a farmhouse. Wallander assumed that it was from there that the call had been made. The firefighters were still spraying foam on the wreck. Martinsson took a pair of wellingtons from the boot. Wallander looked unhappily down at his own shoes, a pair of winter boots, almost brand new. Then they started to make their way through the slippery mud. The man in charge of the fire crew was Peter Edler. Wallander had met him on numerous occasions. He liked him. It was easy for them to work together. Apart from the two fire engines and the ambulance, there was also a patrol car. Wallander nodded at Peters, a patrol officer. Then he turned to Peter Edler.

"What do we have?" he asked.

"Two dead," Edler replied. "I have to warn you that it is not a pretty sight. That's what happens when people burn in petrol."

"You don't have to warn me," Wallander said. "I know what that looks like."

Martinsson came up next to Wallander.

"Find out who made the call," Wallander said. "Probably someone in that farm over there. Find out what the time was. And then someone has to have a serious talk with the control tower at Sturup."

Martinsson nodded and set off towards the farm. Wallander approached the plane. It was lying on its left side, embedded in the mud. The left wing had been torn off completely and had broken into several parts that were strewn out across the field. The right wing was still intact near the fuselage but had been broken off at the tip. Wallander observed that it was a single-engine plane. The propeller was bent and driven deep into the ground. He slowly circled the plane. It was black with soot and covered in foam. He waved Edler over.

"Is it possible to remove the foam?" he asked. "Don't aeroplanes tend to have some kind of markings on the fuselage and under the wings?"

"I think we should let the foam stay on a while longer," Edler said. "You never know with petrol. There may still be some left in the fuel tanks."

Wallander knew he had no choice but to obey Edler's directives. He walked closer and peered into the plane. Edler had been right. It was impossible to discern any facial features. He circled the plane one more time. Then he lumbered out into the muddy field where the largest piece of wing lay. He crouched down. He could not make out any numbers or letter combinations. It was still very dark. He called out to Peters and asked for a torch. Then he studied the wing intently. Scraped the outside with his fingertips. It appeared to have been painted over. Could that mean that someone had wanted to conceal the identity of the plane?

He stood up. He was jumping to conclusions again. It was Nyberg and his team's job to sort this out. He looked over absently at Martinsson, who was making his way to the farm with deliberate strides. Several cars with curious onlookers had pulled over by a dirt road. Peters and his partner were trying to convince them to keep going. Yet another police car had arrived, with Hansson, Rydberg and Nyberg. Wallander walked over and said hello. Explained the situation in brief and asked Hansson to cordon off the area.

"You have two bodies inside the plane," Wallander repeated to Nyberg, who would be responsible for the preliminary forensic investigation.

Eventually, an accident commission would be appointed to investigate the cause of the crash. But at that point Wallander would no longer have to be involved.

"I think it looks as if the wing that was torn off had been repainted," he said. "As if someone wanted to eliminate all possibility of identifying the plane."

Nyberg nodded mutely. He never wasted his words.

Rydberg appeared behind Wallander.

"One shouldn't have to tramp around in the mud at my age," he said. "And this damned rheumatism."

Wallander threw a quick glance at him.

"You didn't have to come out here," he said. "We can handle it. Then the accident commission can take over."

"I'm not dead yet," Rydberg said with irritation. "But who the hell knows . . ." He didn't finish the sentence. Instead he made his way over to the plane, bent down and looked in.

"This one will have to be dental," he said. "I don't think there will be any other way of getting a positive ID."

Wallander ran through the main points for Rydberg's benefit. They worked well together and never had to give each other lengthy explanations. Rydberg was also the one who had taught Wallander what he now knew about being a criminal investigator. That is, after the foundation had been laid in Malmö with Hemberg, who sadly had died in a traffic accident last year. Wallander had departed from his usual habit of never attending funerals and attended the ceremony in Malmö. But after Hemberg, Rydberg had been his role model. They had worked together for many years now. Wallander had often thought that Rydberg must be one of the most skilful criminal investigators in Sweden. Nothing escaped him, no hypothesis was so outlandish that Rydberg did not test it. His ability to read a crime scene always surprised Wallander, who greedily absorbed it all.

Rydberg was single. He did not have much of a social life and did not appear to want one. Wallander was still, after all these years, not sure if Rydberg actually had any interests apart from his work.

On the occasional warm evening in early summer, they would sometimes get together and sit on Rydberg's balcony and drink whisky. Often in a pleasant silence that was broken from time to time with some comment about work.

"Martinsson is trying to establish some clarity with regard to the time of the events," Wallander said. "Then it seems to me that we have to find out why the control tower at Sturup didn't raise the alarm."

"You mean, why the pilot didn't raise the alarm," Rydberg corrected him.

"Maybe he didn't have time?"

"It doesn't take many seconds to send an SOS," Rydberg said. "But you must be right. The plane would have been flying in an assigned air lane. If it wasn't flying illegally, of course."

"Illegally?"

Rydberg shrugged.

"You know the rumours," he said. "People hear aeroplane noise at night. Low-flying, darkened planes slipping covertly into these areas close to the border. At least that's how it was during the Cold War. Perhaps it's not completely over yet. Sometimes we get reports about suspected espionage. And then you can always question if all drugs actually come in by way of the sound. We will never know for sure about this plane. It may simply be our imagination. But if you fly low enough you escape the defence department's radar. And the control tower."

"I'll drive in and talk to Sturup," Wallander said.

"Wrong," Rydberg said. "I'll do that. I leave this mud to you, by the rights of my old age."

Rydberg left. It was starting to get light. One of the technicians was photographing the wreck from various angles. Peter Edler had delegated his responsibilities to someone else and returned to Ystad in one of the fire engines.

Wallander saw Hansson talking to several reporters down on the dirt road. He was happy not to have to do it himself. Then he spotted Martinsson tramping back through the mud. Wallander walked over to meet him.

"You were right," Martinsson said. "There's an old man in there who lives by himself. Robert Haverberg. Seventies, alone with nine dogs. To be honest, it smelled like hell in there."

"What did he say?"

"He heard the roar of a plane. Then it got quiet. And then the sound returned. But at that point it sounded more like a whine. And then he heard the crash."

Wallander often felt that Martinsson was bad at formulating simple and clear explanations.

"Let's go over this again," Wallander said. "Robert Haverberg heard the engine noise?"

"Yes."

"When was this?"

"He had just woken up. Sometime around five o'clock."

Wallander frowned.

"But the plane crashed half an hour later?"

"That's what I said. But he was very firm on this point. First he heard the sound of a passing plane, at a low altitude. Then it grew quiet. He made some coffee. And then the sound returned, and then the explosion."

Wallander reflected on this. What Martinsson had told him was clearly significant.

"How much time elapsed between the first time he heard the sound and the subsequent crash?"

"We worked out that it must have taken around twenty minutes."

Wallander looked at Martinsson.

"How do you account for that?"

"I don't know."

"Did the old man seem sharp?"

"Yes. He also has good hearing."

"Do you have a map in your car?" Wallander asked.

Martinsson nodded. They walked up to the dirt road where Hansson was still talking with the media. One of them saw Wallander and started approaching him. Wallander waved dismissively.

"I have nothing to say," he called out.

They got into Martinsson's car and unfolded the map. Wallander studied it in silence. He thought about what Rydberg had said, about aeroplanes on illegal missions, beyond authorised air lanes and control towers.

"One could imagine the following," Wallander said. "A plane comes in low over the coast, passes by and continues out of earshot. Returns shortly thereafter. And then it goes straight down."

"You mean it dropped something off somewhere? And then turned back?" Martinsson asked.

"Something like that."

Wallander folded the map back up.

"We know too little. Rydberg is on his way to Sturup. Then we have to try to identify the bodies, as well as the plane itself. We can't do any more at the moment."

"I've always been a nervous flyer," Martinsson said. "It doesn't exactly help to see things like this. But it's even worse when Teres talks about becoming a pilot."

Teres was Martinsson's daughter. He also had a son. Martinsson was a real family man. He was always worried that something might have happened and called home several times a day. Often he went home for lunch. Sometimes Wallander was a little envious of his colleague's seemingly problem-free marriage.

"Tell Nyberg we're going now," he said to Martinsson.

Wallander waited in the car. The landscape around him was grey and desolate. He shivered. Life goes on, he thought. I've just turned forty-two. Will I end up like Rydberg? A lonely old man with rheumatism?

Wallander shook off these thoughts.

Martinsson returned and they drove back to Ystad.

At eleven o'clock Wallander stood up to go to the room where a suspected drug dealer by the name of Yngve Leonard Holm was waiting for him. At that moment Rydberg came in. He never bothered to knock. He sat down in the visitor's chair and got straight to the point.

"I've talked to an air traffic controller by the name of Lycke," he said. "He claimed to know you."

"I've spoken to him before, I don't remember the context."

"He was very firm, in any case," Rydberg continued. "No single-engine plane was cleared to pass over Mossby at five o'clock this morning. They have also not received any emergency broadcast from any pilot. The radar screens have been empty. There were no strange signals that may have indicated the presence of an unidentified plane. According to Lycke, the plane that crashed did not exist. They have already reported this both to the defence department and to God knows how many other authorities. Customs, probably."

"So you were right," Wallander said. "Someone was out on an illegal mission."

"We don't know that," Rydberg objected. "Someone was flying illegally. But if it was also an illegal mission, we don't know."

"Who would be out flying around in the dark without a particular reason?"

"There are so many idiots," Rydberg said. "You should know that."

Wallander looked closer at him.

"You don't believe that for a minute, do you?"

"Of course not," Rydberg said. "But until we know who they were or identify the plane, we can't do anything. This has to go to Interpol. I'm willing to wager a pretty penny that the plane came from the outside."

Rydberg left.

Wallander mulled over what he had said.

Then he stood up, took his papers and walked to the room where Yngve Leonard Holm was waiting with his lawyer.

It was exactly a quarter past eleven when Wallander started the tape recorder and began his interrogation.

CHAPTER
TWO

Wallander turned off the tape recorder after one hour and ten minutes. He had had enough of Yngve Leonard Holm. Both because of the man's attitude and the fact that they were going to have to release him. Wallander was convinced that the man on the other side of the table was guilty of repeated and serious drug offences. But there was not one prosecutor in the world who would judge their pre-investigation worthy of taking to trial. Certainly not Per Åkeson, to whom Wallander was going to submit his report.

Yngve Leonard Holm was thirty-seven years old. He was born in Ronneby but had been registered as a resident of Ystad since the mid-1980s. He listed his profession as a paperback-book salesman at outdoor summer markets, specialising in the "Manhattan series". For the last few years he had declared a negligible income. At the same time, he was having a large villa built in an area close to the police station. The house was taxed at several million kronor. Holm claimed to be financing the house with large gambling profits from both the Jägersro and Solvalla tracks, as well as various racetracks in Germany and France. Predictably, he had no receipts for his wins. They had disappeared when the trailer where he had stored his financial records caught fire. The only receipt he could show was a lesser one for 4,993 kronor that he had claimed a couple of weeks earlier. Possibly, Wallander thought, this indicated that Holm knew something about horses. But it hardly meant more than that. Hansson should have been sitting here in my place. He is also interested in racing. They could have talked horses to each other.

Nothing of this altered Wallander's conviction that Holm was the final link in a chain that imported and sold significant amounts of drugs in southern Sweden. The circumstantial evidence was overwhelming. But Holm's arrest had been very poorly organised. The raids should have been synchronised to take place at the same time. One at Holm's house, the other at the warehouse in an industrial area in Malmö where he rented space for his paperbacks. It had been a coordinated operation between the police in Ystad and their colleagues in Malmö.

But something had gone wrong from the start. The warehouse space had been empty, except for a lone box of old, well-thumbed Manhattan books. Holm had been watching TV in his house when they rang the bell. A young woman was curled up at his feet, massaging his toes, while the police searched the house. They found nothing. One of the drug-sniffing dogs they had brought in from customs had spent a long time sniffing a handkerchief they had found in the rubbish. Chemical analysis had only been able to establish that the cloth could have come into contact with a drug. In some way, Holm had been tipped off about the raid. Wallander did not doubt that the man was both intelligent and good at covering up his activities.

"We have to let you go," he said. "But our suspicion of you remains. Or, to be precise, I'm convinced that you're involved in extensive drug trafficking in Skåne. Sooner or later, we will get you."

The lawyer, who resembled a weasel, straightened up.

"My client doesn't have to put up with this," he said. "Slander of this kind against my client is inadmissible under the law."

"Of course it is," Wallander said. "You're welcome to try to have me arrested."

Holm, who was unshaven and appeared sick of the whole situation, stopped his lawyer from continuing.

"I understand that the police are simply doing their job," he said. "Unfortunately you made a mistake in directing your suspicions at me. I'm a simple citizen who knows a lot about horses and bookselling. Nothing else. Moreover, I regularly donate money to Save the Children."

Wallander left the room. Holm would go home and have his feet massaged. Drugs would continue to stream into Skåne. We will never win this battle, Wallander thought as he walked down the corridor. The only room for hope is if future generations of young people reject it entirely.

It was now half past twelve. He felt hungry and regretted not having taken the car this morning. He could see through the window that it had started to rain. There was snow mixed in with the rain. The thought of walking all the way downtown and back in order to eat was not appealing. He pulled out a desk drawer and found the menu of a pizzeria that delivered. He eyed the menu without being able to decide on anything. Finally he closed his eyes and placed his index finger down somewhere at random. He called and ordered the pizza that fate had selected for him. Then he walked over to the window and stared at the water tower on the other side of the road.

The phone rang. He sat down at his desk and picked up. It was his father, calling from Löderup.

"I thought we had agreed that you would come by here last night," his father said.

Wallander sighed quietly.

"We didn't agree to anything."

"Yes we did, I remember it very well," his father said. "You're the one who's starting to get forgetful. I thought the police had notepads. Can't you write down that you're planning to arrest me? Then maybe you'll remember."

Wallander didn't have the energy to get angry.

"I'll come by tonight," he said. "But we had *not* arranged that I was coming over last night."

"It's possible I made a mistake," his father replied, suddenly surprisingly meek.

"I'll be there around seven," Wallander said. "Right now I have a lot to do." He hung up. My father engages in finely tuned emotional blackmail, Wallander thought. And the worst thing about it is that he's continually successful.

The pizza arrived. Wallander paid and took the box back to the break room. Per Åkeson was sitting at a table eating some porridge. Wallander sat down across from him.

"I thought you were going to come by and talk about Holm," Åkeson said.

"And I will. But we had to release him."

"That doesn't surprise me. The whole operation was exceedingly poorly executed."

"You'll have to talk to Björk about that," Wallander said. "I wasn't involved."

To Wallander's surprise, Åkeson salted his porridge.

"I'm taking a leave of absence in three weeks," Åkeson said.

"I haven't forgotten," Wallander replied.

"A young woman will be replacing me. Anette Brolin is her name. From Stockholm."

"I'm going to miss you," Wallander said. "I'm also wondering how a female prosecutor is going to work out."

"Why would that be a problem?"

Wallander shrugged.

"Prejudice, I guess."

"Six months goes by fast. I have to admit that I'm looking forward to getting away for a while. I need to think."

"I thought you were getting some additional education?"

"I am. But that won't stop me from thinking about the future. Should I continue as a public prosecutor for the rest of my life? Or is there something else I should do?"

"You could learn to sail and become a vagabond of the seas."

Åkeson shook his head energetically.

"Nothing like that. But I am thinking about applying for something overseas. Perhaps in a project where one feels one is really making a difference. Perhaps I could be part of building a workable justice system where there was none before? In Czechoslovakia, for example."

"I hope you write and tell me," Wallander said. "Sometimes I also wonder about the future, if I'm going to stay in this business until I retire. Or do something else."

The pizza was tasteless. Åkeson, however, was tucking into his porridge with gusto.

"What's the story with that plane?" Åkeson asked.

Wallander told him what they knew.

"That sounds strange," Åkeson said when Wallander had finished. "Could it be drugs?"

"Yes, it could," Wallander replied and regretted not having asked Holm if he owned an aeroplane. If he could afford to build a house he could probably afford to keep a private plane. Drug profits could be astronomical.

They stood at the sink together and cleaned their plates. Wallander had left half of his pizza uneaten. The divorce was still having an effect on his appetite.

"Holm is a criminal," Wallander said. "We'll get him sooner or later."

"I'm not so sure of that," Åkeson said. "But of course I hope you're right."

Wallander was back in his office a little after one o'clock. He considered calling Mona in Malmö. Linda lived with her right now. She was the one Wallander wanted to talk to. It had been almost a week since they talked last. She was nineteen and a little lost. Lately, she was back to thinking she wanted to work upholstering furniture. Wallander suspected she would change her mind many more times.

Instead Wallander called Martinsson and asked him to come by. Together they went over the events of the morning. It was Martinsson who was going to write the report.

"People have called both from Sturup and the Department of Defence," he said. "There is something not right about that plane. It doesn't seem to have existed. And it seems you were right in thinking the wings and fuselage had been painted over."

"We'll see what Nyberg comes up with," Wallander said.

"The bodies are in Lund," Martinsson went on. "The only way we have of identifying them is through dental records. The bodies were so badly burned they fell to pieces when they were moved onto stretchers."

"We'll have to wait and see, in other words," Wallander said. "I was going to suggest to Björk that you act as our representative in the accident commission. Do you have anything against that?"

"I'll always learn something new," Martinsson said.

When Wallander was alone again he ended up thinking about the difference between Martinsson and himself. Wallander's ambition had always been to become a good criminal investigator. And he had succeeded in this. But Martinsson had other ambitions. What tempted him was the post of chief of police in a not-too-distant future. To perform well in the field was for him only a step in his career.

Wallander dropped his thoughts about Martinsson, yawned, and listlessly pulled over the folder that was at the top of the pile on his desk. It still irritated him that he hadn't asked Holm about the plane. At least to get to see his reaction. But Holm was probably lying in his whirlpool by now. Or enjoying a delicious lunch at the Continental with his lawyer.

The folder remained unopened in front of Wallander. He decided he might as well talk to Björk about Martinsson and the accident commission. Then that could be checked off the list. He walked to the end of the corridor where Björk had his office. The door was open. Björk was on his way out.

"Do you have time?" Wallander asked.

"A few minutes. I'm on my way to a church to give a speech."

Wallander knew that Björk was constantly giving lectures in the most unexpected settings. Apparently he loved performing in public, something that Wallander disliked intensely. Press conferences were a constant scourge. Wallander started to tell him about the morning's events, but apparently Björk had already been briefed. He had no objection to Martinsson's being appointed as police representative to the accident commission.

"I take it the plane was not shot down," Björk said.

"Nothing so far indicates that it was anything other than an accident," Wallander answered. "But there is definitely something fishy about that flight."

"We'll do what we can," Björk said, indicating that the conversation was over. "But we won't exert more of an effort than we have to. We have enough to do as it is."

Björk left in a cloud of aftershave. Wallander shuffled back to his office. On the way he looked into Rydberg's and Hansson's offices. Neither one was around. He got himself a cup of coffee and then spent several hours reviewing the assault case that had occurred the week before in Skurup. New information had turned up that seemed to ensure that the man who had beaten up his sister-in-law could actually be charged with battery. Wallander organised the material and decided he would hand it over to Åkeson tomorrow.

It was a quarter to five. The police station seemed unusually deserted this day. Wallander decided he would go home and get his car and then go shopping. He would still have time to make it to his father's by seven. If he wasn't there on the dot, his father would burst out in a long tirade of accusations about how badly his son treated him.

Wallander took his coat and walked home. The snow-slush had increased. He pulled up his hood. When he sat down in his car he checked that he still had the grocery list in his pocket. The car was hard to start and he would soon have to get a new one. But where would he get the money? He managed to get the engine going and was about to put it in gear when he was struck by a thought. Even though he realised that what he wanted to do was meaningless, his curiosity proved too strong. He decided to put his shopping trip on hold. Instead he turned out onto Österleden and drove in the direction of Löderup.

The thought that had struck him was very simple. In a house just past the Strandskogen Forest, there lived a retired air traffic controller Wallander had got to know a few years earlier. Linda had been friends with his youngest daughter. It occurred to Wallander that he might be able to answer a question that Wallander had been thinking about ever since he had stood next to the wrecked plane and listened to Martinsson's summary of his conversation with Haverberg.

Wallander turned into the driveway of the house where Herbert Blomell lived. As Wallander got out of his car, he saw Blomell standing on a ladder, in the process of repairing a gutter. He nodded pleasantly when he saw who it was and carefully climbed down onto the ground.

"A broken hip can be devastating at my age," he said. "How are things with Linda?"

"Fine," Wallander said. "She's with Mona in Malmö."

They went in and sat in the kitchen.

"A plane crashed outside Mossby this morning," Wallander said.

Blomell nodded and pointed to a radio on the windowsill.

"It was a Piper Cherokee," Wallander continued. "A single-engine plane. I know that you weren't just an air traffic controller in your day. You also had a pilot's licence."

"I've actually flown a Piper Cherokee a few times," Blomell answered. "A good plane."

"If I put my finger on a map," Wallander said, "and then gave you a compass direction, and ten minutes, how far would you be able to fly the plane?"

"A matter of straightforward computation," Blomell said. "Do you have a map?"

Wallander shook his head. Blomell stood up and left. Several minutes later he returned with a rolled-up map. They spread it out on the kitchen table. Wallander located the field that must have been the crash site.

"Imagine that the plane came straight in off the coast. The engine noise is heard here at one point. Then, at most twenty minutes later, it returns. Of course, we cannot know that the pilot held the same course for the duration, but let us assume he did. How far did he go, then, in half that time? Before he turned round?"

"The Cherokee normally flies at around 250 kilometres an hour," Blomell said. "If the load is of a normal weight."

"We don't know about that."

"Then let's assume maximum load and an average headwind."

Blomell computed silently, then pointed to a spot north of Mossby. Wallander saw that it was close to Sjöbo.

"About this far," Blomell said. "But keep in mind that there are many unknowns included in this estimation."

"Still, I know a lot more now than just a moment ago."

Wallander tapped his fingers on the table reflectively.

"Why does a plane crash?" he asked after a while.

Blomell looked quizzically at him.

"No two accidents are alike," he said. "I read some American magazines that refer to various accident investigations. There may be recurring causes. Errors in the plane's electrical wiring, or something else. But in the end there is nonetheless almost always some exceptional reason at the root of any given accident. And it almost always involves some degree of pilot error."

"Why would a Cherokee crash?" Wallander asked.

Blomell shook his head.

"The engine may have stalled. Poor maintenance. You'll have to wait and see what the accident commission comes up with."

"The plane's identifying marks had been painted over, both on the fuselage and the wings," Wallander said. "What does that mean?"

"That it was someone who didn't want to be known," Blomell said. "There is a black market for aeroplanes just as for anything else."

"I thought Swedish airspace was secure," Wallander said. "But you mean that planes can sneak in?"

"There is nothing in this world that is absolutely secure," Blomell answered. "Nor will there ever be. Those who have enough money and enough motivation can always find their way across a border, and back again, without interception."

Blomell offered him a cup of coffee, but Wallander declined.

"I have to look in on my father in Löderup," he said. "If I'm late I'll never hear the end of it."

"Loneliness is the curse of old age," Blomell said. "I miss my air control tower with a physical ache. All night I dream of ushering planes through the air corridors. And when I wake up it's snowing and all I can do is repair a gutter."

They took leave of each other outside. Wallander stopped at a grocery shop in Herrestad. When he drove away again, he cursed. Even though it had been on his list he had forgotten to buy toilet paper.

He arrived at his father's house at three minutes to seven. The snow had stopped, but the clouds hung heavy over the countryside. Wallander saw the lights on in the little side building that his father used as a studio. He breathed in the fresh air as he walked across the yard. The door was ajar; his father had heard his car. He was sitting at his easel, an old hat on his head and his near-sighted eyes close to the painting he had just started. The smell of paint thinner always gave Wallander the same feeling of home. This is what is left of my childhood. The smell of paint thinner.

"You're on time," his father observed without looking at him.

"I'm always on time," Wallander said as he moved a couple of newspapers and sat down.

His father was working on a painting that featured a wood grouse. Just as Wallander had stepped into the studio he had placed a stencil onto the canvas and was painting a subdued sky at dusk. Wallander looked at him with a sudden feeling of tenderness. He is the last one in the generation before me, he thought. When he dies, I'll be the next to go.

His father put away his brushes and the stencil and stood up.

They went into the main house. His father put on some coffee and brought some shot glasses to the table. Wallander hesitated, then nodded. He could take one glass.

"Poker," Wallander said. "You owe me fourteen kronor from last time."

His father looked closely at him.

"I think you cheat," he said. "But I still don't know how you do it."

Wallander was taken aback.

"You think I'd cheat my own father?"

For once his father backed down.

"No," he said. "Not really. But you did win an unusual amount last time."

The conversation died. They drank coffee. His father slurped as usual. This irritated Wallander as much as it always did.

"I'm going to go away," his father said suddenly. "Far away."

Wallander waited for more, but none came.

"Where to?" he asked finally.

"To Egypt."

"Egypt? What are you going to do there? I thought it was Italy you wanted to see."

"Egypt and Italy. You never listen to what I say."

"What are you going to do in Egypt?"

"I'm going to see the Sphinx and the pyramids. Time is running out. No one knows how long I will live. But I want to see the pyramids and Rome before I die."

Wallander shook his head.

"Who are you going with?"

"I'm flying with Egypt Air, in a few days. Straight to Cairo. I'm going to stay in a very nice hotel called Mena House."

"But you're going alone? Is it a charter trip? You can't be serious," Wallander said in disbelief.

His father reached for some tickets on the windowsill. Wallander looked through them and realised that what his father said was true. He had a regular-fare ticket from Copenhagen to Cairo for the fourteenth of December.

Wallander put the tickets down on the table.

For once he was completely speechless.

CHAPTER
THREE

Wallander left Löderup at a quarter past ten. The clouds had started to break up. As he walked to the car he noticed that it had turned colder. This in turn would mean that the Peugeot would be harder to start than usual. But it wasn't the car that occupied his thoughts, it was the fact that he had not managed to talk his father out of taking the trip to Egypt. Or at least wait until a time when he or his sister could accompany him.

"You're almost eighty years old," Wallander had insisted. "At your age, you can't do this kind of thing."

But his arguments had been hollow. There was nothing visibly wrong with his father's health. And even if he dressed unconventionally at times, he had a rare ability to adapt to new situations and the new people he met. When Wallander realised that the ticket included a shuttle bus from the airport to the hotel that was situated close to the pyramids, his concerns had slowly dissipated. He did not understand what drove his father to go to Egypt, to the Sphinx and the pyramids. But he couldn't deny that — many years ago now, when Wallander was still young — his father had actually told him many times about the marvellous structures on the Giza plateau, just outside Cairo.

Then they had played poker. Since his father ended in the black, he was in a great mood when Wallander said his goodbyes.

Wallander paused with his hand on the car-door handle and drew in a breath of night air.

I have a strange father, he thought. That's something I'll never escape.

Wallander had promised to drive him into Malmö on the morning of the fourteenth. He had made a note of the telephone number for Mena House, where his father would be staying. Since his father never spent money unnecessarily, he had of course not taken any travel insurance and so Wallander was going to ask Ebba to take care of it tomorrow.

The car started reluctantly and he turned towards Ystad. The last thing he saw was the light in the kitchen window. His father had a habit of sitting up for a long time in the kitchen before going to bed. If he didn't return to the studio and add yet another few brushstrokes to one of his paintings. Wallander thought about what Blomell had said earlier that evening, that loneliness was a curse of the aged. But Wallander's father lived no differently since he had grown old. He continued to paint his pictures as if nothing had changed, neither anything around him nor himself.

Wallander was back at Mariagatan shortly after eleven o'clock. When he unlocked the front door he saw that someone had slipped a letter through the letter box. He opened the envelope and already knew whom it was from. Emma Lundin, a nurse at the Ystad hospital. Wallander had promised to call her yesterday. She walked past his building on her way home to Dragongatan. Now she was wondering if something was wrong. Why had he not called her? Wallander felt guilty. He had met her a month before. They had fallen into conversation at the post office on Hamngatan. Then they had bumped into each other a few days later at the grocery shop and after only a couple of days they had started a relationship that was not particularly passionate on either side. Emma was a year younger than Wallander, divorced with three children. Wallander had soon realised that the relationship meant more to her than to him. Without really daring to, he had started trying to extricate himself. As he stood in the hall now he knew very well why he hadn't called. He simply had no desire to see her. He put the letter down on the kitchen table and decided he had to end the relationship. It had no future, no potential. They did not have enough to talk about, and too little time for each other. And Wallander knew that he was looking for something completely different, someone completely different. Someone who would actually be able to replace Mona. If that woman even existed. But above all it was Mona's return that he dreamed of.

He undressed and put on his old worn dressing gown. Realised again that he had forgotten to buy toilet paper and found an old telephone book that he put in the bathroom. Then he put the grocery items he had bought in Herrestad into the fridge. The phone rang. It was a quarter past eleven. He hoped that nothing serious had occurred that would make him have to get dressed again. It was Linda. It always made him happy to hear her voice.

"Where have you been?" she asked. "I've been calling all evening."

"You could have guessed," he replied. "And you could have called your grandfather. That's where I was."

"I didn't think of that," she said. "You never go to see him."

"I don't?"

"That's what he says."

"He says a lot of things. By the way, he's going to fly to Egypt in few days to see the pyramids."

"Sounds fun. I wouldn't mind going along."

Wallander said nothing. He listened to her lengthy narrative about how she had spent the past couple of days. He was pleased that she had now clearly recommitted herself to a career in upholstering furniture. He assumed that Mona was not home since she would normally get irritated when Linda talked so much and for so long on the phone. But he also felt a pang of jealousy. Even though they were now divorced, he could not reconcile himself to the thought of her seeing other men.

The conversation ended with Linda promising to meet him in Malmö and see her grandfather off for his trip to Egypt.

It was past midnight. Since Wallander was hungry he went back to the kitchen. The only thing he could be bothered to make was a bowl of porridge. At a half past twelve he crawled into bed and fell asleep almost immediately.

On the morning of the twelfth of December, the temperature had sunk to four degrees below zero. Wallander was sitting in the kitchen, just before seven o'clock, when the telephone rang. It was Blomell.

"I hope I didn't wake you," he said.

"I was up," Wallander said, coffee cup in hand.

"Something occurred to me after you left," Blomell went on. "I'm not a policeman, of course, but I still thought I should call you."

"Tell me."

"I was simply thinking that for someone to hear the engines outside Mossby the plane must have been at a very low altitude. That should mean that even others heard it. In that way you should be able to find out where it went. And perhaps you might even find someone who heard it turn round in the air and head back. If someone, for example, heard it with a break of only several minutes, you may be able to figure out what the turning radius was."

Blomell was right. Wallander should have thought of it himself. But he did not say this.

"We're already on it," he said instead.

"That was all," Blomell said. "How was your father?"

"He told me he's taking a trip to Egypt."

"That sounds like a wonderful idea."

Wallander didn't answer.

"It's getting colder," Blomell concluded. "Winter is on its way."

"Soon we'll have snowstorms upon us," Wallander said.

He went back to the kitchen, thinking about what Blomell had said. Martinsson or someone else could get in touch with colleagues in Tomelilla and Sjöbo. Maybe also Simrishamn to be safe. It might be possible to pinpoint the plane's route and destination by looking for people who were early risers and who had noticed an engine noise overhead, twice in a row if they were lucky. Surely there were still some dairy farmers around who were up at that time of day? But the question remained. What had the two men been doing on their flight? And why had the plane lacked all signs of identification?

Wallander quickly leafed through the paper. The Labrador puppies were still for sale. But there was no house that caught his eye.

Wallander walked in through the doors of the station a little before eight o'clock. He was wearing the sweater he reserved for days of up to five degrees below zero. He asked Ebba to arrange travel insurance for his father.

"That has always been my dream," she said. "To go to Egypt and see the pyramids."

Everyone seems to be envious of my father, Wallander thought as he poured himself a cup of coffee and went to his office. No one even seems surprised. I'm the only one who's worried that something will happen. That he'll get lost in the desert, for example.

Martinsson had placed a report on his desk about the accident. Wallander eyed it quickly and thought that

Martinsson was still far too verbose. Half as much would have been enough. Once Rydberg had told him that that which could not be expressed in a telegram format was either poorly conceived or completely wrong. Wallander had always tried to make his reports as clear and brief as possible. He called Martinsson and told him about his conversation with Björk the day before. Martinsson seemed pleased. Then Wallander suggested a meeting. What Blomell had said was worth following up. Martinsson managed to locate Hansson and Svedberg at half past eight. But Rydberg had still not arrived. They filed into one of the conference rooms.

"Has anyone seen Nyberg?" Wallander asked.

Nyberg walked in at that moment. As usual, he appeared to have been up all night. His hair was standing on end. He sat in his usual seat, somewhat apart from the others.

"Rydberg seems ill," Svedberg said, scratching his bald spot with a pencil.

"He is ill," Hansson said. "He has sciatica."

"Rheumatism," Wallander corrected. "There's a big difference."

Then he turned to Nyberg.

"We've examined the wings," the latter said. "And washed away the fire-retardant foam and tried to puzzle the pieces of the fuselage back together. The numbers and letters had not only been painted over, they had also been scraped away beforehand. But that had only been partly successful, hence the need for paint. The people on board definitely did not want to be traced."

"I imagine there is a number on the engine," Wallander said. "And of course not as many planes are manufactured as cars."

"We're getting in touch with the Piper factory in the United States," Martinsson said.

"There are some other questions that need to be answered," Wallander went on. "How far can a plane like this fly on one tank of fuel? How common are additional fuel tanks? What is the limit to the amount of petrol a plane of this type can carry?"

Martinsson wrote this down.

"I'll get the answers," he said.

The door opened and Rydberg came in.

"I've been to the hospital," he said curtly, "and things always take a long time there."

Wallander could see that he was in pain but said nothing.

Instead, he presented the idea of trying to find others who might have heard the engine noise. He felt a little guilty that he did not give Blomell credit for this insight.

"This will be like in wartime," Rydberg commented. "When everyone in Skåne walked around and listened for planes."

"It's possible it won't yield anything," Wallander said. "But there's no harm in checking with our colleagues in nearby districts. Personally I have trouble believing it could have been anything other than a drug transport. An arranged drop somewhere."

"We should talk to Malmö," Rydberg said. "If they've noticed that the supply seems to have increased dramatically, there could be a connection. I'll call them."

No one had any objections. Wallander brought the meeting to a close shortly after nine o'clock.

He spent the rest of the morning concluding work on the assault case in Skurup and presenting the findings to Per Åkeson. At lunchtime he went downtown, had the hot-dog special, and bought some toilet paper. He even took the opportunity to drop by the state-run off-licence and buy a bottle of whisky and two bottles of wine. Just as he was leaving he bumped into Sten Widén on his way in. He reeked of alcohol and looked worn out.

Sten Widén was one of Wallander's oldest friends. They had met many years ago, united by their interest in opera. Widén worked for his father in Stjärnsund, where they had raised racehorses. They had seen each other less often the past few years. Wallander had started to keep his distance when he realised that Widén's drinking was getting out of control.

"It's been a while," Widén said.

Wallander winced at his breath, which seemed to testify to many drinking bouts.

"You know how it is," Wallander says "These things go in waves."

Then they exchanged some neutral words. Both wanted to end the conversation as soon as possible. In order to meet under different, prearranged circumstances. Wallander promised to call.

"I'm training a new horse," Widén said. "She had such a bad name I managed to get it changed."

"What is she now?"

"La Trottiata."

Widén smiled. Wallander nodded. Then they went their separate ways.

Wallander walked back to Mariagatan with his bags. He was back at the station at a quarter past two. Everything still seemed deserted. Wallander continued to work through his pile of paper. After the assault in Skurup came a burglary in central Ystad, on Pilgrimsgatan. Someone had broken a window in the middle of the day and emptied the house of various valuables. Wallander shook his head as he read through Svedberg's report. It was unbelievable that none of the neighbours had seen anything.

Is this fear starting to spread even in Sweden? he wondered. The fear of assisting the police with the most elementary observations. If this is the case then the situation is far worse that I have wanted to believe.

Wallander struggled on with the material and made notes on who should be questioned and which searches should be made in the files. But he had no illusions that they would be able to solve the burglary case without a large dose of luck or reliable witnesses' accounts.

Martinsson walked into his office shortly before five. Wallander saw that he was starting to grow a moustache, but he said nothing.

"Sjöbo actually did have something to say," Martinsson began. "A man had been out looking for a lost bull calf all night. God only knows how he thought he was going to find anything in the dark. But he called the police in Sjöbo that morning and said he had seen

386

strange lights and heard an engine noise shortly after five."

"Strange lights? What did he mean by that?"

"I've asked the Sjöbo colleagues to interview the man in more detail. Fridell was his name."

Wallander nodded.

"Lights and engine noise. That could confirm our hypothesis about a scheduled drop."

Martinsson spread out a map on Wallander's desk. He pointed. Wallander saw that it was in the area that Blomell had circled.

"Good work," Wallander said. "We'll have to see if it leads us anywhere."

Martinsson folded up the map.

"It's terrible if it's true," he said. "If this really is the case then we're unprotected. If any old plane can come in across the border and drop off drugs without being sighted."

"We have to get used to it," Wallander said. "But of course I agree with you."

Martinsson left. Wallander left the station a little later. When he got home he cooked a real dinner for once. At half past seven he sat down with a cup of coffee to watch the news. The phone rang as the top stories were being announced. It was Emma. She was just leaving the hospital. Wallander didn't really know what he wanted. Another evening alone. Or a visit from Emma. Without being sure that he really wanted to see her, he asked if she wanted to stop by. She said yes. Wallander knew this meant that she would stay until a little after midnight. Then she would get dressed and go home. In order to steel himself for the visit he had two glasses of whisky. He had already showered before while he was waiting for the potatoes to boil. Quickly, he changed the sheets on the bed and threw the old bed-linen into the wardrobe, which was already overflowing with dirty laundry.

Emma arrived shortly before eight. Wallander cursed himself when he heard her on the stairs. Why couldn't he put an end to it, since it had no future?

She arrived, she smiled and Wallander asked her in. She had brown hair and beautiful eyes, and was short. He put on the kind of music he knew she liked. They drank wine and shortly before eleven they went to bed. Wallander thought of Mona.

Afterwards they both fell asleep. Neither one of them had said anything. Just before he fell asleep, Wallander noticed a headache coming on. He woke up again when she was getting dressed, but he pretended to be asleep. When the front door had shut, he got out of bed and drank some water. Then he returned to bed, thought about Mona for a bit longer, and fell back asleep.

The telephone started to ring deep inside his dreams. He woke immediately. Listened. The rings continued. He glanced at the clock on the bedside table. A quarter past two. That meant that something had happened. He lifted the receiver as he sat up in bed.

It was one of the officers who worked the night shift, Näslund.

"There's a fire on Möllegatan," Näslund said. "Right on the corner of Lilla Strandgatan."

Wallander tried to visualise that block.

"What's burning?"

"The Eberhardsson sisters' sewing shop."

"That sounds like a case for the fire brigade and a patrol unit."

Näslund hesitated before answering.

"They're already there. It sounds like the house may have exploded. And the sisters live above the shop."

"Did you get them out?"

"It doesn't look like it."

Wallander didn't need to think any further. He knew there was only one thing to do.

"I'm coming," he said. "Who else have you called?"

"Rydberg."

"You could have let him sleep. Get Svedberg and Hansson."

Wallander hung up. Checked the time again. Seventeen minutes past two. While he put his clothes on he thought about what Näslund had said. A sewing shop had been blown up. That sounded implausible. And it was serious if the two owners had not managed to escape.

Wallander walked out onto the street and realised he had left his car keys. He cursed, then ran back up the stairs, noticing how out of breath he became. I should start playing badminton with Svedberg again, he thought. I can't manage four flights without losing my breath.

Wallander pulled up on Hamngatan at half past two. The whole area had been blocked off. The smell of fire was perceptible before he even opened the door. Flames and smoke were rising into the sky. The fire

389

brigade had all their engines on the scene. Wallander ran into Peter Edler for the second time that day.

"It looks bad," Peter Edler shouted, raising his voice to be heard above the din.

The whole house was in flames. The firefighters were spraying the surrounding buildings to restrict the damage.

"The sisters?" Wallander shouted.

Edler shook his head.

"No one has come out," he replied. "If they were home, they're still in there. We have a witness who says the building just blew up. It started to burn everywhere at once."

Edler left to continue directing the operation. Hansson appeared at Wallander's side.

"Who the hell sets fire to a sewing shop?" he asked.

Wallander shook his head.

He had no answer.

He thought about the two sisters who had worked in their sewing shop for as long as he had lived in Ystad. Once, he and Mona had bought a zip there for one of his suits.

Now the sisters were gone.

And if Peter Edler was not completely mistaken, this fire had been started in order to kill them.

CHAPTER
FOUR

Wallander rang in this St Lucia's Day, 1989, with lights other than those of a children's Lucia procession. He stayed at the scene of the blaze until dawn. By then he had sent home both Svedberg and Hansson. When Rydberg turned up, Wallander also told him to go home. The night cold and the heat of the flames would do nothing good for his rheumatism. Rydberg listened to a short report about the two sisters' likely death, and then he left. Peter Edler gave Wallander a cup of coffee. Wallander sat in the driver's cab in one of the fire engines and wondered why he didn't simply go home and sleep instead of staying here, waiting for the fire to be put out. He didn't manage to come up with a good answer. He thought back to the evening before, with discomfort. The erotic dimension between him and Emma Lundin was completely devoid of passion. Hardly more than an extension of their earlier inane conversations.

I can't go on like this, he thought suddenly. Something has to happen in my life. Soon, very soon. The two months that had gone by since Mona had left him felt like two years.

The fire was out at dawn. The building had burned to the ground. Nyberg arrived. They waited for Peter Edler to give the go-ahead for Nyberg to enter the smouldering remains with the fire brigade's own forensic technicians.

Then Björk turned up, impeccably dressed as usual, accompanied by a scent of aftershave that managed to overpower even the smoke.

"Fires are tragic," he said. "I hear the owners have died."

"We don't know that yet," Wallander said. "But there are no indications to the contrary, unfortunately."

Björk looked at his watch.

"I have to push on," he said. "I have a breakfast meeting with Rotary." He left.

"He's going to lecture himself to death," Wallander said.

Nyberg followed him with his eyes.

"I wonder what he says about the police and our work," Nyberg said. "Have you ever heard him speak?"

"Never. But I suspect he doesn't tell them about his accomplishments at the desk."

They stood quietly, waiting. Wallander felt cold and tired. The whole block was still closed to traffic, but a reporter from *Arbetet* had managed to duck his way past the blockades. Wallander recognised him. He was one of the reporters who usually wrote what Wallander actually said, so he was given the little information they had. They still could not confirm that anyone had died. The reporter let himself be satisfied with this.

Another hour went by before Peter Edler could give them the green light. When Wallander had left home the night before, he had been smart enough to put on rubber boots, and now he stepped carefully into the scorched rubble where beams and the remains of walls lay jumbled in a mess of water. Nyberg and some of the firefighters carefully made their way through the ruins. After less than five minutes, they stopped. Nyberg nodded for Wallander to come.

The bodies of two people lay a few metres away from each other. They were charred beyond the point of recognition. It occurred to Wallander that he had now experienced this sight for the second time in forty-eight hours. He shook his head.

"The Eberhardsson sisters," he said. "What were their first names?"

"Anna and Emilia," Nyberg answered. "But we don't yet know if it is actually them."

"Who else would it be?" Wallander said. "They lived alone in this house."

"We'll find out," Nyberg said. "But it will take a couple of days."

Wallander turned and went back out onto the street. Peter Edler was smoking.

"You smoke?" Wallander said. "I didn't know that."

"Not very often," Edler replied. "Only when I'm very tired."

"There must be a thorough examination of this fire," Wallander said.

"I shouldn't jump to any conclusions, of course, but this looks like nothing less than deliberate arson.

Though one may wonder why anyone wanted to take the lives of two old spinsters."

Wallander nodded. He knew that Peter Edler was an extremely competent fire chief.

"Two old ladies," Wallander remarked. "Who sold buttons and zips."

There was no longer any reason for Wallander to stay. He left the scene, got in his car and went home. He ate breakfast and conferred with the thermometer about which sweater to wear. He decided on the same one as yesterday. At twenty minutes past nine he parked in front of the station. Martinsson arrived at the same time. This is unusually late for him, Wallander thought. Martinsson offered up the explanation without being asked.

"My niece, who is fifteen, came home drunk last night," he said sombrely. "That hasn't happened before."

"Some time has to be the first," Wallander said.

He did not miss his days as a patrol officer, when St Lucia's Day was always a raucous affair, and he recalled that Mona had called several years ago and complained that Linda had come home and thrown up after late-night Lucia festivities. Mona had been very upset. That time, to his surprise, Wallander was the one who had been more relaxed about the whole incident. He tried to explain this to Martinsson as they walked up towards the station. But his colleague was resistant. Wallander gave up and stopped talking.

They halted in the reception area and Ebba came over to them.

"Is it true what I hear?" she asked. "That poor Anna and Emilia have burned to death?"

"That's what it looks like," Wallander said.

Ebba shook her head.

"I've bought buttons and thread from them since 1951," she said. "They were always so friendly. If you needed anything extra, they always took care of it with no additional charge. Who on earth would want to take the lives of two old ladies in a sewing shop?"

Ebba is the second person to ask that, Wallander thought. First Peter Edler, now Ebba.

"Is it a pyromaniac?" Martinsson asked. "In that case he's chosen a particularly apt evening to get started."

"We'll have to wait and see," Wallander replied. "Has anything more come in about the crashed plane?"

"Not as far as I know. But Sjöbo was going to have another talk with the man who was looking for his calf."

"Call the other districts just to be sure," Wallander reminded him. "It could turn out that they received calls about an engine noise too. There can hardly be that many aeroplanes flying around at night."

Martinsson left. Ebba gave Wallander a piece of paper.

"The travel insurance for your father," she said. "Lucky man, he gets to leave this weather and see the pyramids."

Wallander took the paper and went to his office. When he had hung up his coat, he called Löderup. There was no answer, even though he let the phone ring fifteen times. His father must be out in the studio.

Wallander put down the phone. I wonder if he remembers that he's supposed to travel tomorrow, he thought. And that I'm picking him up at seven o'clock.

But Wallander was looking forward to spending a couple of hours with Linda. That always put him in a good mood.

He pulled over a pile of papers, this one about the burglary on Pilgrimsgatan. But he ended up lost in thought about other things. What if they had a pyromaniac on their hands? They had been spared that for the past couple of years.

He forced himself to return to the burglary, but Nyberg called at ten-thirty.

"I think you should come down here," he said. "To the scene of the fire."

Wallander knew Nyberg would not have called unless it was important. It would be a waste of time to start asking questions over the phone.

"I'm on my way," he said and hung up.

He took his coat and left the station. It took him only a couple of minutes by car to get downtown. The cordoned-off area was smaller, but some traffic was still being redirected around Hamngatan.

Nyberg was waiting next to the ruins of the house, which were still smoking. He got straight to the point.

"This was not only arson," he said. "It was murder."

"Murder?"

Nyberg gestured for him to follow. The two bodies in the ruin had now been dug out. They crouched down next to one and Nyberg pointed to the cranium with a pen.

"A bullet hole," he said. "She's been shot, assuming it is one of the sisters. But I suppose we are assuming that."

They stood up and walked over to the second body.

"Same thing here," he said and pointed. "Just above the neck."

Wallander shook his head in disbelief.

"Someone shot them?"

"Looks like it. What's worse is that it was execution-style. Two shots to the back of the head."

Wallander had trouble taking in what Nyberg had just said. It was too preposterous, too brutal. But he also knew that Nyberg never said anything he wasn't absolutely sure about.

They walked back out to the street. Nyberg held up a small plastic bag in front of Wallander.

"We found one of the bullets," he said. "It was still stuck in the cranium. The other one exited through the forehead and has melted in the heat. But the medical examiner will of course do a thorough examination."

Wallander looked at Nyberg while he tried to think.

"So we have a double murder that someone tried to cover up with a fire?"

Nyberg shook his head.

"That doesn't make sense. A person who executes people by shooting them in the back of the head most likely knows that fires normally leave skeletons intact. After all, it's not a crematorium."

Wallander realised that Nyberg had said something important.

"What's the alternative?"

"The murderer may have wanted to conceal something else."

"What can you conceal in a sewing shop?"

"That's your job to figure out," Nyberg replied.

"I'll go and get a team together," Wallander said. "We'll start at one." He checked his watch. It was eleven. "Can you make it?"

"I won't be done here, of course," Nyberg said. "But I'll come by."

Wallander returned to his car. He was filled with a feeling of unreality. Who could have a motive for executing two old ladies who sold needles and thread and one or two zips? This was beyond anything he had been involved in before.

When he reached the station he walked straight to Rydberg's office. It was empty. Wallander found him in the break room, where he was eating a rusk and drinking tea. Wallander sat down and told him what Nyberg had discovered.

"That's not good," Rydberg said when Wallander was finished. "Not good at all."

Wallander stood up. "I'll see you at one," he said. "For now, let Martinsson focus on the plane. But Hansson and Svedberg should be there. And try to get Åkeson. Have we ever had anything like this?"

Rydberg considered. "Not that I can remember. There was a lunatic who planted an axe in a waiter's head about twenty years ago. The motive was an unpaid debt of thirty kronor. But I can't think of anything else."

Wallander lingered at the table.

"Execution-style," he said. "Not particularly Swedish."

"And what is Swedish, exactly?" Rydberg asked. "There are no longer any borders. Not for aeroplanes nor serious criminals. Once Ystad lay at the outskirts of something. What happened in Stockholm did not happen here. Not even things that occurred in Malmö were typical in a small town like Ystad. But that time is over."

"What happens now?"

"The new era will need a different kind of police, particularly out in the field," Rydberg said. "But there will still be a need for those like you and me, the ones who can think."

They walked together along the corridor. Rydberg walked slowly. They parted outside Rydberg's door.

"One o'clock," Rydberg said. "The double murder of two old ladies. Is that what we should call this? The case of the little old ladies?"

"I don't like it," Wallander said. "I don't understand why anyone would shoot two honourable old ladies."

"That may be where we have to begin," Rydberg said thoughtfully. "By examining if they were actually as honourable as everyone appears to believe."

Wallander was taken aback.

"What are you insinuating?"

"Nothing," Rydberg said, and smiled suddenly. "It's possible that one sometimes draws conclusions too quickly."

Wallander stood by the window in his office and absent-mindedly watched some pigeons flapping around the water tower. Rydberg is right, he thought. As usual. If there are no witnesses, if we don't get any observations from outside, then this is where we have to start: who were they really, Anna and Emilia?

They were all assembled in the conference room at one o'clock. Hansson had tried to get hold of Björk, without success. But Per Åkeson was there.

Wallander gave an account of the discovery that the two women had been shot. A sombre mood spread through the room. Evidently everyone had been to the sewing shop at least once. Then Wallander turned to Nyberg.

"We're still digging around in the rubble," Nyberg said. "But so far we haven't found anything of interest."

"The cause of the fire?" Wallander asked.

"It's too early to tell," he replied. "But according to the neighbours there was a loud blast. Someone described it as a muted explosion. And then, within the span of a minute, the whole building was on fire."

Wallander looked around the table.

"Since there is no immediately apparent motive, we have to begin by finding out what we can about these sisters. Is it true, as I believe, that they didn't have any relatives? Both were single. Had they ever been married? How old were they? I thought of them as old ladies already when I moved here."

Svedberg answered that he was sure that Anna and Emilia had never been married, and that they had no children. But he would find out more in greater detail.

"Bank accounts," said Rydberg, who had not said anything until then. "Did they have money? Either stuffed under the mattress at home or at the bank. There are rumours about such things. Can that have been the reason for the murder?"

"That doesn't explain the execution-style method," Wallander said. "But we need to find out about this. We need to know."

They divvied up the usual tasks among themselves. They were the same methodical and time-consuming tasks that had to be performed at the beginning of every investigation. When it was a quarter past two, Wallander had only one more thing to say.

"We need to speak to the media," he said. "This will interest them. Björk should be present, of course. But I would be happy to get out of it."

To everyone's surprise, Rydberg offered to speak to the reporters. Normally he was as reticent as Wallander on such occasions.

They broke up. Nyberg returned to the fire scene. Wallander and Rydberg stayed behind for a moment.

"I think we have to place some hope in the public," Rydberg said. "More than usual. It's clear that there must have been a motive for killing these sisters. And I have trouble thinking it could have been anything other than money."

"We've encountered this before," Wallander said. "People who don't own a penny but who get attacked because there are rumours of wealth."

"I have some contacts," Rydberg said. "I'll do a little investigating on the side."

They left the room.

"Why did you take on the press conference?" Wallander asked.

"So that you wouldn't have to do it for once," Rydberg said and went to his office.

Wallander managed to reach Björk, who was at home with a migraine.

"We're planning a press conference at five o'clock today," Wallander said. "We're all hoping you can be there."

"I'll be there," Björk said. "Migraine or not."

The investigative machine had been set in motion, slow but thorough. Wallander went back to the scene of the fire once more and talked to Nyberg, who was up to his knees in rubble. Then he returned to the station. But when the press conference started, he stayed away. He arrived home around six o'clock. This time his father answered when Wallander called.

"I've already packed," his father said.

"I should hope so," Wallander said. "I'll be there at half past six. Don't forget your passport and tickets."

Wallander spent the rest of the evening consolidating what they knew of the previous evening's events. He called Nyberg at home and asked him how the work was going.

Slowly, Nyberg said. They would continue in the morning as soon as it was light. Wallander also called the station and asked the officer on duty if any information had come in. But there was nothing that he considered noteworthy.

Wallander went to bed at midnight. In order to be sure of waking on time in the morning, he ordered a telephone wake-up call.

He had trouble falling asleep even though he was very tired.

The thought of the two sisters who had been executed worried him.

Before he fell asleep at last, he had managed to convince himself that it would be a long and difficult investigation. If they did not have the good fortune of tripping over the answer at the very beginning.

The following day he got up at five. At exactly half past six he turned into the driveway in Löderup.

His father was sitting outside on his suitcase, waiting.

CHAPTER
FIVE

They drove to Malmö in darkness. The daily commute from the Skåne region into Malmö had not yet begun in earnest. His father was wearing a suit and a strange-looking pith helmet. Wallander had never seen it before and imagined that his father must have picked it up at a flea market or a second-hand shop. But he said nothing. He didn't even ask if his father had remembered to bring his tickets or his passport.

"You're really going" was all he said.

"Yes," his father replied. "This is the day."

Wallander could sense that his father did not want to talk. It gave him the opportunity to focus on his driving and lose himself in his own thoughts. He was worried about the recent developments in Ystad. Wallander tried to get a handle on it. Why someone would cold-bloodedly shoot two old ladies in the back of the head. But he drew a blank. There was no context, no explanation. Only these brutal and incomprehensible executions.

As they turned into the small car park by the ferry terminal, they saw Linda already waiting outside. Wallander noticed that he didn't like how she greeted her grandfather first, then her father. She commented

404

on her grandfather's pith helmet, saying she thought it suited him.

"I wish I had as nice a hat to show off," Wallander said as he hugged his daughter. To his relief she was wearing a remarkably ordinary outfit. The opposite was often the case, which always bothered him. Now it struck him that this habit was something that she may have inherited from her grandfather. Or he'd been an influence, at least.

They accompanied him into the terminal. Wallander paid for his ferry ticket. Once he had climbed aboard, they stood out in the darkness and watched the vessel chug out through the harbour.

"I hope I'll be like him when I'm old," Linda said.

Wallander did not reply. To become like his father was something he feared more than anything.

They had breakfast together at the Central Station restaurant. As usual, Wallander had very little appetite so early in the morning. But in order to stave off a lecture from Linda about how he wasn't taking proper care of himself, he filled his plate with various sandwich toppings and several pieces of toast.

He watched his daughter, who talked almost continuously. She was not really beautiful in the traditional and banal sense of the word. But there was something confident and independent about her manner. She did not belong among the scores of young women who did their utmost to please all the men they met. From whom she had inherited her loquaciousness he could not say. Both he and Mona were rather quiet. But he liked listening to her. It always raised his spirits.

She continued to talk about going into the business of restoring furniture. Informed him of the possibilities in the field, what the challenges were, cursed the fact that the apprenticeship system had almost died out, and astonished him at the end by imagining a future where she set up her own shop in Ystad.

"It's too bad that neither you nor Mum have any money," she said. "Then I could have gone to France to learn."

Wallander realised she was not in fact chastising him for not being wealthy. Nonetheless, he took it this way.

"I could take out a loan," he said. "I think a simple policeman can manage that."

"Loans have to be paid back," she said. "And anyway, you are actually a criminal inspector."

Then they talked about Mona. Wallander listened, not without some satisfaction, to her complaints about Mona, who controlled her daughter in everything she did.

"And to top it off I don't like Johan," she finished.

Wallander looked searchingly at her.

"Who's that?"

"Her new guy."

"I thought she was seeing someone called Sören?"

"They broke up. Now his name is Johan and he owns two diggers."

"And you don't like him?"

She shrugged.

"He's so loud. And I don't think he's ever read a book in his life. On Saturdays he comes over and he's bought some comic book. A grown man. Can you imagine?"

Wallander felt a momentary relief at the fact that he had never bought a comic book. He knew that Svedberg sometimes picked up an issue of *Superman*. Once or twice he had flipped through it to try to recapture the feeling from childhood, but it was never there.

"That doesn't sound so good," he said. "I mean, that you and Johan don't get along."

"It's not so much a question of us," she said. "It's more that I don't understand what Mum sees in him."

"Come and live with me," Wallander said impulsively. "Your room is still there, you know that."

"I've actually thought about it," she said. "But I don't think that would be a good idea."

"Why not?"

"Ystad is too small. It would drive me crazy to live there. Maybe later, when I'm older. There are towns where you simply can't live when you're young."

Wallander knew what she was talking about. Even for divorced men in their forties, a town like Ystad could start to feel cramped.

"What about you?" she asked.

"What do you mean?"

"What do you think? Women, of course."

Wallander made a face. He didn't want to bring up Emma Lundin.

"You could put an ad in the paper," she suggested. "'A man in his best years looking for a woman.' You would get a lot of responses."

"Sure," Wallander said, "and then it would take five minutes before we'd simply end up sitting there staring vacantly at each other, realising we have nothing to say."

She surprised him again.

"You need to have someone to sleep with," she said. "It's not good for you to walk around with so much pent-up longing."

Wallander winced. She had never said anything like that to him before.

"I have all I need," he said evasively.

"Can't you tell me more?"

"There's not much to say. A nurse. A decent person. The problem is just that she likes me more than I like her."

Linda did not ask any more questions. Wallander immediately started to wonder about her sex life. But the very thought filled him with so many ambivalent feelings that he didn't want to get into it.

They stayed in the restaurant until it was past ten o'clock. Then he offered to drive her home, but she had errands to run. They parted in the car park. Wallander gave her three hundred kronor.

"You don't need to do this," she said.

"I know. But take it anyway."

Then he watched her walk off into the city. Thought that this was his family. A daughter who was finding her way. And a father who was right now sitting on a plane taking him to scorching-hot Egypt. He had a complicated relationship with both of them. It was not only his father who could be difficult, but also Linda.

★　★　★

He was back in Ystad at half past ten. During the trip back he had an easier time thinking about what now awaited him. The meeting with Linda had given him new energy. The broadest possible approach, he said to himself. That's the way we have to proceed. He stopped on the outskirts of Ystad and ate a hamburger, promising himself it would be the last one of the year. When he walked into the reception area, Ebba called out to him. She looked a little tense.

"Björk wants to talk to you," she said.

Wallander hung his coat up in his office, then walked to Björk's room. He was let in at once. Björk stood up behind his desk.

"I have to express my great dismay," he said.

"With what?"

"That you go to Malmö on personal business when we are in the midst of a difficult murder case, one that you moreover are in charge of."

Wallander could not believe his ears. Björk was actually reprimanding him. That had never happened before, even if Björk had often had ample reason to do so on previous occasions. Wallander thought about all the times that he had acted too independently during an investigation, without informing the others.

"This is extremely unfortunate," Björk concluded. "There will be no formal reprimand. But it was, as I said, a show of poor judgement."

Wallander stared at Björk. Then he made an about-face and left without saying a word. But when he was halfway back to his office, he turned and walked back, pulling open the door to Björk's office and saying, through clenched teeth:

"I'm not going to take any shit from you. Just so you know. Give me a formal reprimand if you want. But don't stand there talking nonsense. I won't take it."

Then he left. He noticed that he was sweating. But he didn't regret it. The outburst had been necessary. And he was not at all worried about the consequences. His position at the station was strong.

He got a cup of coffee in the break room and then sat down at his desk. He knew that Björk had gone to Stockholm to take a leadership course of some kind. He had probably learned he should scold his colleagues from time to time in order to improve the climate of the workplace, Wallander thought. But if so, he had chosen the wrong person to start with.

Then he wondered who had passed on the fact that Wallander had spent the morning driving his father to Malmö.

There were several possibilities. Wallander could not recall to whom he had mentioned his father's impending trip to Egypt.

The only thing he was sure of was that it was not Rydberg. The latter regarded Björk as a necessary administrative evil. Hardly anything more. And he was always loyal to those he worked with. His loyalty would never be corrupted, though of course he would not spare his colleagues if they acted irresponsibly. Then Rydberg would be the first to react.

Wallander was interrupted in this train of thought by Martinsson, who looked in.

"Is this a good time?"

Wallander nodded at his visitor's chair.

They began by talking about the fire and the murder of the Eberhardsson sisters. But Wallander soon realised that Martinsson had come in about something different.

"It's about the plane," he said. "Our Sjöbo colleagues have worked quickly. They've located an area just south-west of the village where lights were allegedly observed that night. From what I gather, it's a non-residential area. That could also corroborate the idea of an air drop."

"You mean that the lights would have been guiding lights?"

"That is one possibility. There's also a myriad of small roads through that area. Easy to get to, easy to leave."

"That strengthens our theory," Wallander said.

"I have more," Martinsson went on. "The Sjöbo team has been diligent. They've checked to see who actually lives in that area. Most of them are farmers, of course, but they found one exception."

Wallander sharpened his attention.

"A farm called Långelunda," Martinsson said. "For a couple of years it's been a haven for a variety of people who have caused problems for the Sjöbo police from time to time. People have moved in and out, the ownership has been unclear and there have been drug seizures. Not great quantities, but still."

Martinsson scratched his forehead.

"The colleague I spoke with, Göran Brunberg, gave me a few names. I wasn't paying that much attention, but when I hung up I started thinking. There was one name I thought I recognised. From a case we had recently."

Wallander sat up.

"You don't mean that Yngve Leonard Holm lives up there? That he has a place there?"

Martinsson nodded.

"He's the one. It took a while for me to put it together."

Damn it, Wallander thought. I knew there was something about him. I even thought of the plane. But we had to let him go.

"We'll bring him in," Wallander said and banged a fist firmly on his desk.

"That was exactly what I told our Sjöbo colleagues when I made the connection," Martinsson said. "But when they got out to Långelunda, Holm was gone."

"What do you mean, 'gone'?"

"Disappeared, gone, vanished. He did live there, even if he was registered in Ystad for the last couple of years. And built his mansion here. The Sjöbo colleagues talked to a couple of other individuals living there. Rough types, from what I gather. Holm was there as recently as yesterday. But no one has seen him since then. I went to his house here in Ystad, but it's locked up."

Wallander thought it over.

"So Holm doesn't usually disappear like this?"

"The people in the house actually seemed a little concerned."

"In other words, there could be a connection," Wallander said.

"I was thinking that Holm may have been intending to leave on the plane that crashed."

"Not likely," Wallander said. "Then you're assuming the plane had somewhere to land and pick him up. And the Sjöbo police haven't found any place like that, have they? An improvised landing strip? It would also exceed the time frame."

"A sport plane with a skilled pilot may only need a small level area to land and take off from."

Wallander hesitated. Martinsson could be right, even though Wallander doubted this was the case. On the other hand, he had no difficulty imagining that Holm could be involved in decidedly larger drug operations than they had believed.

"We'll have to continue working on this," Wallander said. "Unfortunately, you'll be more or less alone on it. The rest of us have to focus on the murdered sisters."

"Have you found a possible motive?"

"We have nothing other than an incomprehensible execution and an explosive fire," Wallander replied. "But if there's anything to be found in the remains of the fire, Nyberg will get it."

Martinsson left. Wallander noticed that his thoughts were alternating between the downed plane and the fire. It was two o'clock. His father would have landed in Cairo by now, if the plane had left on time from

Kastrup. Then he thought about Björk's strange behaviour. He felt himself getting upset again and at the same time felt pleased that he had given his boss a piece of his mind.

Since he was having trouble concentrating on his paperwork he drove down to the scene of the fire. Nyberg was on his knees in the rubble together with the other technicians. The smell of smoke was still strong. Nyberg saw Wallander and made his way out onto the street.

"The fire burned with an intense heat, according to Edler's people," he said. "Everything appears to have melted. And that of course strengthens the suspicion of arson, about a fire started in several places at once. Perhaps with the help of petrol."

"We have to get the people who did this," Wallander said.

"That would be a good thing," Nyberg said. "One gets the feeling that this is the work of a madman."

"Or the opposite," Wallander said. "Someone who really knew what he was after."

"In a sewing shop? Run by two old unmarried sisters?"

Nyberg shook his head disbelievingly and returned to the ruins. Wallander walked down to the harbour. He needed some air. It was a couple of degrees below freezing and there was almost no breeze. He stopped outside the theatre building and saw that there was going to be a performance by the National Theatre. *A Dream Play* by Strindberg. If only it had been an opera, he thought. Then I would have gone. But he hesitated to attend a regular play.

He walked out onto the pier in the yacht harbour. A ferry to Poland was just leaving the large terminal that lay adjacent to it. Absent-mindedly he wondered how many cars were being smuggled out of Sweden this time.

He returned to the station at half past three. He wondered if his father had reached the hotel and settled in. And if he would receive a new reprimand from Björk for an unexplained absence. At four o'clock he gathered with his colleagues in the conference room. They reviewed the findings of the day. Their collected material was still thin.

"Unusually thin," Rydberg said. "A building burns down in Ystad. And no one has noticed anything out of the ordinary."

Svedberg and Hansson reported what they had found. Neither of the sisters had been married. There were a number of distant relatives, cousins and second cousins. But no one who lived in Ystad. The sewing shop yielded an unremarkable declared income. Nor had they uncovered any bank accounts with large savings. Hansson had located a safe-deposit box at Handels Bank. But since they lacked keys, Per Åkeson would have to submit a request that the box be opened. Hansson calculated that it could be done by the following day.

Afterwards a heavy silence descended on the room.

"There has to be a motive," Wallander said. "Sooner or later we'll find it. If we only have patience."

"Who knew these sisters?" Rydberg asked. "They must have had friends and a bit of spare time now and again when they weren't working in the shop. Did they belong to any kind of organisation? Did they have a summer cabin? Did they take holidays? I still feel that we haven't scratched below the surface."

Wallander thought Rydberg sounded irritable. He's probably in a lot of pain, Wallander thought. I wonder what is really wrong with him. If it isn't only rheumatism.

No one had anything to add to what Rydberg had said. They would go forward and delve deeper.

Wallander remained in his office until close to eight o'clock. He made his own list of all the facts they had about the Eberhardsson sisters. As he read through what he had written he realised in earnest how thin it was. They had absolutely no leads to pursue.

Before leaving the office he called Martinsson at home. Martinsson told him that Holm had still not turned up.

Wallander went to his car. It took a long time for the engine to sputter into life. He angrily decided to take out a loan and get a new car as soon as he had the time.

When he came home he booked a time for the laundry room and then opened a can of luncheon meat. Just as he was about to sit down in front of the TV with his plate perched on his lap the phone rang. It was Emma. She asked if she could come by.

"Not tonight," Wallander said. "You've probably read about the fire and the two sisters. We're working round the clock right now."

She understood. After Wallander hung up he wondered why he couldn't tell her the truth. That he didn't want to be with her any more. But of course it was inexcusable cowardice to say this over the phone. Therefore he had to steel himself to go over to her place some evening. He promised himself he would as soon as he had time.

He started to eat his food, which had already grown cold. It was nine o'clock.

The telephone rang again. Annoyed, Wallander put the plate down and answered.

It was Nyberg, who was still at the scene of the fire, calling from a patrol car.

"Now I think we've found something," he said. "A safe, the expensive kind that can withstand extreme heat."

"Why didn't you find it earlier?"

"Good question," Nyberg answered, without taking offence. "The safe had been lowered into the foundation. We found a heat-insulated trapdoor under all the rubble. When we managed to force it open we found a space underneath. And there was the safe."

"Have you opened it?"

"With what? There are no keys. This is a safe that will be difficult to force open."

Wallander checked his watch. Ten minutes past nine.

"I'm on my way," he said. "I wonder if you might have uncovered the lead we were looking for."

When Wallander got down to the street he couldn't get the car to start. He gave up and walked to Hamngatan.

At twenty minutes to ten he stood at Nyberg's side and studied the safe, illuminated by a lone spotlight.

At about the same time the temperature began to fall, and a gusty wind was moving in from the east.

CHAPTER
SIX

Shortly after midnight on the fifteenth of December, Nyberg and his men had managed to lift up the safe with the help of a crane. It was loaded onto the back of a truck and immediately taken to the station. But before Nyberg and Wallander left the scene, Nyberg examined the space under the foundation.

"This was put in after the house was built," he said. "I have to assume it was constructed expressly to hold this safe."

Wallander nodded without a reply. He was thinking about the Eberhardsson sisters. The police had searched for a motive. Now they may have found it, even if they didn't yet know what was in the safe.

But someone else may have known, Wallander thought. Both that the safe existed. And what was inside.

Nyberg and Wallander left the scene of the fire and walked out to the street.

"Is it possible to cut into the safe?" Wallander asked.

"Yes, of course," Nyberg answered. "But it requires special welding equipment. This is not the kind of safe that a regular locksmith would dream of trying to crack open."

"We have to open it as soon as possible."

Nyberg pulled off his protective suit. He looked sceptically at Wallander.

"Do you mean that the safe should be opened tonight?"

"That would be best," Wallander said. "This is a double homicide."

"Impossible," Nyberg said. "I can only get hold of people with the requisite welding equipment tomorrow at the earliest."

"Are they here in Ystad?"

Nyberg reflected.

"There is a company that's a sub-contractor for the armed forces," he said. "They probably have the equipment that would do the trick. I think their name is Fabricius. They're on Industrigatan."

Nyberg looked exhausted. It would be insane to drive him onward right now, Wallander thought. He himself shouldn't press on either.

"Seven o'clock tomorrow," Wallander said.

Nyberg nodded.

Wallander looked around for his car. Then he remembered that it hadn't started. Nyberg could drop him off, but he preferred to walk. The wind was cold. He passed a thermometer outside a shop window on Stora Östergatan. Minus six degrees Celsius. Winter is creeping in, Wallander thought. Soon it will be here.

One minute to seven on the morning of the fifteenth of December, Nyberg entered Wallander's office. Wallander had the telephone directory open on his desk. He had already inspected the safe, which was being stored in a temporarily empty room next to reception. One of the officers just going off the night shift told him that they had needed a forklift to get the safe inside. Wallander nodded. He had noticed the marks outside the glass doors and seen that one of the hinges was bent. That won't make Björk happy, he thought. But he'll have to live with it. Wallander had tried to move the safe, without success. He had wondered again what it contained. Or if it was empty.

Nyberg called the company on Industrigatan. Wallander went to get some coffee. Rydberg arrived at the same time. Wallander told him about the safe.

"It was as I suspected," Rydberg said. "We know very little about these sisters."

"We're in the process of trying to find a welder who can take on this kind of safe," Wallander said.

"I hope you'll tell me before you open it," Rydberg said. "It will be interesting to be there."

Wallander returned to his office. He thought it seemed as if Rydberg was in less pain today.

Nyberg was just getting off the phone when Wallander walked in with two cups of coffee.

"I've just spoken to Ruben Fabricius," Nyberg said. "He thought they would be able to do the job. They'll be here in half an hour."

"Tell me when they arrive," Wallander said.

Nyberg left. Wallander thought about his father in Cairo. Hoped that his experiences were living up to his expectations. He studied the note with the telephone number of the hotel, Mena House. Wondered if he should call. But suddenly he was unsure of what the time difference was, or if there even was one. He dropped the thought and instead called Ebba to see who had come in.

"Martinsson called in to say that he was on his way to Sjöbo," she answered. "Svedberg hasn't arrived yet. Hansson is showering. He's apparently had a water leak at home."

"We're going to open the safe soon," Wallander said. "That may get noisy."

"I went in to take a look at it," Ebba said. "I thought it would be bigger."

"One that size can hold a lot as well."

"Of course," she said. "Ugh."

Wallander wondered later what she had meant by her last comment. Did she expect that they would find a child's corpse in the safe? Or a decapitated head?

Hansson appeared in the doorway. His hair was still wet.

"I've just talked to Björk," he said cheerily. "He pointed out that the doors of the station were damaged last night."

Hansson had not yet heard about the safe. Wallander explained.

"That may provide us with a motive," Hansson said.

"In the best-case scenario," Wallander said. "In the worst case, the safe is empty. And then we understand even less."

"It could have been emptied by the people who shot the sisters," Hansson objected. "Perhaps he shot one of them and forced the other to open the safe?"

This had also occurred to Wallander. But something told him it was not what had actually happened. Without being able to say why he had that feeling.

At eight o'clock, under Ruben Fabricius's direction, two welders started the work of cutting open the safe. It was, as Nyberg had predicted, a difficult task.

"A special kind of steel," Fabricius said. "A normal locksmith would have to devote his whole life trying to open this kind of safe."

"Can you blow it up?" Wallander asked.

"The risk would be that you'd take the whole building with you," Fabricius answered. "In that case I would first move the safe to an open field. But sometimes so much explosive is needed that the safe itself is blown to pieces. And the contents either burn or are pulverised."

Fabricius was a large, heavyset man who punctuated each sentence with a short laugh.

"This kind of safe probably costs a hundred thousand kronor," he said and laughed.

Wallander looked astonished.

"That much?"

"Easily."

One thing at least is certain, Wallander thought as he recalled yesterday's discussion about the dead women's financial situation. The Eberhardsson sisters had much more money than they had reported to the authorities. They must have had undeclared income. But what can you sell of value in a sewing shop? Gold thread? Diamond-studded buttons?

The welding equipment was turned off at a quarter past nine. Fabricius nodded to Wallander and chuckled.

"All set," he said.

Rydberg, Hansson and Svedberg had arrived. Nyberg had been following the work from the beginning. Using a crowbar, he now forced out the back piece that had been freed with a welding torch. Everyone who was crowded around leaned forward. Wallander saw a number of plastic-wrapped bundles. Nyberg picked up one that lay on top. The plastic was white and sealed with tape. Nyberg placed the bundle on a chair and cut open the tape. Inside there was a thick wad of notes. American hundred-dollar bills. There were ten wads, each a stack of ten thousand dollars.

"A lot of money," Wallander said.

He carefully pulled out a bill and held it up to the light. It appeared genuine.

Nyberg took out the other bundles, one after another, and opened them. Fabricius stood in the background and laughed each time a new package of money was revealed.

"Let's take the rest to a conference room," Wallander said.

Then he thanked Fabricius and the two men who had cut open the safe.

"You'll have to send us a bill," Wallander said. "Without you, we would never have been able to get this open."

"I think this one's on us," Fabricius said. "It was an experience for a tradesman. And a wonderful opportunity for professional training."

424

"There is also no need to mention what was inside," Wallander said and tried to sound serious.

Fabricius let out a short laugh and saluted him. Wallander understood that it was not intended to be ironic.

When all of the bundles had been opened and the wads of notes counted, Wallander made a swift calculation. Most of it had been in US dollars. But there had also been British pounds and Swiss francs.

"I estimate it to be around five million kronor," he said. "No insignificant sum."

"There would also not have been room for more in this safe," Rydberg said. "And this means, in other words, that if this cash was the motive then he or they who shot the sisters did not get what they had come for."

"We nonetheless have some kind of motive," Wallander said. "This safe had been concealed. According to Nyberg, it appeared to have been there for a number of years. At some point the sisters must therefore have found it necessary to buy it because they needed to store and hide large sums of money. These were almost entirely new and unused dollar bills. Therefore it must be possible to trace them. Did they arrive in Sweden legally or not? We also need to find answers as quickly as possible to the other questions we're working on. Who did these sisters socialise with? What kind of habits did they have?"

"And weaknesses," Rydberg added. "Let us not forget about that."

Björk entered the room at the end of the meeting. He gave a start when he saw all the money on the table.

"This has to be carefully recorded," he said when Wallander explained in a somewhat strained manner what had happened. "Nothing can be lost. Also, what has happened to the front doors?"

"A work-related accident," Wallander said. "When the forklift was lifting the safe."

He said this so forcefully that Björk did not make any objections.

They broke up the meeting. Wallander hurried out of the room in order not to be left alone with Björk. It had fallen to Wallander to contact an animal protection association where at least one of the sisters, Emilia, had been an active member, according to one of the neighbours. Wallander had been given a name by Svedberg, Tyra Olofsson. Wallander burst out laughing when he saw the address: Käringgatan — "käring" meant old woman or shrew — number 11. He wondered if there was any other town in Sweden that had as many unusual street names.

Before Wallander left the station he called Arne Hurtig, the car salesman he usually did business with. He explained the situation with his Peugeot. Hurtig gave him a few suggestions, all of which Wallander found too expensive. But when Hurtig promised a good trade-in price on his old car, Wallander decided to get another Peugeot. He hung up and called his bank. He had to wait several minutes until he could speak to the person who normally helped him. Wallander asked for a loan of twenty thousand kronor. He was informed that this would not be a problem. He would be able to come in the following day, sign the loan documents and pick up the money.

The thought of a new car put him in a good mood. Why he always drove a Peugeot, he couldn't say. I'm probably more stuck in my ways than I like to think, he thought as he left the station. He stopped and inspected the damaged hinge on the front doors of the station. Since no one was around, he took the opportunity to give the door frame a kick. The damage became more noticeable. He walked away quickly, hunched over against the gusty wind. Of course he should have called to make sure that Tyra Olofsson was in. But since she was retired, he took the chance.

When he rang the doorbell, it opened almost at once. Tyra Olofsson was short and wore glasses that testified to her myopia. Wallander explained who he was and held up his ID card, which she held several centimetres from her glasses and studied carefully.

"The police," she said. "Then it must have to do with poor Emilia."

"That's right," Wallander said. "I hope I'm not disturbing you."

She invited him in. There was a strong smell of dogs in the hall. She led him out into the kitchen. Wallander counted fourteen food bowls on the floor. Worse than Haverberg, he thought.

"I keep them outside," Tyra Olofsson said, having followed his gaze.

Wallander wondered briefly if it was legal to keep so many dogs in the city. She asked if he wanted coffee.

Wallander thanked her but declined. He was hungry and planning to eat as soon as his conversation with Tyra Olofsson was over. He sat down at the table and looked in vain for something to write with. For once he had remembered to put a notepad in his pocket. But now he didn't have a pen. There was a small stump of a pencil lying on the windowsill, which he picked up.

"You're right, Mrs Olofsson," he began. "This is about Emilia Eberhardsson, who has died so tragically. We heard through one of the neighbours that she had been active in an animal protection association. And that you, Mrs Olofsson, knew her well."

"Call me Tyra," she said. "And I can't say I knew Emilia well. I don't think anyone did."

"Was her sister Anna ever involved in this work?"

"No."

"Isn't that strange? I mean, two sisters, both unmarried who live together. I imagine they would develop similar interests."

"That is a stereotype," Tyra Olofsson said firmly. "I imagine that Emilia and Anna were very different people. I worked as a teacher my whole life. Then you learn to see the differences in people. It's already apparent in young children."

"How would you describe Emilia?"

Her answer surprised him.

"Snooty. The kind who always knows best. She could be very unpleasant. But since she donated money for our work, we couldn't get rid of her. Even if we wanted to."

Tyra Olofsson told him about the local animal protection association that she and a few other like-minded individuals had started in the 1960s. They had always worked locally and the impetus for the association was the increasing problem of abandoned summer cats. The association had always been small, with few members. One day in the early seventies, Emilia Eberhardsson had read about their work in the *Ystad Allehanda* and got in touch. She had given them money every month and participated in meetings and other events.

"But I don't think she really liked animals," Tyra said unexpectedly. "I think she did it so she would be thought of as a good person."

"That doesn't sound like such a nice description."

The woman on the other side of the table looked cheekily at him.

"I thought policemen wanted to know the truth," she said. "Or am I wrong?"

Wallander changed the subject and asked about money.

"She donated a thousand kronor a month. For us that was a lot."

"Did she give the impression of being rich?"

"She never dressed expensively. But I'm sure she had money."

"You must have asked yourself where it came from. A sewing shop is hardly something one associates with a fortune."

"Not one thousand kronor a month either," she answered. "I'm not particularly curious. Perhaps it's because I see so badly. But where the money came from or how well their shop did, I know nothing about."

Wallander hesitated for a moment, and then he told her the truth.

"It has been reported in the papers that the sisters burned to death," he said, "but it has not been reported that they were shot. They were already dead when the fire started."

She sat up.

"Who could have wanted to shoot two old ladies? That's as likely as someone wanting to kill me."

"That is exactly what we are trying to understand," Wallander said. "That's why I'm here. Did Emilia ever say anything about having enemies? Did she appear frightened?"

Tyra Olofsson did not have to reflect.

"She was always very sure of herself," she said. "She never said a word about her and her sister's life. And when they were away she never sent a postcard. Not once, even with all the wonderful postcards with animal motifs that you can get these days."

Wallander raised his eyebrows.

"You mean they travelled a lot?"

"Two months out of every year. November and March. Sometimes in the summer."

"Where did they go?"

"I heard it was Spain."

"Who took care of their shop?"

"They always took turns. Perhaps they needed time apart."

430

"Spain? What else do the rumours say? And where do these rumours come from?"

"I can't remember. I don't listen to rumours. Perhaps they went to Marbella. But I'm not sure."

Wallander wondered if Tyra Olofsson was really as uninterested in rumours and gossip as she seemed. He had only one remaining question.

"Who do you think knew Emilia best?"

"I would think it was her sister."

Wallander thanked her and walked back to the station. The wind was even stronger. He thought about what Tyra Olofsson had said. There had been no meanness in her voice. She had been very matter-of-fact. But her description of Emilia Eberhardsson had not been flattering.

When Wallander reached the station, Ebba told him that Rydberg had been looking for him. Wallander went straight to his office.

"The picture is becoming clearer," Rydberg said. "I think we should get the others and have a short meeting. I know they're around."

"What's happened?"

Rydberg waved a bunch of papers.

"VPC," he said. "And there's a great deal of interest in these papers."

It took Wallander a moment to remember that VPC stood for the Swedish securities register centre, which, among other things, recorded stock ownership.

"For my part I've managed to establish that at least one of the sisters was a genuinely unpleasant person," Wallander said.

"Doesn't surprise me in the least," Rydberg chuckled. "The rich often are."

"Rich?" Wallander asked.

But Rydberg did not answer until they were all assembled in the conference room. Then he explained himself in detail.

"According to the Swedish securities register centre, the Eberhardsson sisters had stocks and bonds totalling close to ten million kronor. How they managed to keep this from being subject to the wealth tax is a mystery. Nor do they appear to have paid income tax on their dividends. But I've alerted the tax authorities. It actually appears that Anna Eberhardsson was registered as a resident of Spain. But I'm not clear on the details of this yet. In any case, they had a large portfolio of investments both in Sweden and abroad. The Swedish securities register centre's ability to check international investments is of course minimal; this is not their job. But the sisters invested heavily in the British weapons and aviation industries. And in this they appear to have shown great skill and daring."

Rydberg put down the documents.

"We can thus not exclude the possibility that what we see here is only the tip of the proverbial iceberg. Five million in a safe and ten million in stocks and bonds. This is what we have uncovered in the space of a few hours. What happens after we've been working for a week? Perhaps the amount will increase to one hundred million?"

Wallander reported on his meeting with Tyra Olofsson.

432

"The description of Anna isn't flattering either," Svedberg said when Wallander had finished. "I talked to the man who sold the sisters the house five years ago. That was when the market was getting soft. Until then they had always rented. Apparently it was Anna who negotiated. Emilia was never present. And the estate agent said Anna was the most difficult customer he ever had. Apparently she had managed to find out that his company happened to be in crisis at that time, with regard to both solidity and liquidity. He said that she had been completely ice-cold and more or less blackmailed him."

Svedberg shook his head.

"This isn't exactly how I would have imagined two old ladies who sold buttons," he said and the room fell silent.

Wallander was the one who broke the silence.

"In a way this has been our breakthrough," he started. "We still have no leads on who killed them. But we have a plausible motive. And it is the most common of all motives: money. In addition, we know that the women committed tax fraud and concealed great sums of money from the authorities. We know that they were rich. It won't surprise me if we turn up a house in Spain. And perhaps other assets, in other parts of the world."

Wallander poured himself a glass of mineral water before continuing.

"Everything we know now can be summed up in two points. Two questions. Where did they get the money? And who knew that they were rich?"

Wallander was about to lift the glass to his lips when he saw Rydberg flinch, as if he had been given a shock.

Then his upper body slumped over the table.

As if he was dead.

CHAPTER
SEVEN

Later, Wallander would remember that for a few seconds he had been entirely convinced that Rydberg had died. Everyone who was in the room when Rydberg collapsed thought the same thing: that Rydberg's heart had suddenly stopped. It was Svedberg who reacted first. He had been sitting next to Rydberg and could tell that his colleague was still alive. He grabbed the telephone and called for an ambulance. Wallander and Hansson lowered Rydberg onto the floor and unbuttoned his shirt. Wallander listened to his heart and heard it beating very quickly. Then the ambulance arrived and Wallander accompanied it on its short drive to the hospital. Rydberg received immediate treatment, and after less than half an hour Wallander had been informed that it was not likely to have been a heart attack. Rather, Rydberg had collapsed for some as yet unknown reason. He was conscious at this point but shook his head when Wallander wanted to talk to him. He was judged to be in stable condition and admitted to the hospital for observation. There was no longer any reason for Wallander to stay. A patrol car was waiting outside to drive him back to the station. His colleagues had remained in the conference room. Even Björk was present. Wallander could inform them that the situation was under control.

"We work too hard," he said and looked at Björk. "We have more and more to do. But our numbers have not increased. Sooner or later what happened to Rydberg can happen to all of us."

"It is a troubling situation," Björk admitted. "But we have limited resources."

For the next half an hour the investigation was set aside. Everyone was shaken and talked about the working conditions. After Björk left the room, the words became sharper. About impossible planning, strange priorities and a continual lack of information.

At around two o'clock, Wallander felt they had to move on. Not least for his own sake. When he saw what had happened to Rydberg he had thought about what could happen to himself. How long would his own heart put up with the strain? All the unhealthy food, the frequently recurring bouts of broken and lost sleep? And, above all, his grief after the divorce.

"Rydberg would not approve of this," he said. "That we're wasting time talking about our situation. We'll have to do that later. Right now we have a double murderer to catch. As soon as we possibly can."

They ended the meeting. Wallander went to his office and called the hospital. He was told that Rydberg was sleeping. It was still premature to expect an explanation for what had happened.

Wallander hung up the phone, and Martinsson walked in.

"What happened?" he asked. "I've been in Sjöbo. Ebba was all shaken up out there."

Wallander told him. Martinsson sat down heavily in the visitor's chair.

"We work ourselves to death," he said. "And who appreciates it?"

Wallander became impatient. He didn't want to think about Rydberg any more, at least not right now.

"Sjöbo," he said. "What do you have for me?"

"I've been out in a variety of muddy fields," Martinsson replied. "We've been able to pinpoint the location of those lights quite well. But there were no traces anywhere of either spotlights or marks from a plane landing or taking off. On the other hand, some information has turned up that probably explains why this aeroplane couldn't be identified."

"And what is it?"

"It simply doesn't exist."

"What do you mean?"

Martinsson took a while to search through the papers he had taken out of his briefcase.

"According to the records of the Piper factory, this plane crashed in Vientiane in 1986. The owner back then was a Laotian consortium that used it to transport its managers to various agricultural centres around the country. The official cause of the crash was listed as a lack of fuel. No one was injured or killed. But the plane was wrecked and removed from all active registers and from the insurance company, which apparently was a kind of daughter company to

Lloyd's. This is what we know after looking up the engine registration number."

"But that turned out not to be correct?"

"The Piper factory is naturally very interested in what has happened. It's not good for their reputation if a plane that no longer exists suddenly starts to fly again. This could be a case of insurance fraud and other things that we have no idea about."

"And the men in the plane?"

"We're still waiting for them to be identified. I have a couple of good contacts in Interpol. They've promised to expedite the matter."

"The plane must have come from somewhere," Wallander said.

Martinsson nodded.

"That gives us yet another problem. If you refurbish a plane with extra fuel tanks, it's able to fly long distances. Nyberg thinks he may have identified the remains of something that could have been a spare fuel tank. But we don't know yet. If this is the case, the plane could have come from virtually anywhere. At least Britain and Continental Europe."

"But it must have been observed by someone," Wallander insisted. "You can't cross borders with complete impunity."

"I agree," Martinsson said. "Therefore Germany would be an educated guess, because you fly over open water until you reach the Swedish border."

"What do the German aviation authorities say?"

"It takes time," Martinsson said. "But I'm working on it."

Wallander reflected for a moment.

"We actually need you on this double homicide," he said. "Can you delegate this work to someone else? At least while we wait on a positive identification of the pilots, and whether the plane came from Germany?"

"I was about to suggest the same thing," Martinsson said.

Wallander checked the time.

"Ask Hansson or Svedberg to get you up to speed on the case," he said.

Martinsson got out of the chair.

"Have you heard from your father?"

"He doesn't call without a good reason."

"My father died when he was fifty-five," Martinsson said abruptly. "He had his own business. A car-repairs shop. He had to work constantly in order to make ends meet. Right when things were starting to look up, he died. He wouldn't have been more than sixty-seven now."

Martinsson left. Wallander did his best to avoid thinking about Rydberg. Instead he again reviewed everything they knew about the Eberhardsson sisters. They had a likely motive — money — but no trace of the killer. Wallander jotted a few words on his notepad.

The double life of the Eberhardsson sisters?

Then he pushed the pad away. When Rydberg was out, they lacked their best instrument. If an investigative team is like an orchestra, Wallander thought, we've lost our first violinist. And then the orchestra doesn't sound as good.

At that moment he made up his mind to have his own talk with the neighbour who had provided the information about Anna Eberhardsson. Svedberg was often too impatient when he talked to people about what they might have seen or heard. It's also a matter of finding out what people think, Wallander said to himself. He found the name of the neighbour, Linnea Gunnér. Only women in this case, he thought. He dialled her phone number and heard her pick up. Linnea Gunnér was at home and happy to receive him. She gave him the code to the front door of her building and he made a note of it.

He left the station shortly after three o'clock and kicked the damaged hinge again. The dent was getting worse. When he reached the scene of the fire, he saw that the ruins of the building were already in the process of being razed. There were still many curious onlookers gathered around the site.

Linnea Gunnér lived on Möllegatan. Wallander entered the door code and took the stairs to the first floor. The house dated back to the turn of the century and had beautiful designs on the walls of its stairwell. On the door to Gunnér's apartment was posted a large sign about residents not wishing to receive any advertisements. Wallander rang the bell. The woman who opened the door was the opposite of Tyra Olofsson in almost every way. She was tall, with a sharp gaze and a firm voice. She invited him into her apartment, which was filled with objects from all over the world. In the living room there was even a ship's figurehead. Wallander looked at it for a long time.

440

"This belonged to the barque *Felicia*, which sank in the Irish Sea," Linnea Gunnér said. "I bought it once for an insignificant sum in Middlesbrough."

"Then you've been at sea?" he asked.

"My whole life. First as a chef, then as a steward."

She did not speak with a Skåne dialect. Wallander thought she sounded more as if she came from Småland or Östergötland.

"Where are you from?" he asked.

"Skänninge in Östergötland. About as far from the sea as one can get."

"And now you live in Ystad?"

"I inherited this apartment from an aunt. And I have a view of the sea."

She had put out coffee. Wallander thought it was probably the last thing his stomach needed. But he still said yes. He had immediately felt he could trust Linnea Gunnér. He had read in Svedberg's notes that she was sixty-six years old. But she appeared younger.

"My colleague Svedberg was here," Wallander started.

She burst into laughter.

"I have never seen someone scratch his forehead as often as that man."

Wallander nodded.

"We all have our ways. For example, I always think there are more questions to be asked than one may initially think."

"I only told him about my impressions of Anna."

"And Emilia?"

"They were different. Anna spoke in quick, choppy bursts. Emilia was quieter. But they were equally disagreeable. Equally introverted."

"How well did you know them?"

"I didn't. Sometimes we bumped into each other on the street. Then we would exchange a few words. But never more than was necessary. Since I like to embroider, I often went to their shop. I always got what I needed. If something had to be ordered, it arrived quickly. But they were not pleasant."

"Sometimes one needs time," Wallander said. "Time to allow one's memory to catch things one thought one had forgotten."

"What would that be?"

"I don't know. You know. An unexpected event. Something that went against their habits."

She thought about it. Wallander studied an impressive brass-inlaid compass on a bureau.

"My memory has never been good," she said finally. "But now that you mention it, I do remember something that happened last year. In the spring, I think it was. But I can't say if it's important."

"Anything could be important," Wallander said.

"It was one afternoon. I needed some thread. Blue thread, as I recall. I walked down to the shop. Both Emilia and Anna were behind the counter. Just as I was about to pay for the thread, a man entered the shop. I remember that he started, as if he hadn't been expecting anyone else to be in the shop. And Anna became angry. She gave Emilia a look that could kill.

442

Then the man left. He had a bag in his hand. I paid for my thread and then I left."

"Could you describe him?"

"He was not what one would call Swedish-looking. Swarthy, on the short side. A black moustache."

"How was he dressed?"

"A suit. I think it was of good quality."

"And the bag?"

"An ordinary black briefcase."

"Nothing else?"

She thought back.

"Nothing that I can recall."

"You only saw him that one time?"

"Yes."

Wallander knew that what he had just heard was important. He could not yet determine what it meant. But it strengthened his impression that the sisters had led a double existence. He was slowly penetrating below the surface.

Wallander thanked her for the coffee.

"What was it that happened?" she asked when they were standing in the hall. "I woke up with my room on fire. The light from the flames was so bright that I thought my own apartment was burning."

"Anna and Emilia were murdered," Wallander answered. "They were dead when the fire started."

"Who would have wanted to do something like that?"

"I would hardly be here if I knew the answer," Wallander said and took his leave.

When he came back out onto the street he stopped for a while next to the scene of the fire and watched absently as a backhoe filled a truck with rubble. He tried to visualise the case clearly. Do what Rydberg had taught him. To enter a room where death had wreaked havoc and try to write the drama backwards. But here there is not even a room, Wallander thought. There is nothing.

He started walking back in the direction of Hamngatan. In the building next to Linnea Gunnér's there was a travel agency. He stopped when he noticed a poster in the window that depicted the pyramids. His father would be home again in four days. Wallander felt he had been unfair. Why couldn't he be happy that his father was realising one of his oldest dreams? Wallander looked at the other posters in the window. Majorca, Crete, Spain.

Suddenly something occurred to him. He opened the door and walked in. Both of the sales agents were busy. Wallander sat down to wait. When the first of them, a young woman hardly older than twenty, became free he got up and sat down at her desk. He had to wait a couple of minutes longer as she answered the phone. He saw from a nameplate on the desk that her name was Anette Bengtsson. She put down the receiver and smiled.

"Do you want to get away?" she asked. "There are still spaces left around Christmas and New Year."

"My errand is of a different nature," Wallander said and held up his ID card. "You have of course heard

444

that two old ladies burned to death across the street from here."

"Yes, it's terrible."

"Did you know them?"

He received the answer he had been hoping for.

"They booked their trips through us. It's so awful that they're gone. Emilia was planning to travel in January. And Anna in April."

Wallander nodded slowly.

"Where were they going?" he asked.

"To the same place as always. Spain."

"More precisely?"

"To Marbella. They had a house there."

What she said next surprised Wallander even more.

"I've seen it," she said. "I went to Marbella last year. We have ongoing professional training. There's stiff competition between travel agencies these days. One day when I had time, I drove out and looked at their house. I knew the address."

"Was it large?"

"It was palatial. With a huge garden. High walls all around, and guards."

"I would appreciate it if you could write down the address for me," Wallander said, unable to conceal his eagerness.

She looked through her folders and then wrote it down.

"You said that Emilia was planning to travel in January?"

She entered something into her computer.

"The seventh of January," she said. "From Kastrup at 9.05a.m., via Madrid."

Wallander helped himself to a pencil from her desk and made a note.

"So she didn't take charter trips?"

"Neither of them did. They travelled first class."

That's right, Wallander thought. These ladies were loaded.

She told him which airline Emilia had booked her flight with. Iberia, Wallander wrote.

"I don't know what happens now," she said. "The ticket has been paid for."

"I'm sure it will sort itself out," Wallander said. "How did they pay for their travel, by the way?"

"Always in cash. In thousand-kronor notes."

Wallander slipped his notes into his pocket and got up.

"You've been a great help," he said. "The next time I travel anywhere I'll come and book my trip here. But for me that will mean charter."

It was close to four o'clock. Wallander walked past the bank, where he was due to pick up his loan documents and money for the car tomorrow. He braced himself against the wind as he crossed the square. He made it back to the station by twenty past four. Again he directed a ritual kick at the hinge. Ebba told him that Hansson and Svedberg were out. But, more important, she had called the hospital and been able to speak to Rydberg. He had said that he was feeling fine. But he was being kept in overnight.

"I'll go look in on him."

446

"That was the last thing he said," Ebba replied. "That under no circumstances did he want to have any visitors or phone calls. And absolutely no flowers."

"Well, that doesn't surprise me," Wallander said. "If you think about how he is."

"You all work too hard, eat too much junk and don't get enough exercise."

Wallander leaned over towards her.

"That goes for you too," he said. "You aren't as slim as you once were, you know."

Ebba burst into laughter. Wallander went to the break room and found half a loaf of bread that someone had left. He made several sandwiches to bring back to his office. Then he wrote a report on his conversations with Linnea Gunnér and Anette Bengtsson. He was done at a quarter past five. He read through what he had written and asked himself how they should proceed with the case from here. The money comes from somewhere, he thought. A man is on his way into the shop but turns round on the doorstep. They had a system of signs worked out.

The question is simply what is behind all this. And why were the women murdered all of a sudden? Something has been set in motion but then all at once it collapses.

At six o'clock he tried once more to get in touch with the others. The only one he managed to reach was Martinsson. They decided to hold a meeting at eight o'clock the next morning. Wallander put his feet up on his desk and went through the double homicide in his mind one more time. But since he didn't feel that he

447

was getting anywhere he decided he might as well continue his thinking at home. And anyway, he needed to clean out his car before he got rid of it tomorrow.

He had just put his coat on when Martinsson walked in.

"I think it's best that you sit down," Martinsson said.

"I'm fine standing up," Wallander said grumpily. "What is it?"

Martinsson appeared conflicted. He was holding a telex message in his hand.

"This just came in from the Ministry of Foreign Affairs in Stockholm," he said.

He handed the piece of paper to Wallander, who read the message without understanding anything. Then he sat down at his desk and read it again, word for word.

Now he understood what was written there, but he refused to believe that it was true.

"It says here that my father had been arrested by the Cairo police, and that he would be brought before a judge if he did not immediately pay a fine of approximately ten thousand kronor. He had been accused of 'unlawful entry and forbidden ascent'. What the hell does 'forbidden ascent' mean?"

"I called the foreign ministry," Martinsson said. "I also thought it seemed strange. Apparently he was trying to climb the Cheops pyramid. Even though it's against the law."

Wallander stared helplessly at Martinsson.

"I think you're going to have to fly there and bring him home," Martinsson said. "There are limits to what the Swedish authorities can do."

Wallander shook his head.

He refused to believe it.

It was six o'clock. The fifteenth of December, 1989.

CHAPTER
EIGHT

At ten past one the following day, Wallander sank down into an SAS seat on a DC-9 aircraft called *Agne*. He sat in 19C, an aisle seat, and he had a vague understanding that the plane, after stops in Frankfurt and Rome, would take him to Cairo. The arrival time was set at 10.15. Wallander still did not know if there was a time difference between Sweden and Egypt. In fact, he knew very little in general about what had jerked him out of his life in Ystad, from the investigation of a plane crash and a brutal double homicide, to an aircraft in Kastrup preparing for take-off, headed for North Africa.

The evening before, when the contents of the telex from the foreign ministry had actually sunk in, he had completely lost it. He left the station without a word, and even though Martinsson accompanied him as far as the car park and declared himself willing to help, Wallander had not so much as answered him.

When he got home to Mariagatan, he had two large tumblerfuls of whisky. Then he re-read the crumpled telex several more times in the hopes that there was an encoded message in it explaining that it was all an invention, a joke, one that perhaps even his own father had played on him. But he had realised that the Ministry of Foreign Affairs in Stockholm meant business. There was no way out for him other than to accept this as a fact: his demented father had started climbing a pyramid, with the result that he had been apprehended and was now being held in police custody in Cairo.

Shortly after eight o'clock, Wallander called Malmö. As luck would have it, Linda answered. He told her what had happened and asked for her advice. What should he do? Her answer had been very firm. He had no option but to travel to Egypt the following day and see to it that her grandfather was released. Wallander had many objections, but she dismissed them one after another. Finally he realised that she was right. She also promised him to find out what available connections there were to Cairo tomorrow.

Wallander slowly calmed himself. Tomorrow he was supposed to go to the bank to pick up a car loan for twenty thousand kronor. No one would ask him what he was going to use the money for. He had enough money to buy a ticket and he could change the rest of the cash to British pounds or dollars in order to pay his father's fine. At ten o'clock Linda called and said that there was a flight the following day at ten past one. He also decided to ask Anette Bengtsson for help. Earlier that day, when he had promised to avail himself of the travel agency's services, he had not dreamed it would be so soon.

He tried to pack at around midnight, realising he knew nothing about Cairo. His father had gone there with an ancient pith helmet on his head. But he was unhinged beyond a doubt and could not be taken seriously. Finally, Wallander tossed some shirts and underwear into a bag and decided that would be enough. He was not going to stay away any longer than absolutely necessary.

Then he had a couple more glasses of whisky, set his alarm clock to wake him at six and tried to sleep. A restless slumber carried him towards the dawn at an interminable crawl.

When the bank opened the following day he was the first customer to step through the doors. It took him twenty minutes to sign the loan documents, get his money and exchange half of it for British pounds. He hoped that no one would ask why half of the payment for the car was to be paid in pounds. From the bank he went straight to the travel agency. Anette Bengtsson couldn't believe her eyes when he walked in through the door. But she was immediately willing to help him book the ticket. The return had to remain open for now. He was astonished to hear the price. But he simply pulled out his thousand-kronor notes, took his tickets and left the agency.

Then he took a taxi to Malmö.

He had taken a taxi to Ystad from Malmö before in a state of inebriation. But never in the opposite direction, and never sober. He would never be able to afford a new car now. Perhaps he should consider getting a moped or a bike.

Linda met him by the ferry terminal. They only had a few minutes together. But she convinced him he was

452

doing the right thing. And she asked if he had remembered his passport.

"You'll need a visa," she said. "But you can buy that at the airport in Cairo."

Now he was sitting in 19C and felt how the aeroplane gathered speed and tilted up towards the clouds and the invisible air corridors, headed south. He still felt as if he were standing in his office at the station, with Martinsson in the doorway, the telex in his hand, looking miserable.

Frankfurt airport became a memory of an endless series of corridors and stairs. He took his aisle seat again and, when they came to Rome in order to make the last connection, he took off his coat, as it had suddenly become very warm. The plane thudded down at the airport outside Cairo, delayed by half an hour. In order to lessen his worry, his fear of flying and his nervousness about what awaited him, Wallander had had far too much to drink during the flight. He was not drunk when he stepped out into the stifling Egyptian darkness, but he was not sober either. Most of the money was in a cloth bag squeezed in under his shirt. A tired passport controller directed him to a bank where he could buy a tourist visa. He ended up with a large number of dirty notes in his hand and was suddenly through both passport control and customs. Many taxi drivers then crowded round, prepared to drive him to any place in the world. But Wallander had the presence of mind to look around for a van heading to Mena House, which he imagined to be quite large. His plan went this far: to stay at the same hotel as his father. In a small bus, sandwiched between some loud American women, he then went through the city towards the hotel. He felt the warm night air on his face, discovered suddenly that they were crossing a river that might be the Nile, and then they were there.

When he stepped out of the bus he was sober again. From here on he did not know what to do. A Swedish policeman in Egypt could feel very insignificant, he thought gloomily as he stepped into the magnificent foyer of the hotel. He walked up to the reception desk, where a pleasant young man who spoke perfect English asked if he could be of service. Wallander explained his situation and said he had not reserved a room. The helpful young man looked concerned for a moment and shook his head. But then he managed to find a room.

"I think you already have a guest by the name of Wallander."

The man searched in his electronic database and then nodded.

"That's my father," Wallander said and groaned inwardly over his poor English pronunciation.

"Unfortunately, I cannot give you a room close to his," the young man said. "We only have simple rooms left. Without a view of the pyramids."

"That suits me fine," Wallander said. He didn't want to be reminded of the pyramids more than was necessary.

He registered, was given a key and a small map, and then made his way through the labyrinthine hotel. He gathered that it had been expanded many times over the years. He found his room and sat down on the bed.

454

The air conditioning was cool. He took off his shirt, which was drenched in sweat. He looked at his face in the bathroom mirror.

"Now I am here," he said out loud to himself. "It's late at night. I need to eat something. And sleep. Above all, sleep. But I can't, since my crazy father is being held at a police station somewhere in this city."

He put on a clean shirt, brushed his teeth and returned to the reception desk downstairs. The young man who had recently helped him was nowhere to be seen. Or else Wallander did not recognise him. He approached an older receptionist who was standing motionless and appeared to be surveying everything that happened in the lobby. He smiled when Wallander turned up in front of him.

"I have come here because my father has found himself in difficulty," he said. "His name is Wallander and he is an elderly man who arrived here several days ago."

"What type of difficulty?" the receptionist asked. "Has he become ill?"

"He appears to have tried to climb one of the pyramids," Wallander answered. "If I am right he chose the highest one."

The receptionist nodded slowly.

"I have heard about it," he replied. "It was very unfortunate. The police and the Ministry of Tourism did not approve."

He retreated behind a door and returned shortly with another man, also older. They spoke rapidly for a short while. Then they turned to Wallander.

"Are you the old man's son?" one of them asked.

Wallander nodded.

"Not only that," Wallander said, "I am also a policeman."

He displayed his identification, which clearly stated the word "police". But the two men did not appear to understand.

"You mean, you are not his son, you are police?"

"I am both," Wallander said. "*Both* his son *and* police."

They pondered what he had said for a while. A couple of other receptionists who didn't have anything to do for the moment joined the group. The incomprehensible conversation resumed. Wallander noticed that he was drenched in sweat again.

Then they asked him to wait. They pointed to a group of sofas in the lobby. Wallander sat down. A veiled woman walked past. Scheherazade, Wallander thought. She could have helped me. Or Aladdin. I could have used someone in that league. He waited. An hour went by. He got up and started to walk back to the reception desk. But immediately someone pointed to the sofas again. He felt very thirsty. The clock had struck twelve a long time ago.

There were still many people in the lobby. The American women from the bus left with a guide who was apparently going to take them out into the Egyptian night. Wallander closed his eyes. He jumped when someone touched his shoulder. When he opened his eyes the receptionist was there, together with a number of police officers in impressive uniforms.

456

Wallander got up from the sofa. A clock on the wall read half past two. One of the police officers, who appeared to be about his own age and who was also wearing the most stripes on his uniform, saluted him.

"I hear you have been sent here by the Swedish police," he said.

"No," Wallander said. "I *am* a police officer. But above all I am Mr Wallander's son."

The policeman who had saluted him immediately exploded into an incomprehensible torrent of words directed at the receptionists. Wallander thought that the best thing he could do would be to sit down again. After about a quarter of an hour the policeman brightened.

"I am Hassaneyh Radwan," he said. "I now have a clear picture. It is a delight to meet a Swedish colleague. Come with me."

They left the hotel. Wallander felt like a criminal surrounded by officers who were all carrying weapons. It was a very warm night. He sat down beside Radwan in the back of a police car that immediately revved into action and turned on its sirens. Just as they were driving away from the hotel grounds, Wallander saw the pyramids. They were illuminated by large spotlights. It happened so fast he could not believe his eyes. But they were actually the pyramids that he had seen depicted so many times. And then he thought with dread about the fact that his father had tried to climb one.

They drove east, the same way he had come from the airport.

"How is my father doing?"

457

"He is a very determined man," Radwan answered. "But his English is unfortunately difficult to understand."

He doesn't speak any English at all, Wallander thought helplessly.

They drove through the city at high speed. Wallander caught sight of some heavily loaded camels moving with slow dignity. The bag inside Wallander's shirt was rubbing against his skin. Sweat streamed down his face. They crossed the river.

"The Nile?" Wallander asked.

Radwan nodded. He took out a packet of cigarettes but Wallander shook his head.

"Your father smokes," Radwan remarked.

No, he doesn't, Wallander thought. With increasing trepidation, he now started to question if they were in fact on their way to see his father, who had never smoked in all his life. Could there be more than one old man who had tried to climb the pyramids?

The police car slowed down. Wallander had seen that the name of the street was Sadei Barrani. They were outside a large police station where armed guards stood in small sentry boxes outside the tall doors. Wallander followed Radwan. They came to a room where garish neon tubes glowed in the ceiling. Radwan pointed to a chair. Wallander sat down and wondered how long he now had to wait. Before Radwan left Wallander asked him if it would be possible to buy a soft drink. Radwan called over a young policeman.

"He will help you," Radwan said and then left.

Wallander, who was extremely unsure of the value of his notes, gave the policeman a small wad of them.

"Coca-Cola," he said.

The policeman looked wide-eyed at him. But he said nothing, he simply took the money and left.

A little while later he returned with a carton of Coke bottles. Wallander counted fourteen in all. He opened two of them with his penknife and gave the rest to the policeman, who shared them with his colleagues.

It was half past four. Wallander watched a fly that was sitting still on one of the empty bottles. The sound of a radio came from somewhere. Then he realised there was actually something that this police station and the one in Ystad had in common. The same night-time peace. The waiting for something to happen. Or not. The policeman who had sunk down into his newspaper could have been Hansson poring over his horse races.

Radwan came back. He gave Wallander a sign to follow him. They walked down an endless succession of winding corridors, up and down stairs, and at last stopped outside a door where a policeman was standing guard. Radwan nodded and the door opened. Then he signalled for Wallander to step inside.

"I'll be back in half an hour," he said and left.

Wallander stepped inside. Inside the room, which was illuminated by the ubiquitous neon tubes, were a table and two chairs. His father was sitting on one of them, dressed in a shirt and trousers but barefoot. His hair was sticking up. Wallander suddenly felt pity for him.

"Hello, old man," he said. "How are you?"

His father looked at him without the slightest trace of surprise.

"I intend to protest," he said.

"Protest what?"

"That they prevent people from climbing the pyramids."

"I think we should wait on that protest," Wallander said. "The most important thing right now is for me to get you out of here."

"I am not paying any fines," his father replied angrily. "I want to wait out my punishment instead. Two years, they said. That will go by quickly."

Wallander quickly considered getting angry, but that could simply egg his father on.

"Egyptian prisons are probably not particularly comfortable," he said carefully. "No prisons are. I also doubt they would allow you to paint in your cell."

His father stared back at him in silence. Apparently he had not considered this possibility.

He nodded and stood up.

"Let's go then," he said. "Do you have the money to pay the fine?"

"Sit down," Wallander said. "I don't think it's quite that simple. That you can just stand up and leave."

"Why not? I haven't done anything wrong."

"According to what I understand, you tried to climb the Cheops pyramid."

"That was why I came here. Ordinary tourists can stand among the camels and look. I wanted to stand on the top."

"That's not allowed. It's also very dangerous. And what would happen if everyone started to climb all over the pyramids?"

"I'm not talking about everyone else, I'm talking about me."

Wallander realised it was futile to try to reason with his father. At the same time he couldn't help but be impressed with his intractability.

"I'm here now," Wallander said. "I'll try to get you out tomorrow. Or later today. I'll pay the fine and then it's over. We'll leave this place, go to the hotel and get your suitcase. Then we'll fly home."

"I've paid for my room until the twenty-first."

Wallander nodded patiently.

"Fine. I'm going home. You stay. But if you climb the pyramids one more time you're on your own."

"I never got that far," his father said. "It was difficult. And steep."

"Why did you want to get to the top?"

His father hesitated before answering.

"It's a dream I've had all these years. That's all. I think that one should be faithful to one's dreams."

The conversation died away. Several minutes later Radwan returned. He offered Wallander's father a cigarette and lit it for him.

"Have you started smoking now?"

"Only when I'm in jail. Never anywhere else."

Wallander turned to Radwan.

"I assume there's no possibility that I can take my father with me now?"

"He must appear before the court today at ten o'clock. The judge will most likely accept the fine."

"Most likely?"

"Nothing is certain," Radwan said. "But we have to hope for the best."

Wallander said goodbye to his father. Radwan followed him out to a patrol car that was waiting to take him back to the hotel. It was now six o'clock.

"I will send a car to pick you up a little after nine," Radwan said as they parted. "One should always help a foreign colleague."

Wallander thanked him and got into the car. Again he was thrown back against the seat as it sped off, sirens blaring.

At half past six Wallander ordered a wake-up call and collapsed naked on the bed. I have to get him out, he thought. If he ends up in prison he'll die.

Wallander sank into a restless slumber but was awakened by the sun rising over the horizon. He had a shower and dressed. He was already down to his last clean shirt.

He walked out. It was cooler now, in the morning. Suddenly he stopped. Now he saw the pyramids. He stood absolutely still. The feeling of their enormity was overwhelming. He walked away from the hotel and up the hill that led to the entrance to the Giza plateau. Along the way he was offered rides on both donkeys and camels. But he walked. Deep down he understood his father. One should stay faithful to one's dreams. How faithful had he been to his own? He stopped close to the entrance and looked at the pyramids. Imagined his father climbing up the steeply inclined walls.

He ended up standing there for a long time before he returned to the hotel and had breakfast. At nine o'clock he was outside the hotel entrance, waiting. The patrol car arrived after several minutes. Traffic was heavy and the sirens were on as usual. Wallander crossed the Nile for the fourth time. He saw now that he was in a huge metropolis, incalculable, clamorous.

The court was on a street by the name of Al Azhar. Radwan was standing on the steps, smoking, as the car pulled up.

"I hope you had a few hours of sleep," he said. "It is not good for a person to go without sleep."

They walked into the building.

"Your father is already here."

"Does he have a defence lawyer?" Wallander asked.

"He has a court-assigned assistant. This is a court for minor offences."

"But he could still receive two years in prison?"

"There is a big difference between a death sentence and two years," Radwan said thoughtfully.

They walked into the courtroom. Some cleaners were walking around, dusting.

"Your father's case is the first of the day," Radwan said.

Then his father was led in. Wallander stared horrified at him. His father was in handcuffs. Tears welled up in Wallander's eyes. Radwan glanced at him and put a hand on his shoulder.

A lone judge walked in and sat down. A prosecutor seemed to appear out of thin air and rattled off a long tirade that Wallander assumed to be the charges. Radwan leaned over.

"It looks good," he whispered. "He claims that your father is old and confused."

As long as no one translates that, Wallander thought. Then he really will go crazy.

The prosecutor sat down. The court assistant made a very brief statement.

"He is making the case for a fine," Radwan whispered. "I have informed the court that you are here, that you are his son and that you are a policeman."

The assistant sat down. Wallander saw that his father wanted to say something. But the court assistant shook his head.

The judge struck the table with his gavel and uttered a few words. Then he banged the gavel again, got up and left.

"A fine," Radwan said and patted Wallander on the shoulder. "It can be paid here in the courtroom. Then your father is free to go."

Wallander took out the bag inside his shirt.

Radwan led him to a table where a man calculated the sum from British pounds into Egyptian pounds. Almost all of Wallander's money disappeared. He received an illegible receipt for the amount. Radwan made sure his father's handcuffs were removed.

"I hope that the rest of your journey is pleasant," Radwan said and shook both their hands. "But it is not advisable for your father to attempt to climb the pyramids again."

Radwan had a patrol car take them back to the hotel. Wallander made a note of Radwan's address. He realised that this would not have been so easy without Radwan's help. In some way he wanted to thank him. Perhaps it would be most appropriate to send him a painting with a wood grouse?

His father was in high spirits and commented on everything that they drove past. Wallander was simply tired.

"Now I will show you the pyramids," his father said happily when they reached the hotel.

"Not right now," Wallander said. "I need to sleep for a few hours. You too. Then we'll look at the pyramids. When I've booked my return flight."

His father looked intently at him.

"I must say that you surprise me. That you spared no expense in flying out here and getting me out. I would not have thought that of you."

Wallander did not answer.

"Go to bed," he said. "I'll meet you here at two o'clock."

Wallander did not manage to fall asleep. After writhing on his bed for an hour he went to the reception desk and asked them for help in booking his return flight. He was directed to a travel agency located in another part of the hotel. There he was assisted by an unbelievably beautiful woman who spoke perfect English. She managed to get him a seat on the plane that was leaving Cairo the following day, the eighteenth of December, at nine o'clock. Since the plane only stopped in Frankfurt, he would already be in Kastrup at two o'clock that afternoon. After he had confirmed his seat, it was only one o'clock. He sat down in a cafe next to the lobby and drank some water and a cup of very hot coffee that was much too sweet. At exactly two o'clock his father appeared. He was wearing his pith helmet.

Together they explored the Giza plateau in the intense heat. Wallander thought several times that he was going to faint. But his father seemed unaffected by the heat. Down by the Sphinx Wallander at last found some shade. His father narrated and Wallander realised that he knew a great deal about the Egypt of old where the pyramids and the remarkable Sphinx had once been built.

It was close to six o'clock when they finally returned to the hotel. Since he was travelling very early the next morning they decided to eat dinner in the hotel, where there were several restaurants to choose from. At his father's suggestion they booked a table at an Indian restaurant and Wallander thought afterwards that he had rarely had such a good meal. His father had been pleasant the entire time and Wallander understood that he had now dismissed all thoughts of climbing the pyramids.

They parted at eleven. Wallander would be leaving the hotel at six.

"Of course I'll get up and see you off," his father said.

"I'd rather you didn't," Wallander said. "Neither of us likes goodbyes."

"Thank you for coming here," his father said. "You're probably right about it being hard to spend two years in prison without being able to paint."

"Come home on the twenty-first and everything will be forgotten," Wallander answered.

"The next time we'll go to Italy," his father said and walked away towards his room.

That night Wallander slept heavily. At six o'clock he sat in the taxi and crossed the Nile for the sixth and hopefully final time. The plane left at the assigned time and he landed in Kastrup on time. He took a taxi to the ferries and was in Malmö at a quarter to four. He ran to the station and just made a train to Ystad. He walked home to Mariagatan, changed his clothes and walked in through the front doors of the station at half past six. The damaged hinge had been replaced. Björk knows where to set his priorities, he thought grimly. Martinsson's and Svedberg's offices were empty, but Hansson was in. Wallander told him about his trip in broad strokes. But first he asked how Rydberg was doing.

"He's supposed to be coming in tomorrow," Hansson said. "That was what Martinsson said."

Wallander immediately felt relieved. Apparently it had not been as serious as they had feared.

"And here?" he asked. "The investigation?"

"There has been another important development," Hansson said. "But that has to do with the plane that crashed."

"What is it?"

"Yngve Leonard Holm has been found murdered. In the woods outside Sjöbo."

Wallander sat down.

"But that isn't all," Hansson said. "He hasn't only been murdered. He was shot in the back of the head, just like the Eberhardsson sisters."

Wallander held his breath.

He had not expected this. That a connection would suddenly appear between the crashed plane and the two murdered women who had been found in the remains of a devastating fire.

He looked at Hansson.

What does it mean, he thought. What is the significance of what Hansson is telling me?

All at once the trip to Cairo felt very distant.

CHAPTER
NINE

At ten o'clock in the morning on the nineteenth of December, Wallander called the bank and asked if he could increase his loan by another twenty thousand kronor. He lied and said he had misheard the price of the car he intended to buy. The bank loan officer replied that it shouldn't present any difficulties. Wallander could come by and sign the loan documents and collect the money the same day. After Wallander hung up the phone, he called Arne, who was selling him the car, and arranged for him to deliver the new Peugeot to Mariagatan at one o'clock. Arne would also either try to bring the old one to life or tow it back to his garage.

Wallander made these two calls right after the morning meeting. They had met for two hours, starting at a quarter to eight. But Wallander had been at the station since seven o'clock. The night before, when he had learned that Yngve Leonard Holm had been murdered and that there was a possible connection between him and the Eberhardsson sisters, or at least with their killer, he had perked up and sat with Hansson for close to an hour, learning all the available facts. But then he had suddenly felt exhausted. He had gone home and stretched out on the bed in order to rest before undressing but had fallen asleep and slept through the night. When he woke up at half past five he felt restored. He stayed in bed for a while and thought about his trip to Cairo, which was already a distant memory.

When he reached the station, Rydberg was already there. They went to the break room, where they found several bleary-eyed officers who had just finished the night shift. Rydberg had tea and rusks. Wallander sat down across from him.

"I heard you went to Egypt," Rydberg said. "How were the pyramids?"

"High," Wallander said. "Very strange."

"And your father?"

"He could have gone to prison. But I got him out by paying almost ten thousand kronor in fines."

Rydberg laughed.

"My dad was a horse-trader," he said. "Have I told you that?"

"You've never said anything about your parents."

"He sold horses. Travelled around to markets, checking the teeth, and was apparently a devil at inflating the price. That old stereotype about the horse-trader's wallet is actually true. My dad had one of those filled with thousand-kronor notes. But I wonder if he even knew that the pyramids were in Egypt. It's even less likely that he knew the capital was Cairo. He was completely uneducated. There was only one thing he knew and that was horses. And possibly women. All his dalliances drove my mother crazy."

470

"One has the parents one has," Wallander said. "How are you feeling?"

"Something is wrong," Rydberg said firmly. "One doesn't collapse like that from rheumatism. Something is wrong. But I don't know what it is. And right now I'm more interested in this Holm who got a bullet in the back of his head."

"I heard about it from Hansson yesterday."

Rydberg pushed his teacup away.

"It is of course an incredibly compelling thought that the Eberhardsson sisters might turn out to have been involved in drug trafficking. Something like that would strike at the very foundations of the Swedish sewing supplies industry. Out with the embroidery, in with the heroin."

"The thought has crossed my mind," Wallander said. "I'll see you in a while."

As he walked to his office he thought that Rydberg would never have been as open about his health if he wasn't convinced that something was wrong. Wallander felt himself starting to worry.

Until a quarter to eight he went through some reports that had piled up on his desk during his absence. He had spoken to Linda the day before — just after he had got home and put his bag down. She had promised to go to Kastrup and meet her grandfather and make sure he made it home to Löderup. Wallander had not dared to hope that he would really be approved for a new loan and therefore be able to get a new car and pick up his father in Malmö.

He found a message that Sten Widén had called. And his sister. He saved these messages. His colleague Gösta Boman in Kristianstad had tried to reach him. Boman was a police officer he got together with from time to time after they had met at one of the countless National Police Commission seminars. He also put this message aside. The rest of them he swept into the bin.

The investigative meeting started with Wallander briefly describing his adventures in Cairo and the helpful police officer Radwan. Then a discussion broke out about when exactly the death penalty had been abolished in Sweden. There were many guesses. Svedberg claimed that convicts had been executed by firing squad as late as the 1930s, which was firmly dismissed by Martinsson, who maintained that no executions had taken place in Sweden since Anna Månsdotter had her head cut off at the Kristianstad prison sometime in the 1890s. It ended with Hansson calling a crime reporter in Stockholm who shared his interest in horse racing.

"Abolished in 1910," he said when he got off the phone. "It was the first and last time the guillotine was used in Sweden. On a man by the name of Ander."

"Didn't he fly in a balloon to the North Pole?" Martinsson said.

"That was Andrée," Wallander said. "And now let's move on."

Rydberg had sat quietly throughout. Wallander had the feeling that he was in some way absent from the proceedings.

Then they discussed Holm. Administratively, he was on the borderline. The body had been found within the Sjöbo police district, but just a couple of hundred metres from the dirt road where Ystad's police district began.

"Our Sjöbo colleagues are happy to give him to us," Martinsson said. "We can symbolically carry the corpse across the dirt road and then it is ours. Especially considering that we have already had dealings with Holm."

Wallander asked for a timetable of events, which Martinsson was able to supply. Holm had gone missing shortly after he was brought in for questioning on the day that the aeroplane crashed. While Wallander was in Cairo, a man out walking in the woods had discovered the body. It had been lying at the end of a forest road. There were car tracks. But Holm still had his wallet, so it had not been a case of robbery-homicide. No observations of any interest had been called in to the police. The area was deserted.

Martinsson had just finished when the door to the conference room was opened. An officer popped his head in and said that a communication had arrived from Interpol. Martinsson went to get it. While he was gone, Svedberg told Wallander about the violent energy with which Björk had gone about getting the front doors repaired.

Martinsson returned.

"One of the pilots has been identified," he said. "Pedro Espinosa, thirty-three years old. Born in

Madrid. He'd been imprisoned in Spain for embezzlement and in France for smuggling."

"Smuggling," Wallander said. "That fits perfectly."

"There's another thing that's interesting," Martinsson said. "His last known address is in Marbella. That's where the Eberhardsson sisters' big villa is."

The room fell silent. Wallander was clear on the point that it could still be a coincidence. A house in Marbella and a dead pilot who happened to have lived in the same place. But deep down he knew that they were in the process of uncovering a baffling connection. He did not yet know what it would mean. But now they could begin to focus their work in a particular direction.

"The other pilot is still unidentified," Martinsson went on. "But they're working on it."

Wallander looked around the table.

"We need more help from the Spanish police," he said. "If they're as helpful as Radwan in Cairo, they should be able to search the Eberhardsson sisters' villa very soon. They should look for a safe. And they should look for drugs. Who did the sisters know down there? This is what we need to find out. And we need to find out soon."

"Should one of us go down there?" Hansson asked.

"Not yet," Wallander said. "Your sunbathing will have to wait until next summer."

They reviewed the material one more time and assigned the tasks to be performed. Above all they were going to focus on Yngve Leonard Holm. Wallander noticed that the pace in the team had picked up.

They ended the meeting at a quarter to ten. Hansson reminded Wallander about the traditional Christmas buffet that would be celebrated at the Hotel Continental on the twenty-first of December. Wallander tried to think of a good excuse for missing it, without success.

After Wallander had made his telephone calls, he put down the receiver and closed the door. Slowly he went back through the material they had uncovered so far, regarding the plane that had crashed, Yngve Leonard Holm and the two Eberhardsson sisters. He drew a triangle on his notepad: each of the three components marked a corner. Five dead people, he thought. Two pilots, one of whom came from Spain. In an aeroplane that was literally a Flying Dutchman since it had supposedly been scrapped after an accident in Laos. An aeroplane that flew in across the Swedish border at night, turned round just south of Sjöbo and crashed next to Mossby Strand. Lights had been observed on the ground, which could mean that the plane had dropped something.

This is the first point of the triangle.

The second point is the two sisters, who ran their sewing shop in Ystad. They are killed with shots to the head and their building is burned down. They turn out to have been wealthy, with a safe built into the foundation and a villa in Spain. The second point, in other words, consists of two sisters who lived a double life.

Wallander drew a line between Pedro Espinosa and the Eberhardsson sisters. There was a connection there. Marbella.

The third point consisted of Yngve Leonard Holm, who had been executed on a forest road outside Sjöbo. About him they knew that he was a notorious drug dealer who possessed an unusually well-developed ability to cover his tracks.

But someone caught up with him outside Sjöbo, Wallander thought.

He got up from the desk and studied his triangle. What did it say? He made a point in the middle of the triangle. A centre, he thought. Hemberg and Rydberg's constant question: where was the centre, a midpoint? He continued to study his sketch. Then all at once he realised that what he had drawn could be interpreted as a pyramid. The base was a square. But from a distance, the pyramid could look like a triangle.

He sat down at the desk again. *Everything that I have in front of me tells me one thing. That something has happened that has disturbed a pattern. The most likely thing is that the plane crash is the beginning. It has set a chain reaction in motion that has resulted in three murders, three executions.*

He started over from the beginning. He couldn't drop the thought of a pyramid. Could it be that a kind of strange power play had been enacted? Where the triangle points consisted of the Eberhardsson sisters, Yngve Leonard Holm and the downed plane? But where there was still an unknown centre?

Slowly and methodically he proceeded through all the known facts. Now and again he wrote down a question. Without him noticing the time pass, it was suddenly twelve o'clock. He dropped the pen, took his coat and walked down to the bank. It was a couple of degrees above zero and drizzling. He signed his loan documents and received another twenty thousand kronor. Right now he did not want to think about all the money that had disappeared in Egypt. The fine was one thing. What gnawed at him and ate away at his parsimonious inner recesses was the price of the plane ticket. He held out no hopes that his sister would agree to help defray the costs.

At exactly one o'clock the car salesman arrived with his new Peugeot. The old one refused to start. Wallander did not wait for the tow truck. Instead he took a drive in the new dark blue car. It was worn and reeked of smoke. But Wallander noticed that the engine was good. That was the most important thing. He drove towards Hedeskoga and was about to turn when he decided to continue. He was on the road to Sjöbo. Martinsson had explained in detail where Holm's body had been found. He wanted to see the place with his own eyes. And perhaps even stop by the house where Holm had lived.

The place where Holm had been found was still cordoned off. But there were no police. Wallander stepped out of the car. There was silence all around. He stepped over the police tape and looked about. If someone wanted to kill a person, this was an excellent location. He tried to imagine what had happened. Holm had arrived here with someone. According to Martinsson there were only tracks from one car.

A confrontation, Wallander thought. Certain goods are handed over, a payment is to be made. Then something happens. Holm is shot in the back of the head. He is dead before he falls to the ground. The person who has committed the murder vanishes without a trace.

A man, Wallander thought. Or more than one. The same person or people who killed the Eberhardsson sisters a few days earlier.

Suddenly he felt close to something. There was yet another connection here that he would be able to see if only he made an effort. That it had to do with drugs appeared obvious, even if it was still hard to accept that two sisters who owned a sewing shop would have been mixed up in something like that. But Rydberg had been right. His first comment — what did they really know about the two sisters? — had been justified.

Wallander left the forest road and drove on. He could see Martinsson's map clearly in his head. He had to turn right at the large roundabout south of Sjöbo. Then another road, a gravel road, to the left, to the last house on the right, a red barn next to the road. A blue mailbox that was about to fall to the ground. Two junked cars and a rusty tractor on a field next to the barn. A barking dog of indeterminate breed in a dog run. He had no trouble finding it. He heard the dog before he even got out of the car. He stepped out and walked into the yard. The paint on the main house was peeling. The gutters hung in pieces at the corners. The dog barked desperately and scratched at the fence. Wallander wondered what would happen if the fence gave way and the dog was let loose. He walked over to the door and rang a bell. Then he saw that the wiring was loose. He knocked and waited. Finally he banged on the door so hard that it opened. He called out to see if anyone was home. Still no answer. I shouldn't go in, he thought. I will break many rules that pertain not only to the police but to all citizens. Then he pushed the door open further and went in. Peeling wallpaper, stale air, a mess. Broken couches, mattresses on the floor. Yet there was a large-screen television and a relatively new video recorder. A CD player with large speakers. He called out again and listened. No answer. There was indescribable chaos in the kitchen. Dishes piled up in the sink. Paper bags, plastic bags, empty pizza cartons on the floor to which various lines of ants led.

A mouse scuttled past in a corner. The place smelled musty. Wallander walked on. Stopped outside a door that had been spray-painted with the words "Yngve's Church". He pushed open the door. There was a real bed inside, but only a bottom sheet and a blanket on it. A chest of drawers, two chairs. A radio in the window. A clock that had stopped at ten minutes to seven. Yngve Leonard Holm had lived here. While he was having a large house built in Ystad. On the floor there was a tracksuit top. He had been wearing it when Wallander questioned him. Wallander sat down gingerly on the edge of the bed, afraid that it would give way, and looked around. A person lived here, he thought. A person who lived by herding other people into various forms of drug hell. He shook his head with distaste. Then he leaned over and looked under the bed. Dust. A slipper and some porn magazines. He stood up and pulled out the chest drawers. More magazines with undressed, splay-legged women. Several of them frighteningly young. Underwear, painkillers, Band-Aids.

Next drawer. An old kerosene blowtorch. The kind you used to start engines on fishing boats. In the final drawer, piles of papers. Old report cards. Wallander saw that Holm had been proficient only in what was also his own favourite subject, geography. Otherwise his marks were forgettable. Some photographs. Holm at a bar somewhere with a glass of beer in each hand. Drunk. Red-eyed. Another photograph: Holm naked on a beach. Grinning straight at the camera. Then an old black-and-white photograph of a man and a woman on a road. Wallander turned it over. Båstad, 1937. It could be Holm's parents.

He continued to search among the papers. Stopped at an old aeroplane ticket. Took it over to the window. Copenhagen — Marbella, return. The twelfth of August, 1989. The return dated the seventeenth. Five days in Spain, and not on a charter ticket. He was unable to determine if the code was tourist or business class. He tucked it into his pocket and closed the drawer after a few more minutes of searching.

There was nothing of interest in the wardrobe. More clutter and chaos. Wallander sat back down on the bed. Wondered where the other people who lived in the house were. He walked into the living room. There was a telephone on the table. He called the station and spoke to Ebba.

"Where are you?" she asked. "People have been asking for you."

"Who is asking for me?"

"You know how it is. As soon as you aren't here everyone wants you."

"I'm on my way," Wallander said.

Then he asked her to look up the number of the travel agency where Anette Bengtsson worked. He made a mental note of it, finished his conversation with Ebba and dialled the agency. It was the other girl who answered. He asked to speak with Anette. It took several minutes but then she picked up. He told her who it was.

"How was the trip to Cairo?" she asked.

"Good. The pyramids are very high. Remarkable, really. It was also very warm."

"You should have stayed longer."

"I'll have to do that another time."

Then he asked her if she could tell him if Anna or Emilia Eberhardsson had been in Spain between the twelfth and seventeenth of August.

"That will take a while," she said.

"I'll wait," Wallander said.

She put the receiver down. Wallander again caught sight of a mouse in a corner. He could not of course be sure that it was the same mouse. Winter is coming, he thought. The mice are on their way back into the house. Anette Bengtsson came back.

"Anna Eberhardsson left Ystad on the tenth of August," she said. "She returned at the beginning of September."

"Thanks for the help," Wallander replied. "I would very much like to have an inventory of all of the sisters' trips last year."

"What for?"

"For the police investigation," he said. "I'll come in tomorrow."

She promised to help him. He hung up. Thought that he would probably have fallen in love with her if he had been ten years younger. Now it would be senseless. She would look on advances from him with distaste. He left the house and thought alternately of Holm and Emma Lundin. Then his thoughts returned to Anette Bengtsson. He couldn't be completely sure that she would be offended. But she probably already had a boyfriend. Although he could not recall seeing a ring on her left hand.

The dog barked like crazy. Wallander walked up to the dog run and screamed at it and then it went quiet. As soon as he turned round and left it started to bark again. I should be grateful, he thought, that Linda doesn't live in a house like this. How many people in Sweden, how many normal, unthinking citizens, are familiar with these environments? Where people live in constant mists, misery, despair. He got into the car and drove away. But first he had checked the mailbox. There was a letter in it, addressed to Holm. He opened it. It was the final notice of a bill from a car-hire agency. Wallander put the letter in his pocket.

He was back at the station at four o'clock. A note from Martinsson was on his desk. Wallander went to Martinsson's office. He was on the phone. When

Wallander turned up in the doorway, he said he'd call back. Wallander assumed he had been talking with his wife. Martinsson hung up.

"The Spanish police are searching the villa in Marbella right now," he said. "I've been in touch with a colleague by the name of Fernando Lopez. He speaks excellent English and seems to be a very high-ranking officer."

Wallander told him about his excursion and his conversation with Anette Bengtsson. He showed Martinsson the ticket.

"That bastard flew business class," Martinsson said.

"Be that as it may," Wallander said, "we now have another connection. No one can still say this is a coincidence."

That was also what he said at the case meeting at five o'clock. It was very brief. Per Åkeson sat in on it without saying anything. He's already finished, Wallander thought. He's physically here, but mentally he's already away on his leave.

When there was nothing more to say, they finished the meeting. Each of them went back to his tasks. Wallander called Linda and told her he now had a car that worked and could pick up her grandfather in Malmö. He went home a little before seven. Emma Lundin called. This time Wallander said yes. She stayed until just past midnight, as usual. Wallander thought of Anette Bengtsson.

The following day he stopped by the travel agency and picked up the information he had requested. There were many customers looking for seats for Christmas.

Wallander would have liked to stay for a while and talk to Anette Bengtsson, but she didn't have time. He also stopped outside the old sewing shop. The rubble had now been cleared. He walked into town. Suddenly he realised there was only a week left until Christmas. The first one since the divorce.

That day nothing happened that took the investigation further. Wallander pondered his pyramid. The only addition he made was a thick line between Anna Eberhardsson and Yngve Leonard Holm.

The next day, the twenty-first of December, Wallander drove to Malmö to pick up his father. He felt great relief when he saw him walk out of the ferry terminal. He drove him back to Löderup. His father talked non-stop about his wonderful trip. He appeared to have forgotten the fact that he had been in prison and that Wallander had actually also been to Cairo.

That evening Wallander went to the annual police Christmas function. He avoided sitting at the same table as Björk. But the toast the police chief made was unusually successful. He had taken the trouble to look into the history of the Ystad police. His account was both entertaining and well presented. Wallander chuckled on several occasions. Björk was without a doubt a good orator.

He was drunk when he came home. Before falling asleep he thought of Anette Bengtsson. And decided in the next moment to immediately stop thinking about her.

On the twenty-second of December they reviewed the state of the investigation. Nothing new had happened. The Spanish police had not found anything noteworthy in the sisters' villa. No hidden valuables, nothing. They were still waiting for the second pilot to be identified.

In the afternoon, Wallander went and bought himself a Christmas present. A stereo for the car. He managed to install it himself.

On the twenty-third of December they were able to add to the existing case data. Nyberg informed them that Holm had been shot with the same gun used on the Eberhardsson sisters. But there was still no trace of this weapon. Wallander made new lines in his sketch. The connections grew, but the top of the pyramid was still missing.

The work was not supposed to stop during Christmas, but Wallander knew it would slow down. Not least because it would be hard to track people down, hard to get information.

It rained in the afternoon on Christmas Eve. Wallander picked Linda up at the station. Together they drove out to Löderup. She had bought her grandfather a new scarf. Wallander had bought him a bottle of cognac. Linda and Wallander made dinner while his father sat at the kitchen table and told them about the pyramids. The evening went unusually well, above all because Linda had such a good relationship with her grandfather. Wallander sometimes felt as if he were on the outside. But it didn't bother him. From time to time he thought about the dead sisters, Holm and the plane that had crashed into a field.

After Wallander and Linda had returned to Ystad they sat up and talked for a long time. Wallander slept late the following morning. He always slept well when Linda was in the apartment. Christmas Day was cold and clear. They took a long walk through Sand Forest. She told him about her plans. Wallander had given her a promise for Christmas. A promise to cover some of the costs, as much as he could afford, if she decided to pursue an apprenticeship in France. He accompanied her to the train station in the late afternoon. He had wanted to drive her to Malmö, but she wanted to take the train. Wallander felt lonely in the evening. He watched an old film on TV and then listened to *Rigoletto*. Thought that he should have called Rydberg to wish him a merry Christmas. But now it was too late.

When Wallander looked out of the window on Boxing Day, just after seven in the morning, a gloomy mix of snow and rain was falling over Ystad. He suddenly recalled the warm night air in Cairo. Thought that he should not forget to thank Radwan for his help in some way. He wrote it down on the pad of paper on the kitchen table. Then he cooked himself a substantial breakfast for once.

It was close to nine when he finally got to the police station. He talked to some of the officers who had worked during the night. Christmas had been unusually calm in Ystad this year. As usual, Christmas Eve had resulted in a number of family quarrels, but nothing had been really serious. Wallander walked down the deserted corridors to his office.

Now he would take up the murder investigations in earnest again. There were still technically two cases, even though he was convinced that the same person, or people, had killed the Eberhardsson sisters and Yngve Leonard Holm. It was not simply the same weapon and the same style. There was also a common motive. He got himself a cup of coffee in the break room and sat down with his notes. The pyramid with its base. He drew a large question mark in the middle. The apex, which his father had been aiming for, he now had to find himself.

After two hours of thinking, he was sure. They now had to concentrate most forcefully on the missing link. A pattern, perhaps an organisation, had collapsed when the plane crashed. Then one or several unknown individuals had hastily stepped out of the shadows and acted. They had slain three people.

Silence, Wallander thought. Perhaps that is what all this is about? To prevent information from trickling out. Dead people do not speak.

That could be what it was. But it could also be something completely different.

He went over and stood by the window. The snow was falling more thickly now.

This will take time, he thought.

That's the first thing I'll say when we have our next meeting.

We have to count on the fact that it will take time to solve this case.

CHAPTER
TEN

The night before the twenty-seventh of December Wallander had a nightmare. He was back in Cairo again, in the courtroom. Radwan was no longer at his side. But now he could suddenly understand everything that the prosecutor and judge were saying. His father had been sitting there in handcuffs at his side and Wallander had listened in horror as his father was sentenced to death. He had stood up in order to protest. But no one had heard him. At that point he had kicked himself out of the dream, up to the surface, and when he woke up he was covered in sweat. He lay completely still, staring into the darkness.

The dream had made him so unsettled that he got out of bed and went to the kitchen. It was still snowing. The street lamp was swaying gently in the wind. It was half past four. He drank a glass of water, then stood for a while fingering a half-empty bottle of whisky. But he let it be. He thought about what Linda had said, that dreams were messengers. Even if dreams were about other people, they consisted foremost of messages to the self. Wallander had always doubted the value of trying to interpret dreams. What could it mean for him to imagine that his father had been sentenced to death?

Had the dreams pronounced a death sentence on him? Then he thought that perhaps it had to do with the concern he felt for Rydberg's health. He had another glass of water and went back to bed.

But sleep would not come. His thoughts wandered. Mona, his father, Linda, Rydberg. And then he was back to his constant point of departure. Work. The murders of the Eberhardsson sisters and Yngve Leonard Holm. The two dead pilots, the one from Spain and the other as yet unidentified. He thought about his sketch. The triangle with a question mark in the middle.

But now he was lying in darkness, thinking about the fact that a pyramid also has different cornerstones.

He tossed and turned until six o'clock. Then he got out of bed, ran a bath and made a cup of coffee. The morning paper had already arrived. He turned the pages until he reached the property section. There was nothing of interest to him there today. He took his coffee cup with him into the bathroom. Then he lay and dozed in the warm water until close to six-thirty. Thinking about going out into the weather was unpleasant. This endless slush. But now at least he had a car that would presumably start.

He turned the key in the ignition at a quarter past seven. The engine started at once. He drove to the station and parked as close to the entrance as possible. Then he ran through the snow and slush and almost slipped on the front steps. Martinsson was in reception, skimming the police magazine. He nodded when he spotted Wallander.

"It says here that we're supposed to get better at everything," he said with a note of despondence. "Above all, we're supposed to improve our relations with the general public."

"That sounds excellent," Wallander said.

He had a recurring memory, something that had happened in Malmö over twenty years ago. He had been accosted by a girl at a cafe who accused him of hitting her with a baton at a Vietnam demonstration. For some reason he had never forgotten this moment. That she had been partly responsible for his almost being stabbed to death with a knife at a later time was of a lesser concern. It was her expression, her complete contempt, that he had never forgotten.

Martinsson threw the magazine onto the table.

"Don't you ever think about quitting?" he asked. "Doing something else?"

"Every day," Wallander answered. "But I don't know what that would be."

"One could apply to a private security company," Martinsson said.

This surprised Wallander. He had always imagined that Martinsson nurtured a heady dream of one day becoming police chief.

Then he told him about his visit to the house that Holm had lived in. Martinsson expressed concern when he heard that only the dog had been home.

"At least two others live there," Martinsson said. "A girl around twenty-five. I never saw her. But a man was there. Rolf was his name. Rolf Nyman, I think. I don't remember her name."

"There was only a dog," Wallander repeated. "It was such a coward it crawled on its belly when I raised my voice."

They agreed to wait until around nine before meeting in the conference room. Martinsson was not sure if Svedberg was coming. He had called the night before and said that he had come down with a bad cold and a temperature.

Wallander walked to his office. As usual it was twenty-three steps away from the beginning of the corridor. Sometimes he wished that something would suddenly have happened. That the corridor would turn out to be longer or shorter. But everything was normal. He hung up his coat and brushed off a couple of hairs that had stuck to the back of the chair. He brushed his hand along the back and top of his head. With every year he became more worried that he was going to lose his hair. Then he heard rapid steps outside in the corridor. It was Martinsson, waving a piece of paper.

"The second pilot has been identified," he said. "This came just now from Interpol."

Wallander immediately stopped thinking about his hair growth.

"Ayrton McKenna," Martinsson read. "Born 1945 in Southern Rhodesia. A helicopter pilot since 1964 in the then Southern Rhodesian military. Decorated many times during the 1960s. For what, one might ask. For bombing a lot of black Africans?"

Wallander only had a very vague sense of what had transpired in the former British colonies in Africa.

"What is Southern Rhodesia called today?" he asked. "Zambia?"

"That was Northern Rhodesia. Southern Rhodesia is Zimbabwe today."

"My knowledge of Africa isn't what it should be. What else does it say?"

Martinsson continued to read.

"At some point after 1980, Ayrton McKenna moved to England. Between 1983 and 1985 he was in prison in Birmingham for drug smuggling. From 1985 on there are no records until he suddenly turns up in Hong Kong in 1987. There he is suspected of smuggling people from the People's Republic. He escapes from a prison in Hong Kong after shooting two guards to death and has been a wanted man ever since. But the identification is definitive. He was the one who crashed with Espinosa outside Mossby."

Wallander mulled this over.

"What do we have?" he said. "Two pilots with criminal histories. Both with smuggling on their records. In an aeroplane that does not exist. They cross illegally over the Swedish border for a few short minutes. They are probably on their way out again when the plane crashes. That leaves us with two possibilities. They were either leaving or collecting something. Since there are no indications that the plane landed, this seems to indicate that something was tossed out. What is dropped from a plane? Besides bombs?"

"Drugs."

Wallander nodded. Then he leaned over the table.

"Has the accident commission begun its work yet?"

"Things have proceeded very slowly. But nothing indicates that the plane was shot down, if that's what you're getting at."

"No," Wallander said. "I'm only interested in two things. Did the plane have extra fuel tanks, that is, from how far away could it have come? And was it an accident?"

"If it wasn't shot down, it could hardly have been anything other than an accident."

"There is a possibility that it was sabotage. But perhaps that's remote."

"It was an old plane," Martinsson said. "We know that. It probably ran into the hillside outside Vientiane. And was then put back together again. It could, in other words, have been in bad shape."

"When is this accident commission going to get started for real?"

"The twenty-eighth. Tomorrow. The plane's been transported to a hangar in Sturup."

"You should probably be there," Wallander said. "This matter of the extra fuel tanks is an important one."

"I think it would need a great deal to be able to fly here from Spain without landing somewhere in between," Martinsson said hesitantly.

"I don't believe that either. But I want to know if the flight could have originated from the other side of the sea. Germany. Or one of the Baltic States."

Martinsson left. Wallander made some notes. Next to the name Espinosa he now wrote McKenna, unsure of the exact spelling.

The investigators met at half past eight. Their group was down to the bare bones. Svedberg did in fact turn out to have a cold. Nyberg had gone to Eksjö to visit his ninety-six-year-old mother. He would have been back this morning but his car had broken down somewhere south of Växjö. Rydberg looked tired and harried. Wallander thought he caught a whiff of alcohol. Probably Rydberg had spent the holidays alone, drinking. Not to the point of drunkenness, since he rarely did. But a steady, quiet drinking. Hansson complained that he had eaten too much. Neither Björk nor Per Åkeson showed up. Wallander studied the three men around the table. You don't see this on TV very often, he thought. There they have young, fresh and enthusiastic policemen in action. Martinsson could possibly fit such a context. Apart from him this squad is not such an edifying sight.

"There was a stabbing incident last night," Hansson said. "Two brothers who ended up in a fight with their father. Drunk, of course. One of the brothers and the father are in the hospital. Apparently they attacked each other with various tools."

"What kind of tools?" Wallander asked.

"A hammer. A crowbar. Screwdriver maybe. At least, the father has stab wounds."

"We'll have to deal with that when we have time," Wallander said. "Right now we have three murders on our plate. Or two, if we combine the sisters into one."

"I don't really understand why Sjöbo can't deal with Holm on their own," Hansson said with irritation.

494

"Because Holm has to do with us," Wallander replied, just as irritated. "If both of us investigate these things on our own we'll never get anywhere."

Hansson did not back down. He was apparently in a very bad mood this morning.

"Do we know that Holm had anything to do with the Eberhardssons?"

"No," Wallander said. "But we know everything indicates that the same person killed them. I think that's enough of a connection to bind the cases and for us to lead a coordinated investigation from Ystad."

"Has Åkeson weighed in on this?"

"Yes," Wallander said.

It was not true. Per Åkeson had not said anything. But Wallander knew that he would have backed him up.

Wallander marked the end of this discussion with Hansson by turning to Rydberg.

"Do we have any updates on the drug trade?" he asked. "Has anything happened in Malmö? Have the prices changed, or the supply?"

"I called," Rydberg said, "but there didn't appear to be anyone working there over Christmas."

"Then we'll have to proceed with Holm," Wallander decided. "Unfortunately, I suspect this investigation will prove both long and difficult. We need to dig deeper. Who was Holm? Who did he associate with? What was his position in the drug-trade hierarchy? Did he even have a position? And what about the sisters? We know too little."

"Absolutely correct," Rydberg said. "Digging down usually takes one forward."

Wallander decided to store these words in his memory.

Digging down usually takes one forward.

They ended the meeting with Rydberg's words of wisdom buzzing in their ears. Wallander drove down to the travel agency to speak to Anette Bengtsson. But to his disappointment she had taken time off over Christmas. Her colleague did, however, find an envelope to give to him.

"Have you found him yet?" she asked. "The one who killed the sisters?"

"No," Wallander answered. "But we're working on it."

On the way back to the station, Wallander suddenly remembered that he had signed up for the laundry room this morning. He stopped at Mariagatan, walked up to the apartment and carried down all the dirty laundry that had accumulated in his wardrobe. When he reached the laundry room there was a note taped to the front of the washer saying it was out of order. Wallander was so furious he carried all the laundry out to his car and threw it in the boot. There was a washing machine at the station. As he turned onto Regementsgatan he was almost hit by a motorcycle approaching at high speed. He pulled over to the side of the road, turned off the engine and closed his eyes. I'm stressed, he thought. If a broken washer almost causes me to lose control then there's something wrong with my life.

He knew what it was. Loneliness. The increasingly anaemic late-night hours with Emma Lundin.

Instead of driving to the station he decided to pay a visit to his father out in Löderup. It was always a risky proposition to arrive without prior notice. But right now Wallander felt the need to experience the smell of oil paints in the studio. The dream from last night still haunted him. He drove through the grey landscape and wondered where he should begin in order to achieve a change in his existence. Perhaps Martinsson was right and he should seriously consider whether or not he should remain a police officer for the rest of his life. Sometimes Per Åkeson would speak dreamily about a life beyond all charges, all leaden and uniform hours in courtrooms and questioning chambers. Even my father has something that I lack, he thought as he turned into the driveway. The dreams that he has decided to stay faithful to. Even if they cost his only son a small fortune.

He got out of the car and walked towards the studio. A cat strutted out through the half-open door and regarded him suspiciously. When Wallander bent down to pet it, it slunk away. Wallander knocked and went in. His father was leaning forward in front of his easel.

"You here?" he said. "That's unexpected."

"I was in the neighbourhood," Wallander said. "Am I disturbing you?"

His father pretended not to hear the question. Instead he talked of his trip to Egypt. As if it were a vivid but already very distant memory. Wallander sat down on an old sledge and listened.

"Now only Italy remains," his father concluded. "Then I can lie down to die."

"I think we'll wait with that trip," Wallander said. "At least a couple of months."

His father painted. Wallander sat quietly. Now and again they exchanged a few words. Then more silence. Wallander noticed that he was more relaxed. His head felt lighter. After about half an hour he stood up to leave.

"I'll come by for New Year," he said.

"Bring a bottle of cognac," his father replied.

Wallander returned to the police station, which still gave the impression of being almost completely deserted. He knew that everyone was now lying low in preparation for New Year's Eve, when there would be a flurry of activity, as usual.

Wallander sat down in his office and reviewed the Eberhardsson sisters' trips during the past year. He tried to discern a pattern, without being sure of what he was really looking for. I know nothing about Holm, he thought. Or these pilots. I have nothing that I can apply like a grid to these trips to Spain. There are no fixed points, other than this single trip that Holm made at the same time as Anna Eberhardsson.

He put all the papers back into the envelope and put that into the folder where he kept all the documents having to do with the murder investigations. Then he wrote himself a reminder to buy a bottle of cognac.

It was already past noon. He felt hungry. In order to break his habit of downing a couple of hot dogs at a stand, he walked down to the hospital and had a sandwich at the cafe. Then he leafed through a ripped magazine that had been left on the table next to him. A pop star had almost died of cancer. An actor had fainted during a performance. Photographs from the parties of the rich. He tossed the magazine aside and started walking back to the station. He felt like an elephant lumbering around in a ring bounded by the city of Ystad. Something has to happen soon, he thought. Who has executed these three people, and why?

Rydberg was sitting in the reception area, waiting for him. Wallander sat down on a sofa next to him. As usual Rydberg got right to the point.

"Heroin is flowing into Malmö," he said. "In Lund, Eslöv, Landskrona, Helsingborg. I talked to a colleague in Malmö. He said that there were clear signs that the market had received a boost in supply. It could, in other words, coincide with a drug drop from the plane. In this case, there is only one important question."

Wallander understood.

"Who was there to receive it?"

"In this, we can play with several different scenarios," Rydberg went on. "No one counted on the fact that the plane would crash. A wreck of a plane from Asia that should have been junked a long time ago. Something must then have happened on land. Either the wrong person picked up the package that was dropped in the night. Or else there was more than one predator stalking this prey."

Wallander nodded. He had also thought this far.

"Something went wrong," Rydberg said. "And this led to the execution-style slayings of the Eberhardsson sisters and subsequently Holm. With the same weapon and by the same hand, or hands."

"But I still resist this thought," Wallander said. "We know by now that Anna and Emilia were not nice old ladies. And yet from there, the step of saying they were involved in illegal narcotics transactions feels too great."

"I actually think so too," Rydberg said. "But nothing surprises me any longer. Greed knows no bounds when it sinks its claws into people. Perhaps the sewing shop was doing worse and worse? If we analyse their tax returns we'll get a clearer picture. It should also be possible to tell from the numbers when something happens. At which point they no longer have to care about the profitability of the sewing shop. Perhaps they dreamed of a life in a sunny paradise. They could never have achieved this by selling snaps and silk thread. Suddenly something happens. And they are caught in the web."

"You can also look at it from the reverse perspective," Wallander said. "A better cover than two older women in a sewing shop can hardly be imagined. They were the personification of innocence."

Rydberg nodded.

"Who was there that night to receive the package?" he repeated. "And one more question: who was behind all this? More precisely: who is behind it?"

"We're still searching for a midpoint," Wallander said. "The apex of the pyramid."

Rydberg yawned and got up from the sofa with some effort.

"We'll figure it out sooner or later," he said.

"Has Nyberg returned yet?" Wallander asked.

"According to Martinsson he's still in Tingsryd."

Wallander returned to his office. Everyone seemed to be waiting for something to happen. Nyberg called at four o'clock and said that his car had finally been fixed. They had a meeting at five. No one really had anything new to bring to the table.

That night Wallander slept heavily, without dreaming. The next day it was sunny and five degrees above zero Celsius. He left the car at home and walked to the station. But when he was halfway there, he changed his mind. He thought of what Martinsson had told him, about the two people who lived in the house where Holm had a room. It was only a quarter past seven. He would have time to drive up there and see if they were in before his meeting at the station.

He turned into the front yard at a quarter to eight. The dog was in its fenced run, barking. Wallander looked around. The house appeared as abandoned as the day before. He walked up to the door and knocked. No answer. He felt the handle. It was locked. Someone must have been there. He stepped away in order to walk around the house. Then he heard the front door open behind him. He jumped involuntarily. A man wearing an undershirt and sagging jeans was standing there staring at him. Wallander walked over and introduced himself.

"Are you Rolf Nyman?" he asked.

"Yes, that's me."

"I need to speak to you."

The man looked hesitant.

"The house is a mess," he said. "And the girl who lives here is sleeping."

"My place is also messy," Wallander said. "And we don't need to sit next to her bed."

Nyman stepped aside and led Wallander to the cluttered kitchen. They sat down. The man made no gesture to offer Wallander anything. But he appeared friendly. Wallander assumed he was embarrassed at the mess.

"The girl has big problems with drugs," Nyman said. "Right now she's trying to detox. I'm helping her as much as I can. But it's hard."

"And you?"

"I never touch anything."

"But isn't it strange then to live in the same place as Holm? If you want her to get over a drug addiction."

Nyman's reply was swift and convincing.

"I had no idea he was involved with drugs. We lived here cheaply. He was nice. I had no idea what he did. To me he said he was studying astronomy. We used to stand outside in the garden in the evenings. He knew the name of every single star."

"What do you do?"

"I can't hold down a permanent job until she gets better. I work at a disco from time to time."

"Disco?"

"I play records."

"You're a DJ?"

"Yes."

Wallander thought he made a sympathetic impression. He did not appear anxious about anything other than disturbing the girl who was sleeping somewhere.

"Holm," Wallander said. "How did you meet him? And when was that?"

"In a disco in Landskrona. We started talking. He told me about this house. A couple of weeks later we moved in. The worst thing is that I don't have the energy to clean. I did earlier. Holm did too. But now all my time goes to taking care of her."

"You never suspected what Holm was up to?"

"No."

"Did he ever have visitors?"

"Never. He was usually gone during the day. But he always said when he was coming back. It was only the last time, when he didn't come back, that he said where he was going."

"Had he appeared nervous that day? Was there anything different about him?"

Rolf Nyman thought back.

"No, he was like normal."

"And how was that?"

"Happy. But reserved sometimes."

Wallander thought about how best to proceed.

"Did he have a lot of money?"

"He certainly didn't live in luxury. I can show you his room."

"That won't be necessary. Are you sure he never had any visitors?"

"Never."

"But there must have been telephone calls."

Nyman nodded.

"It was as if he always knew when someone was going to call. Sat down next to the phone and it rang. If he wasn't at home or nearby, it never rang. That was the strangest thing about him."

Wallander had reached the end of his questions and stood up.

"What will you do now?" he asked.

"I don't know. Holm rented the house from someone in Örebro. I guess we'll have to move."

Rolf Nyman followed him out onto the front steps.

"Did you ever hear Holm mention the Eberhardsson sisters?"

"The ones who were killed? No, never."

Wallander realised he had one final question.

"Holm must have had a car," he said. "Where is it?"

Rolf Nyman shook his head.

"I don't know."

"What kind was it?"

"A black VW Golf."

Wallander held out his hand and said goodbye. The dog was silent as Wallander walked to the car.

Holm must have concealed his business well, he thought on the way back to Ystad. Just as he concealed his true self well when I questioned him.

He parked the car outside the station at a quarter to nine. Ebba was at her desk and said that Martinsson and the others were waiting for him in the conference room. He hurried over. Nyberg had also arrived.

"What's going on?" Wallander said before he had even sat down.

"Big news," Martinsson said. "Our Malmö colleagues have made a routine search of a well-known drug dealer. In his house they found a .38 calibre pistol."

Martinsson turned to Nyberg.

"The technicians have worked quickly," he said. "Both the Eberhardsson sisters and Holm were shot with a weapon of that calibre."

Wallander caught his breath.

"What's the name of the dealer?"

"Nilsmark. But he's known as Hilton."

"Is it the same pistol?"

"We can't answer that question yet. But the possibility exists."

Wallander nodded.

"Good," he said. "This may be our breakthrough. And then we have a shot at wrapping this up before the new year."

CHAPTER
ELEVEN

They worked intensively for three days, until New Year's Eve. Wallander and Nyberg drove into Malmö on the morning of the twenty-eighth. Nyberg went in order to talk to the Malmö police technicians, Wallander in order to take part, and in part to take over, the questioning of the drug dealer known as Hilton. He turned out to be a man in his fifties, overweight yet able to move with a surprising agility. He was dressed in a suit and tie and appeared bored. Before the start of his questioning, Wallander had been briefed on the man's history by a detective inspector named Hyttner, whom Wallander had met before.

Hilton had done some time at the beginning of the 1980s for dealing drugs. But Hyttner was convinced that the police and prosecutors had only been able to skim the surface that time and put him away for just a small portion of his criminal activities. He had clearly been able to retain control of his business from the prison in Norrköping where he had served his time. During his absence, the Malmö police had not been able to detect a power struggle among those who controlled the drug supply into the southern parts of Sweden.

506

When Hilton had got out of prison he had immediately celebrated the event by getting divorced and marrying a young Bolivian beauty. Thereafter he had moved to a large estate just north of Trelleborg. What they also knew was that he had started to extend his hunting grounds as far as Ystad and Simrishamn and was on his way to establishing himself in Kristianstad. On the twenty-eighth of December, the police felt they had enough evidence against him to get the public prosecutor to issue a search warrant for his estate. That was when they found the gun. Hilton had immediately confessed that he had no licence for the weapon. He explained that he had bought it in order to defend himself since his home was so remotely located. But he had firmly denied any involvement in the murders of the Eberhardsson sisters and Yngve Leonard Holm.

Wallander sat in on the drawn-out questioning of Hilton. Towards the end he posed some of his own questions, among them what exactly Hilton had been doing on the two dates in question. In the case of the Eberhardssons, the timetable was very precise. It was less certain when Holm had been shot. Hilton claimed to have been in Copenhagen when the Eberhardssons were killed. Since he had travelled alone, it would take time to confirm this claim. During the time that had elapsed between Holm going missing and when he had been found murdered, Hilton had done many different things.

Wallander wished Rydberg was there. Wallander could usually tell fairly quickly if the person before him was telling the truth or not. But it was hard with Hilton. If Rydberg had been there they could have compared their impressions. After the session, Wallander had coffee with Hyttner.

"We've never been able to link him to any violent incidents before," Hyttner said. "He has always used other boys when needed. And they haven't always been the same ones. From what we can tell, he's brought in people from the Continent when he's had to break someone's leg who hasn't performed up to snuff."

"All of them will have to be tracked down," Wallander said, "if it turns out that the weapon matches."

"I have a hard time believing that it's him," Hyttner said. "He's not the type. He has no qualms about selling heroin to schoolkids. But he's also the kind who faints when he has to give a blood sample."

Wallander returned to Ystad at the start of the afternoon. Nyberg remained in Malmö. Wallander noticed that he was hoping more than he believed that they were nearer to solving the case.

At the same time another thought had started to gnaw at him. Something he had overlooked. A conclusion he should have drawn, or an assumption he should have made. He searched his mind without finding an answer.

On his way back to Ystad he turned off by Stjärnsund and stopped for a while at Sten Widén's horse ranch. He found Widén out in the stables with an older woman who apparently owned one of the horses being trained. She was on her way out when Wallander arrived. Together, he and Widén watched the BMW drive away.

"She's nice," Sten Widén said. "But the horses that she is swindled into buying don't make anybody happy. I always tell her to ask me for advice before she buys. But she thinks she knows best. Now she has one called Jupiter who is guaranteed never to win a race."

Widén threw his arms out.

"But she keeps me alive," he said.

"La Trottiata," Wallander said. "I'd like to see her."

They walked back through the stables where the horses were stomping in various boxes. Sten Widén stopped next to one of the horses and stroked its muzzle.

"La Trottiata," he said. "Not particularly wanton, I have to say. She's mostly just afraid of the stallions."

"Is she any good?"

"Could be. But she has frail hind legs. We'll have to see."

They walked outside again. Wallander had picked up a faint trace of alcohol on Widén's breath when they were in the stables. Widén wanted to invite him in for a cup of coffee but Wallander said no.

"I have a triple homicide to solve," he said. "I assume you've read about it in the papers."

"I only read the sport pages," Sten Widén answered.

Wallander left Stjärnsund. He wondered if he and Sten would ever find their way back to the ease of understanding that had once existed between them.

When Wallander came back to the station he bumped into Björk in the reception area.

"I hear you've solved those murders," he said.

"No," Wallander said firmly. "Nothing has been solved."

509

"Then we'll have to continue to hope," Björk said.

Björk left through the front doors. It is as if our confrontation had never taken place, Wallander thought. Or else he's more afraid of conflict than I am. Or nurses a grudge longer.

Wallander gathered the squad together and reviewed the developments in Malmö.

"Do you think it's him?" Rydberg asked when Wallander was finished.

"I don't know," Wallander answered.

"That means, in other words, that you don't think it's him?"

Wallander did not answer. He only shrugged somewhat despondently.

As they ended the meeting, Martinsson asked if Wallander would consider switching New Year's Eve duty with him. Martinsson was on duty and would rather get out of it if he could. Wallander thought it over. Perhaps it would be best to work and keep his hands busy instead of thinking of Mona the whole time, but he had promised his father he would spend the evening in Löderup. That carried the most weight.

"I've promised to be with my father," he said. "You'll have to try someone else."

Wallander stayed behind in the conference room after Martinsson had left. He searched for the thought that had started nagging at him on the way back from Malmö. He went over to the window and stared absent-mindedly out across the car park to the water tower. Slowly he reviewed all of the events in his mind.

Tried to catch something he had missed. But it was in vain.

The rest of the day, nothing significant occurred. Everyone was waiting. Nyberg returned from Malmö. The forensic ballistics specialists were working at full speed on the weapon. Martinsson managed to switch his New Year's Eve with Näslund, who was on bad terms with his wife and wanted to avoid being home. Wallander walked to and fro in the corridor. He kept searching for the thought that was just out of reach. It continued to gnaw on his subconscious. He knew enough to realise it was only a detail that had flashed by. Perhaps a single word that he should have caught and examined more closely.

It was six o'clock. Rydberg left without saying anything. Together, Wallander and Martinsson reviewed everything they knew about Yngve Leonard Holm. He was born in Brösarp and, as far as they could tell, had never held down a real job in his life. Small-time stealing in his youth had led to increasingly serious crimes. But no violence. In this he reminded them of Nilsmark. Martinsson excused himself and left. Hansson was absorbed in his racing tables, which he quickly stuffed into a drawer if anyone came into his office. In the break room Wallander talked with a couple of officers who were going to run a drunk-driving campaign over New Year. They were going to focus on the smaller roads, the "alcohol routes" that were used by drivers with good local knowledge who were over the legal limit and still planned to drive themselves home. At seven o'clock

Wallander called Malmö and spoke to Hyttner. Nothing had happened there either. But the heroin was now flowing as far north as Varberg. There, the drug trade controlled from Gothenburg took over.

Wallander went home. The washing machine had still not been repaired. And the dirty laundry was still in his car. He angrily returned to the station and stuffed the washer full. Then he sat doodling in his notebook. Thought about Radwan and the mighty pyramids. By the time his laundry was dry it was past nine o'clock. He went home, opened a can of hash and ate in front of the TV while he watched an old Swedish film. He vaguely remembered it from his youth. He had seen it with a girl who had not allowed him to place a hand on her thigh.

Before he went to bed he called Linda. This time it was Mona who answered. He could immediately tell from her voice that he had called at the wrong time. Linda was out. Wallander simply asked Mona to give Linda his greetings. The conversation was over before it had even begun.

He had just crawled into bed when Emma Lundin called. Wallander pretended to have been woken up. She apologised for disturbing him. Then she asked him about New Year's Eve. Wallander told her he was planning to spend it with his father. They arranged to get together on New Year's Day. Wallander regretted this even before he replaced the receiver.

The following day, the twenty-ninth of December, nothing happened other than that Björk was in a minor traffic accident. It was a smirking Martinsson who delivered the news. Björk had seen a car too late as he was making a left turn. It had been slick and the cars had skidded into each other and received some superficial damage.

Nyberg was still waiting for the forensic ballistics report. Wallander spent the day trying to work through his piles of paper. In the afternoon Per Åkeson came into his office and asked for an update on the latest developments. Wallander told him the truth, that they were just hoping they were on the right track. But there was still a great deal of groundwork to be done.

It was Åkeson's last day of work before his leave of absence.

"My replacement is a woman," he said. "But I've already told you that, haven't I? Her name is Anette Brolin and she's coming down from Stockholm. You should be happy. She's much more attractive than I am."

"We'll see," Wallander said. "But I expect we'll miss you."

"Not Hansson," Per Åkeson said. "He's never liked me. Why, I don't know. The same goes for Svedberg."

"I'll try to find out why that is while you're gone."

They wished each other a happy new year and promised to stay in touch.

That evening Wallander talked to Linda for a long time on the phone. She was planning to celebrate New Year's Eve with friends in Lund. Wallander was disappointed. He had thought, or at least hoped, that she would join them in Löderup.

"Two old men," she said kindly. "I can think of a more exciting way to spend the evening."

After the call, Wallander realised that he had forgotten to buy the bottle of cognac his father had asked for. He should also buy a bottle of champagne. He wrote two notes. He put one on the kitchen table and one in his shoe. That night he sat up for a long time listening to an old recording of *Turandot* with Maria Callas. For some strange reason his thoughts wandered to the horses in Sten Widén's stables. Only when the time was close to three did he fall asleep.

On the morning of the thirtieth there was a heavy snowfall over Ystad. It could be a chaotic New Year's Eve if the weather did not improve. But already at ten o'clock the skies cleared and the snow started to melt away. Wallander wondered why the ballistics team was taking such an inordinate amount of time to decide whether it was the same weapon. Nyberg grew angry and said that forensic technicians did not earn their measly wages by performing substandard work. Wallander immediately crawled on his knees. They made up and then spent some time talking about the low wages of the police. Not even Björk had a particularly good salary.

In the afternoon, the investigative squad assembled for what turned out to be a slow-moving meeting since there were so few new items. The police in Marbella had sent an impressively detailed report of their search of the Eberhardsson sisters' villa. They had even included a photograph. The picture was now passed around the table. The house really was palatial. But nonetheless the report did not yield anything new to the investigation. There was no breakthrough, only this waiting.

Their hopes were dashed on the morning of the thirty-first. The forensic ballistic specialists were able to determine that the weapon that had been found in Nilsmark's home had not been the one used to kill either the Eberhardsson sisters or Holm. For a moment, the investigative squad was deflated. Only Rydberg and Wallander had suspected that the message would most likely be in the negative. The Malmö police had also been able to confirm Nilsmark's trip to Copenhagen. He could not have been in Ystad when the sisters were slain. Hyttner also believed that Nilsmark would be able to produce an alibi for the time period of Holm's death.

"That puts us back at square one," Wallander said. "In the new year we are going to have to start again at full speed. Review the material again and work deeper."

No one made any more comments. During the new year's holiday, the investigation would be put on hold. Since they had no immediate leads Wallander felt that what they needed most was to rest. Then they wished one another a happy new year. Finally, only Rydberg and Wallander were left.

"We knew this," Rydberg said. "Both you and I. That it would have been too easy with that Nilsmark. Why the hell would he have kept the weapon? It was wrong from the start."

"But we still had to look into it."

"Police work often consists of doing what one knows from the start to be meaningless," Rydberg said. "But it is as you say. No stone can be left unturned."

Then they talked about New Year's Eve.

"I don't envy my colleagues in the big cities," Rydberg said.

"It can get messy here too."

Rydberg asked Wallander what he was going to do.

"I'll be out with the old man in Löderup. He wants cognac, we'll have a bite to eat, play cards, yawn and then drink a toast at midnight. Then I'll go home."

"I try to avoid staying up," Rydberg said. "New Year's Eve is a ghost. It's one of the few times during the year that I take a sleeping pill."

Wallander wanted to ask how Rydberg was feeling, but he decided to let it be.

They shook hands, as if to mark the day as special.

Then Wallander went to his office, put out an almanac for 1990 and cleaned out his drawers. It was a habit he had acquired over the past few years. New Year's Eve was for cleaning out drawers, to rid himself of old paper.

Wallander was amazed at all the old junk he found. A bottle of glue had leaked in one of the drawers. He fetched a knife from the break room and started to scrape it away. From the corridor he could hear an outraged drunk let it be known that he did not have time to waste at the station because he was on his way to a party. It's already started, Wallander thought, and he took the knife back to the break room. He threw the bottle of glue into the bin.

At seven o'clock he went home, had a shower and changed his clothes. Shortly after eight he was out in Löderup. On the road he had continued to grope around for the thought that bothered him, without success. His father had made a fish gratin that was surprisingly tasty. Wallander had managed to buy cognac and his father nodded approvingly when he saw that it was Hennessy. The bottle of champagne was put in the fridge. They drank beer with their dinner. His father had put on his old suit for the occasion and also a tie that he had tied in a way Wallander had never seen before.

A little after nine they sat down and played poker. Wallander got three of a kind two times but threw one of his cards away each time so that his father could win. At around eleven, Wallander walked outside to relieve himself. It was clear and had grown colder. The stars were sparkling. Wallander thought of the pyramids. The fact that they were lit by strong spotlights meant the Egyptian night sky had been all but invisible. He went back inside. His father had downed several glasses of cognac and was starting to get drunk. Wallander only had small sips since he was planning to drive back. Even though he knew where the traffic controls were going to be, it was unacceptable for him to drive while over the legal limit. Not on New Year's Eve. Sometimes it ended up happening, and each time Wallander told himself he would never let it happen again.

Linda called at half past eleven. They took turns talking to her. In the background Wallander heard the sounds of a stereo turned up very high. They had to shout at each other.

"You would have had a better time with us," Wallander shouted.

"You don't know anything about it," she yelled back, but it sounded friendly.

They wished each other a happy new year. His father had yet another glass of cognac. He was starting to spill as he refilled his glass. But he was in good spirits. And that was the only thing that mattered to Wallander.

They sat in front of the TV at twelve and watched Jarl Kulle ring in the new year. Wallander glanced at his father, who actually had tears in his eyes. He was not touched himself, only tired. He also thought with dread about the coming day when he would get together with Emma Lundin. It was as if he was cheating at cards with her. If he was going to make a New Year's resolution this evening it should be to tell her the truth as soon as possible, that he did not want to continue the relationship.

But he made no resolution.

He went home a little before one. But first he had helped his father into bed. He had taken off his shoes and spread a blanket over him.

"We'll go to Italy soon," his father said.

Wallander cleaned up in the kitchen. His father's snores were already rolling through the house.

On the morning of New Year's Day, Wallander woke up with a headache and a sore throat. He said as much to Emma Lundin when she came by at twelve o'clock.

Since she was a nurse and Wallander was both hot and pale she didn't doubt that it was true. She checked his throat.

"A three-day cold," she pronounced. "Stay home."

She made some tea that they drank in the living room. Wallander tried several times to tell her what he was thinking. But when she left at around three they had not arrived at anything except that Wallander would be in touch with her when he felt better.

Wallander spent the rest of the day in bed. He started to read several books without being able to concentrate. Not even *The Mysterious Island* by Jules Verne, his favourite, was able to kindle his interest. But he was reminded of the fact that one of the characters in the book had the same name — Ayrton — as one of the dead pilots who had finally been identified.

For long periods of time he lay in a kind of half-stupor. The pyramids returned again and again in his thoughts. His father climbed and fell, or else he found himself deep down in a narrow passageway where enormous masses of stone were suspended above his head.

In the evening he managed to find a packet of dried soup in one of the kitchen drawers, which he made. But he poured almost all of it out. His appetite was almost non-existent.

The following day he still felt ill. He called Martinsson and said he was planning to stay in bed. He was told that New Year's Eve had been a calm affair in Ystad but unusually troublesome in other parts of the country. At around ten o'clock he went out and bought groceries, since his fridge and pantry were almost empty. He also went by the chemist and bought some headache tablets. His throat felt better, but now his nose was running. He sneezed as he was about to pay for the painkillers. The cashier looked disapprovingly at him.

He went back to bed and fell asleep again.

Suddenly he woke up with a start. He had dreamed about the pyramids again. But it was something else that had awakened him. Something that had to do with the thought that had eluded him.

What is it that I don't see? he wondered. He lay in absolute stillness and stared out into the darkened room. It had something to do with the pyramids. And with New Year's Eve at his father's in Löderup. When he had been standing out in the garden, staring up at the sky, he had seen the stars. Since it was dark all around him. The pyramids outside Cairo had been illuminated by strong lights. They had detracted from the light of the stars.

He finally grasped the thought that had nagged at him.

The plane that had sneaked in over the Swedish coast had dropped something. Lights had been observed beyond the woods. An area had been marked out in order for the plane to find it. Spotlights had been set up in the fields and then taken down again.

It was the spotlights that had nagged at him. Who had access to strong lights of this kind?

The idea was a long shot. Nonetheless he trusted his intuition. He thought about it for a while, sitting up in bed. Then he made up his mind, got up, put on his old dressing gown and called the police station. He wanted to talk to Martinsson. It took a couple of minutes for him to get to the phone.

"Do me a favour," Wallander said. "Call Rolf Nyman. The guy who shared that house with Holm outside Sjöbo. Call and make it sound like a routine inquiry. Some facts that need to be filled in. Nyman told me he worked as a DJ at various discos. Ask him in passing for the names of all the places where he's worked."

"Why is this important?"

"I don't know," Wallander said. "But please do me this favour."

Martinsson promised to get back to him. Wallander had already started to doubt himself. It was too much of a long shot. But it was as Rydberg always said: no stone should be left unturned.

The hours went by. It was already afternoon. Martinsson did not call. Wallander's fever was starting to go down. But he was still plagued by sneezing attacks. And a runny nose. Martinsson called at half past four.

"No one answered the phone until just now," he said. "But I don't think he suspected anything. I have a list here of the four discos. Two in Malmö, one in Lund, and one out in Råå, outside Helsingborg."

Wallander wrote down the names.

"Good," he said.

"I hope you realise that I'm curious."

"It's just an idea I've had. We'll talk about it tomorrow."

Wallander finished the conversation. He got dressed without a second thought, let a couple of painkillers dissolve in a glass of water, had a cup of coffee and took out a roll of toilet paper to bring along. At a quarter past five he was in his car and on his way.

The first disco was housed in an old warehouse in the Malmö Frihamn area. Wallander was in luck. Just as he stopped the car, a man walked out of the closed disco. Wallander introduced himself and learned that the person in front of him was called Juhanen, from Haparanda, and the owner of the disco Exodus.

"How does someone from Haparanda end up in Malmö?" Wallander asked.

The man smiled. He was around forty and had bad teeth.

"He meets a girl," he said. "Most people who move do so for one of two reasons. To find work. Or because they meet someone."

"I actually want to ask you about Rolf Nyman," Wallander said.

"Anything wrong?"

"No," Wallander answered. "Routine questions. He works for you sometimes?"

"He's good. Perhaps a little conservative in his music selection. But skilled."

"A disco lives on the high volume of its music and its light effects," Wallander said, "if I'm not completely mistaken?"

"Correct," Juhanen said. "I always stuff my ears, or I would have lost my hearing a long time ago."

"Rolf Nyman never borrowed any lighting equipment, did he?" Wallander asked. "Some of the high-intensity spotlights?"

"Why would he do that?"

"It's just a question."

Juhanen shook his head firmly.

"I keep an eye on both the staff and the equipment," he said. "Nothing disappears around here. Or gets borrowed."

"That's all I needed to know," Wallander said. "Also, I would rather you didn't mention this to anyone for now."

Juhanen smiled.

"You mean, I shouldn't tell Nyman?"

"Exactly."

"What's he done?"

"Nothing. But we have to snoop around in secret sometimes."

Juhanen shrugged.

"I won't say anything."

Wallander drove on. The second disco was located in the inner city. It was open. The volume hit Wallander's head like a club as he walked in the door. The disco was owned by two men, one of whom was present. Wallander convinced him to walk out onto the street. He also had a negative answer to give. Rolf Nyman had never borrowed any lights. Nor had any equipment gone missing.

Wallander got back in his car and blew his nose into some toilet paper. This is meaningless, he thought. What I am doing right now is just throwing away my efforts. The only result will be that I'll end up staying ill longer.

Then he drove to Lund. The sneezing attacks came and went in waves. He noticed that he was sweating. He was probably running a temperature again. The disco in Lund was called Lagårn — the Barn — and was in the eastern corner of the city. Wallander made several wrong turns before he found it. The sign was not illuminated and the doors were locked. Lagårn was located in a building that had earlier been a dairy, Wallander was able to read from the facade. He wondered why the disco had not been given that name instead, the Dairy. Wallander looked around. There was some small industry on either side of the disco. A little further away there was a house with a garden. Wallander walked over, opened the gate and rang the doorbell. A man around his own age opened it. Wallander heard opera music in the background.

Wallander showed him his police ID. The man let Wallander into the hall.

"If I'm not mistaken, it's Puccini," Wallander said.

The man looked more closely at him.

"That's right," he said. "*Tosca*."

"I'm actually here to talk about a different kind of music," Wallander said. "I'll keep this brief. I need to know who owns the disco next to you."

"How on earth would I know that? I'm a genetic researcher. Not a disc jockey."

524

"But you are neighbours, after all," Wallander said.

"Why not ask your colleagues?" the man suggested. "There are often fights outside. They would know."

He's right, Wallander said.

The man pointed to a telephone on a table in the hall. Wallander had the number of the Lund police memorised. After being transferred several times he got the information that the disco was owned by a woman with the last name Boman. Wallander made a note of her address and telephone number.

"It's easy to find," the officer he spoke to said. "She lives in the building downtown that's across from the station."

Wallander hung up.

"That is a very beautiful opera," Wallander said. "The music, I mean. I have unfortunately never seen it performed."

"I never go to the opera," the man said. "The music is enough for me."

Wallander thanked him and left. Then he drove around for a long time until he managed to find the station in Lund. The pedestrian streets and dead ends seemed innumerable. He parked in a no-parking zone. Then he tore off a number of sheets of toilet paper, put them in his pocket and walked across the street. He pressed the button with the name Boman. The door lock buzzed open and Wallander walked in. The apartment was on the second floor. Wallander looked around for a lift, but there was none. Even though he walked slowly, he got out of breath. A woman who was very young, hardly twenty-five, was standing in the doorway waiting for him. She had very short hair and several rings in her ears. Wallander introduced himself and showed her his ID. She didn't even glance at it but asked him to come in. Wallander looked around with astonishment. There was almost no furniture in the apartment. The walls were bare. And yet it was cosy somehow. There was nothing in the way. It only contained what was absolutely necessary.

"Why do the police in Ystad want to speak with me?" she asked. "I have enough trouble with the cops in Lund."

He could tell that she was not overly fond of the police. She had sat down in a chair and was wearing a very short skirt. Wallander searched around for a spot next to her face where he could direct his gaze.

"I'll get right to the point," Wallander said. "Rolf Nyman."

"What about him?"

"Nothing. But does he work for you?"

"I have him as a reserve. In case one of my regular DJs gets ill."

"My question may strike you as strange," Wallander said. "But I have to ask it."

"Why aren't you looking me in the eye?" she asked abruptly.

"That is probably because your skirt is so very short," Wallander replied, surprised at his own directness.

She burst into laughter, reached for a blanket and laid it across her legs. Wallander looked at the blanket and then her face.

"Rolf Nyman," he repeated. "Has he ever borrowed any lighting equipment from your establishment?"

"Never."

Wallander caught an almost imperceptible cloud of uncertainty that crossed her face. His attention sharpened at once.

"Never?"

She bit her lip.

"The question is odd," she said. "But the fact is that a number of lights disappeared from the disco about a year ago. We reported it to the police as a burglary. But they never found any leads."

"When was that? Was it after Nyman started to work for you?"

She thought back.

"Exactly one year ago. In January. After Nyman had started."

"You never suspected that it could be an inside job?"

"No, actually."

She got up and quickly left the room. Wallander looked at her legs. After a moment's absence she returned with a pocket calendar in her hand.

"The lights disappeared sometime between the ninth and twelfth of January. And now that I look I can see that it was actually Rolf who was working then."

"What kind of lights?" Wallander asked.

"Six spotlights. Not really useful for a disco. They're more for theatre work. Very strong, around two thousand watts. There were also a number of cables that went missing."

Wallander nodded slowly.

"Why are you asking about this?"

"I can't tell you that right now," Wallander said. "But I have to ask you one thing, and I want you to regard it as an order. That you don't mention this to Rolf Nyman."

"Request granted as long as you have a word with your Lund colleagues and ask them to leave me alone."

"I'll see what I can do."

She followed him out into the hall.

"I don't think I ever asked you for your first name," he said.

"Linda."

"That's my daughter's name. Therefore it's a very beautiful name."

Wallander was overcome by a sneeze. She drew back a few steps.

"I won't shake your hand," he said. "But you gave me the answer I had been hoping for."

"You realise, of course, that I'm curious?"

"You'll get your answer," he said, "in time."

She was just about to close the door when Wallander realised he had yet another question.

"Do you know anything about Rolf Nyman's private life?"

"No, nothing."

"So, you don't know about his girlfriend who has a drug addiction?"

Linda Boman looked at him for a long time before she answered.

"I don't know if he has a girlfriend who takes drugs," she said finally. "But I do know that Rolf has serious problems with heroin. How long he'll manage to control it, I have no idea."

Wallander went back down onto the street. The time was already ten o'clock and the night was cold.

We are through, he thought.

Rolf Nyman. Surely he's the one.

CHAPTER
TWELVE

Wallander was almost back in Ystad when he decided not to go straight home. At the second roundabout on the edge of town he turned north instead. It was ten minutes to eleven. His nose continued to run, but his curiosity drove him on. He thought that what he was doing again — how many times now, he had no idea — was at odds with the most fundamental rules governing police work. Above all, the rule that forbade placing yourself in dangerous situations alone.

If it was true, as he was now convinced, that it was Rolf Nyman who had shot Holm and the Eberhardsson sisters, Nyman definitely counted as potentially dangerous. In addition, he had tricked Wallander. And he had done so effortlessly and with great skill. On his car ride from Malmö, Wallander had been wondering what could be driving him. What was the crack that had appeared in the pattern? The answers he came up with pointed in at least two different directions. It could be a power struggle or about influence over the drug trade.

The point in the whole situation that worried him most was what Linda Boman had said about Nyman's own drug habit. That he was a heroin addict. Wallander had almost never come across drug dealers above the

absolute bottom level who were also addicts. T
question went around in Wallander's head. There wa
something that did not make sense, a piece that wa
missing.

Wallander turned by the road that led to the house
where Nyman lived. He turned off the engine and
the headlights. He took out a torch from the glove
compartment. Then he carefully opened the door after
first turning off the interior lights. Listened out into the
darkness and then closed the car door as quietly as he
could. It was about a hundred metres to the yard
entrance. He shielded the torch with one hand and
directed the beam in front of him. The wind was cold,
he felt. Time for a warmer sweater. But his nose had
almost dried up. When he reached the edge of the
woods, he turned out the torch. One window in
the house was lit up. Someone must be home. Now
comes the dog, he thought. He walked back the way he
had come, about fifty metres. Then he went into the
woods and turned the torch back on. He was going to
approach the house from the back. As far as he could
recall, the room with the lighted window had windows
both to the front and back of the house.

He moved slowly, trying to avoid stepping on twigs.
He was sweating by the time he had reached the back
of the house. He had also started to question himself
more and more as to what he thought he was up to. In
the worst-case scenario the dog would bark and give
Rolf Nyman the first warning that someone was
watching him. He stood still and listened. All he could
hear was the sighing of the trees. In the distance a plane

was coming in for landing at Sturup. Wallander waited until his breathing was back to normal before he carefully walked up to the house. He crouched down and held the torch only a few centimetres from the ground. Just before he entered the area lit up by the window, he turned off the torch and drew back into the shadows next to the house. The dog was still quiet. He listened with his ear pressed against the cold wall. No music, no voices, nothing. Then he stretched up and carefully peered in through the window.

Rolf Nyman was sitting at a table in the middle of the room. He was leaning over something that Wallander could not immediately see. Then he realised that Rolf Nyman was playing a game of patience. Slowly, he turned over card after card. Wallander asked himself what he had been expecting. A man who was measuring out tiny bags of white powder on some scales? Or someone with a rubber tube around his upper arm, injecting himself?

I'm wrong, he thought. This is a mistake from beginning to end.

But he was still convinced. The man sitting at the table playing a game of patience had recently killed three people. Brutally executed them.

Wallander was just about to pull away from the house wall when the dog at the front of the house started to bark. Rolf Nyman jumped. He looked straight at Wallander. For one second, Wallander thought he had been discovered. Then Nyman quickly stood up and walked to the front door, at which point Wallander was already on his way back into the woods.

If he lets the dog loose I'm in trouble, he thought. He directed the torch at the ground that he was stumbling over. He slipped and felt a branch cut his cheek. In the background he could still hear the dog barking.

When he reached the car he dropped the torch but did not stop to pick it up. He turned the key and wondered what would have happened if he had had his old car. Now he was able to put the car in reverse without a problem and drive away. Just as Wallander got into the car he heard a tractor approach on the main road. If he could get the sound of his own engine to coincide with the sound of the other vehicle then he would be able to get away without Rolf Nyman hearing him. He stopped and quietly turned and sneaked slowly into third gear. When he got out onto the main road he saw the tail lights of the tractor. Since he was going downhill he turned off the engine and let the car coast. There was no one in his rear-view mirror. No one had come in pursuit. Wallander stroked his cheek and felt blood and then felt around for the toilet paper. In a brief moment of inattentiveness he almost drove into a ditch. At the last moment he was able to straighten the car.

It was already past midnight when he reached Mariagatan. The branch had made a deep cut in his cheek. Wallander briefly considered going to the hospital, but he settled for cleaning the wound himself and applying a large Band-Aid. Then he put on a pot of strong coffee and sat down at the kitchen table with one of his many half-full notepads in front of him.

He reviewed his triangle-shaped pyramid once more and replaced the question mark in the middle with Rolf Nyman. He knew from the start that the material was very thin. The only thing that he could produce against Nyman was the suspicion that he had stolen the lights that were later used to mark the area for the plane drop.

But what else did he have? Nothing. What relationship had Holm and Nyman shared? Where did the plane and the Eberhardsson sisters fit in? Wallander pushed the notepad away. They would need a more thoroughgoing investigation in order to move forward. He was also wondering how he could convince his colleagues that despite how it looked, he really had found the lead that they should concentrate on. How far could he go by simply citing his intuition again? Rydberg would understand, perhaps even Martinsson. But both Svedberg and Hansson would dismiss it.

It was two o'clock before he turned out the light and went to bed. His cheek ached.

In the morning, the third of January, it was cold and clear in Skåne. Wallander got up early, changed the bandage on his cheek, and arrived at the station shortly before seven. Today he was in before even Martinsson. In reception he was told about a serious traffic accident that had happened an hour earlier, just outside Ystad, involving several deaths, including a young child, which always evoked a particularly sombre mood among his colleagues. Wallander went to his office and was grateful for the fact that he no longer found himself called out to the scene of traffic accidents. He poured himself some coffee and then sat down and thought back to the events of the evening before.

But his doubts from the day before remained. Rolf Nyman could turn out to be a red herring. But there were still grounds for investigating him thoroughly. Wallander also decided that they should put his house under discreet surveillance, not least in order to find out when Nyman would be out. Technically this fell to the Sjöbo police, but Wallander had already decided simply to keep them informed. The Ystad police would insist on undertaking this work themselves.

They needed to get into the house. But there was an additional complication. Rolf Nyman was not alone. There was also a woman, whom no one had seen, and who had been sleeping when Wallander stopped by.

Wallander suddenly wondered if the woman even existed. Much of what Nyman had told him had turned out not to be true. He looked at his watch. Twenty minutes past seven. It was probably very early for a woman who ran a disco. But he still searched around for Linda Boman's telephone number in Lund. She picked up almost immediately. Wallander could hear that she was groggy.

"I'm sorry if I woke you up," he said.

"I'm awake."

She is like me, Wallander thought. Doesn't like to admit that she has been woken up. Even if this is a perfectly decent hour to still be sleeping.

"I have some more questions," Wallander said. "And unfortunately they can't wait."

"Call me in five minutes," she said and hung up.

Wallander waited for seven minutes. Then he dialled the number again. Her voice was less hoarse now.

"This is in regard to Rolf Nyman, of course," he said.

"Are you still not planning to tell me why you're interested in him?"

"I can't do that right now. But I promise you'll be the first to know."

"I feel honoured."

"You said that he had a serious heroin addiction."

"I remember."

"My question is very simple: how do you know this?"

"He told me. It took me by surprise. He didn't try to hide it, and that made an impression on me."

"He told you?"

"Yes."

"Does this mean that you never noticed that he had a problem?"

"He always did his job."

"He never appeared high?"

"Not that I could tell."

"And he never appeared nervous or anxious?"

"No more so than anyone else. I can also be nervous and anxious. Especially when the police in Lund bother me and the disco."

Wallander sat quietly for a moment and wondered if he should ask his Lund colleagues about Linda Boman. She waited.

"Let me go through this one more time," he said. "You never saw him when he was under the influence. He only told you that he was a heroin addict."

"I have a hard time believing that a person would lie about something like that."

"I agree," Wallander said. "But I want to assure myself that I've understood this correctly."

"Is that why you're calling at six o'clock in the morning?"

"It's half past seven."

"Same difference."

"I have one more question," Wallander continued. "You said that you never heard about a girlfriend."

"No, I didn't."

"You never saw him with one?"

"No, never."

"So if we assume that he said he had a girlfriend you couldn't verify if this were true or not?"

"Your questions are getting stranger and stranger. Why wouldn't he have a girlfriend? He isn't worse-looking than other guys."

"Then I have no more questions for the moment," Wallander concluded. "And what I said yesterday is still very much in effect."

"I won't say anything. I'm going to sleep."

"It's possible that I'll be in touch again," Wallander said. "Do you know, by the way, if Rolf has any close friends?"

"No."

The conversation came to a close.

Wallander went to Martinsson's office. Martinsson was combing his hair and looking into a small hand-held mirror.

"Eight-thirty," Wallander said. "Can you get everyone together?"

"It sounds like something's happened."

"Maybe," Wallander replied.

Then they exchanged a few words about the traffic accident. Apparently a car had crossed over onto the wrong side of the road and driven head-on into a Polish tractor.

At half past eight Wallander informed his colleagues about the latest developments. About his conversation with Linda Boman and the missing lighting equipment. He did not, however, mention his nighttime visit to the remote house outside Sjöbo. As he had predicted, Rydberg found the discovery important while Hansson and Svedberg had a number of objections. Martinsson said nothing.

"I know it's thin," Wallander said after listening to the discussion. "But I'm still of the opinion that we should concentrate on Nyman right now, though not discontinue the investigations we're already pursuing."

"What does the public prosecutor have to say about this?" Martinsson asked. "Who is the public prosecutor right now, anyway?"

"Her name is Anette Brolin and she's in Stockholm," Wallander said. "She'll be coming down next week. But I had been planning to talk to Åkeson. Even if he no longer has formal responsibility in charge of the pre-investigation."

They went on. Wallander argued that they needed to get into the house outside Sjöbo but without Nyman's knowledge, which was immediately greeted with new protests.

"We can't do that," Svedberg said. "That's illegal."

"We have a triple homicide on our hands," Wallander said. "If I'm correct, Rolf Nyman is very cunning. If we're going to find something, we have to observe him without his knowledge. When does he leave the house? What does he do? How long is he gone? But above all we have to find out if there really is a girlfriend."

"Maybe I'll dress up as a chimney sweep," Martinsson suggested.

"He'll see through it," Wallander said, ignoring his ironic tone of voice. "I had been thinking we would proceed more indirectly. With the help of the country postman. Find out who handles Nyman's post. There is not one rural postman in this country who doesn't know what goes on in the houses in their district. Even if they never set foot in a house, they know who lives there."

Svedberg was stubborn.

"Maybe that girl never receives any post?"

"It's not only about that," Wallander replied. "Postmen just know. That's how it is."

Rydberg nodded in agreement. Wallander felt his support. It spurred him on. Hansson promised to contact the post office. Martinsson grudgingly agreed to organise surveillance of the house. Wallander said he would speak to Åkeson.

"Find out everything you can about Nyman," Wallander said in closing. "But be discreet. If he is the bear I think he is, we don't want to wake him."

Wallander signalled to Rydberg that he wanted to speak to him in his office.

"Are you convinced?" Rydberg asked. "That it's Nyman?"

"Yes," Wallander said. "But I'm aware that I could be wrong. That I could be steering this investigation in the wrong direction."

"The theft of the lighting equipment is a strong indicator," Rydberg said. "For me that is the deciding factor. What made you think of it, by the way?"

"The pyramids," Wallander answered. "They're illuminated by spotlights. Except for one day a month, when the moon is full."

"How do you know that?"

"My old man told me."

Rydberg nodded thoughtfully.

"It's unlikely that drug shipments follow the lunar calendar," Rydberg said. "And they may not have as many clouds in Egypt as we have in Skåne."

"The Sphinx was actually the most interesting," Wallander said. "Half man, half animal. Holding guard to make sure the sun returns every morning. From the same direction."

"I think I've heard of an American security firm that uses the Sphinx as a symbol," Rydberg said.

"That fits," Wallander said. "The Sphinx keeps watch. And we keep watch. Whether or not we're police officers or night guards."

Rydberg burst into laughter.

"If you told new recruits about this kind of thing they would make fun of us."

540

"I know," Wallander said. "But perhaps we should tell them anyway."

Rydberg left. Wallander called Per Åkeson at home. He promised to inform Anette Brolin.

"How does it feel?" Wallander asked. "Not to have any criminal cases pending?"

"Good," Åkeson said. "Better than I could have imagined."

The investigative squad met two more times that day. Martinsson arranged the surveillance of the house. Hansson left in order to meet up with the rural postman. During this time the others continued with the task of establishing the facts of Rolf Nyman's life. He did not have a police record, something that made the process more difficult. He was born in 1957, in Tranås, and moved to Skåne with his parents in the mid-1960s. They had initially lived in Höör and later in Trelleborg. His father had been employed by a power plant as a systems operator, his mother stayed at home, and Rolf was an only child. His father had died in 1986 and the mother had then moved back to Tranås, where she had died the following year. Wallander had a growing feeling that Rolf Nyman had lived an invisible life. As if he had deliberately swept up any traces of himself. With the help of their Malmö colleagues they learned that he had never been mentioned in the circles that worked on illegal drug activity. He is too invisible, Wallander thought several times during the afternoon. All people leave traces. Everyone except Rolf Nyman.

Hansson returned, having spoken to the postal worker, whose name was Elfrida Wirmark. She had been very firm in stating that there were two people in the house, Holm and Nyman. Which meant there was only one person there these days, as Holm was in the mortuary, waiting to be buried.

They met in the conference room at seven that evening. According to the reports that Martinsson had received, Nyman had not left the house during the day other than to feed the dog. No one had come by to see him. Wallander asked if the officers who were keeping Nyman under surveillance had been able to tell if he was on his guard, but no such reports had been issued. Then they discussed the postal worker's statement for a while. In the end they were able to reach a consensus that Rolf Nyman had most likely invented his girlfriend.

Wallander made the final case review of the day.

"There are no indications that he is a heroin addict," he started. "That is his first lie. The second is that he has a girlfriend — he's alone in that house. If we want to get in there we have two choices. Either we wait until he leaves, which he has to do sooner or later, if for no other reason than to buy groceries. If he doesn't have extensive provisions. But why would he have something like that? Or else we find a way to lure him out of the house."

They decided to wait him out, at least for a few days. If nothing happened, they would revisit the situation.

They waited on the fourth, and they waited on the fifth. Nyman left the house twice in order to feed the dog. There were no indications that he had grown more watchful than before. During that time they continued to work on mapping his life. It was as if he had lived in a strange vacuum. Via the tax authorities they could see that he had a low annual income from his work as a DJ. He never claimed any exemptions, which seemed unusual. He applied for a passport in 1986. He received his driver's licence in 1976. There did not appear to be any friends.

On the morning of the fifth of January, Wallander sat down with Rydberg and closed the door. Rydberg said that they should probably continue for a couple more days, but Wallander presented an idea that would make it possible to lure Nyman out of the house. They decided to present this idea to the others that same afternoon. Wallander called Linda Boman in Lund. The following evening the disco was going to be open, and a Danish DJ was scheduled that night. Wallander explained his idea. Linda Boman asked who would cover the extra costs since the DJ from Copenhagen had a contract with Linda's disco. Wallander told her she could send the bill to the Ystad police if need be. He promised to get back to her within a couple of hours.

At four o'clock in the afternoon on the fifth of January, a bitingly cold wind had started to blow in over Skåne. A snow front was passing from the east and could possibly nudge the southern tip of Skåne. At the same time Wallander gathered his team in the conference room. As succinctly as possible, he explained the idea that he had discussed earlier with Rydberg.

"We have to smoke out Rolf Nyman," he said. "Apparently he doesn't go anywhere unnecessarily. At the same time it seems that he doesn't suspect anything."

"Maybe the whole thing is too far-fetched," Hansson interjected. "Maybe because he has nothing to do with the murders?"

"That possibility does exist," Wallander admitted. "But right now we're assuming the opposite. And that means we need to get into the house without him finding out. The first thing that we have to do is find a way to get him out, but not for a reason that will arouse any suspicion."

Then he laid out the plan. Linda Boman was going to call Nyman and tell him that the scheduled DJ had cancelled. Could Rolf cover for him? If he said yes, the house would be empty all evening. They could post someone at the disco who could keep in contact with the people inside the house. When Rolf Nyman returned to Sjöbo in the early morning, the house would be empty. No one except the dog would know they had been there.

"What happens if he calls his DJ colleague in Copenhagen?" Svedberg asked.

"We've thought of that. Linda Boman is going to tell the Dane not to answer the phone. The police will cover his regular fee. But we're happy to take that on."

Wallander had expected more objections. But none came. He realised it was because of a growing impatience among the team. They weren't getting anywhere. They had to do something.

Wallander looked around the table. No one had anything more to add.

"Then we're agreed? The plan is to do this soon, tomorrow night."

Wallander reached for the telephone on the table and called Linda Boman.

"Let's do it," he said when she answered. "Call me in an hour."

Wallander hung up, checked his watch and turned to Martinsson.

"Who's on surveillance right now?"

"Näslund and Peters."

"Call them on the radio and tell them to be particularly observant at twenty past five. That's when Linda Boman is going to call Nyman."

"What do you think might happen?"

"I don't know. I just want increased attentiveness."

Then they talked through the programme. Linda Boman was going to ask Nyman to come into Lund early, at eight, in order to look over a number of new records. That meant he should leave Sjöbo around seven. The disco would then stay open until three in the morning. As soon as the person posted at the disco confirmed that Nyman had entered, the others would go into the house. Wallander had asked Rydberg to come along. But Rydberg had in turn suggested Martinsson. So Martinsson it was.

"Martinsson and I will go into the house. Svedberg comes along and keeps watch. Hansson takes the disco in Lund. The rest remain here at the station. In case something happens."

"What are we looking for?" Martinsson asked.

Wallander was about to ask when Rydberg raised his hand.

"We don't know," he said. "We're trying to find what we don't know that we're looking for. But by extension there will be a yes or a no. Was Nyman the one who killed Holm and the two sisters?"

"Drugs," Martinsson said. "Is that it?"

"Weapons, money, anything. Spools of thread bought in the Eberhardsson sisters' shop. Copies of plane tickets. We don't know."

They sat around the table for a little longer. Martinsson left in order to get in touch with Näslund and Peters. He returned, nodded, and sat down.

At twenty minutes past five, Wallander was sitting with the clock in his hand.

Then he dialled Linda Boman's number. The line was busy.

They waited. Nine minutes later the phone rang. Wallander picked up the receiver. He listened and then hung up.

"Nyman has agreed," he said. "Now we're in business. Let's see if this leads us in the right or wrong direction."

The meeting broke up. Wallander held Martinsson back.

"It's best for us to be armed," he said.

Martinsson looked surprised.

"I thought Nyman was going to be in Lund?"

"Just in case," Wallander replied. "That's all."

★ ★ ★

The snowstorm never reached Skåne. The next day, the sixth of January, the sky was covered in clouds. A faint wind was blowing, there was rain in the air, and it was four degrees above zero. Wallander stood indecisively in front of his sweaters for a long time before he was able to select one. They met at six o'clock in the conference room. By then Hansson had already left for Lund. Svedberg was stationed behind a clump of trees where he had a view of the front of Nyman's house. Rydberg was doing crossword puzzles in the break room. Wallander had reluctantly taken out his gun and strapped on the holster that never quite fit properly. Martinsson had his weapon in his coat pocket.

At nine minutes past seven they received a dispatch from Svedberg. *The bird has flown.* Wallander had not wanted to take any unnecessary risks. Police dispatches were always being listened to. Therefore they were referring to Rolf Nyman as *the bird.* Nothing else.

They waited. Six minutes to eight came Hansson's dispatch. *The bird has landed.* Rolf Nyman had driven slowly.

Martinsson and Wallander stood up. Rydberg looked up from his crossword puzzle and nodded.

They arrived at the house at half past eight. Svedberg greeted them. The dog barked. But the house was dark.

"I've checked the lock," Svedberg said. "A simple pass key is enough."

Wallander and Svedberg held up their torches while Martinsson picked the lock. Svedberg left to resume his post as lookout.

They went in. Wallander turned on all the lights, which took Martinsson by surprise.

"Nyman is playing records at a disco in Lund," Wallander said. "Let's get started."

They proceeded slowly and methodically through the house. They found no traces of a woman anywhere. Apart from the bed that Holm had used there was only one other single bed.

"We should have brought a drug-detection dog," Martinsson said.

"I think it's unlikely he keeps any supplies at home," Wallander said.

They searched the house for three hours. Shortly before midnight Martinsson contacted Hansson on the police dispatch radio.

"There are a lot of people here," Hansson said. "And the music is thundering like hell. I'm staying outside. But it's cold."

They continued to search. Wallander had started to worry. No drugs, no weapons. Nothing that indicated any involvement on Nyman's part. Martinsson had searched the basement and the outlying building thoroughly. No lighting equipment. Nothing. Just the dog that was barking like crazy. Several times Wallander had felt an urge to shoot it. But he loved dogs, deep down. Even dogs that barked.

At half past one Martinsson got in touch with Hansson again. Still nothing.

"What did he say?" Wallander asked.

"That a lot of people were crowded around outside."

At two o'clock they could get no further. Wallander had started to realise that he had made a mistake. There was no indication that Rolf Nyman was anything other than a DJ. The lie about a girlfriend could hardly be considered criminal. And they had also not found any indications that Nyman was a drug addict.

"I think we can wrap this up," Martinsson said. "We haven't found anything."

Wallander nodded.

"I'm staying behind for a while," Wallander answered. "But you and Svedberg can go home. Leave me the radio."

Martinsson put the radio, which was turned on, on the table.

"Time to call it quits," Wallander said. "Hansson will have to wait until I call him, but everyone at the station can go home."

"What do you think you'll find when you're alone?"

Wallander caught the sarcastic tone in Martinsson's voice.

"Nothing," he said. "Perhaps I just need more time to realise I've led us in the wrong direction."

"We'll start over tomorrow," Martinsson said. "That's life."

Martinsson left. Wallander sat down and looked around the room. The dog was barking. Wallander cursed under his breath. He was convinced he was right. It was Rolf Nyman who had killed the two sisters and Holm. But he found no evidence. He found nothing. He remained seated for a while longer. Then he started to walk around and turn out the lamps.

Then the dog stopped barking.

Wallander stopped. Listened. The dog was quiet. Immediately he sensed danger. Where it came from, he didn't know. The disco was supposed to be open until three in the morning. Hansson had not contacted him.

Wallander did not know what made him react. But suddenly he realised he was standing in a window that was clearly illuminated from the inside. He threw himself to the side. At that moment, the window-pane shattered. Wallander lay motionless on the floor. Someone had fired a shot. Confused thoughts went through his head. It could not be Nyman. Hansson would have told him. Wallander pressed himself against the floor while he tried to pull out his own gun. He tried to crawl deeper into the shadows but saw that he was about to enter the light again. The person who had fired the shot may have made it up to the window by now. Overhead there was a ceiling lamp that was lighting up the room. He got out his weapon and aimed it at the strong bulb. When he pressed the trigger his hand was shaking so hard that he missed. He aimed again, holding it with two hands now. The shot shattered the bulb. The room became darker. He sat still, listening. His heart was pounding in his chest. What he needed most of all was the police dispatch radio. But it was on the table several metres away. And the table was in a pool of light.

The dog was still silent. He listened. Suddenly he thought he heard someone in the hall. Almost inaudible steps. He aimed the weapon at the doorway. His hands shook. But no one came in. How long he waited, he didn't know. The whole time he was feverishly trying to understand what was happening. Then he noticed that the table was on a rug. Carefully, without putting his gun down, he started to pull on the rug. The table was heavy. But it was moving. He saw how it was moving closer, extremely gently. But just when he had the radio within reach, a second shot rang out. It hit the radio, which shattered. Wallander curled up into the corner. The shot had come from the front of the house. Wallander knew that he would no longer be able to shield himself if the shooter walked round to the back of the house. I have to get out, he thought. If I stay here I'm dead. He tried desperately to come up with a plan. He had no chance of getting at the outside lights. The person out there would shoot him first. So far, the person shooting had shown himself to have a steady hand.

Wallander knew he had only one choice. A thought that was more repellent to him than anything. But he had no choice. He took several deep breaths. Then he got to his feet, rushed out into the hall, kicked open the door, threw himself to the side, and aimed three shots into the dog run. A howl signalled that he had hit the mark. Every second that went by, Wallander expected to die. But the dog's howls gave him time to slip into the shadows. Then he spotted Rolf Nyman. He was standing in the middle of the yard, momentarily bewildered by the shooting of the dog. Then he saw Wallander.

Wallander closed his eyes and fired two shots. When he opened his eyes again he saw that Rolf Nyman had fallen to the ground. Slowly Wallander walked up to him.

He was alive. A bullet had caught him in the side. Wallander took the weapon out of his hand, and then went up to the dog run. The dog was dead.

Wallander heard sirens approaching in the distance.

His whole body shaking, he sat down on the front steps and waited.

At that moment he noticed that it had started to rain.

EPILOGUE

At a quarter past four, Wallander was sitting in the station break room drinking a cup of coffee. His hands were still shaking. After the first chaotic hour when no one had really been able to explain what had happened, the picture had finally cleared up. When Martinsson and Svedberg had left Nyman's home and contacted Hansson on the police dispatch, the police in Lund had stormed Linda Boman's disco, since they suspected that the number of people inside exceeded the legal limit. In the general chaos that had ensued Hansson had misunderstood what Martinsson had said. He had believed that everyone had left Nyman's house. Then he had also realised too late that Nyman had sneaked out a back door that he had missed due to an oversight when he had inspected the disco. He had asked an officer in charge where the employees were and had been told that they had been brought down to the Lund station for questioning. He had assumed that this group included Rolf Nyman. Then he had decided there was no longer any reason for him to stay in Lund and had driven back to Ystad with the belief that Nyman's house had been empty for more than an hour.

During that time Wallander had lain on the floor, shot at the ceiling light, rushed out into the yard and killed a dog — and injured Rolf Nyman with a bullet to his side.

Wallander had thought several times since returning to Ystad that he should be furious. But he could decide for himself who he should blame. It had been an unfortunate series of misunderstandings that could have ended very badly, with not only a dog left dead. That had not happened. But it had been a close shave.

There is a time to live, and a time to die, Wallander thought. This was a mantra he had carried with him ever since the time he had been stabbed in Malmö many years ago. Now it had been a close call again.

Rydberg came into the break room.

"Rolf Nyman is going to be fine," he said. "You hit him in a good spot. He will suffer no permanent damage. The doctors seemed to think we could talk to him as early as tomorrow."

"I could easily have missed," Wallander said. "Or hit him right between the eyes. I'm a terrible shot."

"Most policemen are," Rydberg said.

Wallander slurped more of the hot coffee.

"I talked to Nyberg," Rydberg went on. "He said that the weapon looked like a probable match with the one that was used to kill the Eberhardsson sisters and Holm. They've also found Holm's car. It was parked on a street in Sjöbo. Nyman probably drove it there."

"So something has been solved," Wallander said. "But we still have no idea what's really behind all this."

Rydberg had no answer to that.

554

★   ★   ★

It would take several weeks for the whole picture to emerge. But when Nyman began to speak, the police were able to uncover a skilfully constructed organisation that managed the importation of large quantities of heavy drugs into Sweden. The Eberhardsson sisters had been Nyman's ingenious camouflage. They organised the supply links in Spain, where the drugs — which had their origin in distant producers in both Central America and Asia — arrived on fishing boats. Holm had been Nyman's henchman. But then, at a moment that they were unable to pinpoint, Holm and the Eberhardsson sisters had joined forces in their greed and decided to oust Nyman. When he had realised what was happening, he had struck back. The plane crash had occurred during this time. Drugs were being transported from Marbella to northern Germany. The night-time air trips to Sweden had taken off from a private airstrip outside Kiel. The plane had always returned there, except this last time when it had gone down. The commission in charge of investigating the accident was never able to determine the actual cause. But there were many indications that the plane was in such poor condition that several factors had worked together.

Wallander himself led the first questioning of Nyman. But when two other serious crimes occurred he had to hand the case over. Nonetheless he had understood from the start that Rolf Nyman was not the head of the pyramid that he had drawn. There were others above him — financiers, invisible men — who behind the facade of blameless citizens saw to it that the flood of drugs into Sweden did not dry up.

Many evenings Wallander thought about the pyramids. To the top that his father had been trying to reach. Wallander thought that this climb could stand as a symbol for his own work. He never reached the summit. There were always some who sat so high and far above everyone else that they could never be reached.

But this morning, the seventh of January 1990, Wallander was simply tired.

At half past five he could no longer take it. Without saying a word to anyone other than Rydberg he went home to the apartment on Mariagatan. He showered and crawled into bed without being able to fall asleep. Only when he managed to find a sleeping pill in an old bottle in the bathroom cabinet was he finally able to sleep, and he did not wake up until two o'clock in the afternoon.

He spent the rest of the day at the station and the hospital. Björk turned up and congratulated Wallander on his efforts. Wallander did not reply. He thought that most of what he had done had been wrong. It had been their luck, not their skill, that had finally felled Rolf Nyman.

Then he had had his first conversation with Nyman at the hospital. The man had been pale but collected. Wallander had expected Nyman to refuse to say a word. But he had answered many of Wallander's questions.

"The Eberhardsson sisters?" Wallander asked before he concluded the session. Rolf Nyman smiled.

556

"Two greedy old ladies," he said. "Who were tempted by the fact that someone rode into their hopeless lives and brought the scent of adventure."

"That sounds implausible," Wallander said. "It's too big a step."

"Anna Eberhardsson had lived a fairly wild life when she was younger. Emilia had always had to keep an eye on her. Perhaps deep down she had wanted to live the same life. What do we know about people? Other than that they have their weaknesses. And those are the things you need to know."

"How did you meet them?"

The answer came as a surprise.

"I bought a zip. It was a time in my life when I mended my own clothes. I saw those old ladies and had a crazy idea. That they could be useful. As a cover."

"And then?"

"I started dropping by. Bought some thread. Talked about my travels around the world. How easy it was to make money. And that life is short. But that nothing was ever too late. I saw that they listened."

"And then?"

Rolf Nyman shrugged.

"One day I made them an offer. How does that go again? An offer they couldn't refuse."

Wallander wanted to ask more. But suddenly Nyman did not want to talk about it any more.

Wallander changed the subject.

"And Holm?"

"He was also greedy. And weak. Too stupid to realise that he wouldn't be able to trick me."

"How did you catch onto their plans?"

Rolf Nyman shook his head.

"I won't give you that answer," he said.

Wallander walked from the hospital to the station. A press conference was going on that to his relief he had managed to get out of. When he got to his office there was a package on the floor. Someone had written a note and said that the package had ended up sitting around in reception by mistake. Wallander saw that it had come from Sofia in Bulgaria. Immediately he knew what it was. Several months earlier he had participated in an international police conference in Copenhagen. While there he had become good friends with a Bulgarian detective who shared his interest in opera. Wallander opened it. It contained a recording of *La Traviata* with Maria Callas.

Wallander wrote up a report on his first conversation with Rolf Nyman. Then he went home. Cooked some food, slept a few hours. Thought of calling Linda but didn't.

In the evening he listened to the record from Bulgaria. Thought that what he needed most right now was a couple of days off.

He only went to bed and fell asleep when it was close to two.

The incoming call was registered by the Ystad police dispatcher at 5.13 a.m., the eighth of January. It was received by an exhausted policeman who had been on duty almost without a break since New Year's Eve. He had listened to the stammering voice on the phone and at first thought that it was a confused elderly person. But something nonetheless alerted his attention. He started to ask questions. When the conversation was over he only had to reflect for a moment before he lifted the receiver again and dialled a number he knew by heart.

When the telephone signals jerked Wallander from his slumber he had been deeply enmeshed in an erotic dream.

He checked his watch as he reached his hand out for the telephone receiver. A car accident, he thought quickly. An icy road, or someone driving too fast. People dead. Or clashes with refugees who arrived on the morning ferry from Poland.

He sat up in bed and pressed the receiver against his cheek, where his stubble stung.

"Wallander!" he barked.

"I didn't wake you, did I?"

"I was awake."

Why do I lie? he wondered. Why don't I tell the truth? That most of all I would like to return to my sleep and catch a fleeting dream in the form of a naked woman.

"I thought I should call you. An old farmer called in, said his name was Nyström and that he lived in Lenarp. He claimed that a neighbouring woman was tied up on the floor and that someone was dead."

Wallander swiftly located Lenarp in his mind. Not so far from Marsvinsholm, in an unusually hilly area for Skåne.

"It sounds serious. I thought it was best to call you directly."

"Who is available right now?"

"Peters and Norén are out looking for someone who broke a window at the Continental. Should I call them in?"

"Tell them to drive to the intersection of Kadesjö and Katslösa and wait until I get there. Give them the address. When did you receive this call?"

"A couple of minutes ago."

"Are you sure it's not some drunk?"

"It didn't sound like it."

Wallander got out of bed and got dressed. The rest that he needed so much was not to be granted him.

He drove out of the city, passing the newly built furniture warehouse by the main road into town, and sensed the dark sea beyond it. The sky was covered in clouds.

The snowstorms are coming, he thought.

Sooner or later they will be on top of us.

Then he tried to concentrate on whatever sight it was that he would encounter.

The patrol car was waiting for him by the road to Kadesjö.

It was still dark.